W9-BUK-036

RATTLESNAKE WELLS, WYOMING

Look for These Exciting Series from
WILLIAM W. JOHNSTONE
with J. A. Johnstone

The Mountain Man

Preacher: The First Mountain Man

Matt Jensen, the Last Mountain Man

Luke Jensen, Bounty Hunter

Those Jensen Boys!

The Family Jensen

MacCallister

Flintlock

The Brothers O'Brien

The Kerrigans: A Texas Dynasty

Sixkiller, U.S. Marshal

Hell's Half Acre

Texas John Slaughter

Will Tanner, U.S. Deputy Marshal

Eagles

The Frontiersman

AVAILABLE FROM PINNACLE BOOKS

RATTLESNAKE WELLS, WYOMING

WILLIAM W. JOHNSTONE
with J. A. Johnstone

PINNACLE BOOKS
Kensington Publishing Corp.
www.kensingtonbooks.com

PINNACLE BOOKS are published by

Kensington Publishing Corp.
119 West 40th Street
New York, NY 10018

Copyright © 2017 J. A. Johnstone

All rights reserved. No part of this book may be reproduced in any form or by any means without the prior written consent of the publisher, excepting brief quotes used in reviews.

To the extent that the image or images on the cover of this book depict a person or persons, such person or persons are merely models, and are not intended to portray any character or characters featured in the book.

PUBLISHER'S NOTE
Following the death of William W. Johnstone, the Johnstone family is working with a carefully selected writer to organize and complete Mr. Johnstone's outlines and many unfinished manuscripts to create additional novels in all of his series like The Last Gunfighter, Mountain Man, and Eagles, among others. This novel was inspired by Mr. Johnstone's superb storytelling.

If you purchased this book without a cover, you should be aware that this book is stolen property. It was reported as "unsold and destroyed" to the publisher, and neither the author nor the publisher has received any payment for this "stripped book."

All Kensington titles, imprints, and distributed lines are available at special quantity discounts for bulk purchases for sales promotions, premiums, fund-raising, educational, or institutional use. Special book excerpts or customized printings can also be created to fit specific needs. For details, write or phone the office of the Kensington sales manager: Kensington Publishing Corp., 119 West 40th Street, New York, NY 10018, attn: Sales Department; phone 1-800-221-2647.

PINNACLE BOOKS, the Pinnacle logo, and the WWJ steer head logo, are Reg. U.S. Pat. & TM Off.

ISBN-13: 978-0-7860-4012-4
ISBN-10: 0-7860-4012-2

First printing: February 2017

10 9 8 7 6 5 4 3 2 1

Printed in the United States of America

Chapter 1

Spring, 1885

Later, Bob Hatfield would remember how still and peaceful that day had started out. A misleading omen, he'd come to reflect, in sharp contrast to the trouble that was soon to rear its ugly head. But, at the start, there was no hint of anything like that . . .

As usual, Bob rose with the sun. After he dressed, he headed for the kitchen. Consuela, his pretty housekeeper and cook, already had a pot of coffee brewed and waiting. They exchanged "good mornings" and she poured him his first cup of the day. He barely had it drunk halfway before she placed in front of him his customary breakfast of two boiled eggs and a generous scoop of spicy fried sausage wrapped in a soft tortilla shell.

They didn't talk much as he ate. He was contemplating his day. She, having already gotten her own breakfast out of the way, was busying herself with the start of the day's remaining tasks that would keep the household running smoothly and efficiently.

Once he'd finished his meal, Bob poured himself

a second mug of coffee. He doctored it with two heaping spoonfuls of sugar and a splash of milk, the single time he treated himself in that manner as opposed to the numerous other cups of mud—some of which were darn near, depending on the source— he took black during the course of most days.

"Shall I wake Bucky now?" Consuela asked.

"Yeah, reckon it's that time. He needs to get up and get ready for school. I don't want him giving you any sass about it after I've left, so tell him to snap to it and come see me before I have to go."

"*Sí.*"

Bucky was Bob's ten-year-old son. Priscilla, Bucky's mother and Bob's late wife, had passed away close to three years earlier, shortly after they'd arrived in Wyoming Territory upon relocating from Texas. She was never far from Bob's thoughts, but each morning when it was time to roust Bucky, she became even more prominent in his mind. He could imagine the smile on her face when she looked at their strong, rambunctious son in the light of each new day.

Bob wasn't a deeply religious man, yet he had enough faith to believe that Priscilla *was* looking on and watching their son grow. But it wasn't like she was *there* to do it . . . where they could see her in return and all could experience such things together. The way it was supposed to be.

Bob carried his mug out to the front porch and sat down near one end so that the morning sunlight slanted in under the porch roof and washed over him, a ritual he followed whenever the weather was nice. Not a breath of air stirred. The leftover chill of night lingered at the early hour, but Bob knew it wouldn't be long before that burned away and the early spring day on tap would be another pleasant one.

He took a long pull of coffee and lowered his arm, exposing the badge pinned to the front of his shirt. It glinted brightly in the sun. As the marshal of Rattlesnake Wells, Bob would take all the pleasant days he could get—not only weather-wise, but in other ways, too. In fact, the way the town was growing and flexing its muscles, an occasional bout of lousy weather sometimes helped tame down other kinds of unpleasantness.

Rattlesnake Wells, it happened, was in the early middle stages of being a boomtown.

Originally it was just a sleepy, peaceful little community. Growth had come from emigrants branching off the Oregon Trail and settling near where they found plentiful water in the form of several spring-fed "wells." Numerous rattlesnake nests also found in the area gave the place its rather unbecoming name, which stuck even after most of the rattler population had been eliminated. Once the town had taken root, so did a handful of small but supportive surrounding ranches—horse and cattle—finding dependable markets supplying Army forts throughout the territory.

And so it was for a number of years. But then some fool struck gold in the Prophecy Mountains that loomed just to the northwest and, almost overnight, the quiet, sleepy little community turned into a boomtown. First came the swarm of eager, determined gold seekers ready to dig and work and sweat for their reward. Following them came the next swarm—the easy profit seekers, the hucksters and shysters and swindlers, the pimps and whores and pickpockets, the petty thieves and the skimmers looking for every kind of score they were willing to dirty their souls for . . . but not their hands.

As marshal, it was Bob Hatfield's job to keep a lid on all of it.

From his porch, he could look down a gentle slope and see pretty much the whole spread of the town. When he and his family had first moved in, the house had been somewhat outlying off the north end of the original layout of homes and businesses and streets that ran at a slight angle from northeast to southwest. These days it was generally referred to as Old Town.

The mishmash of structures and shelters that had hastily sprung up as a result of the boom—tent saloons, gambling joints, greasy spoon eateries, equipment suppliers, boardinghouses, and whore cribs—were all crowded in a single row angling northwest toward the Prophecy Mountains, where the gold had been found. The more recent addition was naturally called New Town and it ran along what had been dubbed Gold Avenue. The combined overall effect was a town laid out in two converging angles that came to a point, like an arrowhead, aiming almost directly at Bob's house.

More than once, he wondered about the omenlike significance of that, too.

As he was enjoying the final sips of his coffee, the house door opened behind him and Bucky came out onto the porch. He squinted fiercely at the bright morning light and stood a minute, letting his eyes adjust. It gave Bob a chance to gaze at him with loving eyes for a long moment without causing the kind of embarrassment a ten-year-old boy was apt to feel under such scrutiny.

Like his father, Bucky had a thatch of thick red

hair—uncombed and spectacularly tousled at the moment—and a solid, square-shouldered frame. He was already big for his age and would no doubt grow to equal or maybe exceed Bob's six-one height. In fact, most of Bucky's features—and mannerisms— were stamped from a pattern mighty similar to his dad's, which shouldn't have come as a surprise for any youngster so proud of and focused on his only parent.

It was mainly in the boy's eyes where Bob could see Priscilla's traits. A depth of kindness and gentleness was there—as yet untapped by its restless, energetic young host. Bob hoped that would shine through as Bucky matured and make him a better, more rounded—though not softened—man. It's what Priscilla had done for Bob, from the outside in, and it appeared as if she'd instilled it inside their son right from the jump.

"Consuela said you wanted to see me, Pa?"

Bob arched an eyebrow. "What? No 'good morning'?"

Bucky looked slightly confused for a second. "Well, uh . . . sure. Good morning, Pa."

"That's better. Good morning to you, too, son."

Bucky continued to look a bit confused and uncertain, not fully woken up yet.

Bob smiled. "That's all I wanted. Just to see you, say good morning, and spend a couple minutes before I have to head off. I may be in for a long day, so I'm not sure when I'll be showing up for supper. The train's making a special trip in today to pick up a herd of horses that the Bar Double J boys are bringing in to ship off and sell to the Army. After the hayburners are loaded up and their jobs are done for the day, you know how frisky some of those wranglers can get when they haven't been to town in a while. Since this is a special run, I figure the train's gonna do a quick turnaround, so I don't think the crew will be staying in town overnight like they sometimes do. Can't ever be certain about that, though. If they change their minds and stay, they could turn out to be feeling a mite frisky, too. With them, how frisky they are usually depends on how long it's been since last payday."

"Aw, I wouldn't worry too much about the Bar Double J bunch," Bucky said, waving a hand dismissively. "They're mostly old codg—uh, what I mean to say is that, unless they've hired on some new hands, it's usually older fellas who show up and hardly ever cause any trouble. They tell good stories about the old days, though, when they're sitting in the back of Krepdorf's store playing cribbage or checkers. Not to say that some jug passin' don't go on, too, while they're back there."

"I won't even ask how you know about the stories and the jug passin' in the back of Krepdorf's," Bob said, putting his eyebrow to work in another skeptical arch. "But I will accept your reassurance about not having to worry much about the Bar Double J fellas. So, except for keeping an eye on the train crew long enough to see what they've got in mind, maybe my day will be nice and uneventful after all."

"I don't know much about the train crew, Pa. I can't help you there," Bucky said earnestly.

Bob chuckled.

"Is that all, Pa? Consuela's making me oatmeal for breakfast and then I gotta finish getting ready for school. I probably ought to get back inside."

"Yeah, I guess we both got other things to take care of"—Bob paused thoughtfully—"although, now that you mentioned school . . . we haven't talked for a few days about how you're doing there. You got anything we need to go over?"

"Uh. Gee. No, Pa, not really."

"That geography stuff you were wrestlin' with? You on top of that?"

"I think so."

"You *think* so? Ain't you got a big test coming up in the next day or so?"

"Yeah . . . Uh, actually it's today."

"That's what I thought. Are you ready for it? And don't say you *think* so."

Bucky heaved a tormented sigh. "I been studying really hard, Pa. Truly I have. But Mr. Fettleford loves that stuff so much that he rambles on for hours it seems about countries and customs all over the place—way more than just the ones we're studying on—and pretty soon I get all the names and maps so scrambled in my head I don't know one from the other."

Bob could feel his son's pain. Nobody hated school studies more than he had as a boy . . . but he was in a different role and had to hold the line. "Well, you've got to keep trying," was his parental advice. "Pay attention, mind your p's and q's, and do the best you can. I can't ask for more. If I hear you tried to weasel out of going by playing on Consuela's sympathy after I leave, or if I find out you played hooky—*that* would be a whole different matter."

"I know better than to try anything like that, Pa."

"I know you do. I was just reminding you of it," said Bob, smiling, reaching out to tousle Bucky's already-tousled head of hair. "Okay. Speaking of p's and q's, here's a pop quiz. Name me a country that starts with *P* and one that starts with *Q*."

Bucky's eyes widened and he looked a little panicked. "Uh . . . Portugal! Portugal, for *P*."

"Good. Now *Q*."

Bucky's expression scrunched with concentration. Then, "How about . . . Cuba?"

Bob shook his head. "Nice try, pal. But I don't think so."

"You sure? It *sounds* right, like it could start with a *q*."

"I may not be the world's greatest speller, but I'm good enough to know that sounds and spellings don't always match. And Cuba don't start with no *q*."

"Wait! I know—the Quater!"

It was Bob's expression that scrunched up. "What?"

"You know. The Quater. That circle around the world that divides . . ." Bucky's voice trailed off. "Never mind. I remember now . . . that's the *E*-quator, and it really ain't even a country. I guess I was reachin' a mite too hard."

Not liking to see the boy look so crestfallen, and frankly unable to think of a country that started with *Q* himself, Bob said, "Tell you what. *Q*'s a tough one. You worry about your test first, then try to come up with an answer for *Q*. Check your maps at school or maybe even ask Mr. Fettleford. We can take it up again this evening. Deal?"

Bucky looked relieved. "Deal, Pa."

Bob held out his emptied coffee mug. "Here, take

this to Consuela when you go in, okay? Tell her I've got to get going. I'm running late."

"Okay. I'll tell her."

Bob gave his son a quick hug and another hair tousle, then stepped off the porch and headed down the slope toward town.

Chapter 2

The sturdy log building that housed the marshal's office and jail was located nearly to the south end of Front Street, the main drag of Old Town, on the corner of Front and Wyoming streets. Only four streets crossed Front, each running a few blocks, serving private homes and a pair of boardinghouses. The structures lining Front Street made up the business district.

At the early hour, except for a few shopkeepers stirring around inside their stores, getting ready to open, hardly any activity appeared on the streets. As Bob strode down Front Street and drew even with Bullock's Saloon, Rattlesnake Wells' oldest and most popular watering hole, Mike Bullock stepped out of his place with a rolled-up floor mat tucked under each thick arm. He was a stout individual with a clean-shaven head, beer-keg torso, and arms as big around as most men's legs. He habitually wore a bowler hat clamped so tight onto his bald dome many claimed it could never be knocked off, even in the fiercest barroom brawl . . . of which Mike was a veteran many times over.

"Mornin', Mike," Bob greeted.

"Same to you, Marshal." Mike dropped one of the mats and unfurled the other, preparing to give it a good shaking out. He paused, looking skyward, and said, "Mighty still this morning. Like the dead quiet you sometimes see ahead of a big storm."

"Could be," Bob said, also glancing skyward. "Ain't a cloud in the sky, though."

"Maybe not. But you never know what's coming over the horizon."

"True enough. It's probably just as well we don't."

"You really think so?" Mike said rhetorically. "I don't. I like to know if trouble's coming. Then I can be prepared."

Bob grinned. "Best thing for that, I reckon, is to just stay prepared all the time."

Mike balled one of his mallet-sized fists and held it up. "That's exactly what I do . . . with this baby right here."

Bob walked on a few steps, then stopped and turned back. "Say, Mike. Can you think of the name of a country that starts with the letter q?"

Mike stopped shaking one of the mats. "Huh? A country where?"

"Anywhere. Anywhere around the globe. It's a question that, er, came out of Bucky's schoolwork."

Mike grunted. "Boy, you picked the wrong fella to ask about school learnin'. I never set foot in a class-room all my days. My old man didn't believe in it. He said payin' attention while you was livin' life was all the schoolin' anybody ever needed." He jabbed a thumb to indicate the saloon behind him. "So all my schoolin' has come from right in there—actually from my old man's beer hall in Brooklyn through a couple dozen other joints in between to my own place right here. And, boy, have I learned a thing or three . . . but I don't know no countries startin' with the letter *q*."

"It was just a question, Mike. Don't worry about it. If you *do* think of something, let me know."

"I'll ask around as customers come in and out today." A rumble of laughter rolled out of his chest. "I guarantee I'll get answers for you. They may not be right, but you can bet there'll be some wild ones."

Bob shook his head, not holding out hope for much in the way of accurate information, and continued on down the street. He hadn't gone far before he stopped again, for a very different reason. He heard a sound unmistakable to his ears. Gunshots. Distant and sporadic at first, but quickly growing louder and more frequent.

Pop! Poppity-pop! Bang! Boom!

It was coming from the north, from the newer section of town, and sounded like all hell was busting loose.

Bob wheeled and moved in that direction. Measured steps at first, then lengthier and faster. The Colt Peacemaker riding in the old but well-oiled holster on his right hip flashed to his fist, and he carried it out front as he broke into a run.

Mike Bullock dropped the mat he was shaking out and took a step out into the street, craning his neck to look north as Bob raced by. "What in hell's going on?"

"I don't know, but it don't sound good," Bob called back over his shoulder. "Ring the fire bell. If the shooting keeps up, send me some help!"

Painted bright red, the large iron bell that served as the town's warning notice for danger hung from a pole right next to the public pump and watering trough fed by an underground stream running down from the largest of the spring wells that had originally drawn folks to settle there. At the point where Front Street and Gold Avenue met and branched off at separate angles, the bell served primarily in case of fire, although in the old days it had also brought armed men running to face an Indian attack or two. In addition to the bell and pump, in an old shed just off the east side of the street, a hand-drawn water wagon sat ready and faithfully kept full of water in case of need.

Bob again urged Mike to ring the bell, even as he ran past it and made the turn up Gold Avenue toward the sound of the shooting, which hadn't given any sign of letting up and, in fact, seemed to be increasing.

Bob ran harder and his breath chugged harder. *I'm a horseman, not a damn foot racer,* he lamented inside his head, but he nevertheless kept on. The fire bell began clanging behind him.

Deputy Fred Ordway was in the outhouse in back of Mabel Nyby's boardinghouse, where he stayed, when he heard the fire bell. Not one given to swearing in general and especially not using the Lord's name in vain, at that moment he couldn't help but cut loose with a very salty tirade at his predicament.

As a proud, badge-wearing representative of the citizens of Rattlesnake Wells, it was incumbent on him to set the tone for a prompt response to any town emergency. In other words, he should have been one of the *first* responders to the fire bell.

Thanks to the taco pie he'd eaten for a late supper at that new Mexican food stand on Gold Avenue, he was in no condition—not to mention *no position*—to go anywhere at the moment.

A short time earlier, he'd woken with a rumbling, tumbling stomach, and it had been all he could do to pull on some pants and make it out to the outhouse in time. Leaving as quickly as he'd arrived did not seem advisable. True, the upheaval in his stomach had largely subsided, but an undeniable queasiness still warned him against leaving the two-hole facility in too big a hurry.

Ahead, near the far end of the New Town row, Marshal Hatfield could see signs of what was causing the commotion. It looked like half a dozen men on horseback were riding about wildly, whooping and shooting and trampling recklessly near where various-sized tents housed everything from cramped bed-by-the-night joints to hawkers of trinkets and trash and snake oil to the cheapest whore cribs.

What the hell for? was all he could think as he ran.

A few heads, drawn by the noise, began poking sleepily out of buildings and tents he was running past.

"Don't just stand there," he shouted to them. "Grab

some men and come help with this! Get McTeague, if he's in town."

Although he didn't know if the hell-raisers would even notice his shots amid all the gunfire they were popping off, Bob aimed his Colt to the sky and fired off two shots. He hated to waste the rounds, inasmuch as the Colt was the only weapon he had on him, but he had to try something and wasn't ready to cut down one or two riders merely to get the attention of the rest.

They were doing plenty of damage and making a lot of noise with their guns but didn't seem to be aiming to shoot or kill anybody. He was hoping that if he drew their attention and they spotted his badge it might serve to tame them down before anybody *did* get hurt.

That notion went out the window pretty quick after his warning shots drew the desired attention.

One of the riders looked around, saw him advancing, and shouted to the others, "We got company, boys!"

Another face whipped around and the man it belonged to said with a sneer, "Let's blast the nosy damn badge-toter."

A second later, the sneering hombre and most of the others swung their guns in Bob's direction and cut loose with a hail of lead that ripped down the street and came shockingly close to ventilating him like a piece of Swiss cheese. Only a diving roll that took him to a skidding halt behind a sturdy, low-slung ore wagon saved him. Bullets thumped and hammered against the thick sides of the wagon and tore long gouges in the middle of the dusty street.

Bob hunkered behind the ore wagon and quickly replaced the Colt's spent cartridges. Not even a full wheel was going to last very long in the shoot-out that seemed on tap, but it was the best way to start. He looked down the street the way he'd come, hoping for some sign of reinforcements at least starting to form. Even though the fire bell had stopped ringing, he saw nothing.

Damn. Well, he'd poked the hornet's nest on his own, and it looked like—at least for the moment and for the foreseeable next few minutes—he'd have to deal with the results on his own.

The bell stopped ringing, signaling that a sufficient number of men had answered its call or were visibly on the way.

But not Fred. He remained seated where he was. *What would the marshal think?* Fred swore again.

"Come on, law dog!" a taunting voice called toward Bob. "You were in a big hurry to join our party just a minute ago. Pop back up and join in for more of the fun!"

That prompted the marshal to do the last thing the taunter or any of his cohorts expected—he *did* pop back up and join in. Rising up suddenly from behind the low wagon, he extended his Colt just below chest level and swept it in a short, level arc as he fanned off four rapid-fire rounds. It not only caught the hell-raisers by complete and utter surprise, it sent two of them flying from their saddles.

Bob dropped back down immediately as another responsive hail of bullets raked the ore cart and sizzled through the air above his head. His heart pounded nearly as hard and fast as the hammering of the incoming slugs, but none of it interfered with his fingers nimbly and automatically reloading the Colt.

Vaguely, but unmistakably, Fred heard gunfire. A lot of gunfire. Its distant sound made him guess it must be coming from New Town, somewhere up Gold Avenue. What in the world could be going on that would result in so much shooting? And was *that* what the bell was ringing for, as opposed to a fire?

Sucking in his substantial gut and gritting his teeth, he put his faith in force of will and the hope that Fate would not be so cruel as to let him lose control during a public emergency. No matter what, he couldn't just sit in the outhouse and let Marshal Hatfield down. He had to take the risk.

Fred hurriedly tucked his long nightshirt—which he hadn't taken time to change out of—into his pants and rushed back to the boardinghouse. In his room, he pulled on his boots and strapped on his gun belt and holster. Without taking time for anything else, not even to clap on his hat or pin on his deputy's badge, he clomped back out and headed in the direction of the gunfire.

Pouring lead, Marshal Hatfield continued to press low and tight against his end of the wagon as the volley roared. When it abruptly eased up—while the riders were doing some reloading of their own, he guessed—he considered trying the pop-up tactic one more time. Unable to convince himself they'd be so dumb as to get caught again without at least one member of their bunch primed and ready for just such a move, he held off. Leaning over nearly to the edge of the wagon, he turned his head to call sharply, "If you'll hold your damn fire and lay down your guns, we can talk out whatever your grievance is without anybody else getting hurt!"

"To hell with that, Marshal! You already drew blood on two of ours, and that don't go unreturned. Wasn't nobody hurt up till then, so that's on you alone."

"Yeah, and alone is strictly what you are, you dumb bastard," another shouted. "You supposed to be somebody so ferocious you expect us to lay down our guns just because you tell us to?"

"All I am is a fella wearin' a badge, trying to keep peace in this town," Bob called back. "I'll tell you what *is* gonna be ferocious, and that's the mob of angry citizens and pissed-off miners who'll be forming up behind me any minute now. If you're dumb enough to want to face that, the hurt that gets handed out from there is gonna be strictly on *you*."

"If you're tryin' to scare us off, you're gonna have to do a helluva lot better than the threat of a few shopkeepers and rock choppers!"

"Your choice," Bob called. "I did my best to give you a fair chance." He looked back down the street again and was relieved to see evidence that he wasn't just making empty threats.

A knot of men was coming around the point and starting up Gold Avenue. Mike Bullock was in the lead, wielding an oversized bung starter that Bob knew was his second-favorite weapon for breaking up barroom brawls. On rare occasions when brute force wasn't enough, Bullock carried a snub-nosed revolver in his pocket. Since he and the men falling in behind him were heading toward gunfire, Bob trusted that the burly saloon man also had the pistol at hand. As for the others making up the reinforcements, they were armed and prepared. A number of rifle barrels poked up along with handguns being brandished.

In their eagerness to respond and come to Bob's aid, the undisciplined group was bunched together as they picked up momentum and charged right up the middle of the street. If the raiders loosed a volley on them the way they already had on Bob, the rain of lead would tear into the pack and chew them to ribbons.

Bob turned his attention back to the raiders and risked a moment of exposure to lean out around the edge of what he'd come to consider *his* wagon. He did this for two reasons. One, to check the positioning of the horsemen and two, to snap off a couple rounds in order to keep them focused on him for as long as he could.

The remaining four raiders on horseback were still positioned much as they'd been—off to the right side of Gold Avenue where he was—their horses milling and trampling in among some low sleeping tents that served mostly as cribs for the cheapest priced working girls. A fifth man was standing as if he might be preparing to mount again.

Bob calculated that his first surprise flurry must have hit pretty good and left down one of the two men he'd unsaddled. Evidently, the second one had been clipped and was attempting to get back in the battle again.

Part two of what Bob had hoped to accomplish with his peek-and-shoot maneuver—to keep the raiders focused on him—worked very well. They let loose with another barrage of lead, hammering the sturdy ore wagon until it shook and shivered like a dog throwing off water.

That was okay. It was fine. It kept them concentrated on Bob and not on the knot of men coming up the street.

When the barrage started to falter, Bob took the moment of relative quiet to shout out to Bullock and the others arriving with him. "Spread out, you damn fools!" he hollered, motioning with his hands. "Take to the sides of the street. Keep to cover and work your way up from there!"

At his command, the group hesitated for a moment then dispersed with surprising speed and smoothness. Half split to the left, half to the right.

That drew the full attention of the mounted raiders, who immediately opened up on the scattering men. As far as Bob could see, no one got hit, but it was a close call for a couple of them. Leaning out once more to throw some return lead, he also saw that the fifth raider had indeed made it back into the saddle. Bob tried his best to knock him right back out of it, but his hurried aim was too wide.

As Bullock and the others made their way up the sides of the street, they did some shooting of their own. Men emerged from some of the structures along the street to join them. The air fairly sang with the whine of bullets and began to fill with layers of gun smoke that hung undispersed in the stillness.

The raiders remained on their horses, spurring them harder, faster, in zigzag patterns in and out among the tents. As erratically moving targets, it was hard for even a reasonably skilled marksman to draw a bead on them.

Several terrified, scantily clad soiled doves darted in all directions, screeching as they looked for a safe haven. For several wild seconds their appearance hampered Bob's men from shooting at the raiders, leaving the horsemen unrestrained from doing all the shooting they wanted.

Making their way up the sides of the street, the men had no problem finding cover. Unfortunately, not much of it was as substantial as the sturdy ore wagon Bob was behind. A tent flap or a flimsy wooden gate with three-inch openings between slats was okay for a bit of concealment, but not for stopping the punch of a bullet. Sharp yelps and groans of pain came from some of the men taking hits as they edged their way forward.

Bob cursed bitterly and ducked back from another exchange of lead.

From behind him, a man cautiously pushed back the door flap of a good-sized tent and peeked out of the opening. He was an older gent with graying whiskers and wide, anxious eyes. "What in thunderation is goin' on, Marshal?" he hollered over the crack of gunfire.

"Raiders are hitting this end of town," Bob answered. "I don't know why, but they mean business and it ain't good."

"I can tell. It sounds like a war out there."

"Who you got in there with you?"

"Three nephews who just showed up from Iowa. Young fools ain't got no more sense than me. Came to scratch in the ground for gold."

"You got guns in there?"

"Sure. A-course."

"Then why don't you join in this turkey shoot to help protect your town?"

The tent opened wider and two more faces—young, not more than a year on either side of twenty—showed themselves.

"We'll fight with you, Marshal," one of them said eagerly. "A fella ought to side with the law, wherever he finds himself."

"Me, too!" From inside came another voice, a younger-sounding one.

"Now wait a minute," said Gray Whiskers. "The one lad in here ain't but fourteen. It ain't right to expose him to no gun battle."

"I can't argue that." Bob's words were nearly lost in a particularly heavy exchange of gunfire. He heard another of the townsmen over on the other side of the street yelp in pain and cut his gaze back to Gray Whiskers. "You said those Iowa boys just got in. They got horses?"

"Yeah. Three of 'em, tied out back."

"There a back way out of that tent?"

"You can lift the bottom and slip under," one of the young faces said.

Bob made a quick decision. "Get ready to cover me and be fixed to yank that door flap open wider. I'm comin' in!"

Chapter 3

Widow Nyby's boardinghouse was on Oregon Street, a block north of the marshal's office and jail, but Fred didn't even bother looking in that direction. He could tell for sure the shooting was coming from somewhere in the opposite direction—up in New Town. If that's where the trouble was, that's where the marshal would be—and where Fred needed to get to.

Turning onto Front Street, he broke into a run . . . for as long as he could last. Possessing an unfortunate amount of extra pounds, the deputy was not a sprinter. He was overweight, generally slow, and shuffle-footed in the normal course of things. Those traits, combined with his amiable nature, made him seem a little comical and hard for some folks to take seriously. But as a number of would-be hardcases could attest—not to mention a few who were no longer in any condition to speak up—Fred was strong as a bull and could move his bulk surprisingly fast when need be . . . in close quarters.

* * *

Bob left the cover of the ore wagon in much the same way he'd arrived behind it. He lunged and went into a diving roll that took him inside the tent with Gray Whiskers and his three nephews. Shots from the raiders chased him and punched holes through the peak of the tent, the slugs making hollow slapping sounds.

"Stay down!" Bob ordered. "Too many tents and other obstacles in the way for them to shoot low at us."

As Gray Whiskers leaned slightly out of the doorway and returned fire with an old Henry repeater, Bob made a quick assessment of the three nephews. The two older ones looked strong and savvy. The fourteen-year-old looked gritty and eager, though he still lacked his late teen height and muscle spurt.

Silently agreeing with the uncle that they could in no way let the teenager mix seriously in the conflict, Bob said to the nephews, "Give me some names."

The two older boys were Peter and Vern, the youngest was Lee.

"Okay. Good." Bob pointed at the converted Navy Colt Peter was holding. "You any good with that?"

"Darn good, sir."

"He is for a fact," Vern confirmed. "I'm better with a rifle."

Looking at Peter, Bob nodded toward the doorway where Gray Whiskers was continuing to fire intermittent rounds. "You think you can make it back out there where I was?"

"You bet."

"Then do it." Bob cut his eyes to Vern. "You come with me. I'm going out the back and taking one of your horses to flank those skunks. I need you to cover me."

"What about me?" said Lee.

Bob pointed. "You go over there by the doorway and reload for your uncle and brother. Stay back a safe distance."

"I can shoot, too. I can shoot good."

"And you can reload, like I said. That's just as important. All three of you shooting and stopping to reload means giving the other hombres a break, see? With you reloading and always having a gun ready, there's no pause for them to take advantage of. Understand?"

"I . . . guess so," said Lee, reluctantly accepting his role. "I never thought of it that way."

"Well, that's the way it is," Bob told him. "Stay low and hold up your end, okay?"

"Yes sir."

In a matter of minutes, Bob and Vern slipped out the back of the tent. Vern quickly slapped a bridle on the horse of Bob's choosing, a blaze-faced black gelding, and the marshal mounted bareback.

"Okay, I mean to sweep out and come in at 'em from the side. Surprise 'em, hopefully," Bob said, talking fast. "They haven't spotted us so far, so hold your fire for as long as you can. When I make my move or whenever they spot me and swing some guns in my direction, give 'em something else to worry about. Okay?"

Vern brandished a lever-action Winchester with the same kind of confidence his brother had shown with the Navy Colt. "I darn well will, sir."

Bob dug his heels into the sides of the gelding and the black shot away, swinging wide around other tents and sheds and a rickety fenced-in area that held some goats and hogs.

* * *

A runner he was not. Just past the intersection of First Street, Fred slowed down. Out of breath, he veered over to the side of the street and leaned on the hitch rail out front of the Starbuck Territorial Bank to rest.

On Gold Avenue the air was thick with fibrous layers of gun smoke hanging nearly motionless in the still air. The intensity of gunfire being traded up and down the street hadn't diminished nor had the amount of reckless trampling and damage the riders were dishing out as they spurred their horses back and forth and in and out of flimsy structures and tents.

Suddenly, the thing Bob had been dreading as much or maybe more than the wanton destruction or flying bullets made its appearance. As he completed his sweep and turned the gelding toward those administering the wreckage, he saw the tongues of flame licking upward out of a flattened tent.

Fire! One of the most devastating, town-destroying, life-ruining forces on the frontier.

"Bastards!" he spat out, his teeth bared in rage. At all costs, he had to end the battle and end it fast. Stop the shooting and concentrate all his energy on the fire before it got the chance to spread uncontrollably.

Bob dug his heels harder into the gelding and rode straight for the nearest of the hell-raisers posing more of a threat to his town than ever.

Somehow, the rider sensed him almost as soon as he started his charge. After shouting to get the attention of a nearby cohort, the rider twisted in his saddle to face the lawman, at the same time swinging a rifle up and around.

Bob fired at the rifleman, but missed. As he was steadying his aim for another try, he heard the crack of a different rifle, distinguishable from all the other guns going off because it didn't come from out on the street but rather from in *back* of the tents and buildings down the line.

Vern was covering the marshal with his Winchester and doing so with all the accuracy he'd laid claim to.

The raider suddenly flung out his arms—rifle falling from his grasp—and pitched from the saddle.

The reprieve was short-lived. The other raider held one arm extended at full length and fired a long-barreled revolver at Bob. One of the slugs cut close enough that Bob heard the unmistakable sound of its passing, a sound that anyone who's ever heard it never forgets.

Bob ducked down low on the gelding's back and swung the horse to face the new threat. In the sudden maneuver, the gelding's feet got tangled in some of the wreckage and stumbled, lurching sharply and nearly dropping to its front knees. Although Bob was a skilled rider, the jolt threw him off the gelding's back.

Once again he hit the ground rolling. The impact knocked only some of the wind out of him as he made sure to fiercely maintain a grip on his Colt. He was damned if he'd let a little horse spill knock him out of the battle. Not with so much at stake.

He shoved determinedly back to his feet, only to find the raider was nearly on top of him. Still mounted, the varmint was clearly aiming to ride right over him, knock him back down, and trample him into the dirt like the rest of the wreckage scattered all around them. Only a desperately nimble last-second dodge saved the marshal from being slammed back down by the raider's horse.

As he jumped to one side, Bob grabbed hold of the rider's leg, clamped it in the crook of his free arm, and pulled as hard as he could, intending to yank the rider from his saddle and either shoot him or brain him with his Colt. Only trouble was, the rider was in a better position to use his own handgun as a club. He beat the marshal to his intentions.

The pistol barrel clanging off the side of his head sent Bob to the ground yet again. As before, he clung to his Colt . . . but wasn't in such a big hurry to clamber back to his feet. He stayed on the ground, waiting and watching as the raider wheeled his horse around for another trampling attempt. Before the man could spur the animal forward, the marshal fired upward from his prone position.

Chapter 4

Had he kept on running, it was likely Fred would never have noticed the activity taking place in the alley that ran along the north side of the bank building. Four horses were tied at the rear where none really belonged. What was more, just as he glanced down the alley, a man ducked inside through the side door that was only used by bank personnel.

It was way too early for any of the bank people to show up for work, except for Abraham Starbuck, owner and president, who was notorious for arriving each morning well in advance of his employees. But the man Fred had caught a glimpse of definitely wasn't Starbuck. Not only that, neither was he at all recognizable to Fred, who knew each member of the bank staff quite well. And the way the man was dressed—shabby, dusty trail clothes with a gun belt around his waist—absolutely did not fit the employee dress code that fastidious old Starbuck strictly enforced.

Something was damned fishy.

All of a sudden, Fred forgot about his queasy

stomach and being out of breath. Every instinct told
him something bad was happening at the bank . . .
and he was the only one in a position to do anything about it. The commotion taking place in New
Town—either staged as a purposeful distraction or a
mighty suspicious coincidence—had the marshal and
most other able-bodied men drawn away from that
part of town. Leaving to go fetch some of them was
out of the question.

It was up to Fred to stay right where he was and
deal with whatever was going on.

Drawing his six-gun from its holster and holding it
at the ready, he started down the alley toward the
door he'd seen the strange man go through. With
nerves jumping around under his skin, he drew
closer to the door, fearful it might suddenly fly open
just as he reached it. The continuing gunfire from up
north didn't help his nerves any.

One of the horses tied at the end of the alley
suddenly chuffed and stamped its feet. Fred gave a
little start, but his gun hand stayed steady.

A moment later, he had cause to move his gun
hand quickly. At the end of the alley, a man stepped
out from behind the corner of the building and
reached to gentle the horse that had snorted. He
wasn't a man, really, just a kid barely into his teens,
but he was wearing a gun low-slung on his hip. A
cigarette hung from one corner of his pinched
mouth, slicing the lower part of his narrow, hard-
looking young face.

Fred got a real good look at those features when
the kid turned his face and looked straight at him.
Centering the muzzle of his .44 square on the young
man he reckoned to be a lookout posted with the

getaway horses, Fred figured bank robbers were paying a call inside.

"Hold it right there," he ordered, forcing his voice steady and firm. "Don't move a muscle."

The kid didn't listen. He was young and scared, probably more nervous than Fred. He knew he'd messed up by not watching the alley more closely and letting Fred get as far as he did. He was either more frightened by repercussions from his partners inside than by Fred's .44 or one of those young gunnies who thought he was fast enough on the draw to pull it off.

Whatever the case, he went for his gun and Fred had no choice but to shoot him. He fired twice, planting both slugs an inch apart in the fool's chest, sending him into a spinning fall. Before hitting the ground, the boy managed to draw his gun and trigger a round into the side of the building with a dying spasm of his fingers.

Close enough to the bank's side door, which wasn't latched all the way tight, Fred heard a gruff voice call out from inside. "Benny! What the hell's going on out there?"

Fred didn't answer right away. His mind raced. Four horses meant three robbers were inside. Likely, they had been waiting to overpower Abe Starbuck when he showed up and had forced him to let them in.

"Benny! Answer me, dammit!"

"Benny can't answer," Fred called back. "He's dead. He didn't give me any choice, but you've got a choice, unless you want to end up the same way. Throw your guns down and come out with your hands up!"

"To hell with you! Here's the only part of my gun you're gonna get!"

Whoever was doing the talking fired four rapid-fire rounds into the door's inner side. If he meant for the slugs to blast through and hit Fred or whoever else might be standing outside, he stupidly failed to take into consideration that the door was reinforced with sheet steel. The door banged and shuddered, but nothing went through. It would have served the shooter right—and suited Fred just fine—if one of the bullets had ricocheted back on the shooter.

Obviously wasn't the case. The man wasted no time going back to hollering. "We've got your bank president in here. We're fixin' to make him just as dead as you made Benny unless you're willin' to make a deal."

"No deals. Turn Starbuck loose and come on out like I told you. That's your only chance."

"Who the hell *are* you, anyway? You speak for the whole town?"

"I'm Marshal Robert Hatfield," Fred said, wishing that was true. Better yet, wishing the marshal was there instead of him. "And, yeah, I speak for the town."

Although no response came right away, he heard some muttering and murmuring from inside.

"Maybe you speak for the town, Marshal, but you sure as hell don't speak for Mr. Bank President here. Listen to what he has to say."

"M-Marshal, p-please do what this villain s-says," came a quavering voice that sounded only vaguely like the normally firm-toned Abe Starbuck. "You must do what he demands or they will surely kill me!"

The other voice followed immediately. "You heard him, Marshal. You stand back, let us ride out of here with him as hostage, and we'll let him go as soon as we're clear of town. That's the only way you're gonna keep him alive. You force us to blast our way clear, I'll make sure my first bullet goes into your banker man."

Convinced the quavering voice he'd heard was Starbuck, Fred's mind churned. He was vaguely aware that the shooting to the north had stopped, but he couldn't worry about what that meant. He had his hands more than full right where he was. "No good," he called back in response to the bank robber's proposed deal. "You'll get clear of town then dump Starbuck after killing him anyway. That's not a deal I'll bite on."

"It's the only one you're gonna get. The only one that'll leave your banker man alive."

"I've got the bank surrounded and a sharpshooter on the roof. You're trapped. The only way for *you* to come out alive is to release Mr. Starbuck unharmed. You follow him with your guns thrown down and your hands in the air, just like I said at the start."

"I think you're bluffin', damn you!"

"Think what you want. But in the end you'll—" Almost too late, Fred discovered that his bluff had already been called.

Marshal Hatfield's bullet skimmed the side of the raider's face, nipping off a piece of his left ear and knocking off his hat, making it pop straight up like a cork out of a bottle. The hombre jerked back in alarm, yanking so violently on his reins that his horse reared high on its hind legs.

When the animal came back down, the raider decided he'd had enough and swung his horse away, spurring it back into the midst of his cohorts. "That's enough," the hatless raider shouted to the others. "We've done our part. We've kept 'em busy as long as we can. Let's get the hell out of here!"

Fred never could say exactly what caused him to look away from the side door of the bank and turn to glance toward the mouth of the alley where it fed out to Front Street. When he did, he saw a man with a gun aimed right at him, leaning around the front corner of the bank.

With a speed fueled by desperation and a survival instinct as old as mankind, Fred reacted. He jerked around with his own gun and got a shot off before the man at the mouth of the alley fired on him. Fred's bullet failed to hit the would-be back shooter, but it came close enough. It struck the corner of the brick bank building and splattered chunks of brick and mortar against the side of the man's face, causing him to twist sharply away as he triggered a round that sailed high and harmless over Fred's head.

Instantly, Fred realized he'd be in a serious pickle if he stayed where he was, trading shots with the man at the mouth of the alley.

The marshal sat up with the intent of firing after the retreaters, but when he raised his gun hand it suddenly felt like it weighed a ton. He left it resting on his thigh and concentrated on catching his breath for a minute.

A minute was all he got . . . and it was damn near the last minute of his life.

As the raiders beat a full retreat and the townsmen

came boiling up the street through the clouds of gun smoke and dust, Bob caught a faint click of sound from behind him. Spinning around on his rump, he spotted the bloodied rifleman Vern had knocked out of the saddle. On his knees, the raider once again raised a weapon—a revolver drawn from the holster on his hip—and aimed it at the marshal.

To his misfortune, the man's wound made him slow and jerky, giving Bob enough time to raise his Colt and snap-fire a round before his would-be assassin could pull the trigger. A red-rimmed black hole appeared in the center of the man's forehead, slamming him backwards to land flat and limp in the puddle of gore that had spouted out the back of his head with the exiting bullet.

The Colt abruptly felt very heavy in Bob's hand once again. With no time to stop and catch another breath or for the men out in the street to pause and enjoy their rout of the raiders, the best he could do was return the Colt to its holster. They still had a fire to put out!

Moving with speed and decisiveness born of desperation, Fred lunged *past* the side door and calculated that while he was trading words with one of the robbers, one of the others had taken Starbuck's key and gone to the front. Seeing that Fred had indeed been bluffing, that robber had slipped out and attempted to catch him by surprise.

It had almost worked.

With no way to escape and nowhere to hide in the narrow alley, he grabbed the handle of the unlatched door, pulling it open along with him as he threw himself against the side of the building and pressed tight. Temporarily, the steel-reinforced door gave him a shield against anyone shooting at him from either the mouth of the alley or from inside.

The effectiveness of his move was put quickly to the test when the would-be back shooter down the alley opened up and sent three rounds pounding against the door. Once again, none of them came close to penetrating.

The robber from inside the bank—the leader, it seemed—called out, "Hold it. Hold it, you jackass! All you're doin' is sendin' ricochets in at us! How the hell did you miss him in the first place?"

"You wouldn't believe how fast that slob can move!" came the reply. "It's just a matter of time now. He tries to make it out from behind that door, I guarantee I won't miss his fat ass again!"

Working up a healthy dose of anger over the disparaging remarks about his weight, of which he was damn well aware but didn't like hearing about from others, especially lowdown back shooters, Fred was caught off guard by an unexpected move from the robber inside the bank. The door suddenly banged hard against his forehead, flattening his nose and pinning him against the rough bricks of the bank's outer wall.

"Come on! Come on! I got him pinned!" came the voice of the robber boss. "Get your ass down here and finish him!"

Ordinarily, Fred's size and strength would never have kept him jammed against the wall for more than a few seconds, but the blow to his forehead had stunned him to a point of dazed weakness.

Fred raised his hands to push back against the

door, but his fingers were spongy, without strength. His gun slipped from his grasp. He was vaguely aware of the sound of the man on the other side of the door, grunting with the effort of keeping it rammed against him . . . and of running feet, coming closer.

Suddenly, he heard the sound of hoofbeats, a running horse closing fast.

A new voice, a hazily familiar one, called, "Hold it right there, you varmints!"

Gunshots.

More curses.

The force of the door pressing against Fred eased momentarily then slammed back harder than ever.

Fred's knees sagged. The last thing he was aware of was the sound of more running feet and additional cracks of gunfire . . .

Chapter 5

Bob Hatfield looked on with a mixture of concern and pride as the doctor tended to Fred.

"There, that ought to do it," the doc announced as he straightened up from completing the task. At six feet and six inches in height, Dr. Amos Tibbs was frequently stooped over in his work. So much so that, even at the relatively young age of thirty-four, he carried his string-bean frame in a kind of hunched-shoulders manner that made some people think he was considerably older. The premature thinning of his hair and the spectacles perched on the end of his nose didn't help, even though his face had a contrasting boyish quality, especially when displaying the eagerness he felt for practicing his profession.

"Well?" Bob said. "How is he?"

"Oh, he'll be fine," Tibbs assured him. "The nose is broken, of course. I've stuffed it with cotton to stanch any bleeding and I've braced it as best I can with some bandages. The cotton can come out later today, but I'd leave the bandage on through tomorrow at least. He'll likely sport a couple shiners for a while. He took two hard raps on the noggin, so he can expect a headache for today anyway . . . but that will go away and the nose will heal. So, like I said, he'll be fine."

"You're right about having a headache," Fred said from where he sat on a straight-backed chair in the doctor's examining room. "I hope you're just as right about it going away pretty soon."

"It will," the doc said. "Try to stay awake throughout the day. Eat a good meal for lunch and another for supper. Maybe a glass of warm milk before you go to bed tonight. Get a good night's sleep and your head should feel good as new when you wake up. Just be careful not to bump your nose for the next few days. If it should start bleeding and won't stop, come back and see me."

"I'll see that he does," Bob said.

"Speaking of bleeding"—Tibbs looked at the marshal—"how about that cut on the side of your head? You going to slow down long enough to let me take a look at that now?"

"It's just a scratch. It's not even bleeding anymore."

"If it was made by a gun barrel clanging off the side of your head, you need to have it taken care of proper," said Fred, standing up. "Your turn in the chair. Take a seat."

Bob scowled at him but nevertheless went over and sat in the chair.

"Besides," Tibbs said as he began gently cleaning away the dried blood on the side of Bob's head, "I want to keep you two around long enough to hear firsthand accounts of all the excitement that took place while I was away. I was out delivering twins for

Mr. and Mrs. Nyquist until just before sunup and didn't get back to town until everything was dying down. Am I to understand that the two events—the raid and fire to the north and the attempted bank robbery here in Old Town—were connected?"

"They were connected all right," confirmed Bob. "The raid was staged as a diversionary tactic to pull all or most of our townsmen up into New Town so the robbery could take place without any interference. They'd have got away with it, too, if Fred here hadn't been on the ball and showed up to knock the hell out of their plan."

"I was doing okay," Fred said, "until I took a pretty good knock of my own from that stupid door. Then another. If you hadn't come riding to the rescue, Marshal, I would have been a goner." He paused, scrunching his face into a frown. "I'm still a little fuzzy, though, on how you knew to leave fighting the fire and ride down to where I was in trouble at the bank."

"After we put the run on those raiders," Bob explained, "everybody immediately swarmed the fire. Luckily, the fire hadn't got too much of a start and we had plenty of men. So, with shovelfuls of dirt and buckets of water, we got the flames under control pretty quick.

"Some of the men, thinking it was a bigger deal than it was, ran back to get the water wagon. That's when they spotted you trying to flush those rascals out of the bank. After one of 'em ran back to tell me, I grabbed the saddled horse of one of the dead raiders and hightailed it down to find out what was what. I was just in time to see two gang members boiling into the alley with you pinned unconscious behind that door. When they saw me coming up the alley behind 'em on a horse, they got a lot more interested in reaching their own horses for a get-away than in sticking around to finish you or finish trying to rob the bank." He shrugged his shoulders. "Either one."

"It sounds like stuff straight out of a dime novel," said Tibbs, excitement showing on his boyish face as he applied a bandage to Bob's gashed head. "Raiders, robbers, shoot-outs, fires, a daring ride to execute a last-second rescue. It's got all the elements of a crackerjack yarn."

"Well, let me tell you," said Fred. "It's a lot more fun to read about that kind of stuff than it is to go through it."

Bob nodded. "That's especially true for the men who died or got wounded—bullet wounds, I'm talking about. A lot more serious than these scratches of ours."

"That's why I took care of them first. At your insistence," Tibbs reminded him. "Fortunately, none of them were all that bad. Including—and I don't know if you'd call this fortunate or not—the one you put in that robber you managed to capture."

"It sure wasn't fortunate that I let the other two get away," Bob muttered bitterly.

Tibbs gave a little laugh. "I wouldn't beat yourself up over it. I can assure you that your grateful public is finding no shortfall in your performance, not based on what I heard while I was tending the wounded men. And that goes for both of you. You drove back a band of menacing raiders, put out a threatening fire, and prevented a bank robbery. Not to mention suffering wounds in the process. *And . . .* the robber you *did* manage to capture is *only* Arlo Sanders, one of the most wanted desperadoes on the Western frontier. I'd say that's a pretty fair morning's work for a pair of small-town lawmen."

Bob looked at Fred and grinned crookedly. "You hear that, Fred? We're a couple of ripsnortin' heroes."

Fred managed a grin, too. "Remind me again when my head quits hurting. I'm sure I'll appreciate it more then."

Once again Tibbs stepped back from his handiwork, saying to Bob, "There. That should do it. I probably should've put a couple stitches in that cut, but that would've meant shaving away some of your hair, and I didn't figure you'd hold still for that. Don't be in a hurry to pull that bandage off. It *will* yank some hair when you do."

"Heck, that won't bother me, Doc," said Bob, rising to his feet. "Us heroes eat pain for breakfast and dine on danger all through the rest of the day. Ain't that right, Fred?"

Fred didn't look so chipper about things. "If we've got Arlo Sanders in our jail, we'll be getting a daily dose of danger, that's for sure, just from having that snake close by."

"Well, that's where he is," Bob said. "Mike Bullock and a couple of his boys are looking after him while we're away. We'd better get down there and spell them."

The two lawmen thanked Tibbs for his services.

As they started for the door, Bob paused and said,

"Send your bill to Mike and he'll see to it the town council gets you paid, Doc."

"Sounds good."

Bob lingered a moment longer. "By the way, Doc . . . can you think of a country that starts with the letter *Q*?"

Chapter 6

Bob and Fred emerged from the doctor's office and found a throng of still-excited citizens milling about, waiting for them. Most of the faces were familiar but, while the lawmen had a cordial enough relationship with the majority of them, they weren't at all used to the way the people were looking at them. Their expressions seemed to be . . . awestruck, adoring. Those were the only words Bob could think of. Accurate or not, it made him feel uncomfortable as hell. Creepy, even.

Among the faces Bob took particular note of was Consuela's. Any way she chose to look at him, he was okay with. He gave her a little smile to let her know everything was okay. Next his gaze came to rest on Curtis Pardee and his three nephews—the Macy boys, Peter, Vern, and Lee. Bob owed them a big debt, especially Vern. He meant to make that fact well known, but for the time being, he simply acknowledged them with a nod.

Quite surprising, the most prominent and vocal of those gathered was none other than Abraham Starbuck, the banker. Normally a gruff, standoffish sort who never mingled much with common folks or exchanged pleasantries with hardly anyone, the recent situation found him acting like another person.

"Here they are now!" he pronounced at the sight of Bob and Fred. "Our city's finest—the brave badge-wearers who led the way to saving the day for all of Rattlesnake Wells. Join me in raising three cheers. Make it loud and make it proud!"

"Hip-hip, hooray! . . . Hip-hip, hooray! . . . Hip-hip, hooray!"

Bob could feel himself blushing furiously. Fred was, too, although Bob could tell he was also soaking up the positive outpouring. While Bob considered Fred a fully competent deputy, his weight and some of the predicaments he'd gotten himself into over the years had made him the brunt of more than a little unkind ribbing and some cruel remarks from certain rude jackasses. Bob told himself any discomfort he felt at the moment was worth enduring for the sake of Fred's enjoyment of it.

Pointing and laying it on even thicker, Starbuck said, "Had it not been for Deputy Fred's brave confrontation with the bank robbers—totally without assistance, mind you—not only would our bank have been robbed, it would have been blown to smithereens."

Starbuck had earlier revealed that the man Fred had first seen ducking back into the bank was returning from the horses, where he'd gone to fetch some dynamite in order to blow the bank safe because Starbuck, even after being beaten, would not reveal the combination.

Said dynamite had since been confiscated and was being held at the sheriff's office.

"And the Lord only knows what fate I would have suffered beyond these bruises and fractures you now see in evidence," Starbuck went on, raising his arms like a fire-and-brimstone preacher calling down the thunder. "But I was saved by the quick action and bravery of Deputy Fred . . . with a last-minute assist from our stalwart Marshal Hatfield, who had already fought a gun battle and helped extinguish a fire in the north part of our town.

"I ask you, ladies and gentlemen, has a citizenry ever been represented by two finer individuals?"

In response, the crowd murmured and stirred and shouted out affirmations.

Bob decided he didn't want to go through another round of hip-hooraying, no matter how good it might make Fred feel. He stepped forward, raising his hand to quell the crowd and prevent Starbuck from continuing. "Thank you, Mr. Starbuck. Thank you very much for all the kind words." Looking out at the crowd, he added, "And thanks for the showing from all of you folks. Me and Fred really appreciate it. But, and I know I speak for Fred too when I say this, we want to remind you that we're just a couple fellas doing our jobs. It's what we get paid for. So, again, thank you for this showing of appreciation, but now we've got other things to attend to as part of our duties . . . just as I'm sure you fine folks have got other things to do . . . so how about we break this up and all go about our business?"

The crowd began to disperse as suggested, but Abe Starbuck wasn't finished yet. Stepping in between the lawmen, he clapped them each on the back, saying, "Yet another example of devotion to duty. Not that I would expect anything less. And that's exactly the kind of thing I want to broadcast to a greater audience. That's why I sent a telegram to the Cheyenne *Gazette* and gave them a brief account of what went on here today. They're sending a reporter and a photographer on the next train to get the full story. You brave boys—and, indeed, our whole brave little town—deserve the recognition."

The reaction from Fred and Bob was in sharp contrast.

Fred's chest puffed up and he beamed like a kid with a new puppy. "Wow. You mean we'll be wrote about and read about all the way to Cheyenne?"

"Maybe farther," said Starbuck. "Maybe some other newspapers will pick up the story and your names and deeds will be read about as far away as New York and Boston."

"Wow," Fred said again.

"What's the matter, Marshal?" Starbuck asked. "You don't look so pleased at such a prospect."

"Like I said before," replied a frowning Bob. "I appreciate the appreciation . . . but some things are better off not played up too big."

Chapter 7

As the two lawmen walked toward the marshal's office and jail, Fred kept casting sidelong glances over at his boss before finally asking, "What's wrong, Marshal? You seemed to be in pretty good humor in the doctor's office, but now you all of a sudden look like you want to bite somebody's head off. Did I do or say something wrong?"

Fred's question and its revelation of his typical low opinion of himself, especially coming so quick on the heels of the way he'd been so pumped up with pride only moments ago, made Bob instantly regret the sour mood he'd slipped into and was doing nothing to hide. He drew to an abrupt halt in the middle of the boardwalk, causing Fred to stop, too.

Facing his deputy and looking him square in the eye, Bob said, "No, Fred, you didn't do a darn thing wrong. Why would you ask that? In fact, let me parrot Starbuck's words and say again, in case I haven't made it clear enough, I've never been prouder of you. Yeah, me and some of the other fellas fought the raiders and the fire and I might have showed up at the last minute to lend you a hand with those robbers, but *you* are the one who saved the day as far as that robbery goes. You not only kept the money from being taken, you also saved old man Starbuck's life. You got every right to be proud of that. So do it, and quit fretting and asking fool doggone questions about if you did anything wrong."

"Okay, Marshal, but I can't help noticing how you've taken on a bad mood. Yeah, I was able to do some good by interfering with those robbers, but it was only because I was running so late in answering the fire bell."

"Well, if you can have as good a luck as you did by running late once in a while, then in this case, I'd say the good outweighed the bad. So go with that," Bob told him. "As far as my mood, I reckon that's my business. Ain't got nothing to do with you. Let's just say I got some things on my mind and leave it at that, okay?"

"Sure, Marshal. Whatever you say," Fred replied.

Bob clapped him on the shoulder. "All right. Now let's get down to the jail so we can take over for Bullock and start spending some time of our own with Arlo Sanders."

At the marshal's office, they found Mike Bullock and Angus McTeague waiting for them as they kept an eye on the new prisoner. Actually, Sanders wasn't just the new prisoner, he was the *only* prisoner. The two men seated out in the office weren't really keeping an eye on him inasmuch as he was locked up back in the cell block. The heavy door to the cell block was propped open so anything the gang leader had to say or any movement he made was easily heard.

Bullock was sitting by the potbellied stove, sipping from a cup of coffee. McTeague was seated behind the marshal's desk lighting up one of the cheap, smelly black cigars he favored even though he could afford the finest on the market.

Bob was surprised to see McTeague present. He remembered calling for someone to fetch the man when he first went running into New Town but never recalled seeing him after that, not during the shoot-out with the raiders or fighting the fire.

"Make him yourself at home," Bob greeted, as he removed his hat and hung it on the hat rack just inside the door.

McTeague smiled and puffed his stinky cigar. He was a beefy individual, thick through the chest and shoulders, with hands the size of shovels and fingers as thick as wagon spokes. His face was broad and fleshy, heavily jowled, framed by coal black sideburns. He'd been one of the first to strike gold in the Prophecies and had parlayed that into a total of three mines—the McT #1, #2, and #3—that he operated with the sweat and labor of others who worked for him. From all reports, he was a tough but fair boss. He got wealthy and he paid his men good. He'd also parlayed his wealth and success into becoming the head of the New Town miners' council, which basically kept order in Rattlesnake Wells' boom wing. They requested minimal help from Marshal Hatfield but were generally cooperative when he felt the need to intervene.

All that prompted McTeague to say, "Understand you did some mighty good work up in my neck of the woods this mornin'. I was up at McT number three overnight and just got in a little bit ago. Thought I'd come by and extend my gratitude and appreciation. Not only for takin' the lead on runnin' off those raiders but also for stoppin' the bank robbery. So happens I got a fair chunk of money in Starbuck's joint."

"A lot of people do," Bob said, then jabbed a thumb toward Fred. "As far as stopping the bank robbers, that was mainly Fred's doing. You can thank him."

"Yeah, that's what I heard. I do indeed thank you, Deputy Fred."

Fred blushed some more. "Just doing my job, sir."

Bob moved toward the stove. "As far as the raiders and the fire up in your neck of the woods—which us folks down here in Old Town happen to consider all part of Rattlesnake Wells' neck of the woods—I had a lot of help from men on both sides of the point."

McTeague nodded. "I heard that, too, and just got done expressin' my gratitude to my counterpart, Mr. Bullock, and asked him to be sure and share it with all who participated. Rest assured if the tide ever swings the other way somehow, me and the men from our . . . well, from the north part of town . . . will come runnin' to help in kind."

"Duly noted," said Bullock, raising his coffee cup in a salute.

From a row of hooks above the stove, Bob took a cup for himself. "Who made the coffee?" he asked, reaching for the pot after picking up a cloth holder to guard his hand against the hot handle.

"I did," said Bullock.

"How is it?"

"Terrible."

Bob twisted his mouth wryly. "Good. Sounds right in line with what we're used to." After pouring himself a cup, he motioned with the pot to Fred and then McTeague.

Fred shook his head.

McTeague arched a shaggy brow and said, "After the glowing testimonial from you two, I think I'll pass."

"After sucking that nasty-smelling cigar smoke in and out of your mouth," observed Bullock, "I'm surprised to hear you find anything distasteful."

"We each suffer our own poisons," McTeague replied as he stood up, making a gesture to Bob. "I imagine you'll be wanting your chair back. You'll pardon me the impertinence, but after a buckboard ride back down the mountain this morning my back was killing me. This chair of yours looked and was very soothing."

"You ought to get yourself one."

"I already have one. Two, in fact. But I wasn't near them. As soon as I leave here, I fully intend to seek out the nearest and sink back into it."

Taking the vacated chair, Bob said, "Well, I appreciate you stopping by. And certainly you, too, Mike, for keeping an eye on the prisoner and all. I imagine both of you have other matters to attend to, so if you need to take your leave, me and Fred can take it from here."

"We'll be doing just that," said McTeague, "but, before we go, Mike and I have been discussing a matter that concerns you and Fred and therefore something we'd like to pursue a bit further with the both of you present."

"Oh? And what might that be?"

"Takin' nothing away from the damn near heroic job you and Fred did this mornin'," Bullock said, "McTeague brought up something a little bit ago that me and the fellas on the Old Town council have touched on a time or two but never really followed up on. After today, I think maybe it's time we did."

"And after today," McTeague added, "I think it's time that me and the New Town miners' council started workin' more closely, at least on certain matters, with Mike and his group."

"I sure see the value in that," Bob said. "I'll be the first to concede that miners and prospectors are a stubborn, special breed unto themselves and yet you and the miners' council have been doing a pretty good job of keeping the lid on things, McTeague. But, like I said before, Gold Avenue and New Town are by any reasonable reckoning a part of Rattlesnake Wells. That means it's only sensible for a joint set of rules and laws to apply to both parts."

"Agreed," said McTeague. "That's what brings up the question of how effective just you and Fred can be—no matter how dedicated and competent you are—if you're spread too doggone thin. You were perfectly adequate for Rattlesnake Wells the way it used to be, but with all the growth due to the gold strike and the way New Town has sprung up . . . well, realistically, how can you possibly cover it all? Especially, when almost as many of the newcomers arriving—fleecers and scam artists and downright crooks—equal the number of honest miners and prospectors."

"In other words," said Bullock, boiling it down, "we're wondering if it wouldn't be a good idea for you to add on another deputy or maybe two. If Angus and the miners' council are willing to pitch in, the cost shouldn't be a problem. We'd even include a raise for you two veterans. What do you think?"

Bob exchanged glances with Fred then cut his eyes back to Bullock and McTeague. "To be honest with you, I've thought about the same thing. Fred and I have even discussed it some. We sure wouldn't have any argument with the raise part. And another deputy or two . . . I can't come up with an argument against that, either. All I ask is that I have final say on anybody we end up pinning a badge on."

"Of course. Goes without saying," agreed Bullock. He turned to McTeague. "You talk to your men, I'll talk to mine. We need to get together and settle this as soon as possible, before it fades from importance again. Right?"

"Couldn't agree more," said McTeague. "And speaking of importance, Bob, do you think there's any chance we may get a return visit from Sanders's gang?"

"Been wondering about that myself. By my count, six of 'em got away. No telling if any of 'em are wounded or otherwise chewed up some. If not, that still leaves a fairly sizable force. Not impossible to think they might work up the notion to try and bust their leader out of jail. Or hit the bank again. Or possibly both."

"But wouldn't they be a little gun-shy about hitting us all over again?" asked Bullock. "I mean, considerin' how they failed at their robbery and got sent packin' the way they did?"

"Be nice to think that. It could be exactly how they'd figure it. On the other hand, they might be pissed off enough to want another crack at us for revenge as much as anything else. Or they might think it would be a good idea to hit us again right away while we're still licking our wounds and softened up some from the first time."

Bullock frowned. "Well, those are some unsettling thoughts to have."

Bob spread his hands. "I'm just saying. I don't want folks to go around jumping at shadows, living in fear. By the same token, we need to stay alert."

"How about a posse to go after the gang? Chase 'em down and remove any threat they could pose?" said McTeague.

"The time for a posse would have been right away this morning, when we could have ridden out hot on their trail," Bob said. "But things were too chaotic. We had people wounded and wreckage all over and we were still putting together the pieces of what exactly had happened. I decided it best to keep all able-bodied men right here."

"What about now? What about leading some men out to track them now?"

Bob shook his head. "No good. We could track them for a while, no doubt. But there's also little doubt they've headed up into the mountains by now, probably the Shirleys, where there's nothing but stands of thick timber, dozens of narrow canyons, and hard ground. You can't track men on rocks. Be a waste of time or, worse yet, an invitation into an ambush."

"So what does that leave?"

"We stay sharp, stay prepared. Be ready if the Sanders gang—or anybody else, for that matter—tries anything. Not too different from the way we've been getting along up to now." Bob's tone hardened. "We can't live scared, can't let the fear of something rattle us. That's not the way this town was forged and built, and this is no time to start living that way."

"By God, I like the sound of that," said McTeague. "I guess that kind of attitude is what makes you Sundown Bob and, once again, why we're damned lucky to have you."

Bob winced a little at the "Sundown Bob" remark. It's what a few of the townsfolk had taken to calling him, based on his fiery red hair and the skill he'd shown a time or two in the past when forced into a gunfight. He'd never cottoned to it much, but since it was usually used in a favorable way, like McTeague was doing, he tended to put up with it.

Rising to his feet, Bullock said, "I guess the only question left is the matter of how long you figure to keep Sanders here in your jail. I think we're all agreed that's asking for trouble, any way you cut it."

"You're probably right about that," Bob said. "As far as keeping him here, I'd just as soon it was as brief as possible. The trouble with that is, he's wanted in so dang many different jurisdictions I don't rightly know who's got priority for laying claim to him. My aim is to send out some telegrams this afternoon and see what I can find out. In the meantime, the circuit judge ain't due to pass through here for another two weeks. I hope to be rid of Sanders by then, but if not, I reckon we'll see what the judge has to say. Hell, we might end up hanging the cuss right here."

Bullock and McTeague exchanged glances.

"All the more reason for us to get authorization for the marshal to have more deputies," said Bullock.

"Absolutely," agreed McTeague. "Let's get on it right away."

The two council leaders were still making plans as they went out the door.

Chapter 8

Appearance-wise, there was nothing special about Arlo Sanders. He was of average height and build, less than a year short of forty. He had dark, suspicious eyes over a bulbous-tipped nose, under which a pencil mustache extended unevenly above a thin-lipped mouth that frequently curled into a sneer he probably imagined was more menacing than it really was.

Stepping into the back to check on the prisoner, Marshal Hatfield found him seated on the edge of his cell bunk, shirtless, with a blanket over his shoulders. Bob could see part of the bandage Doc Tibbs had applied to Sanders's left shoulder after digging out the bullet Bob put there.

Sanders looked up and right away a sneer formed on his mouth. "Well, well. If it ain't Sundown Bob."

The marshal was caught off guard for a moment then remembered the propped-open door would have allowed the prisoner to hear all or most of what was said out in the office area. "You're just lucky," he told Sanders, "that I didn't set *your* sun instead of only putting a bullet in you. For everybody else, it would've simplified things if I had."

"You want to simplify things?" Sanders echoed. "Come dark, just slip the lock on this cracker box and leave me on my way. Just a matter of time before I make it out anyway. Either I'll manage it on my own or my gang will come back and bust me loose. Comes to that, they'll set the sun on this whole stinkin' town while they're at it."

"They didn't have such good luck the first time they tried that," Bob pointed out. "If they were so dead set on keeping you from behind bars, why did they all hightail it and leave you laying in that bank alley in the first place?"

"They were runnin' for their lives," was the quick protest. "For all they knew, I was dead. When word spreads—and it will—that I'm in here alive, you can bet they'll start makin' plans to free me."

"Making plans and getting it done are two different things," Bob said tersely. "If they don't come up with no better idea than riding in and shooting up the place all over again, it could be that a stray bullet might find you in the process. Permanentlike . . . Think on that."

Bob left the cell block, making a point to kick away the wedge of wood holding the door open, and entered the office area.

Fred was holding his heads in his hands as he sat in the chair formerly occupied by Mike Bullock. He looked up. He was pale and it was plain to see he was feeling pretty miserable. As the doctor had warned, the skin under and around his eyes was taking on a greenish-purple tint.

"If you feel as bad as you look," said Bob, "I think you'd better get out of here for a while and do some healing up."

"I'll be all right," Fred insisted. "You got banged up, too. If you can gut it out, I ought to be able to."

"But I didn't get it as rough as you," Bob argued. "I mean it, get out of here for a while. Go home, take some of that medicine the doc gave you, and take it easy. Try not to go to sleep, like he told you. Just rest. If you can, come back by this evening. I want to make our standard rounds, and I want to look in on the men who got wounded chasing off those raiders."

Fred continued to look reluctant. "Are you sure?"

"I said so, didn't I? Now beat it."

Fred stood up.

"One thing you can do for me on the way, though," said Bob. "Stop by the telegraph and ask Feeney to come see me the first chance he gets. I want to get some telegrams off to check on Sanders's wanted status in different places, but I don't want to leave the jail unattended. I can dictate a general message to Feeney, and he can send it off where I tell him."

"See, right there," Fred tried to argue. "I can stick around long enough to—"

"We already covered that. Get out of here and send Feeney. Now beat it, like I told you."

Fred shuffled to the door. "Okay. I'll be sure to make it back before evening."

After Fred had gone, Bob leaned back in his chair, closed his eyes, and sat very still for several minutes. Many things churned through his mind. The events of the morning, naturally. But other events as well. Events from a past that was distant and yet not all that far . . .

Texas, six years earlier

Rafe Hammond had just finished saying grace at the head of the family table when they heard the horses riding up out front. The windows and front door were open to the warm summer night, so the sound easily reached in to them.

Alberto Diaz, seated at the opposite end of the large oval table, frowned at the noise. He was the Hammond ranch foreman, a widower who took his meals at the Hammond table, along with his son and daughter. "I suspect that is Ramos, coming back from town. I'm surprised he is in such a hurry, considering the scolding he is due for arriving late for supper."

Martha Hammond, the matriarch of the gathering, smiled tolerantly. "Oh, don't be too hard on the boy. You know how handsome he is and how the gals flock around him when he goes to town. Are you so old and cranky, Alberto, that you've forgotten how easy it is to lose track of time when you're lingering with a pretty girl?"

Alberto tried to look stern, but a grudging trace of a smile tugged at one corner of his mouth. "Humph. When I used to linger with the mother of Ramos and Consuela—who was the prettiest girl in all of Sonora—I was never late for supper. But sometimes I forgot about supper completely." He laughed gruffly. "I truly knew how to linger."

"Then keep that in mind and don't make a scene when Ramos comes in," said his daughter Consuela.

Before Alberto could reply, a voice called from outside where the arriving riders had reined up. "Mr. Diaz! Mr. Hammond! You need to come out here right away!"

"Ramos has been hurt!" another voice added.

Bob Hammond, Rafe's oldest son and Ramos's best friend, shot to his feet and was out the door ahead of both Rafe and Alberto.

Three men on horseback were at the hitch rail in front of the house. The one in the middle was slumped weakly in his saddle and, even in the gloom of evening, Bob could tell by his fancy shirt and concha-studded vest that it was Ramos. The other two riders were wranglers who worked for the Hammond Slash-H brand.

"What happened?" Bob wanted to know. A moment after he spoke, he saw the dark stains smearing the front of Ramos's shirt.

"He's been shot," said Curley Danielson, the rider to the right of Ramos. "It's pretty bad."

"We wanted to take him to the doctor in town, but he insisted on comin' here," added Smoky Jessup, the other wrangler.

"Shot?" echoed Alberto. "How did such a thing happen?"

"By who?" Bob demanded coldly.

Before anyone could answer, Rafe barged forward. "Somebody give me a hand before he falls out of that saddle."

Bob and Alberto rushed to help him, and the three of them eased Ramos down to the ground as gently as possible. The wounded man groaned from the handling, and when Bob straightened he could feel warm, sticky blood covering his hand.

Remaining on his knees beside the bleeding boy, Rafe called loudly over his shoulder, "Martha, bring a lantern and some clean cloth for bandaging. Hurry!"

Ramos groaned some more and said, his voice very faint, "Oh, Papa . . . It hurts real bad."

Alberto leaned close over his son.

In the faint light, Bob could see the shine of tears rimming his eyes.

"Be still, my son. Try not to move," Alberto said in a hoarse whisper as he squeezed one of Ramos's hands.

Curley climbed down from his saddle and stepped over to

stand beside Bob. Keeping his voice low, he said, "It was Willis Breen. He goaded Ramos into a gunfight. In town they're all sayin' it was a fair fight, that Ramos even drew first. But there was no way he stood a chance against Breen. It was murder plain and simple, Bob. Ain't no other word for it."

Bob's face flushed with anger, turning near as red as his hair. At the same time, he could feel a cold fist balling low in his gut. As he let Curley's words sink in, trying to come to grips with his feelings, his mother and Consuela came rushing out from inside the house. Consuela carried a large lantern, and Martha had a bundle of clean linen.

As Martha also sank to her knees beside Ramos and Consuela hovered close to hold the light, Bob turned and looked back toward the house. His wife Priscilla stood in the open doorway, holding their young son in her arms. She looked pale and wan, the way she did most days lately. Always a bit frail and sickly, she hailed from back east. She'd moved to Texas with her family, but had never really adjusted to the more rugged conditions of the West. It hadn't stopped her from falling in love and marrying Bob, but most of her frailties and delicate ways remained.

"Lord," said Martha. "By the look of that shirt, he's lost a lot of blood, and he's still bleeding. We have to find a way to stop that and do it quick."

"What's worse," said Rafe, "is that I can't find no exit wound. That means the bullet is still in there."

Gut shot! *The two dreaded words screamed inside Bob's head, and a tremor of increased rage passed through him.*

"My God," Consuela whispered. With her free hand she made the sign of the cross over her bosom . . .

* * *

"Señor Bob?"

Consuela's voice—not whispering, not from Texas six years ago, but in the office, in the now—jolted Bob from his reverie. He opened his eyes and sat up straight.

Consuela stood in front of his desk. He hadn't heard her come in.

An impish smile played across her full, lovely lips. "Did I catch you napping on the job?"

"Of course not." Bob scowled. "I was lost in deep thought, that's all."

The impishness moved to a twinkle in Consuela's eyes. "I see. So if Bucky came home from school one day with a note informing you he had fallen asleep in class, but he argued that he was not asleep, only lost in deep thought, you would understand perfectly, no?"

"No," Bob said with finality. "Bucky's a kid. He doesn't have deep thoughts. Especially not in school. If he did, he'd have better grades. On second thought, if he was trying to figure a way to get *out* of school, he might put some hard thought into it."

Seeing that Bob appeared to be in a tense mood, Consuela put away any attempt to tease him further. "I think you are sometimes too hard on the boy about his schooling. Of course, that is not for me to say. What I will say, however, is that Bucky has certainly heard about everything that went on this morning . . . so when he gets out of school and comes tearing here all excited to hear the firsthand details from his hero father, I hope you can manage to be a little bit accommodating and pleasant."

Bob could see that his sour mood had rubbed off

on Consuela. "Aw, come on. Cut me a little slack, will you? I'm sorry if I kinda snapped at you when you were just poking a little fun. But I *do* have a few things on my mind. I hope you can understand that. Especially with that blasted Starbuck carrying on the way he's decided to."

"What's so bad about that?" Consuela said, genuinely puzzled. "Everybody in town is buzzing about how good a job you and Fred did, how brave you are. What's wrong with Mr. Starbuck calling in a newspaper reporter and arranging for you to get a little wider recognition for it?"

"What's wrong with it?" Bob echoed. "Stop and think, Con. You of all people should see the potential risk. Texas may seem like a long way away, but it's not all that far. A fella they called the Devil's River Kid got a lot of newspaper coverage once upon a time, along with having his likeness plastered on wanted posters all over creation. A story might be okay, but if it includes some photographs and it gets picked up by other papers, like Starbuck said it might . . ." His voice trailed off. "You see now what's got me kinda worried?"

Consuela nipped her lower lip between her even white teeth. "But that was years ago, Señor Bob. The Devil's River Kid got caught in a blizzard one winter trying to make it back to his hideout. No one has seen him since and everyone believes he must have died somewhere up in the Devil's River Wilderness that gave him his name."

"No body was ever found," Bob reminded her. "And not everyone is convinced the Kid didn't make it through that blizzard alive somehow and then gave up his outlaw ways to go off and make a new life somewhere."

Neither of them spoke for a minute.

Then Consuela said, "Texas has many stories. So does Wyoming. There's no reason to think that one has need to borrow off the other."

Bob set his jaw. "Let's hope not."

Chapter 9

Abruptly, Bob and Consuela showed mutual awareness that she had been standing the whole time holding a straw basket with a cloth over it.

Bob pointed. "Were you bringing that here? Or are you on your way somewhere else with it?"

"No, it's for you," Consuela said. "I know it's a little early, but it's your lunch. All things considered, I doubted you would be coming home to eat. Plus I wanted to check and see how that head wound of yours is."

"My head's okay. Doc Tibbs took good care of it."

"How about Fred? How is he?"

"He got banged up a little worse than me, but he'll be okay. He went home to take it easy for a while." Bob grinned. "When you see him again, be prepared. It looks like he's gonna end up with two black eyes out of that busted nose."

Consuela giggled at the mental image. "He will look like a big, cuddly raccoon."

"I don't know about the cuddly part."

Consuela placed her basket on the desk. "Well, when he comes back there's a sandwich in here for him, too, if he's hungry."

"We're talking about Fred. Have you ever known him not to be hungry?"

"True. If he is not, you had better take him back to the doctor and have him checked for a more serious injury." Consuela tapped a finger on the basket. "I also put a sandwich in here for your prisoner."

Bob frowned. "I don't know if that skunk deserves decent food."

"You've had other skunks behind bars and we always fed them. You can hardly let this one starve to death."

"Yeah, you're right." Bob pointed a finger at Consuela and scowled for emphasis. "Listen, I don't know how long we're going to have Sanders in our jail, but if there's reason for you to bring his meals here like now, rather send them with me, I don't want you going back in the cell block to give them to him. You got that? Even if he has to wait, only me or Fred will take them back."

Consuela nodded. "Sí. If you say so."

"I say so."

The front door opened then and Harold Feeney, the town's telegraph operator, came in. An elderly gent, somewhere between sixty and a hundred, he was black as a pit, with a smooth dome head and an equally smooth face except for the fine crinkles around his eyes. He had cotton white sideburns, a fringe of the same around the back of his head, and thick white eyebrows that were usually tinted green from the opaque green bill of the eyeshade he always had strapped to his head.

"Mornin', Marshal. Miss Consuela," Feeney greeted them, then focused on Bob. "Fred stopped by a little while ago and said you wanted I should come around when I got a chance."

"That's right. I need to get off some telegrams but don't want to leave the jail unattended. I was hoping I could give you the messages and where I want them to go and you'd send them for me."

"Sure, I can do that," agreed Feeney.

"Sounds like you've got business to tend to, so I'd best be going," said Consuela. "Don't forget to eat your lunch. Will you be home for supper tonight?"

"I plan on it," Bob told her. "I plan on sleeping here in the back room tonight so I at least want to have a meal at home and spend a little time with Bucky before I have to come back here."

"Okay. I'll plan on it, then."

When Consuela had left, Feeney showed a wide, appreciative grin. "There goes one mighty pretty gal."

"Yeah, I suppose she is," said Bob.

Feeney gave him a look. "You *suppose*? Even my rheumy ol' ancient eyes can see it plain. You need lookin' glasses or something?"

"No, I don't need glasses. I need telegrams sent out. Have a seat."

Feeney sat down in front of the desk as Bob produced a pad of yellow lined paper and a pencil and pushed them in front of the telegrapher. Feeney hitched his chair closer and got ready to write.

Twenty minutes later, Feeney had scribbled down a half dozen messages and where to send them. As he got up and started for the door, the marshal thanked him and told him to send his bill to the town council and it would get paid.

After Feeney was gone, Bob put one of Consuela's sandwiches on a tin plate and took it back to Sanders, along with a cup of coffee:

Returning to the office area, he poured himself a cup, took another sandwich out of the basket, and sat back down at the desk. As he ate, he pulled a stack of wanted posters from a desk drawer and leafed through them, checking to see if he'd missed any jurisdictions of significance. He had dictated his messages to Feeney from memory as far as jurisdictions where he knew Arlo Sanders and his gang had struck.

As he ate and leafed through the sheets of paper, Bob couldn't help thinking about a place and time where wanted posters had been no part of his life. Once again, his mind drifted back . . .

Texas, six years earlier

Ramos Diaz died that evening on the ground in front of the house. They hadn't been able to stop the bleeding until his heart stopped and ended it for them. All they could do then was wrap him in clean linen and carry his body into the house.

The women wept. The men cursed.

All except Bob Hammond. He was done cursing. It was time to act.

When he silently strapped on his gun belt and took his hat from the peg where he'd placed it before supper, the others all stopped their lamentations over the corpse that had been

Bob's lifelong best friend. They directed their attention to Bob as he started for the door, still without saying anything.

"No, son. That's not the way," Rafe said, stopping him.

Bob turned. "It's not? Then what is the way, Pa? To do like we've been doing? Excuse me, but that don't seem to have worked so well. We've been pushed, prodded, bullied, threatened . . . and now this. I say it ends here. I say it's time to push back and it starts with Willis Breen."

"You can't go up against Breen."

"I can and I will. I can take him."

"Bob," said his mother. "We're already faced with burying one fine young man whose pride led to tragedy. Don't make it two."

"Plus you've got a wife and son to think of," spoke up Priscilla.

Bob's gaze raked all of them. "None of you understand . . . I can't not do this. Not and live with myself . . . I'm sorry, but that's all there is to it."

Then he was out the door and in the bloody saddle of Ramos's horse and spurring the animal toward town.

Willis Breen worked for Cameron Bell, the largest rancher in the county, well on his way to becoming what some called a cattle baron. In order to grow and expand the reach of his Liberty Bell brand, Bell needed more land—land currently belonging to Rafe Hammond's Slash-H brand, and land Hammond wasn't interested in giving up. Rafe couldn't be bought, nor could he be bullied or intimidated—not even when Bell hired the likes of Breen and his reputation for being a top gunman. So far, Rafe had stopped short of fighting back. All he did was stand fast and stubborn, believing that Bell would eventually seek out another way to expand his empire.

Bob Hammond was tired of just standing fast and enduring the slurs and dirty tricks. He would not merely endure what amounted to the murder of his best friend. He was ready to not only fight back but to take the fight directly to Bell's bully-boy, Willis Breen.

In the town of Calderone, Bob found him drinking and celebrating inside the Broken Spoke Saloon, right where Curley Danielson had suggested he'd be. Drinking and celebrating how he'd gunned down Ramos in the street out front.

When Bob walked in, the place went silent.

Breen watched him closely, all the while wearing a taunting sneer.

"What'll it be, Bob?" asked the nervous barkeep.

"Blood," Bob answered.

"W–What?"

"You heard me. I'm here for blood." Bob turned and rested his elbows on the bar, raising his voice so everybody could hear. "Namely yours, Breen. You goaded Ramos Diaz into a gunfight earlier tonight and gut-shot him. He died a little while ago. Now I'm here to settle the score. I'm calling you out."

"Well, I'll be," said Breen, his sneer widening. "The brave avenger . . . for a lousy damned beaner."

"He was my best friend. And he was worth ten of you," responded Bob.

"But he wasn't worth enough to beat me in a fair-and-square draw."

"He was no fast gun," Bob grated. "You knew that going in or you never would've braced him, you gutless tub."

"And it's a different story with you?"

"*Let's step out in the street and find out.*"

Breen chuckled as he swept his eyes around the table at the other Liberty Bell riders sitting with him. "*You heard him, boys. He cast asparagus on my honor and challenged me without provocation. I got no choice, right?*" He chuckled again. "*And I don't see how Boss Bell will have any choice but to pay me a fat bonus when it's over. I mean, when I'm done gettin' rid of two of the Slash-H's prime young bucks in one night—how can he not?*"

"*I hate benefiting Cameron Bell in any way,*" said Bob, "*but if you'll get off your ass and quit just talking about what you're gonna do, I reckon I'll be saving him that bonus.*"

They made their way outside.

Breen pointed to a dark spot on the ground. "*You want to stand where your buddy was standin' when he got his? Or do you want to christen a fresh patch of ground with your blood?*"

"*Don't worry about me,*" Bob told him. "*Just pick your own spot to die.*"

Breen was fast. But it wasn't even close. To a man, those looking on would later claim they never saw Bob's hand move. One instant it was hovering over his gun, the next it was pointed at Breen, gripping the gun as it roared and spat flame, sending two slugs punching into the gunslinger's chest. Breen hit the ground with his gun never completely cleared of its holster.

Bob continued to hold his own smoking weapon at waist level, his eyes scanning the gawkers who stood with their mouths hanging open. "*Anybody else?*"

Nobody said anything.

Not until Sheriff Tom Garwood and his deputy, Sam

Ramsey, came running up. The sheriff had his handgun drawn, and Ramsey was brandishing a shotgun.

Some men were bending over the still form of Breen.

"Is he dead?" asked Sheriff Garwood.

"Don't get no deader," came the reply.

The sheriff and his deputy swung their guns, aiming them at Bob.

"Drop that hogleg and raise your hands, Bob," Garwood said. "You're under arrest for murder."

Chapter 10

Fred returned to the marshal's office a little before five that evening. Except for the deep purple circles around his eyes, he actually looked considerably better than when he'd left. The color in his face—apart from the eyes—was good, his expression wasn't so hangdog, and he even had some spring in his step.

"Well now," said Bob. "You look like you healed up right smart."

"I finally got rid of that doggone headache," Fred replied. "Man, was that a skull buster. Then you know what? Walking over here, you wouldn't believe how many folks came up to me and congratulated me again on how I dealt with those bank robbers. Not once did anybody even make fun of my black eyes."

"That's because those are like battle scars, man. Badges of honor. They're evidence for everybody to see how hard you fought to save the bank money. They darn well shouldn't be made fun of."

"I guess. I expected to get some ribbing over them

anyway." Fred twisted his mouth wryly. "I'm starting to think now that I'll be sorry to see 'em fade away."

"Don't push it," Bob advised him. "There's still plenty of time for you to get some ribbing over them. Consuela, for instance, hasn't even seen you yet, but she said she expects you'll look like a big, cuddly raccoon."

Fred lifted his eyebrows. "That ain't so bad. At least she said *cuddly*."

"She brought you a sandwich, too," Bob said, pointing at the basket still on the corner of his desk. "That was at lunchtime, though, so it might be a little dry. If you don't want it, we'll give it to Sanders. It'll be good enough for him, no matter how dry it is."

"No, I'll still take it," Fred was quick to say. "Mrs. Nyby made me some soup that was okay, but it didn't stick to the ribs much. I'm sure one of Consuela's sandwiches will go down real good."

"Speaking of eating, now that you're here I'm going to go home for some supper. I might put my feet up and relax for a little bit while I'm there, but I'll be back before too long. I'll bring back some supper for the prisoner before I head out on my rounds. You stick close and don't let Sanders pull any funny business on you, okay?"

"Not a chance. Say, if Consuela makes any extra for supper, maybe you could bring back some for me, too?"

Bob arched a brow. "I thought you were fond of the grub at that Mexican food stand up on Gold Avenue. I thought you were taking all your suppers there lately."

Fred made a ghastly face. "You don't want to know the story on that. Believe me, you don't."

* * *

Bob returned from his supper break an hour and a half later, bearing plates of food for Fred and the prisoner. While Fred was digging eagerly into his, Bob took the other meal back to a sullen, unappreciative Sanders, spent a few minutes chin-wagging with Fred, then headed out to make his usual evening rounds of Rattlesnake Wells.

Everything seemed nice and quiet as if the town was weary after all its morning excitement. As he strolled along, the marshal appreciated that . . . then he remembered how exceptionally calm it had been at the outset of the day and thought wryly that he hoped the end-of-the-day calm didn't take the same kind of sudden turn.

The train making the special run to pick up the horses for the Army had done a quick turnaround, its crew not remaining in town for an overnight stay. And, as Bucky had predicted, the Double Bar J wranglers delivering the horses were an older, quieter bunch who posed nary a hint of the kind of "friskiness" that might result in trouble.

Bob paid visits to the three men who'd answered the call of the emergency bell and had ended up getting wounded in the skirmish with the raiders. Each was in good spirits, their wounds relatively minor, and none expressed any remorse for their participation. On the contrary, all three stated pride in playing their part to rout the outlaws and, in a roundabout way, helping to prevent a bank robbery. The marshal came away feeling a swell of pride for the kind of citizens it was his job to wear a badge for.

He also paid a visit to Curtis Pardee and his three

nephews, the Macy brothers, thanking them once again for the pivotal role they'd played in helping turn the tide against the raiders. They seemed in generally good spirits, except for Vern, who was wrestling with his conscience some over having shot a man for the first time.

"If it makes any difference," Bob told him, "your shot likely saved my life. That hombre was bearing down on me pretty hard and I'd already missed with a shot of my own. Yours was dead-on, although even at that you only wounded him. I ended up killing him a little later on.

"Now I don't take shooting or killing a man lightly, but the thing is, some fellas out here on the frontier have turned so lowdown and bad—like a rabid dog— they don't leave much choice but to be dealt with in a harsh way. It ain't a pleasant thing, but it's all a good man can do in order to keep the rabid ones from overtaking and infecting everything. Leastways, that's the way I see it, and how I can live with doing the harsh dealing when I've had to."

"Those sound to me like some pretty smart words, Vern," Pardee said to his nephew then swept his gaze over Peter and Lee as well. "Smart ones for you lads to hang on to also. The marshal here walks a good path and tells it like it is. You'd all be wise to pay attention."

All three brothers nodded their heads and Vern looked notably relieved of the burden that had been weighing on his mind. Bob hung around and visited a while longer before taking his leave to resume making his rounds.

As he headed north up Gold Avenue, Pardee's words weaved in and out through his thoughts. *The marshal here walks a good path* . . . Bob couldn't help contrasting that assessment with the events that had played out in Texas those bygone years ago. His path had been *right*, the way he saw it. But was that always the same as *good*?

He fought against letting his mind go in that direction again.

He hadn't proceeded much farther before he got some help in finding something else to focus on.

Bob had reached the point near the end of the New Town row where the raiders had done most of their damage. To his right stretched the wreckage of tents that had consisted largely of cheap whore cribs. The blackened patch of ashes where the fire had broken out was roughly in the center.

Some progress toward cleanup had been made, though there was still much to go. Here and there a few salvageable tents had been folded and set aside, presumably to be set back up at some point. Elsewhere, piles of rubble and tattered remnants were stacked, ready to be carted off and burned or maybe just dumped in a convenient gully.

He walked over and stood at the edge of the fire circle for a minute. Traces of acrid smoke still hung in the air.

Ready to turn away and start back down Gold Avenue, he heard a sound, a soft mewling noise. Like a kitten maybe. Slightly muffled, discordant. Maybe an injured kitten. The sound came again, lasting longer. More like a moan, almost a whimper.

A human whimper, he decided, his brow furrowing, his pulse quickening. He went into a slight crouch, his right hand coming to rest on the grips of his revolver. He turned slowly in half a circle, trying to pinpoint where the sound had originated. "Hello? Is somebody there?" he called. "Are you hurt?"

The whimper came again, and Bob was able to identify pretty closely where it came from. Moving quickly, he kicked his way through an area of wreckage where no clearing had yet been done. Flinging aside splintered tentpoles and pulling back torn, collapsed folds of canvas, he uncovered the source of the whimpering. In the gloom of late evening, he could tell it was a young woman. She was nearly nude, smudged with dirt, and curled in a fetal position. Her long dark hair covered her face.

Squatting, Bob reached out and shook her shoulder. "Miss? Are you okay? I mean you no harm. I'm here to help."

She gave no response, except for another whimper as if she was in pain, although he could see no sign of injury. He looked around somewhat desperately. After all the damage caused by the raiders at that far end of the New Town row, he saw no sign of activity or evidence of anyone close by.

He dug a lucifer from his pocket, struck it with his thumbnail, and held it high. In the illumination, he could see the girl was even younger than he'd thought, smooth-skinned and barely conscious, but he could still see no sign of injury. Brushing her silky black hair away from her face, looking for possible damage but finding none, he saw that she was Oriental.

As he shook out the match, he concluded she must have been one of those working the cribs. That was unusual, given that most crib girls were older and pretty well worn, but it was the only explanation he could think of. No matter, she needed help and he had to see that she got it.

Scooping one arm under the backs of her legs and the other under her shoulders, he lifted her up. She was incredibly light.

Turning and picking his way carefully through the wreckage, he worked his way back out to the street and laid her gently into a good-sized, empty pushcart someone had apparently been using to haul away rubble. Pulling loose a section of torn tent canvas, he covered her with it. The girl moaned again and began shivering in the evening chill.

Bob turned the cart around and pushed it toward Old Town and Dr. Tibbs's office.

Chapter 11

"Hold on there, bub. What are you up to with that cart?"

Bob had been so sure no one else was stirring on the wrecked end of town that the gruff voice, coming from behind him, gave him a start. He stopped and turned, his hand once again automatically drifting close to his gun.

In the murkiness, he saw what he had missed before. Across the street from where he'd found the girl was an otherwise weedy, empty area where a collection of abandoned wagons had gathered. Gold seekers flocking in from various points had arrived in those rigs and then left them there. They took the horses or mules, whatever had pulled them that far, and either traded them for equipment or kept them for pack animals when they headed up into the high country to dig for their fortune. A lot of the wagons hadn't arrived in very good shape to begin with. Some of the better ones got stripped for their lumber or hardware. A few remained mostly intact.

In front of a pair of intact rigs—high-wheeled,

with sizable hauling beds covered by tall canopies—stood the man who'd called out. A ways behind him stood a second man. Bob reckoned they must have been inside the wagons, out of sight, when he'd looked around. Maybe they'd had tents or shacks to stay in before the raiders did their trampling and wrecking.

"My name's Hatfield. I'm the marshal here in Rattlesnake Wells," Bob said, hooking a thumb inside the front of his vest and pushing it forward so his badge could be seen more clearly. "I've come across an injured girl. I'm commandeering this cart to haul her to a doctor. I'll see to it the cart gets brought back by morning."

The second man came forward in hurried steps. "You came across a girl, you say?" he asked anxiously.

The first man, the one who'd halted Bob by calling out so gruffly, was a large specimen with sloping shoulders, a gut hanging heavily over his belt buckle, and a broad face dominated by a huge lump of nose that had seen extensive mashing and mauling. The second fellow was taller, skinnier, clad in a shabby swallowtail coat and dented bowler hat, with a narrow wedge of a face highlighted by a flamboyant handlebar mustache.

Bob felt an immediate suspicion for their presence and their interest in what he was up to. Nevertheless, he adopted a civil tone to answer the skinny one's question. "That's right, a young girl. I found her just a few minutes ago, half buried in the rubble across the way. She must have got knocked unconscious during this morning's raid and laid there all day, unseen in the midst of all the damage. What I haven't figured out yet is why nobody's been looking for her or asking about her."

"I can enlighten you on that," the skinny man was quick to say. "As a matter of fact, I assure you there *have* been questions asked and efforts made to find that poor child."

"By who?"

"Why, by me. And also my associate here." The skinny man spread his hands. "Allow me to provide introductions. My name is Neely Pepper. My associate is Iron Lake Iverson. He was born in the Iron Lake region of upper Michigan, you see, and his parents loved the area so much and thought the name carried such strength that they named him after it."

"So what have you got to do with this girl?" Bob asked. "And if you were concerned about her being missing and were looking for her, why wasn't I informed of the matter?"

Neely Pepper licked his lips. "Well, I, er . . . To tell you the truth . . ."

"We got a habit of takin' care of our own problems," Iverson explained bluntly. "We don't believe in runnin' to the law over every little thing."

"I'd hardly call the condition of this girl a little thing," Bob said. "She could have died lying over there all day like that. The chill of the oncoming night was only going to make it worse. Yet you just quit looking?"

Pepper's mouth curved in a nervous, half-sheepish smile. "Shame on us, we sorta came to the conclusion that the little brat had run away. That's why we gave up on the lookin'"

"What is this girl to you, anyway?"

Pepper's eyes shifted around and Bob was certain

he was forming a lie. "Why, we're her, ah, caretakers. Her family met with a terrible tragedy and me and Iron, we've taken it on ourselves to see that she gets took care of. We ain't on the best of times ourselves, but we mean to do all for her that we can."

"That sounds real kind and noble. But, that being the case, why would you figure she had tried to run away from you?" Bob said.

Pepper licked his lips again. "You took a look at her, right? You must have seen she's Oriental. She don't hardly speak no English. She's scared and confused ever since we . . . er, ever since the tragedy to her family. She don't rightly know what to make of me and Iron yet, that we're only to do good for her. She's tried to bolt a time or two before. That's why we thought she'd done it again—you know, out of fear and confusion after those raiders came rippin' through and the fire broke out and all."

Behind Pepper, the marshal saw one of the wagons do some rocking and then a blurred face surrounded by a tangle of reddish curls looked out of the front opening of the canopy. The face, that of a middle-aged woman, appeared only briefly before popping back out of sight.

Bob had a pretty good idea what was going on. "I still find it mighty curious that, if you truly cared about the well-being of this girl and she'd gone missing, you didn't come directly to me or at least to the miners' council about it so a proper search could have been mounted. We can talk about that more later. Right now I need to take this little gal—"

"You don't have to bother about takin' that little gal nowhere, bub," Iverson cut him off. "I done told you once that we got a habit of handlin' our own problems. We're obliged you found the girl, but now we'll be relievin' you of her, and we'll see to it she gets took care of from here." He took a step forward.

Bob quickly held up a hand, signaling him not to take another. "No way in hell, *bub*. Neither of you are gonna get your slimy paws on this gal again. I got you figured out. You're a couple bottom-rung pimps running crib whores. You've got more in those wagons, the usual mostly worn-out kind, I expect. Somehow you got your mitts on this fresh young one, too. I believe you that she probably doesn't speak much English and it's for damn sure she'd want to run away from what you've been putting her through. That ain't gonna be a problem for her anymore, not if she lives. I'll see to that."

Iverson showed yellow stumps of teeth in a wickedly suggestive smile. "Yeah, I bet you'd like to see to that little Chinkie real good, wouldn't you?"

"You shut your filthy mouth or I'll rip your tongue out of your head," Bob warned him.

"Before you get too high and mighty, Marshal," spoke up Pepper, "you might want to consider how that Chinkie has been our top draw by three or four times over ever since we got here. And not just from among these lowly dirt-grubbing, rock-chopping miners, either. Plenty of *gentlemen* from your more prestigious Old Town have found their way to her tent as well. Many of them more than once."

"That don't change a damn thing," Bob said.

But a moment after he gave that reply, things did change. In his anger, he made the mistake of cutting his gaze to Pepper and concentrating on him, giving Iverson the opening to pull a surprise move.

He yanked a snub-nosed, large-bore revolver from

his pocket and aimed it at the marshal. "How about this, you meddlin' damn law dog? Does this make a difference?" taunted the big man. "We been hearin' all day about how you chased off the raiders and stopped a bank robbery and what an all-around rip-snorter marshal and gun hand you are. Are you good enough to draw and fire on me, just a lowly ol' pimp, before I plug your nosy, trouble-makin' ass?"

"You pull that trigger, you fool, you'll have the whole town down on you," Bob told him. "And if I ain't around to stop 'em, they'll hang the both of you before the moon rises."

"By the time a shot draws anybody down to this trampled and burned end of the row," Pepper said in a smug tone, "we'll have that cart dragged out of the way and all they'll find is you layin' in the middle of the street. They'll see us pilin' out of our wagon, too—for the first time, they'll think—and we'll tell how we heard the shot and also the sound of horses tearin' away fast. And then we'll plant the notion that a couple of those cowardly damn raiders must have come back and laid in wait to ambush you. Who'll be able to say any different?"

Bob's eyes narrowed and his voice dripped loathing as he said, "You've got it all figured out, don't you? Hell, in that case what have I got to lose if I make a stab for my gun and try to get at least one of you on my way down? That'd throw a kink in your fancy yarn, wouldn't it?"

The smugness drained from Pepper's face. "Damn it, Iron, what are you waiting for? Go ahead and—"

The sharp crack of a rifle drowned out his words and in the same instant, the gun flew out of Iverson's hand, torn away by a bullet. The big man fell instantly to his knees, his free hand clutching his shattered, bloody former gun hand as he issued a high-pitched squeal of pain. Pepper staggered back a step and a half, looking on in shock and fear.

"Say the word, Marshal," called a familiar voice from over in the tent ruins. "Me and the boys can whittle down the big one the rest of the way and do the same with Derby Hat, too, if you want. Elsewise, they're yours to do with as you wish."

"Hold off any more shooting," Bob said, heaving a sigh of relief. "They're whipped, and they ain't worth the waste of more good lead."

He walked toward the two pimps.

As he reached Iverson, the blubbering giant held up his damaged hand. Two fingers were missing and thin lines of blood were squirting from the stumps. "M-my hand," he wailed. "It's ruined."

"It'll match your face," Bob said offhandedly as he moved past him. "Wrap it in something to stop the bleeding."

Reaching Pepper, the marshal said, "How about you? You got any hideaway guns you're hankering to pull on me?"

"No. No, I don't. I swear," Pepper assured him in a quavering voice.

"Like I'd believe you," Bob grunted. "Raise your hands. High, and hold them there."

Bob patted down the skinny man, unearthing a spring-blade knife tucked in the waistband of his trousers at the small of his back.

"I forgot it was there. Honest to God, I—"

"Shut up! Don't use God's name with your filthy mouth. As for the knife"—the marshal thumbed the button to make the blade flash out—"maybe I oughta stick it in your liver so you won't forget it again."

Pepper's chin trembled. "Please. You wouldn't do that, would you? Please, Gahh . . . I mean, please don't!"

Bob leaned over and snapped the blade under his boot heel. Straightening up, he tossed the broken pieces aside and jerked a thumb at Pepper. "Get over there with your partner. Help him with his hand. I don't want him bleeding all over my street."

Chapter 12

By then, Curtis Pardee and his nephews had converged on the scene. Coming from the tent ruins and carrying his Henry rifle, it was clear Pardee had been the one who'd fired the round that had disarmed Iverson. Peter came from the deep shadows back in among the discarded wagons. Vern and young Lee came walking up the street from the direction of the Pardee tent.

"Once again I find myself deeply indebted to you fellas," Bob said, sweeping his gaze over them. "How did you know I was in a pickle this time?"

"After you left our place a little bit ago," Pardee explained, "I stepped outside to have a pipe. I happened to look up the street just in time to see you loadin' something into this cart. And then I saw these two jaspers step out and start jawin' with you. Right away I got an itchy feelin' they were stickin' their noses in for some no good reason. You see, I had a set-to with this pair only a couple days ago when they cornered Vern and Peter and tried to interest 'em in their sinful business. Needless to say, I spotted 'em for what they was and what they were offerin'. I sent 'em packin' mighty quick.

"Anyway, when my itchy feelin' told me they likely meant to make trouble for you, I grabbed my ol' Henry and rousted the boys. I came up the back way over yonder, sorta like you did this mornin', and sent Peter up the back way on the other side to come in behind those wagons. Told Vern and Lee to stand watch down the street and come a-runnin' if things looked like they was gettin' out of hand. Well, luckily it worked out okay."

Bob grinned. "Luckily for me, yeah. Thanks to you and your itchy feeling."

"So what are you gonna do with the varmints now?" Pardee wanted to know. "Throw 'em in the hoosegow?"

Bob's grin turned into a thoughtful scowl. "Normally, that's exactly what I'd do. For a good long soak. But I've already got one bad hombre behind bars and, even though we have a second cell, I'd as soon not give the two poisons a chance to mingle."

"You gonna just run their asses out of town, then?"

"That's what I'm thinking, yeah."

Iverson looked up from where he and Pepper were huddled together, sudden concern crowding out some of the pain showing on his face. "What about my hand? You're gonna give me a chance to see the doctor, ain't you? You was gonna do as much for that lousy little whore."

Bob's scowl deepened. "You know, I just might have allowed that . . . if you hadn't opened your stupid, evil mouth. Thanks for reminding me what a worthless piece of crud you are and how you don't deserve one damn ounce of consideration."

"But my fingers are shot off and—"

"Shut up. I'll get back to you in a minute. Any more bellyaching out of you, I promise I'll add to your misery."

Pepper glared at him. "You're a mighty hard man, Marshal."

"You should have thought of that before you decided to go tangleways of me. I'd advise you to stow it, too." Turning to the Macy brothers, Bob said, "Vern, Peter, do either of you know where the doctor's office is down in Old Town?"

Peter shook his head. "No, but we can figure it out." Tipping his head, he indicated the amount of activity stirring farther down Gold Avenue as a result of his uncle's rifle shot. "Looks like there'll be plenty of fellas along the way we can ask if need be."

"Good. You do that," Bob said. "I want the two of you to take this cart—you can see there's an injured young girl in it—and go find the doc. His name is Tibbs. Tell him I sent you. Tell him I found this girl unconscious and half-buried in the wreckage left behind by the raiders. He'll know what to do from there. You got that?"

"Yes sir," said Peter and Vern in near perfect unison.

"Tell the doc I'll be along in a little bit. You fellas wait there. Your uncle will be showing up with me."

"What about me?" asked Lee.

"I want you to go along with your brothers. I'm counting on you," Bob said earnestly, "to make sure they don't tarry along the way and get stuck answering questions and such by all those nosy men who'll be trying to slow them down on the way. Can you do that?"

"You bet! I'll tell 'em there's a hurt girl and they better clear the way because it could be a life-or-death emergency."

"That's exactly right," said Bob approvingly. "Now hop to it, all three of you. See to it that girl gets taken care of."

Once the Macy boys had headed off on their mission, Bob turned back to the pimps.

"So that's it?" said Iverson. "You ran the youngsters off so they couldn't see what a cruel sonofabitch their big hero marshal really is?"

Bob took a step toward him. "Did I tell you you could say anything yet?"

Still on his knees, Iverson cringed, leaning back against an ashen-faced Pepper for support.

Bob halted in his advance on the two men. He looked sideways at Pardee. "He's right about me sending away the boys because I'd as soon they didn't see this part. What I'm about to do may seem a mite harsh. If you'd rather not be part of it, either, I'll understand."

Pardee met Bob's look with a flinty gaze of his own. "When I back a man, I back him all the way. Get on with it."

Bob nodded an acknowledgment without further comment. He looked away from Pardee, set his gaze beyond the two pimps, and called out, "Whoever's in those wagons get out here! You women! I know you're there. Get on out here, and make it pronto. And you better not have a notion to try anything funny or it will go bad on your men . . . and you as well."

"Do what he says!" Pepper was quick to add. "Don't try anything foolish. Just get out here and be quick about it!"

At the urging of the men, five women came piling out of the wagons—three out of one, two out of the other. All had shawls over their shoulders but were wearing short, flimsy gowns that left their legs and feet bare. The five included two plumpish blondes, the redhead who'd poked her head out briefly a few minutes back, a slat-thin brunette, and a tall Negress with the emptiest, weariest-looking eyes Bob had ever seen. The women shuffled listlessly forward until they crowded together behind their pimps.

"What's this all about?" said the redhead. "Why you shooting up our men?"

"It's the least they deserve," Bob told her. "Calling that pair of varmints *men* is a bigger insult than you can probably imagine."

The redhead's mouth curved into a lewd smile. "Oh, I can imagine a lot of things, Mr. Marshal. Come on back to one of those wagons with me and I'll show you. I'll let my imagination run plumb wild."

"Knock it off, Marvelle. This is serious," Pepper growled over his shoulder then cut his anxious gaze toward Bob. "So what are you gonna do with us? Let's get it over with."

"You already heard it. It's real simple," Bob said. "You're leaving town. Right now. Tonight."

"You're really gonna do that without givin' proper attention to Iron's hand?"

"When you were trying to get me to hand over

the young girl to you and not bother taking her to the doctor," Bob reminded him, "you kept assuring me you could take care of her just fine. Well, now you can do the same for your pet ape."

"What about Mee-Kee?" asked the redhead, showing a trace of genuine concern on her face. "Is she gonna be all right?"

"Is that the Oriental girl's name? Mee-Kee?" Bob asked.

"It's what we called her."

"Whether or not she's gonna be all right, I can't say. She's been taken to our town doctor. He's a good man and will bring her around if anybody can. But no matter. She's not going anywhere again with you and your so-called men."

"On top of the cruelty you're showing Iron, that's flat-out robbery!" Pepper protested. "I paid good money for that Chink whore."

"That's your tough luck," Bob said. "What's more, I'll put this to the rest of your women. Do you any of you want to make the break from these two and stay behind in Rattlesnake Wells? If so, I'll give you a fair shot to try and make it on your own, however you can, as long as you obey the law, don't force yourselves on those who ain't interested, and otherwise cause no trouble."

Pepper glared furiously, hating Bob with his eyes. But he knew enough not to say anything.

As for the women, their response to Bob's offer was a mixture of mildly confused looks and totally blank stares. Finally, Marvelle, the redhead who seemed to be the senior member and spokesperson for the group, said, "That's a real intriguing proposition, honey, but I'm afraid you're laying it out about ten or twenty years too late. You see, gals like us have come to know our lot in life. Everything is behind us and not much is ahead, except continuing to get by on our backs. We stay here, we'd just end up the same, maybe worse. You ever hear the saying, *Better the devil you know?* With Pepper and Iron, we know we'll be fed, we'll have some kind of shelter over our heads, and we won't be roughed up too much. So when they roll out, we'll be stickin' with 'em."

Bob hadn't known exactly what to expect nor really what he was hoping for. He was glad he at least made the offer, but he was sort of relieved that none of the women took him up on it.

To Pepper, he said, "That's it, then. Commence to making ready to roll out. You came in those canopied wagons, I figure, so where are the horses or mules that pulled 'em?"

"At the livery stable in Old Town. Horses, four of them," answered Pepper in a strained voice. "I paid some up front, probably owe more by now."

"No need for you to go after them. I'll square your bill with the liveryman, just to make sure you've got no excuses, and have the nags fetched here to you. You see to it you're ready to hitch 'em up when they arrive and then are on your way damn quick after that. I'll be back to check and you'd better hope you're long gone when I do." With that, Bob turned and started away, Pardee on his heels.

"Marshal?" Marvelle called after him.

Bob paused and looked back.

The redhead was wearing a deeply saddened

expression and for a moment he thought she was going to say she'd changed her mind.

She said, "Tell Mee-Kee that Marvelle said I hope the best for her, will you? And tell her I . . . hell, never mind. She won't understand a damn word of it, anyway."

Chapter 13

"She suffered a pretty hard blow to the crown of her head," Doc Tibbs explained. "There's a bruise and some swelling, but it would have been hard for you to see, Marshal, due to her thick hair and the fact the skin wasn't broken so there was no bleeding. Additionally, she is suffering from the accumulated effects of being regularly drugged with some sort of opiate. Even before she got knocked out she likely was very listless and lethargic. On top of that, her physical condition was very near total exhaustion."

"Those bastards," Curtis Pardee said, not quite under his breath. "I got half a notion to go back and pay those pimps another visit."

"It's a tempting thought," Bob said, "but it won't do little Mee-Kee any good now, one way or the other. We've got her separated from them, and they're on their way out of town. Let's just leave it go at that."

Bob and Pardee were in Tibbs's waiting room. The Macy brothers were there, too. Mee-Kee was resting quietly on a bed in the adjoining examining room.

The door was slightly ajar so the doctor could hear if she stirred any.

"So what does all that mean, Doc?" Bob asked. "Is she gonna come out of it okay? Is she gonna be all right?"

"From everything I can tell right now, I don't see why not. A lot of rest, getting the poisons flushed out of her system and replacing them with some solid nutrition . . . She should be fine. It will take some time and I can't say what her mental state might be, but, physically, I see nothing less than a full recovery."

"When will she wake up?"

"I could force her awake now, but she needs rest. I expect she'll sleep through until morning, and I believe that would be for the best. She can stay right where she is. I have a cot I can fold out in the office here, so I'll be close by when she does wake."

"That'd be swell, Doc. I really appreciate it," Bob said. "If it's any consolation, I'm sleeping on a cot at the jail tonight. So neither one of us will be getting a choice night's sleep. I'll check with you first thing in the morning and from there I'll make some kind of arrangement for putting Mee-Kee up after that. Good night."

Outside on the boardwalk, Bob paused to talk a bit longer with Pardee and his nephews. "I want to say again how grateful I am for all the help you fellas have been," he told them sincerely. "It's been a long day for me, but, if not for you four, at a couple different points it might have been shortened permanentlike."

"No need to make more of it than it was, Marshal," Pardee replied. "Just doin' the right thing and glad we was on hand to pitch in."

"Okay, then. Let's talk about that," said Bob.

"Something has crossed my mind. I don't have the whole say, not without the town council backing me. And you may not be interested at all. I'm just tossing this out to see which way the milkweed blows . . .

"When we visited earlier, Curtis, you were saying how you're worried that your small claim is gonna have a hard time supporting you and all three boys now that they've shown up. I don't want to get anybody's hopes up, but what if, instead of them going back up on the mountain to work your claim with you, I could offer Peter and Vern decent paying jobs here in town, starting right away? If they're interested, that is."

"We'd be interested," Peter was quick to say. "We didn't come all this way to be a burden to Uncle Curtis, our ma's only brother, or with the sole intent of diggin' for gold. We understand how chancy that is. After the fever took Ma and Pa back home, nothing was left for us there. Since we were faced with havin' to take a chance one way or the other, we figured we might as well come West to do it."

"Whether it's back in Iowa or here in Wyoming Territory," Vern added, "no Macy has ever looked down his nose at the prospect of honest work."

"I think I already got an idea," Pardee said measuredly, "but just what kind of work are you talkin' about?"

"Deputy marshals. Working for me," Bob said flatly. "Rattlesnake Wells is getting bigger practically by the day and, as you've all well seen, so is the trouble that comes with the growth. As I was talking with a couple council men just today, it's becoming clear that me and one deputy are spread too thin to handle it all. Like I said, I'll have to get authorization from the full council, but I'm pretty sure I can persuade 'em. Especially after today's raid and attempted bank robbery."

"You don't think these boys are a mite young for the danger that can come with puttin' on a badge?"

"They're young, true," Bob said. "But what makes a sensible, capable man ain't always just a matter of years. I'd say Peter and Vern have proven themselves able to fit the bill for what I need . . . if they continue to have the interest, that is."

"We're interested," the brothers said again in almost perfect unison.

Pardee pursed his lips. "Reckon I got no argument. What about Lee, the youngster?"

"We can make arrangements for him to stay here in town with his brothers, if that's what you want. I don't know how far along he is in school, but we got a good teacher who covers all grades and learning levels. Otherwise, I thought maybe you'd want to take him along with you."

"I've had enough schoolin'," Lee spoke up. "I want to go prospectin' with Uncle Curtis . . . until I'm old enough to pack a badge, too."

"When were you planning on going back to work your claim, Curtis?" Bob asked.

"I got my supplies bought and ready. I was figurin' on headin' up tomorrow, but I can hold off another day."

"Good enough," said Bob. "You've got some things to hash over and I'll do some hashing over of my own, first thing in the morning with the town council. I'll come by your place after that and we can decide where we stand. How does that sound?"

Pardee nodded. "We'll look for you tomorrow, then."

Chapter 14

"So it's settled then," declared Reese Modello. He took a final drag of his cigarette before flipping the smoldering butt into the campfire. "We go back and hit that damn town double hard. We bust it wide open this time, along with cleaning out that bank and freeing Arlo from behind bars. We're all in agreement, right?"

"I'm damn sure in agreement." Ace Greer reached up to gingerly touch his bandage-covered left ear. "I can't wait for another crack at that stinkin' town and its busybody marshal who shot my ear off."

"Your ear ain't shot off," said Salt River Jackson, somewhat wearily, from where he sat next to Greer. "Just a little piece nicked away, is all. I oughta know. I'm the one who put that bandage on it for you, while you was howlin' and carryin' on like you was crappin' out a thorny cactus."

"It was a damn sight more than a *little* piece," Greer argued. "And I was howlin' because it hurt like blazes. Still does, if you'd like to know."

"Tired as I am of hearin' about Ace's ear, he makes

a valid point when it comes to the Rattlesnake Wells town marshal," said Modello. "I don't have the same personal grudge against him, but Ace called him a busybody. That's the part I mean to key on. Whoever that badge-totin' hombre is, he not only was busy during that fracas this morning, but he didn't back down from no part of it. He was all-fired lucky when it came to dodgin' our bullets and flat hell on wheels at triggerin' ones of his own. In a matter of minutes, he came from the north part of town, where he killed Chester and Earl and shot Ace's ear, then showed up outside the bank, where he wounded Arlo and made it so hot for Pete and me, we had to hightail it out of there with no chance to go back for him."

"Exactly what are you sayin', Reese?" asked Charles "Bad Luck Chuck" Ainsley, his deeply lined face pulled long by a bewildered frown. "You ain't suggestin' we oughta be afraid of this hell-on-wheels law dog, are you?"

Reese Modello was a tall, rawboned specimen with a square jaw and narrow, flinty eyes set too close on either side of a broad, blunt nose. He shot Ainsley a hard look that caused his flinty eyes to narrow into even tighter slits than normal, a look anyone who knew him recognized as a sign of his quick temper boiling near to the surface.

"If you think you heard me say anything about being afraid of that bumpkin marshal, Ainsley, it's time for you to clean the horse shit out of your ears. And if you're sayin' that *you* think I'm scared, it's time for the two of us to have a real serious disagreement."

"No. No, Reese, I never meant it that way at all," protested Ainsley, a small, spindly man with streaks of white running through his otherwise rust-colored hair, marking him as the oldest member of the gang. "Jesus, I'd never say anything like that! Not even hint it."

"You'd damn well better not," Modello seethed. "And you'd better be a whole lot more careful about choosin' your words from now on, or I might forget about us already bein' shorthanded and throw your bony old ass over the side of this mountain just to make sure you never misspeak again."

"Jesus, Reese, I was just tryin' to get clear on what you was tellin' us, that's all," muttered Ainsley.

"Is it so hard to understand?" Modello held up his hands, fingers splayed wide. He swung his gaze in a wide, slow arc, touching each grim, shadow-cut face of the other gang members encircling the campfire in the remote, hidden canyon of the Shirley Mountains. Unlike its neighbor, the gold-bearing Prophecy range to the west, the Shirleys had survived numerous early prospecting attempts without ever yielding any sign of valuable ore and so remained largely an untouched wilderness, providing any number of good places for hiding out.

"My whole purpose in bringing up that damn marshal," Modello continued, "was to drive home the point that we can't afford to take him lightly . . . like I think we did when we hit his town. Even his fat deputy, who showed up first at the bank and killed Benny, turned out to be more than we reckoned on. When we go in again, I repeat, it needs to be double hard and merciless. All guns blazin'."

"I'm with you all the way, Reese," said Salt River Jackson, a soft-spoken Southerner with a mean glint in his pale blue eyes that, for anyone paying attention, deserved to be measured against his slow drawl and generally mild-mannered outward demeanor. He was also the second oldest member of the gang, not too far behind Ainsley.

Where the years and hardships had taken their toll on Bad Luck Chuck and often made him seem as much a burden as a benefit, on Salt River they had bestowed a layer of leathery toughness and accumulated wisdom, to which the others showed a fair amount of respect. Everyone paid attention when he continued. "Here's something more I think we need to consider. True, we need to go in harder and stronger than we did last time . . . but we also need to go in smarter."

Modello nodded. "Well, yeah. Sure, Salt River. That goes without sayin', don't it? What are you drivin' at?"

Jackson shrugged. "Smarter is smarter. We know for sure the town is there and we know the bank is there. Do we know with the same certainty that Arlo is in the jail?"

"Where else would he be?"

"Nowhere else, if he's still alive."

"I saw him get hit and grab his shoulder. As he went down he hollered for me and Pete to keep goin', to save ourselves." Modello frowned at the memory. "He went down, but he wasn't hurt that bad. Not bad enough where he would've died from it. Ain't that the way you saw it, Pete?"

Pete Stuben gave a nod, keeping his tone matter-of-fact. "Sure is. I saw him grab his shoulder and blood running out between his fingers. Arlo's too tough to die from a shoulder wound like that." A trim, dark-complexioned gent, Stuben was a former gambler, with handsome facial features except for cold, lifeless eyes.

Back in his card-playing days, his eyes had conveyed no emotion or clue of what he was holding and had made him a very successful gambler, a trade he'd still be following if he hadn't foolishly gotten into a fight over a loose woman and killed another of her admirers—a young lout who happened to be the son of a very powerful politician who saw to it a high-profile murder charge was slapped on Stuben's head, making him an outlaw on the run ever since.

"I'm not questioning any of that," Jackson said. "But what none of us knows for certain is that they didn't shoot him again later. Or beat him to death—or maybe even hung him by now."

"Jesus, Salt River, you're awful bent on paintin' a dreadful fate for ol' Arlo, ain't you?" Ace Greer was another tall, rawboned, lantern-jawed sort, cut along lines very similar to Modello, but without the flintiness in his eyes. His, under a shelf of thick, black brows, had an intensity of their own and were conveying a mixture of anxiety bordering on anger. "You almost sound like you *want* something like that to have happened."

"Don't be ridiculous," Jackson snapped. "All I'm trying to drive home is that robbin' a bank or bustin' somebody out of jail are pretty ambitious undertakings strictly on their own. Combine 'em together, on top of tearin' up the town on our way in and out, and you can see we're gonna have a mighty full plate for only seven men to chew through. If we hit the jail and it turns out that—for whatever reason—Arlo ain't in there, we will have wasted a lot of precious time and put ourselves at extra risk for nothing."

Modello eyed him. "So by goin' in *smarter*, you're sayin' we need to make sure what the situation is with Arlo."

"That's part of it. The biggest part. In general, though, it also wouldn't hurt to have some idea about the mood of the town. Are they expecting another try on the bank? Or on tryin' to break Arlo out of jail, if that's where he is? Are they makin' preparations for any of that? If so, what kind? . . . See what I mean?"

"I see, yeah," said Modello, making a sour face. "But how the hell are we supposed to find out any of that? We've been on the run or hidin' out ever since we hightailed it out of there amidst flyin' bullets early this mornin'."

Jackson arched a brow. "That's kinda my whole point. We don't know a damn thing about what we left behind. Before we go tearin' back in, we oughta find out."

"Which brings us right back to *how*," said Greer.

"By holdin' off long enough for one of us to go back and do some sniffin' around. See what the mood is, what the talk is," Pete pointed out.

In response to Stuben's remark, Greer said, "And just which one of us would go waltzin' back in there and do all this sniffin'? Whoever did would not only be takin' one hell of a risk for himself but would also risk queerin' the whole deal for the rest of us."

"Not necessarily," said Jackson. "Ironically, not only does Stuben have the right idea, I think he is probably the best candidate for pulling it off."

"How so?" said Modello.

Jackson grinned somewhat whimsically. "Just look at him. Yeah, he's a bit of a handsome rascal—not as handsome as *he* thinks he is, mind you, and not so much that it makes him stand out to the point of it bein' a problem. Otherwise, he's about as average as you can get. Average height, average build, and so on. The way we were spurrin' our horses back and forth during the raid this morning, especially after the gun smoke started gatherin' so thick it was like a murky haze, I don't believe anything about him would've stuck in anybody's mind enough for him to be recognized if he showed up in Rattlesnake Wells again. So he goes to a saloon gaming table, does his gamblin' thing—makin' sure not to draw attention by bein' a big winner—and in the course of listenin' and observin' he should be able to get a pretty good handle on the things it would be good for us to know."

Modello had begun nodding his head even before Jackson was finished talking. "I gotta admit I wasn't so sure at first, but I like the sound of it. It seems like something that would work and would provide us some important details we can't be sure of otherwise. You up for bein' the one who goes in, Stuben?"

The former gambler didn't need a lot of time to come back with his answer. "Sure. I think it's a good idea, too. Plus, from my standpoint, it'll be kinda nice to sit down at a card table again, even if it's only for a little while."

"What about those wanted papers on your head," said Ainsley. "Don't you risk bein' spotted on account of them?"

Stuben smiled wryly. "Lotta time and hard miles between then and now, Ernie. I've changed. Besides, this is a boomtown we're talkin' about, remember? So many new faces passing through that mine—even in spite of my dashing good looks—won't draw a second glance. Except from the ladies, of course."

"Just remember what got you on those wanted posters in the first place," Jackson said.

"Don't worry, I'm not likely to forget that."

"Good. See to it you don't," said Modello. "Otherwise, it's a done deal. You head in at first light. The rest of us will be waitin' here, anxiouslike, to hear your report when you get back."

Even Johnny Three Ponies, the only gang member who hadn't spoken during any part of the discussion—which wasn't necessarily unusual since he seldom spoke more than a dozen words on any given day—gave a final nod of approval and muttered, "It is a good idea."

Chapter 15

Bob Hatfield slept considerably better on the cot in the cramped storeroom off one end of the cell block than he'd expected. Most surprising, thoughts of those long-ago events in Texas that had haunted the corners of his mind all day did not pay any visits to his dreams. In fact, as far as he could remember, he hadn't dreamed at all. That, in itself, wasn't especially unusual. Sometimes he dreamed, sometimes he didn't; it seemed to go in streaks. He was particularly glad he hadn't—at least, not the Texas dreams he'd more or less anticipated.

Like always, he rose with the sun. Since he hadn't bothered to undress for a turn on the lumpy cot, all he had to do was pull his boots on before making his way into the office area. Once he had some coffee brewing, he went back into the cell block to clean up for the day. The washstand was shared with prisoners, at least the ones who weren't so far removed from soap and water that using the facility would have been too distasteful to contemplate, for all parties concerned.

Bob made no special effort to be quiet as he performed his morning ablutions, yet there were no signs that his moving about in any way disturbed Sanders. On the other side of the bars, the prisoner lay on his back on his cot, forearm over his eyes, and continued to snore peacefully. Through the store-room door he'd left open a crack, Bob had heard that same snoring buzz on the couple occasions he'd wakened during the night. It occurred to him that, for somebody who boasted so boldly about jail not being able to hold him, Sanders sure seemed at ease while he was penned up.

Returning to the office area, Bob unlocked the front door, poured himself a cup of coffee, and sat down at his desk. He regretted not being home for his standard morning treat of adding milk and sugar. He regretted not being home for a lot of other reasons, too, but the sacrifices a lawman sometimes had to make included more than the risks and danger that came with the job.

Thinking of those things and the excitement others tended to see in them caused Bob to recall the excitement displayed by his son Bucky when the boy had gotten out of school yesterday and came rushing to hear the details of the raid and the bank robbery attempt. A smile played across the marshal's lips as he recalled the pride Bucky had displayed for the role his dad had played in ruining the plans of "the bad guys." A father always wants his son to be proud of him. The flip side of that, unfortunately, was the devastation that would hit Bucky if anything ever happened to his father. The boy had already been forced to endure the loss of one parent.

Thinking about the danger element, Bob's mouth

formed a thin, tight line. Although he found a great deal of satisfaction in being the marshal of Rattlesnake Wells, now and then he considered seeking another line of work—finding a job that would cut down the chances of anything happening to him, not so much for his own sake, but for Bucky's.

Bob took another drink of his bitter coffee and shook off the unpleasant turn his thoughts had taken. The best way *not* to let anything happen to him, he told himself, was to stay prepared and alert and keep from getting distracted by negativity. The same held true for Fred and the new deputies he hoped to bring aboard. Bob felt fairly confident he could convince Bullock and McTeague and their respective council members to go along with hiring the Macy brothers. He just needed to meet with them, pitch his case, and get the matter settled—which he would proceed with as soon as Fred showed up to relieve him.

Expecting it would take most of the morning to get the matter resolved, he hoped to have some responses to the telegrams he'd sent out to various jurisdictions in order to determine who had the most convincing claim to Arlo Sanders.

Although he hadn't said so to anyone else, the marshal couldn't help thinking there was about a fifty-fifty chance the members of Sanders's gang still on the loose might return to Rattlesnake Wells in order to make another try on the bank. If their captured leader was still behind bars, that would only increase the odds of them showing up and attempting to break him out at the same time.

All the more reason for getting some added deputies hired and getting Sanders transferred somewhere else as soon as possible.

The gold boom had brought enough activity to Rattlesnake Wells to warrant the building of a spur railroad line that fed off the main Union Pacific tracks to the south. Trains traveled the spur line twice a week, sometimes more for a special reason, like the quick run that had come and gone to transport the Bar Double J horses for the Army. The next regularly scheduled train in was due the next day.

It was probably too much to hope for, but if Bob could get a definitive answer on where to transfer Sanders, then he *might* be able to get the prisoner shipped off when that train pulled out again. Otherwise it would be three or four more days before he'd have another such opportunity, even if the question of proper claim was resolved.

That was the potential good news about the next scheduled train.

The bad news was that riding the same iron horse would be the newspaper reporter and photographer Abe Starbuck had summoned. Bob was looking forward to them about as much as coming down with a case of shingles. The thought of the pending newspaper coverage soured his mood all over again.

His spirits were lifted only a short time later, however, when the front door opened and Bucky marched in, followed by Consuela bearing another of her straw baskets, a larger one than before. Bob had stopped home after finishing his rounds and checking to make sure the wagons containing the banished pimps and their women had left town, but Bucky was already in bed asleep. Bob had missed tucking him in and saying their evening prayers together, a routine they'd begun when Priscilla was still alive and had maintained ever since her passing.

He was happy to see his son off to school and knew he had Consuela to thank for arranging it.

"G' morning, Pa. We got up early so we could come down and have breakfast with you," Bucky announced, confirming Bob's thoughts.

"I hope it is okay," said Consuela. "This early, I didn't think you would be too busy to have a little time."

"Of course not," Bob assured her. "No better way to start a day than with my two favorite people."

Consuela smiled. "I've got boiled eggs and fresh baked biscuits with honey. And I brought a little jar with some sugar and milk stirred together inside it for your coffee."

"You hear that, Bucky?" Bob said. "*There* is a woman who thinks of everything."

As Consuela was spreading out the contents of her basket on Bob's desk, Bucky was pulling up chairs for them to sit on.

"I also brought food for the prisoner," said Consuela.

"He can wait," Bob told her.

Once they'd begun eating, Consuela prodded Bucky. "Don't you have something you wanted to tell your father?"

"Oh, yeah. In all the excitement yesterday, I forgot to tell you the good news, Pa—I passed my geography test." He paused, scowling earnestly. "It wasn't real great, I only got a C minus. But that's passing. And Mr. Fettleford said if I keep workin' as hard as I did these past couple weeks he knows I can bring it up even higher."

Bob grinned. "I know you can, too. I also know

how hard you worked to get it that far, so I'm darn proud of you."

"And there's more. I looked and looked but I couldn't find no country that started with the letter *Q*. So I finally asked Mr. Fettleford, like you said I could, and you know what? He couldn't think of one, either. He had to dig and dig through practically every geography book he has before he finally found one. Even then he said it kinda didn't count as a real country. He called it a monarchy. Said it's a peninsula—whatever that is—somewhere over in Arabia, called Qatar. It's pronounced like *Cutter* he says, but it's spelled *Q-A-T-A-R*."

"Well," said Bob, twisting his mouth ruefully, "I don't have much choice but to take his word for it. The spelling, the way it's pronounced, and the whole ball of wax. Reason being, after I sicced you on it, I was dogged if I could come up with anything myself."

Consuela arched a brow somewhat chidingly. "Maybe next time you will think twice before challenging the boy with a puzzle you cannot solve."

"Maybe," Bob said. "Or maybe next time I just won't admit it."

Fred Ordway arrived, reporting for duty, just as Consuela and Bucky were leaving. When he heard Consuela had brought breakfast, the fear that he'd missed out made him look crestfallen. Only upon learning some biscuits and honey had been set aside for him was he able to heave a big sigh of relief.

The morning was Bucky's first chance to get a look at Fred's blackened eyes. The colorization was in full bloom—a deep, purplish, almost black hue—making them quite a sight to behold. For a few minutes, Bucky seemed almost as awestruck just looking at the display as he was by hearing another telling of how Fred got the shiners.

Shortly after Consuela and Bucky were gone, Bob ran the idea of hiring the Macy brothers as added deputies past Fred. Although he hadn't yet met Peter or Vern, Fred was perfectly comfortable with Bob's judgment. As long as he was assured that he would be considered the chief deputy, he more than welcomed the thought of having some added help in keeping the peace around town.

Shortly thereafter, Bob headed out to call on Bullock and McTeague and other necessary council members in order to make his pitch.

Like he had anticipated, it took most of the morning to get full authorization for the hiring. It wasn't that the idea met with any strong resistance, it just took time to contact all the necessary folks and get their buy-in. Some had reluctance when it came to the proposal of hiring *two* new deputies, but Abe Starbuck, who logically was the treasurer for the Old Town council, helped overcome that when he made the offer for the bank to put up part of the second deputy's salary on the proviso that said individual would spend at least half of his time serving as an on-site guard for the bank. Bob had no trouble agreeing. He found it a very sensible idea.

Part of the morning was also taken up by matters involving the young woman he had rescued from the tent wreckage the previous night. He stopped by Dr. Tibbs's office to check on her, and found her very much awake and very frightened. She was proving quite a handful for the doctor when it came to preventing her from running away. The fact that she didn't understand a word being spoken to her—and vice versa—didn't help the situation any.

Bob said her name. "Mee-Kee," and that seemed to soothe her a bit. While he took a turn staying with her to keep her from bolting, he set in motion an idea he'd thought of earlier but hadn't yet had time to follow up on. He sent Doc Tibbs to Bullock's saloon and told him to fetch a girl named Kim, who worked there.

Bullock's was considered the highest class drinking establishment in town. Still, considering Rattlesnake Wells was only a relatively small place—boom or no boom—in the middle of Wyoming Territory, that didn't exactly take it to lofty heights. Like most saloons in the West, Mike had working girls on hand.

They preferred to be called hostesses or barmaids and they did indeed serve drinks part of the time. Quite at their own discretion, they frequently escorted men up to their rooms for some private service. Kim was one of the hostesses. She also happened to be Oriental, capable of speaking decent English as well as her native tongue. It was the marshal's hope that she would be able to communicate with Mee-Kee and help settle her down.

In a lousy mood for having been rousted so early after the late hours she kept, Kim calmed down after she heard Bob's account of how he'd found Mee-Kee and what her circumstances had been, followed by his explanation of why he'd sent for Kim. She quickly showed compassion for the girl's plight.

Her compassion increased as the two began to converse. Mee-Kee wept openly, so happy was she to find someone she could understand and talk to. Without going into too much detail, at least not right at the moment, Kim confirmed to Bob that everything he'd speculated on and pieced together had been reasonably accurate. To the marshal's gratitude and relief, Kim then offered to take the girl back to her quarters and look after her there until more permanent arrangements could be made.

With that problem settled, at least for the time being, Bob finished out the morning finalizing authorization for hiring two deputies. When he took the news and the pay offer to Curtis Pardee and the Macy brothers, he was pleased to find them all receptive. Among themselves, they had decided that, providing the deputy jobs worked out, Lee would remain with his uncle and they would head out for Pardee's digs first thing in the morning. Peter and Vern would continue to rent the big Gold Avenue tent they'd all been sharing, at least until they'd drawn some wages and could afford some better accommodations. Pardee had a cabin up at his digs for him and Lee.

After saying his good-byes to Pardee and the youngster and leaving it with Vern and Peter that they would report in the morning for swearing in and duty, Bob wrapped up the first half of the day feeling everything had turned out pretty well. He decided to go home for lunch before returning to his office, where he hoped some telegrams would continue the good trend by providing him clear direction on what he should do with Arlo Sanders.

Chapter 16

It was the middle of the morning when Pete Stuben rode back into Rattlesnake Wells. After coming down from the Shirley Mountains hideout, he'd swung a good distance west before turning south again for the final leg into town. Just in case anybody was paying attention, it would appear as if he was coming from the direction of the Prophecy range where the gold strikes were, and he'd look like part of the steady flow of traffic that passed between the gold fields and Gold Avenue. Coming from the direction of the Shirleys might strike some nosy parker as suspicious, and that was the last thing he wanted on his little foray. He couldn't be too careful.

As he rode past the tent wreckage and the burnt area, the result of the raid he'd participated in, Stuben couldn't keep one corner of his mouth from quirking back somewhat smugly. Men were picking through the ruins, salvaging what they could and hauling away in pushcarts what was damaged beyond hope.

Damn fools never knew what hit 'em, Stuben

thought. Before they were done reeling from that episode, if everything went according to plan, they were going to get spun around by another dose.

Halfway down the street, he spotted an establishment with a façade of fresh-cut pine logs hammered together without particular skill. Behind the pine front stretched a long, high-peaked tent. Nailed above the front door was a wide plank, painted white with bright red lettering that read BEER—WHISKEY—POKER. Below that, in smaller letters also red in color, was added COME IN—WET YOUR WHISTLE—TRY YOUR LUCK.

Stuben grinned. It looked like a good place to begin. With the wreckage he'd passed, he had the perfect starting point for striking up a conversation—playing it up as a newcomer to town, which he basically was, and asking what the heck had happened.

Forty minutes later, he assessed that things were going fairly well. For early in the day, the joint had a decent crowd and he'd had no problem finding an in-progress poker game to sit in on. Enough other patrons milled about so their movement and conversation did a good job of preventing his talk and questions from making him stand out to any degree.

In short order, he had the events of the recent raid and attempted bank robbery related to him with lots of enthusiasm yet not quite as much embellishment as he might have expected. The number of raiders involved was amusingly inflated, though he could hardly offer a correction. Otherwise, the account was pretty straightforward. What was more, he got confirmation that the notorious gang leader Arlo Sanders was indeed behind bars in the local jail with only a relatively minor wound.

The men Stuben was playing cards with—alleged prospectors who, from every indication, didn't have a lot of ambition for doing the actual work of *digging* for gold—were such dreadful poker players it created a big problem for him. He found it difficult to keep from winning pot after pot, as he'd been warned not to do for the sake of drawing undue attention to himself.

Furthermore, he came to understand that the men, all recent arrivals due to the gold boom, had no real sense of the town's overall mood or what measures of preparedness might be in the works in case of another raid. For that, Stuben realized, he needed to go to the older, more established part of town and see what the talk was there. He had plenty of time before he needed to head back to the hideout. With luck, he'd find another establishment with another poker game that would offer a challenge so he could maybe enjoy himself a little while gathering some additional information.

Just before noon, on the south end of Front Street, another stranger rode into town. He was a tall man, broad across the shoulders, wearing a flat-crowned black Stetson, a black frock coat, and gray-striped trousers. His wide, fleshy face featured a tobacco-brown walrus mustache and above that alert, restlessly moving eyes of the same color. On his right hip, prominently displayed by a swept back fold of his coat, rode a Colt .45 revolver with grooved bone grips.

The stranger rode directly to the marshal's office, swung somewhat wearily down from the saddle, and tied his horse casually to the hitch rail. Entering through the front door, he found Deputy Fred seated behind the desk, fidgeting with some telegrams that had been delivered by Harold Feeney.

Fred looked up. "Hello. Can I help you with something?"

The brief hint of a smile touched the stranger's mouth. "I hope so. Are you Marshal Hatfield?"

"No, I'm his deputy. Chief Deputy Fred Ordway."

"Pleased to meet you, Deputy Ordway. My name's Brock. Vernon Brock. I'm a U.S. marshal up from Kansas." As verification, he pulled back his lapel and revealed a U.S. marshal's badge pinned to his shirt.

Fred's eyebrows lifted. "Kansas, you say. Wow, you're pretty far off your range, ain't you?"

"Happens sometimes with this job. Speaking of what comes with the job, mind me asking if that's how you got those prizewinning shiners you're packing around there?"

With a note of pride, Fred said, "That's exactly how I got 'em. We had some owlhoots make a try at robbing our bank just yesterday morning. I got these, along with a busted nose, in the act of stopping them. Well, me and the marshal, that is."

"Sounds like some mighty good work, apart from the damage and discomfort to you."

"Aw, it ain't no big thing. It don't hardly hurt any more today."

"That's good, then. Where is your marshal, by the way?"

"He's been out most of the morning taking care of matters with the town council and whatnot. Considering the time, he may be at lunch now. I expect him back right after the noon hour, though. Do you have some business with him?"

"Yes, I believe I do. You see, I have to admit that I arrived here already knowing about your trouble from yesterday—the raid and the attempted bank robbery. I heard about it down in Laramie, where I was trying to pick up the trail of a certain fugitive I had reason to believe had fled up this direction. Ironically, when I heard it was the Arlo Sanders gang that hit you and that you ended with ol' Arlo himself behind bars, well, that sort of changed my priorities."

Brock reached inside the front of his coat, withdrew a folded sheet of paper, and shook it open. It proved to be a wanted poster for Arlo Sanders. Holding it up for Fred to see, he continued. "As it says right here, our Dodge City office has been after Sanders for a good long while. Since he's wanted on federal charges, that not only puts me in a good position, but it gives me the full right to take him off your hands and transfer him into my custody."

Fred looked impressed. "I guess that would work out pretty good all the way around. I know that Bob— er, Marshal Hatfield that is—has been wondering what to do with this varmint. You know . . . because him and his gang have cut such a wide swath over the past couple years and are wanted in so many different jurisdictions." For some reason he didn't feel inclined to mention the telegrams that had come in about that very subject.

Brock waved the wanted poster. "Like I said, this is a federal claim. That trumps all lesser jurisdictions."

"What about other federal charges, though? You know, for crimes committed in places besides Kansas."

Brock went tight around the mouth and for a

minute Fred thought he was going to turn angry. The moment passed and half the mouth lifted in a lopsided grin. "Look, I'm just a fella who runs 'em down and hauls 'em in. Not that much different from what you do, right? Who has the first claim or the biggest claim or any of that crap is for the courts and judges and shyster lawyers to figure out, you know what I'm saying? The main thing is that the dirty skunk is captured. None of the rest of it can happen at all until that part gets done."

"That's for sure," agreed Fred.

"So I'll hash it over with Hatfield when he gets back, and we can decide how to play it from there."

"That's a good idea. That would be best."

"In the meantime, how's chances I can go back and have a word with the prisoner?"

Fred's brow puckered with uncertainty. "Jeez, I dunno, Mr. Brock. I mean, seeing as how you're a lawman and all, I guess it should be okay. But the marshal has really drilled into me that we need to be extra cautious about anything and everything concerned with this Sanders hombre. I hope you understand why that makes me sorta reluctant to—"

"What the hell? Do you think I'm going to try and break him out or something?" Brock snapped.

"Well, no, of course not. It ain't that, but—"

"What then?" Brock insisted. A flush of color showed on his face and once again he looked ready to turn very angry. Then once more, he calmed himself and exhaled a deep, even breath. "Never mind. I wouldn't want you to do anything you're not comfortable with or something that might get you in trouble with your boss. I rode hard all yesterday afternoon and this morning and haven't had much rest or a decent meal in all that time. I guess I'm a little testy. Sanders has been on the run somewhere out ahead of me, not to mention a lot of other folks, for a long while now. I reckon another hour or so until the marshal gets back and I can talk directly with him won't make that much difference."

Fred looked relieved. "I think that would be best. Listen, if you want to catch some lunch for yourself, there are some good cafés and restaurants in town. As you can probably tell, I know 'em all pretty good." Fred patted his thickened middle to emphasize the point. "This time of day, Bullock's Saloon puts out a nice spread of fresh baked bread, cold cuts, cheese, and other stuff for practically no charge as long as you're doing some drinking."

Brock grinned. "Well now. A cold beer or two and a feast such as you describe sounds mighty appealing. Where might I find this Bullock's?"

Fred jerked a thumb. "Three blocks up the street, opposite side. You can't miss it."

Chapter 17

Bob enjoyed a nice, leisurely lunch at home with Consuela. It was the first chance he had to tell her about the new deputies he'd be adding. She was very glad to hear this, saying she hoped it meant a reduction in the long days she felt he too often put in and would result in more time for him to spend with Bucky.

What Consuela left unsaid was that it would also mean more time for him to spend around her. It was a thinly veiled secret in their relationship that Consuela was in love with Bob. Had been since she was quite young, actually, and developed a huge crush on her big brother's best friend.

Unfortunately, for too long that was all Bob saw her as in return—Ramos's pesky kid sister, always hanging around and getting in the way. By the time Consuela's crush had solidified into genuine love and Bob finally got around to noticing that the pesky kid sister had turned into a very lovely young woman, his heart was already being won over by Priscilla.

Consuela could only look on and pine for what apparently could never be.

When Priscilla's health began to diminish after Bucky was born, it was Consuela who stepped in to help care for the child as well as the frail mother. Looking back, she often asked herself if it was purely the result of compassion on her part, or if it was done more as a means for her to stay close to Bob. All these years later, after the passing of Priscilla and caring for the boy and his grieving father, Consuela still could not be certain.

The only thing she knew for sure was that she continued to love Bob and—even after the dark, bloody time associated with the Devil's River Kid—found him to be one of the finest, most decent men she'd ever met. She also clung to the belief that he had developed a fondness for her in return, but it was the inherent decency in him that prevented him from expressing it or acting on it in any way. Not yet anyway. But someday . . .

Over lunch, Bob also told Consuela about his discovery of Mee-Kee and her former pimps that he'd subsequently run out of town, things he hadn't been able to discuss in front of Bucky at breakfast.

Consuela saw his rescue of and concern for the abused Oriental girl as further evidence of his decency. "But what will become of her now?"

"Don't rightly know at this point," Bob was forced to admit. And then he stubbornly added, "But anything is a darn sight better than the way she was living before."

* * *

Bob thought about Consuela's question regarding Mee-Kee's future as he walked down the slope from his house and made the turn onto Front Street. Now that he'd intervened and had taken her away from everything she'd ever known—both good and bad— what *was* he going to do with her? Not that it had to be his problem exclusively, but since he'd done what he had, he felt primarily responsible for what would become of her next.

He was still pondering the new predicament he'd more or less heaped on himself as he started past Bullock's Saloon. Something caught his eye and he slowed his steps. One of a half dozen horses tied at the hitch rail in front of the popular establishment was a solid-looking blue roan with some unusual white streaking in its mane. After a couple more steps, he stopped walking completely to study the animal. Something about it was making the short hairs on the back of his neck prickle, trying to tell him something. What was it about this nag that . . .

And then he knew. In his mind's eye, he envisioned it clearly, backlit by the illumination of rising flames. He had seen this very horse, with the odd marking in its mane, being ridden by one of the raiders who made the diversionary hit on New Town two nights ago!

With the certainty surging inside him, Bob's hand dropped to the grips of the .44 holstered at his side and he took a step toward Bullock's front door. But he halted again. While he was positive about his identification of the horse, the man who'd been riding it was just a shadowy form with a murky face. Bob would never be able to pick the man out amid the lunch-hour crowd. If he simply barged in, flashing his badge and demanding to know who belonged to the roan, one of two things would likely result. Either the rider would stay cool and calm and do nothing to give himself away, or he might panic, go for his gun, and unleash a shoot-out, putting a whole bunch of other patrons at risk.

He could hang back, wait and see who came out and got on the roan. That could take hours, and Bob knew he didn't have that much patience, especially not in this instance. He wanted to flush that skunk and do it quick.

As the marshal stood there pondering a reasonable way to go about getting the roan's rider to show his hand, Joe Peterson, who ran the town's main livery stable, emerged from Bullock's, sucking on a toothpick.

An idea quickly formed in Bob's head. "Joe. Come here a minute." He motioned urgently.

"What's up, Marshal?" Peterson said, walking over, a frown forming on his face.

"Listen. I need your help and I don't have time for a lengthy explanation."

Peterson's frown deepened. "Well . . . sure, Marshal. I'll do what I can. I ain't gonna end up in the middle of a bunch of flyin' lead, am I?"

"Not if you do what I ask and then just stand back out of the way."

"What is it you're askin' me to do?"

"Turn around and go right back inside. Act a little excited. Then holler out that whoever has this blue roan stud out here on the hitch rail had better come a-runnin' because his horse is kicking up a big fuss and threatening to pull free."

Peterson's eyes went to the row of horses lined up at the hitch rail. "*That* blue roan? But Bob, he ain't kickin' up no fuss."

Bob expelled an impatient breath. "I know that and you know that, Joe. But the fella I'm hoping to flush out from inside don't know that."

Peterson's expression changed, indicating he was starting to get the picture. "Is he some kind of varmint?"

"That he is. I'll find out for sure once I get him out here, but for right now you're gonna have to take my word."

"That's good enough for me, Marshal."

"Once you make your announcement, stand back out of the way."

"Don't worry about that." Peterson squared his shoulders, swallowed hard, then turned and marched back through the batwing doors.

Bob stepped up on the boardwalk and edged over to one side of the doorway, poised, ready.

He didn't have to wait long. The batwings popped back open only about half a minute after Peterson had gone through them and an average-sized man wearing an anxious expression came hurrying out.

Bob took a step toward him and said in a clear, commanding tone, "Hold it right there, mister. My name's Hatfield, and I'm the marshal here in town. You stay real still and keep your hands out away from your body."

"What the hell, Marshal?" said the man in a tense voice. "What's this all about?"

"We'll be getting to that," Bob told him. "Let's start by you telling me who you are. What's your name?"

"It's Stu—Stewart. Paul Stewart."

Bob knew he'd just been told a lie. "Where you from, Stewart?"

"Nebraska, before comin' here." His voice was smoother, the lies coming easier. "I was punchin' cattle for a rancher in the Sandhills."

"How long you been in town?"

"Just got in this morning. Camped last night only a short ways off to the southwest."

"What brings you to these parts?"

The man who called himself Stewart showed a smug grin. "Same as everybody else. Came for my share of the gold."

"Uh-huh. And you came all the way from Nebraska on that roan?"

"You bet. He's a keeper."

"Yeah, I can see he's a good-looking animal. Real pretty, what with that unusual white streaking in his mane."

The man went tense all over. Not just his voice, his whole body, too. He tried another grin, but it had a nervous twitch to it. "Yeah, he cuts a mighty handsome figure with that mane. And don't think he don't know it, the way he struts his stuff around the fillies." The phony Stewart cleared his throat. "But I don't know about that marking being so unusual. I've seen plenty of other—"

"You got any papers or anything to back up who you say you are or that you're fresh out of Nebraska?"

The man hesitated. "I, uh . . . Yeah, I got some personal stuff in my saddlebags."

"I'd like to have a look."

"Listen, I don't think I deserve—"

"You'll get what you deserve, good or bad," Bob said, cutting him off again. "But I'll be the one to decide it. And the best chance for you to come out on the good side is to do like I ask."

"All right. Whatever you say."

The man started down off the boardwalk to where the roan was tied. So focused was Bob on the suspect's every move that he barely noticed how the display they were putting on had sent ripples of tense awareness up and down the street, causing folks going about their regular business to swing wide around them or hold back altogether.

Taking note of the gun holstered on the suspect's right hip, Bob said, "Reach up in those saddlebags with your left hand only. Keep your right out where I can see it."

The man made no reply, just reached up with his left hand and began fumbling rather awkwardly with the saddlebag's tie thongs. As he leaned into the task, he turned his body, as if inadvertently, and for just a moment his right hand was blocked from Bob's view. In that moment, the hand slipped up the front of the man's body and darted inside his jacket to grasp the over-under .44 caliber derringer Pete Stuben always wore in a spring-loaded shoulder holster whenever he sat in on a poker game.

Even though he could still see the man's sidearm, Bob could tell by the hunching of his shoulders that the suspect was up to something no good. When the damn fool whirled around and started to extend his arm with the derringer clenched in his fist, Bob was ready. With an eyeblink-fast draw, he had his own gun in his fist and was triggering a shot before the man ever got turned all the way. The round took the hat off the suspect's head and sent it sailing into the street. The hat's owner instantly froze, knowing he'd been beat, knowing he had no chance to succeed with the derringer.

Through the partly opened batwing doors of Bullock's Saloon, two more shots thundered out, so close together it sounded almost like a single blast. The slugs pounded into the chest of the man holding the derringer and sent him staggering wildly backwards into the street, where he toppled heavily to the ground. The derringer slipped from dead fingers and was painted bright scarlet a moment later by one of two arcs of blood gushing up from the fallen man's chest.

Bob whirled about, turning to face the saloon doorway and the tall, walrus-mustached man who stood there holding a smoking .45 caliber Colt. The two men's eyes locked and held over the muzzles of their drawn guns.

"Take it easy, Marshal," said the man with the mustache in a calm, level voice. "I'm on your side."

It was then that Bob's gaze dropped down and took note of the U.S. marshal's badge pinned to the man's shirt, prominently displayed by the way the lapel of his frock coat was pushed back.

"Mister," Bob said through clenched teeth, "I don't know who the hell you are or what you think you were doing, but you just interfered in a serious piece of business and cost me a valuable lead to something I wanted real bad."

The federal marshal frowned. "That's a mighty poor showing of gratitude, pal. The way I see it, I just saved your life. Your shot missed and that hombre was—"

"My shot didn't *miss*, damn it," snapped Bob. "I hit

what I was aiming at and succeeded in stopping that jackass from finishing his fool attempt with the derringer. I needed him alive, not shot full of holes!"

"That's too damn bad, then," said the federal man. "Because when *I* shoot to stop a man, I aim to stop 'em permanentlike."

Chapter 18

Shoving his iron disgustedly back into its holster, Bob stepped off the boardwalk and went out to the fallen man. Squatting down, it didn't require a very close examination to confirm the man was sure as hell dead.

He straightened up as the federal lawman came out and stood next to him. "So what the hell is your story?" Bob wanted to know. "Who are you?"

"Because we're in your town and standing in front of your people, I'm going to cut you some slack for a little while longer," came the low-voiced reply, "but you'd better lose that tone and show me some respect or—"

"I asked you a question," Bob cut him off. "A man gets my respect when he earns it, not because he's got a fancy piece of tin on his shirt. So far, you're falling a mite short of getting the job done."

Again the two men locked eyes.

After several beats, the federal man's glare lost some—but not all—of its heat. "My name's Brock. Vernon Brock. I operate out of the Kansas U.S. marshals headquarters but was up in Laramie yesterday when word came in about your trouble with the Arlo Sanders gang and how you'd taken Sanders himself into custody. So happens I've got papers on him for past crimes, federal ones, down from where I hail, so I rode here to take him off your hands."

A crowd was starting to gather by that point—people up and down the street who'd been holding back and shying away as Bob confronted the suspect, others edging out of the shops and other businesses, men boiling out of Bullock's where the whole thing, in a manner of speaking, had started.

One of the latter was Titus O'Malley, the town undertaker, looking every bit the part, as he habitually did, dressed in a black top hat, black suit, and bright red cravat. Elbowing his way to the front of the Bullock's pack, he cleared his throat and inquired, "Is that another customer for me, Marshal Hatfield?"

Bob gave him a wry look. "Can't see him keeping an appointment anywhere else, Titus. Get your wagon and get him off the street as soon as you can, okay?"

The marshal swung his gaze in a full circle around him. "The rest of you folks go on about your business. Nothing more here to see or hear about until I get some additional things figured out."

As the crowd started to disperse, Joe Peterson walked up. "Did I do okay, Marshal? I guess I did, but . . . Jeez, I didn't figure I was sendin' a fella out to meet his maker."

"Wasn't exactly the way I had it planned, either, Joe," said Bob, tossing Brock a sidelong glance. "He brought it on himself, I reckon, going for his gun the way he did."

Mike Bullock joined them. "What was behind this? Who was this character?"

"Said his name was Paul Stewart," Bob answered. "But I don't think I believe that. I made him for—"

"His real name was Pete Stuben," Brock interjected. "He rode with the Arlo Sanders gang."

"What? What the hell brought him back into town?" Bullock blurted. Then, as an afterthought, he swiveled his bullet head suddenly, looking up and down the street.

"Take it easy, Mike," said Bob. "I don't think there's any more of 'em around. I never would have spotted this one—in fact, I *couldn't* have spotted him. I'd never have been able to recognize him on his own— if not for his horse. On the night of the raid, I got a good look at a blue roan with white streaks in its mane." The marshal tipped his head toward the roan at the nearby hitch rail. "When I was coming down the street a minute ago and noticed that fella there . . . well, it's too uncommon a marking to shrug off as just a coincidence."

"So that was the whole business about havin' me go in and raise a false alarm about the horse," said Peterson. "You couldn't identify the varmint unless he revealed himself by showin' interest in the roan."

"That took a pretty sharp eye to notice the horse in the first place," said Brock. "And a clever plan for flushing out Stuben."

"Reason I wanted so bad to take him alive," Bob said, "was to find out what he was up to back in town and get him to tell me where the rest of the gang is holed up."

"Damn. I wrecked the hell out of that by reading everything wrong, didn't I?" said Brock, climbing down off his high horse a little and finally showing a trace of remorse. "I never noticed Stuben when I first went inside. He was playing cards at a table off in one corner. When the fella came in hollering about the feisty roan outside and Stuben jumped up in response to that is when I recognized him and followed him to the door. When I saw him go for the hideaway gun and you only blew his hat off . . . Well, I already told you the way I saw it and why I did what I did."

"So my question still stands," said Bullock gruffly. "What was he—this Stewart or Stuben or whatever the hell his name was—up to back in town?"

Bob sighed. "I don't know the answer to that, Mike. Not yet, anyway. But I do know that the best way to talk about it and try to figure it out ain't standing here in the middle of the street. Me and Marshal Brock here are gonna go on down to my office and see if we can't iron some things out." He clapped one hand on Bullock's shoulder. "You'd probably best go on back in and take care of your customers. You can do me a big favor when you get in there—get me the names of the men Stuben was playing cards with and tell them I might be coming around to talk to them a little later. I'll want to find out what they were talking about, what he might've showed any interest in, things like that. Will you do that for me?"

"Sure. Sure, of course I will."

"Good. I'll see you after a while, then."

"What about me, Marshal? You done with me?" asked Peterson.

"Joe, you've done plenty and I really appreciate it. Tell you what, though. You can take that blue roan off the street and on down to your place. Okay? I'll come around later and we can decide what to do with him."

"You got it, Marshal."

As Peterson went to unhitch the roan, Bob turned

his attention to Brock. "Seems like that leaves you and me to conduct some business probably best taken care of in my office."

"Seems like. Lead the way."

Fred was waiting when they got back to the jail, standing outside the front door with a scattergun cradled in one arm. "I heard the shooting, so I grabbed this baby and started in that direction. When I saw you two standing up there and everything looked okay, I decided it'd be best for me to stick right here close. You know, in case it was another one of those diversionary tricks to draw us all away from the jail."

"That was good thinking, Fred," Bob told him. "Right here watching over the prisoner is exactly where I wanted you to stay."

They all three went inside.

"So what happened?" Fred asked. "What was that all about?"

"That, we haven't quite figured out yet."

"Who was the fella I saw laying on the ground?"

Bob gestured as he sank into his chair behind the desk. "According to Marshal Brock, his name was Pete Stuben. According to the way the fella told it, his name was something else. I'll let you guess which one I believe, but by whatever name, he was a member of the Arlo Sanders gang."

Fred's mouth gaped into a wide circle for a moment before he clapped it shut for a moment. "No foolin'? He was bold enough to show up in town so soon after what they tried to pull? What was he up to?"

"Now you're back to the part we haven't figured out yet," Brock answered.

As Fred turned from putting the scattergun back on its pegs in the wall-mounted gun rack, Bob said, "Is there any coffee left in the pot?"

"Yeah, there is. About half." Fred poured a cup and handed it to Bob then turned to the federal man. "Marshal Brock?"

Brock shook his head. "No, I'm good. I had a beer and a monstrous thick sandwich at Bullock's, like you recommended. I need to let that settle."

Fred grinned. "Was it as good as I said?"

"Every bit."

"Speaking of eats," Bob said, "Consuela will be coming by with lunch for the prisoner in a little bit. She'll no doubt bring something for you too, Fred, but in the meantime you could stand a snack of your own at Bullock's, couldn't you?"

Fred frowned. "Well, yeah. You know I can most always make room for a snack. You're usually the one telling me to cut back some, so what are you getting at?"

"The thing is," Bob explained, "that hombre Stuben was playing cards with some fellas there in Bullock's before I flushed him out. I told Mike to get the names of who he was playing with and that I'd be around to talk to them, see what he talked about and acted like during the time he sat in with 'em. You know, hoping maybe he let something slip that would give us a clue what he was up to. The sooner somebody hits 'em with some questions, the fresher their memories are gonna be. Since I'm likely to be tied up here with Marshal Brock for a while, it strikes me that maybe you could go question them and grab a bite of lunch at the same time."

Fred's expression brightened. "Why, sure. I could do that."

"Knew you could. Don't be afraid to lean on them boys a little, make 'em think about everything Stuben said. Might be a long shot, but it's worth a try."

"I'll find out everything they got." Halfway out the door, Fred paused and looked back over his shoulder. "Those telegrams you've been expecting came in, Marshal, they're there on the desk . . . and, er, if Consuela does bring me something for lunch, just hang onto it for me, okay?"

Chapter 19

After Fred was out the door, Brock settled into a chair in front of Bob's desk. "He could fool a person with his slow, pudgy look, but I'm thinking you've got a pretty good deputy there."

Bob nodded. "You'd be thinking right. He's been known to fool one or two hombres plumb to death."

"Uh-huh. I been thinking something else, too."

"What's that?"

"Just speculation, but I think I've got a pretty good idea what Stuben might've been doing in town all by himself."

Bob took a drink of his coffee. "I'm listenin'."

"Reconnoitering."

Bob made no reply, waiting for Brock to do some building on his single-word answer.

"Stop and think," Brock continued. "If things went the way I've been told, the Sanders gang took off from here knowing only a limited number of things for certain: They knew they'd failed at getting any money out of the bank, and they knew they'd left some men behind, one of them being Arlo himself.

What they didn't know was if their men were dead or behind bars, if you were working up a posse to give chase, or what preparations the town was making—if any—to be ready for another try on the bank or to bust Arlo out of jail, if that's where he was."

"You think they're planning another hit on us?"

"I sure wouldn't discount it as a possibility."

"On the bank or to get Arlo out?"

Brock spread his hands. "That I can't even guess. Depends on how tight the gang is these days, how loyal the other members feel toward Arlo. Last I knew, he still had a few old-timers with him—Stuben, Salt River Jackson, Reese Modello. Fellas like that who've run with Arlo for quite a while I expect would make a try to save him if they knew he was still alive."

"And you think the overall situation is what Stuben came to find out."

"Speculation, like I said. He was a pretty average-looking fella, right? Not too big, not too small, not likely to stick out in a crowd. A skilled card player who could sit in on any kind of action and shoot the breeze comfortably while he was playing, take his time working in a question here and there to find out what he wanted to know . . ." Brock let his words trail off and replaced them with a wry grin. "If only he hadn't been careless riding in on a blue roan with odd markings that a certain sharp-eyed marshal had etched in his memory."

Bob made a sour face. He couldn't quite decide how he felt toward this federal man who'd robbed him—albeit with good intentions—of what could have been a crucial lead. "Fat lot of good it did me," he muttered, "with you and your quick trigger showing up so hell-bent on saving my hide."

"Speaking of quick," said Brock, "that draw you made against Stuben was about as fast as any I've seen. I guess that should've been another clue to me—anybody that good with a gun would likely hit what he was aiming at."

Bob shrugged. "Water under the bridge now."

Brock leaned forward in his chair. "I'm ready with an offer that would go a long way toward making amends for my initial wrong reading." He patted his chest where the inner pocket of his coat held the wanted papers he'd brought with him. "I've got a federal claim on Sanders right here, the one I showed your deputy earlier. My headquarters has wanted that scoundrel for a long time. Say the word, I'll be happy to take him off your hands and head out of the territory with him.

"We'll make a show of leaving, so everybody knows. That won't solve all your worries, but it will narrow 'em down. If what's left of the gang hits your town again, you'll know damn well they're coming after the bank."

Bob put down his coffee and leaned back, lacing his fingers over his stomach. "I gotta say, that's a mighty tempting offer from my side of things. You'd be heaping an awful lot on yourself, wouldn't you? Suspecting Sanders's gang is still in the area, you're willing to light out on your own, with him as your prisoner?"

"I've never lost a prisoner out on the trail yet," Brock said proudly. "In fact, I'll put my record for holding on to 'em up against quite a few jails or other kinds of lockups I could name."

"Gutsy call, I'll give you that."

"Like I said, my office has been wanting to get hold

of Sanders for a long time. Be a favorable mark on my record if I was the one who brought him in."

Bob gestured. "Let me see the papers you got on him."

Brock handed them over. "While you're having a look at those, how about letting me go back and have a few words with Sanders? I want to see the look on his face when he finds out I'm practically standing on his spurs."

Bob considered for a moment, then nodded. "Guess it'd be okay. Try not to agitate him any more than you have to. And I guess I don't have to tell you to be careful around him."

"Oh, I'll be sure to do that."

Bob jabbed a thumb over his shoulder, indicating the heavy door that led back to the cell block. "Through there. Leave the door open a mite, if you will."

Brock got up and made his way back to the cell area. While he was thus occupied, Bob scanned the papers he'd handed over. They were standard-issue wanted notices for crimes committed in the Dodge City area, dating back a couple years. They looked familiar, and Bob suspected he probably had a copy of both of them in one of his desk drawers.

Setting aside the wanted papers, he took up the telegram responses that had come in and started reading through them. He could hear a back-and-forth of voices coming from the cell block, but Brock had left the thick door only slightly ajar so they were muffled to the point of not being understandable. Had Bob concentrated hard enough, he probably could have made out most of what they were saying, but for the time being he was more interested in what the telegrams had to say.

There were three of them. Two basically put the decision of what to do with Sanders back on Bob and his authority. The third, however, came from the territorial headquarters of the U.S. marshals in Cheyenne and laid out somewhat clearer guidelines for him to follow. What it came down to was a line that read *Hold until a judicial review can be attained here and then you will be further advised.*

Somewhat clearer. But nothing firm and final. All it accomplished was telling him to keep Sanders locked up in Rattlesnake Wells—as opposed to allowing Brock to take custody, which Bob had been leaning toward—until notified further. When he might get said advisement was left wide open. It might be later today, it might be tomorrow . . . it might be in a damn week. Bob mentally cursed. If he hadn't sent the inquiry in the first place, he could have handled the matter with a judgment call and turned Sanders over to Brock. But since he *had* raised the question and had gotten a response from a higher territorial authority, he pretty much had to pay attention.

A sudden rise in the volume of the voices coming out of the cell block tore Bob's attention away from the telegram. The voices turning his head were not only louder, they had grown very heated in tone. Bob hadn't expected an exchange of friendly banter between the pair, but the eruption sounded serious.

He got up, shoved the door open wide, and strode into the cell block. Marshal Brock was leaning against the wall opposite Sanders's cell, wearing a crooked, somewhat taunting smile. Sanders was pressed against the bars, squeezing them hard with white-knuckled fists, his face flushed an angry red, mouth twisted into a grimace.

"What in tarnation's going on?" Bob wanted to know.

"Get this sonofabitch outta here!" Sanders seethed. "He's got no right to be here and you got no right to hand me over to him. Is that what you're fixin' to do, like he claims?"

"If it is, that's sort of between him and me," Bob said. "As far as rights, bub, I hate to be the one to break it to you . . . but you ain't in no position to have very many of those. You should have worried about that when you turned down the outlaw trail and started stompin' all over *honest people's* rights."

Brock chuckled. "You tell him, Marshal. Lay it on good and thick."

Bob gave him a look. "Real glad you were paying such close attention when I asked you not to agitate the situation."

"I can't help it he's so touchy that he looks at me and sees the hangman's noose he's bound for."

Sanders jerked on his bars. "You go to hell. Both of you! We'll see how much chucklin' you do out the bullet holes my gang is gonna fill you full of when they show up to bust me out of this cracker box."

"Why, Marshal," said Brock, pushing nonchalantly away from the wall, "I fear he is wholly unappreciative of the hospitality you've shown him here."

"If I had an hour or so to spare, I'd tell you how much I don't give a damn about that. For the time being, I think you two have done enough rekindling of your deep friendship. Let's leave him to his daydreams about his gang coming back to break him out."

Sanders's eyes narrowed into slits as thin as two

razor slashes. "You wait and see, *Sundown Bob*. They're comin' back sure enough. And when they do, like I already told you, I'll see to it your sun gets set once and for all."

The lawmen returned to the office area.

Brock said, "What was that Sundown Bob business?"

Bob waved a hand dismissively. "Aw, just a silly nickname some folks have tried to stick me with. On account of my sundown red hair."

Brock grinned. "Sundown Bob. I like it. It's sorta catchy."

"Yeah, well, I'd be grateful if you didn't make a habit of using it. *Wild Bill Hickock* was a pretty catchy nickname, too, but it didn't do him a helluva lot of good in the end, did it?"

Brock picked up his wanted papers from the desk, refolded them, and slipped them back inside his coat. "So when do I take custody of Sanders?"

Bob dropped back into his chair. "Funny thing about that. Only a few minutes ago I was ready to hand him over as soon as you were ready to take him off my hands. But all of a sudden"—he pushed the Cheyenne telegram across the desktop toward Brock—"we got a new wrinkle."

Frowning, the muscles at the hinge of his jaw tightening, Brock picked up the piece of paper and read it. His frown deepened as his eyes moved back and forth. When he was done, he tossed the paper back on the desk. "So what does that prove? It's from a U.S. marshal's office. I'm a U.S. marshal. The charges against Sanders—down where I come from, up here in your territory, and plenty of other places—are federal charges. It's all the same ball of wax. So what's the wrinkle to me going ahead and taking Sanders?"

"That one little word right there," said Bob, tapping the telegram with his forefinger, "telling me to hold him here. Hold until judicial review, to be exact. And it comes from territorial authority higher than me . . . *after* I asked for their advice."

"Judicial review, my foot," said Brock disdainfully. "It's all legal mumbo jumbo. Bureaucratic bull crap! It just ties things up, slows everything down. You know that as well as I do."

"Maybe I see it the same way, maybe I don't," said Bob. "The fact remains, the words in that message amount to orders. To me. And no matter how I personally feel—and, believe me, I was never looking forward to having Sanders as a guest for any longer than I had to—I don't have much choice but to hang on to him until I hear otherwise."

"More bull crap! You could turn him over to me if you wanted to. Just say I showed up and we'd already made the transfer before you got that wire. I'll even promise to swing by Cheyenne when I leave here and back up your story, get it cleared with them."

Bob gave a reluctant shake of his head. "That's tempting, don't think it's not. But I—"

"Then do it, dammit! Show some backbone and hand him over to me if that's what you want." Brock's voice rose to a near strident level and for added emphasis, he banged the edge of his fist down on Bob's desk.

Bob sat very still and for several beats just looked at the spot on his desk where the federal man's fist had landed. Then he lifted his face, eyes flat and cold, and said in a low voice, "I already cut you some slack for shooting a suspect out from under me. I told you once how I feel about respect, then gave you the chance to earn some from me. It didn't work. Now I'm telling you it's time to leave my office."

Brock stood up. "To hell with you, then. I'll send my own wire to Cheyenne and get them to see the sense in me taking custody of Sanders so everything will be nice and tidy for you."

"You come back with a wire from this same office"—Bob once again tapped the slip of paper before him—"authorizing you to take the prisoner, we can go ahead and settle it. Until then, you and me have no further business with one another."

Chapter 20

Shortly after Brock left, Consuela showed up with lunch for the prisoner. As expected, she had some for Fred as well. When she discovered he wasn't there, she set his plate of ham, beans, and cornbread on the stove next to the coffeepot to keep warm.

Turning back to where Bob remained sitting behind his desk, she held out the plate she'd prepared for Sanders and said, "I suppose you don't want me to take this back."

"You suppose right," Bob told her. "Just set it here on the desk and I'll take it back in a minute."

Consuela brought the plate over and then sat down in the chair recently vacated by Brock. "What's wrong? You look deeply troubled, angry."

Bob would never understand how women were able to do that. He thought he was holding his expression perfectly neutral, but somehow Consuela had seen through it to the turmoil of thoughts underneath. Priscilla used to be able to do that . . . until she became so ill her sense of awareness seldom extended past her pain. Consuela had taken up the habit without ever missing a beat and, if anything, seemed even keener at it.

"I heard about the shooting up the street a little while ago," Consuela went on. "I didn't catch all the details, but I understand another man got killed. Is that what's bothering you?"

"I've got a lot of things gnawing at me, Con," Bob said, using the shortened version of her name like only he ever did, dating back to when they were kids. "They're all sort of tangled together and, yeah, that shooting in front of Bullock's is part of it. If it had gone different, it might have helped a lot toward untangling some of the rest."

"So, in other words, you don't want to talk about it."

"I'm not ready. Like I said, it's still all in tangles."

Consuela rose from the chair. "I guess I should be on my way then. I'll leave you to feed the prisoner and tend to your . . . untangling."

Bob could tell she was hurt because he wouldn't open up to her, but he couldn't help it. He had more to worry about than her bruised feelings. "Listen, from now on you don't need to concern yourself with fixing any more meals for this prisoner. In fact, I'd just as soon you stayed clear of here altogether for a while. Bucky, too. Actually, I'd appreciate it if you'd intercept him when he gets out of school today and not let him come by here like he usually does before heading home. I'll try to explain it more, to both of you, at supper tonight."

Consuela's expression turned troubled in a different way. "You'll be home for supper, then?"

"I intend to, yes."

"But later, you'll be sleeping here at the jail again."

"Afraid so."

"Very well. I'll keep Bucky from coming here until you have the chance to talk to him."

When Bob took the plate of food and a cup of coffee back to Sanders a few minutes later, he found the gang leader in quite a different mood.

"Thanks, Marshal," he said after the meal had been passed through to him. "I don't know who you got cookin' this grub, but it's some of the best I ever had. And I don't mean just jail food. It's damned good by any standards."

Bob eyed him skeptically.

"What?" said Sanders under the scrutiny. "Don't you think I can say a civil word now and then?"

"Haven't heard too many up to now."

"Yeah, well, we ain't exactly in a situation here that lends itself to friendly chitchat."

"No, and I don't see that changing anytime soon," Bob told him. "As a matter of fact, the cooking you're enjoying so much is fixing to change on account of your constant threats about your gang coming to bust you out. I don't want the current cook put in danger, so enjoy what you got. From now on it may not be as good."

"Well, ain't that a lousy break," said Sanders.

"I'll still go ahead and pass your compliment along for what you've had so far."

"Yeah, you do that," said Sanders on the verge of getting surly again. "No matter how good the grub, I ain't about to trade puttin' this joint behind me for the chance to eat some more of it."

Bob grinned wryly. "Dream all you want . . . but it ain't gonna fill your belly." He turned away.

Sanders spoke again, halting him. "Wait a minute, Marshal."

Bob tuned back and waited, giving him the chance to say something more.

A look of sadness appeared to settle over Sanders's face. "When Brock was here before, he said that another of my men got gunned down in town this morning. That right?"

Bob nodded. "It is."

"Pete Stuben?"

"That's what Brock said his name was. I wouldn't have known a name. I just recognized him from the raid up in New Town."

Sanders's mouth pressed into a thin line turned downward at the corners. "Poor damn Pete. He'd rode with me for a long time."

"Every indication was that he'd come back to town alone. Any idea why he'd do that?"

Sanders gave a minimal shake of his head. "Best I could do is a guess."

"Care to say what that would be?"

"Scopin' out the layout of your jail is the only thing I can figure."

"You really think what's left of your gang is gonna try to bust you out?"

"Damn right."

"You hit us the other night with ten men, by my count. Now you're behind bars and four others are dead. Maybe more wounded . . . Strikes me that, having had such poor luck on the first go-round, there might be room for a few discouraging thoughts when it comes to trying anything more."

"You don't know my men."

"No, I don't . . . except for the ones we've already killed."

"That's a helluva cold thing to say."

"They came here, put themselves in our gun sights. Nobody went looking for them."

Sanders seemed to sag against the bars. "Boy, you know how to cut to it, don't you? Yeah, they came here and ended up in your gun sights. But they didn't put themselves there . . . I led 'em."

"It'll be more of the same if they come again to try and free you. Even if they succeed, there'll be a heavy cost."

"Nothing I can do to stop it. If they decide to make a try—and I believe they will—I couldn't change it if I wanted to."

Bob said, "I hope to hell you're wrong."

Sanders regarded him intently. "You want to talk about somebody who's wrong? What about U.S. Marshal Vernon Brock? I'm probably wastin' my breath thinkin' there's any chance you'll believe me, but that man ain't what he seems. He might still be wearin' a U.S. marshal's badge on his shirt, but it ain't legitimate. Not no more. It's just a way of gettin' everybody to cooperate and cut him the slack he needs to get what he's after."

"And what's that?" Bob said.

"Me," Sanders stated flatly.

Bob grunted. "Him and half the lawmen between here and the Missouri River."

"Only with him it ain't the same. It's personal. You turn me over to him, I'll never see the inside of a courtroom or another jail . . . or even a gallows. He gets his hands on me, it'll be something a lot worse."

"Why?"

Sanders turned away and took a couple steps toward the middle of his cell. He stood there for a minute with his head hung. "I did him a bad hurt once a long time ago. He's out for revenge, plain and simple. In his place, I can't say I blame him. But that still don't mean I want to face up to whatever he's got in mind."

"What past hurt did you do him?"

"I'd just as soon not say. I expect you already think low enough of me, no sense addin' to it. Not that I care particularly . . . or maybe I do. Hell, I don't know." He turned back to face Bob. "All I know is that what Brock has in mind for me won't have nothing to do with the law and it ain't right that he's using a badge to get to me.

"Whatever else, I see you as a man who takes the law and things like right and wrong serious. That's why I'm beggin' you not to turn me over to Brock."

When Fred got back, Bob sat down with him to hear what he'd found out, if anything, and then to update him on some conclusions the marshal had come to as far as how they would do some things in the foreseeable future.

For Fred's part, he hadn't found out a whole lot from the men Stuben had played cards with other than their talk had covered a standard range of topics. Included in the mix, not surprisingly, was some rehashing of the raid and attempted bank robbery and how the town was a little bit on edge about the possibility of another visit from the outlaw gang.

Stuben had seemed mildly interested, but not any more so than in most of the other things they'd talked about.

While Fred ate the food Consuela had brought, Bob broke it to him that might it be the last good meal he'd be enjoying for a while.

"Maybe I'm being too gullible or just plain spooking too easy," Bob said, "but Sanders—and Brock, too, a little bit—has got me convinced that his gang is bound to make a try at busting him out of here. The Stuben fella showing up to do some fresh nosing around only adds to the likelihood. That means we've got to stay on guard and be ready around the clock. The best way I can see to do that is to fort up right here at the jail—you, me, and the new deputies that are coming on board tomorrow. We'll go out on rounds and such in pairs while the other pair stays right here at the jail. You or me will always be one of the ones here."

Fred wiped at his mouth with a napkin. "Wow. You really are taking this serious."

"You'd better believe it. If Sanders's gang *does* show up, we'll make believers out of them, too."

Fred frowned. "You mentioned Brock, that U.S. marshal. Aren't you gonna turn Sanders over to him?"

"No," Bob said bluntly. "Number one, if you read those telegrams that came in you saw how Cheyenne is telling me to hold off doing anything until they have a chance to review the situation. Apart from that, something about Brock strikes me as fishy. He's too damn eager to get his hands on Sanders.

I'd be reluctant to hand the prisoner over to him, regardless."

"So he won't be joining us in this forting up we're gonna do, either."

"Not likely. Not unless something changes. For right now, him and me ain't exactly seeing eye to eye."

Fred set aside his empty plate. "Okay. So what do we need to do to get ready? Make that, what do *I* need to do?"

Bob set his jaw. "Well, I can't see Sanders's gang trying anything right away. For the time being, if we're right about what Stuben was doing in town, they'll be waiting for him to get back with his report. Once they figure out he ain't coming back, they'll have to decide what their next move is. That means sometime after tonight. If they make up their minds that they're still gonna try to free Sanders, I'd guess they won't wait too long to go for it."

"What about the bank? You think they'll make another try for that, too?"

"They've only got five men left . . . unless they found a way to add more, and that don't seem likely." Bob shrugged. "Be a big bite to chew if they think they can pull off both at once . . . but we'll have to try and stay ready for anything."

Chapter 21

Reese Modello wore a deep, concerned frown as he gazed out from a high point partly up the wall of the hideout canyon where the remains of the Sanders gang were holed up. He could feel the knot of tension growing tighter in his gut. What was more, he could also feel the growing tension ebbing up from the rest of the men. The gray, descending shadows of dusk seemed to fit the mood descending on all of them.

The scrape of a boot heel on rock and the puff of labored breathing behind him caused Modello to look around. He saw Salt River Jackson climbing up to his position.

"Christ A-mighty," the older man panted as Modello reached down to assist him the last few feet. "You think you're a damned eagle or something, perched way the devil up here?"

"Just wanted a good lookout spot to watch for Stuben," explained Modello.

Jackson squinted out through the thickening

murkiness. "You been up here near an hour. No sign of nothing?"

"Not a puff of dust or shiver of a bush," Modello said grimly. "Damn it. He should've showed long before this—when there was still plenty of daylight left."

"What are you thinkin'?"

"Hell, I don't know. I don't know what to think." Modello took the makings from his jacket pocket and started building a cigarette. The evening air was cooling rapidly and a wind was picking up, fluttering the rolling paper. He carefully spread some tobacco. "All I know is that him not showin' can't be anything good."

"Way I see it, there can only be a couple likely explanations. Either he somehow got spotted for being part of us, or he decided things was fallin' apart and it was time to light a shuck while he had the chance."

Modello raked a lucifer match across a slab of rock and cupped the flame to the tip of his cigarette. "No," he said, streaming smoke, "Pete wouldn't bolt like that. He's too solid, rode with us too long. If he decided it was time to make dust, he'd say it straight up and tell us adios to our faces."

"You don't reckon he got caught up in the cards and the booze—maybe a floozie turned his head— and the damn fool has just lost track of time?"

"That'd be more likely than the other," Modello said. "But I can't hardly see that neither, not with so much on the line. Much as I hate to think it, I'm favorin' that he gave himself away somehow and they either shot him or threw him in the clink. One way or the other, we got to figure he ain't comin' back."

Jackson's eyes narrowed. "Where does that leave the rest of us, then? If he's still alive, you think he'd blow on us, on where we're hidin'?"

Modello took a long drag on his quirley. "It wouldn't come easy out of him, but you and me both know that if you put the screws hard enough to a man, he can be made to spill."

"So what does that leave?"

"For starters, we'll make ready to move our camp first thing in the morning. Try to leave no traces we were ever here and make double damn sure we leave no sign that can be followed where we move to. In these rocks and blind canyons, that should be possible."

Jackson nodded. "We got Johnny Three Ponies, remember. He not only can track a pissant through a pine forest but knows about erasin' our own sign to boot."

"By the time we get relocated, we'll have to have made up our minds on hittin' that town again or not."

"Which way you leanin'?" Jackson said.

Modello finished his cigarette, dropped it, and crushed it underfoot. "My loyalty to Arlo should go without question. I hope you, above anybody else, knows that." He gave the older man a look but went on without waiting for a response. "I think you also know that, as a group, we are on pretty hard times when it comes to basic supplies—food, ammo, fresh horses, right down the line. And the money pot for restockin' any of it is about as empty as anything. We were in bad enough shape when we came here to hit that bank in the first place. And now, with lost time and damages, it sure as hell ain't got no better."

"I think most of the fellas are aware we're scrapin near bottom, though maybe not quite how close."

Modello looked over his shoulder and down at the campsite below, the crackling fire with the three others gathered close. "Well, then I reckon it's time to make 'em full aware of how it is. I hope they'll understand why I'm gonna recommend we go in and make another try at that bank."

Jackson looked uneasy. "And leave Arlo in jail?"

"*If* he's in the jail, and *if* he's in any condition to ride if we did bust him out," insisted Modello. He glared at Jackson. "You were the one who raised those questions in the first place, remember? You said if we hit that town again we had to do it smart. So the smartest thing, the way I see it, is to go for the bank. We need a score too bad to do anything else and, with only five of us now, making a try on the bank *and* the jail would spread us too thin and risk queering the chances to succeed at either one."

Jackson licked his lips. "You're right. You're flat right, ain't no two ways about it. But it's a bitch of a decision to make."

"Tell me about it," Modello said with a rueful twist to his mouth. He shifted his stance to face Jackson full on. "I reckon the boys see you and me, together, since we been part of this pack from the start, as sorta bein' in charge of things with Arlo out of the picture. You agree?"

"I'd say they do, yeah."

"So you gonna side me on this?"

"Ain't like we got a lot of options," Jackson said glumly. "I agree, what you're sayin' is the smartest play left for us."

Modello heaved a sigh. "Not that I'm lookin' forward to it, but let's go down and pitch it to the rest and see how it goes."

Chapter 22

That night, on the cot in the storeroom off the cell block, the dreams Bob had been expecting the previous night came calling very vividly . . .

Texas, six years earlier

It had long been suspected that Sheriff Tom Garwood and his chief deputy, Sam Ramsey, were bought and controlled by Cameron Bell. There'd been more than one instance where it was pretty damn evident to some, yet the majority of folks around Calderone still refused to believe it.

Bob Hammond had been fairly convinced the two lawmen were corrupt, but couldn't prove it beyond a doubt. However, the night he heard Garwood declare him "under arrest for murder" immediately after Bob shot and killed Willis Breen in a fair fight—the same circumstances under which Breen had shot Ramos only a few hours earlier yet was left to freely go about his business—he knew the corruption was real and that it ran deep.

With a chilling certainly, Bob also knew something else. If he allowed Garwood and Ramsey to put cuffs on him and *lead him off to jail, he would never live long enough to see a fair trial or have any chance for exoneration.*

With the same enraged decisiveness that had brought him to face Breen in the first place, he once again did what he saw as his only choice.

He broke free.

When Ramsey stepped close and reached to put a pair of cuffs on him, Bob spun around and kicked him in the groin as hard as he could. As the deputy doubled over, bug-eyed and gagging in pain, Bob snatched away the shotgun Ramsey had tucked under one arm in order to handle the cuffs and whipped its twin barrels in a savage, slashing arc to the side of Garwood's head.

With the two lawmen sprawled on the ground, Bob swung the confiscated shotgun in a slow sweep, covering the men who'd spilled out of the Broken Spoke Saloon to initially watch him and Breen shoot it out.

"You all damn well saw the truth of what happened between Breen and me," he said through clenched teeth. "But just like none of you have had the guts to stand up to Cameron Bell or his corrupt sheriff or any of the rest of the wrongs you've watched take place all around you, I don't expect any of you to speak up for me. That's fine. I advise you to keep being gutless. Don't try to stop me when I ride out of here or it will go mighty hard on you."

So saying, Bob backed slowly, cautiously to where he'd left Ramos's horse tethered. Keeping the shotgun trained on the men from the saloon, he swung lithely into the saddle, pointed the shotgun skyward, and triggered both barrels in a thunderous roar. Flinging away the smoking weapon, he spurred off into the night.

* * *

An hour later, in the kitchen of the main house at the Hammond ranch, Bob sat partly in shadow from a single lantern burning low in the middle of the table and related to his family the events that had taken place in Calderone.

"I'll be branded an outlaw now," he summed up in a dull voice, "so that's how I'll live, what I'll become. They're the ones who set the ball rolling, but I'm the one who's gonna keep it in motion. They don't know what they started yet, but by the time I'm done, they will. I mean to make 'em pay and pay hard. And I mean to make 'em sorry."

"But what kind of life will that be for you?" said Priscilla.

"Better than one spent crawlin' under the likes of Cameron Bell and everything he has influence over," insisted Bob.

"And what will it mean for Bucky and me, and for your whole family?"

"I know it will be tough on everybody," Bob said. "As long as I stay clear, no one will bother you. Retaliation against any of you on account of me would be too obvious, too blatant. Bell is smart enough to realize that the so-called law-abiding citizens who've looked the other way from some of his shenanigans would balk at something like that."

"But surely you're not intending to be an outlaw and a fugitive forever," said Bob's father.

Bob shook his head. "No, not forever. Just long enough to raise so much hell and harass everything and everybody corrupted by the Liberty Bell brand that the Texas Rangers will eventually have to be called in. When they arrive and start digging, they won't stop until they uncover the truth about the things Bell has been getting away with through intimidation and bribery and all the rest. Just like turning over a big rock and watching the bugs and crawly critters scatter for fresh cover, that's what the Rangers will cause to happen. Then Calderone County will be clean again, a place where *decent folks can live and prosper without having to lick the boots of somebody like Cameron Bell in order to get by."*

"Why not go to the Rangers now?" said Bob's mother. "Tell them what's going on, plead your case, have them come investigate now."

Bob shook his head once again. "The time's not right, Ma. It's too soon. Bell has too many layers protecting him. Too much money, too many reputable people he's bought or blackmailed or just plain cowed who will lie and cover for him. I've got to first shake those layers apart, wreck some of them if I have to, so they're no longer solid enough to stand up under a tough, fair investigation."

"The only way to do that is to become an outlaw?" said Priscilla.

"That's how I've already been branded. Not by any properly administered law, but by crooked yellow dogs who are supposed to be upholding it," Bob replied bitterly. "Being outside the law when that's who represents it—yeah, maybe it is the only way!"

And so it began.

For the next several months, Bob Hammond lived the wild, lonely life of an outlaw. In a wide variety of ways and over a wide range of countryside, he plagued Bell's interests tirelessly—stampeding cattle, blowing up irrigation dams, setting fire to grain storage bins, tearing down holding pens, and scattering stock gathered and ready to ship to market. Known associates to Bell were posted with warnings—break with Bell or face the consequences.

Attempts to trap or chase down Bob always met with the same results. He would disappear into the wilderness along the Devil's River, where he and Ramos had trapped and hunted since they were barely dry behind the ears. Even

*though everyone well knew who the perpetrator of such acts
actually was, many took to calling him the Devil's River
Kid. The name stuck and the tales of his exploits grew. Before
long some compared him to a Texas Robin Hood.*

*But not the local law and sure as hell not Cameron Bell.
No romanticized interpretation of his deeds clouded their
minds. They saw Bob as a pain in their collective butts, an
elusive marauder, a growing threat not only to an expand-
ing sphere of Bell influence but to the existence of what was
already established. Plain and simple, they saw him as a
troublemaker who had to be stopped. No matter what it took.*

*From the start, he tried not to make any more killing a
part of his strikes against Bell interests. He clung to the belief
that, since his shooting of Breen had been justified, if he re-
frained from gunning any more men, he still stood a chance
of being cleared once the Rangers came in and got to the
bottom of things. Any additional men he killed would make
it that much harder to reach such a conclusion.*

*Bell started bringing in more hired guns, making it in-
creasingly difficult for Bob to keep from being captured or
killed without defending his hide with lead.*

*It also got harder and harder to sneak in visits to his wife
and son, and his folks. While Bucky was growing like a
weed, Priscilla appeared more worn down and frail each
time he saw her. Alberto Diaz, Ramos's father, passed away
in the fall . . . from grief over his son, many speculated. Consuela naturally took those losses very hard, but endured them
largely by immersing herself in the care of Bucky and tending Priscilla in her state of steadily declining health.*

*The life he was leading began to take its toll on Bob as well,
from exhaustion, improper nourishment, and worry over
Priscilla's worsening condition. What was more, his plans to
shake apart the layers of protection surrounding Cameron
Bell seemed to be failing. As long as Bob was unwilling to*

kill, those under Bell's thumb were evidently more fearful of falling out of favor with the cattle baron than suffering harassment from the Devil's River Kid . . .

Marshal Hatfield jolted awake and out of the dreams tormenting his slumber. He swung his feet to the floor and sat on the edge of the bed, dragging the palms of his hands down over his face. It was dark in the windowless room except for a vertical line of soft light where the door was slightly ajar, leaking in from the low-burning lantern mounted on a wall of the cell block. Also leaking in from the cell block was the familiar buzz of Arlo Sanders's snoring, accompanied by the less regular, half-snorting, half-roaring snores of Fred Ordway, who was occupying a cot in the block's second cell.

Bob smiled dubiously. It was a wonder Sanders was able to sleep at all, let alone snore peacefully, given Fred's noisy rumbling in such close proximity. It might even be considered a form of prisoner torture. Bob was just glad he had the mostly closed door as a sound buffer for himself.

From an old canteen hanging on the storeroom wall he took a couple swallows of stale water. Hanging the canteen back up, he told himself he needed to remember to get the vessel refilled with some fresher contents if he was going to be spending very many nights in the storeroom. At home, Consuela saw to it there was a pitcher of fresh water by his bed each night before he turned in.

Lying back on the cot once more, Bob felt a sudden pang of loneliness for home—almost as sharp as some of the moments he'd experienced back in the Devil's River wilderness when he was hiding out on the wrong side of the law. Somewhat to his surprise, and guilt, he realized the home he was longing for was strictly the one just across town with Bucky and Consuela. For a moment, Priscilla had been more distant in his thoughts than at any time since her passing.

That troubled Bob.

He didn't know for sure what time it was but suddenly knew he wouldn't be able to go back to sleep no matter the hour. He got up, picked up his boots, and carried them quietly out through the cell block and into the office area, closing the heavy door behind him. On reflection, as he sat down in his chair and tugged on the boots, he didn't know why he'd put so much effort into being stealthy. With all the racket Fred was making, Bob could have marched out of the storeroom banging a tin pan and probably never been noticed.

The clock on the office wall said four-thirty.

He poked a fire to life in the stove, fed in some fresh splits of wood, and set a pot of coffee to brewing. While he was waiting for it to get done, he unlocked the front door and stepped outside.

The predawn air had a bite to it. Brisk, damp.

Storm coming, Bob thought. It was that uncertain time of early spring when it could rain or have a chance for some snow. It all depended on how much the day would warm up. Bob was pulling for rain. He'd had his fill of winter for another year.

He looked down the length of Front Street. The blurred shapes of the buildings were all dark and silent. Nothing moved. He liked the sense of solitude it provided, even if only fleeting.

One of the few fond memories he had from his time as an outlaw was waking to similar mornings deep in the Devil's River wilderness with that same sensation. Of course, that had all been fleeting, too. The moments of peaceful solitude had never lasted long enough, and the rest of it—the chases, the danger and the hiding out, the empty stretches apart from his family—had dragged on too long. He couldn't seem to get thoughts of those days out of his mind.

They added to the current matters darkening his mood. The threat of Sanders's gang, for one, likely poised to return and make a try to break their leader out of jail . . . if Bob had it figured right.

Not to mention the certainty of that damnable reporter from Cheyenne due in, thanks to the good intentions of Abe Starbuck.

It was plain to Bob the dreams and stray thoughts of the past that kept crowding in were being generated by the risk of upheaval the reporter's story would cause in his life. Unfortunately, he didn't know how to put a stop to either one—not the reporter, not the freshly stirred thoughts of the past.

It didn't help a damn bit that he'd chosen to largely isolate himself from Bucky and Consuela until the business with Sanders and his gang played out. He'd had supper with them and had used the opportunity to make them understand why he was calling for such measures, explaining how he had reason to believe the Sanders gang would strike again soon to free their leader. That was why Bob needed to stick close to the jail and why he didn't want Bucky or Consuela anywhere near there or him until the threat was past. They *said* they understood, but he could tell by their sullen attitudes that they really didn't and, even if they did, they didn't like it very much. As if he felt otherwise.

Bob had also paid a call on Kim and Mee-Kee at Bullock's. He was surprised and pleased to find how well the two of them were hitting it off. Through interpretation, Mee-Kee had even thanked him for rescuing her, both from where she'd been half-buried in the rubble and from Pepper and Iverson. Kim had taken the night off from any other duties and was keeping close to Mee-Kee in order to continue getting her acclimated to different surroundings and a different life.

Exactly what that different life would turn out to be remained undecided. Maudie Sartain, Mike Bullock's right-hand gal when it came to running the saloon and who also served as a sort of house mother to the girls working there, had pulled Bob aside on his way out. She reminded him that Bullock's was not a halfway house for troubled girls who did nothing to earn their keep. Furthermore, due to his savior role, he bore a certain responsibility for helping to determine Mee-Kee's future.

Maudie—a voluptuous, dark-haired beauty in her own right, a rather curious yet nonetheless smoldering mix of Creole and Armenian blood—tried to be stern and demanding about it, but she and Bob went back too far and had toyed with romantic inclinations toward one another too long for her to be effectively intimidating. Nevertheless, he agreed he bore part of the responsibility for Mee-Kee and would shoulder his share.

Something more to weigh on his mind.

Chapter 23

The Macy brothers reported bright and early with their bedrolls and personal gear to assume their duties as New Town deputies. Bob had stopped by during his rounds the previous evening to inform them about his plan for sticking close to the jail.

Once their gear was unloaded onto the cots Fred had set up for them against the side wall of the office area, they were properly introduced to him, sworn in, and provided their badges. The genuine pride each young man beamed with as they pinned on their stars was heartening to see.

With that taken care of, Bob announced he would take a turn around town with Peter and Vern, familiarize them with certain procedures, show them off a bit, and introduce them to some of the town council members who'd authorized their hire. Fred would stay behind and keep an eye on things at the jail.

The day had dawned overcast and cool, continuing to carry the feel of an imminent—though not immediate—storm. Activity up and down Front Street did not appear deterred by the turn in the weather. If anything, things may have been a bit heavier due to folks wanting to get their shopping or other business out of the way before a storm actually arrived.

At the Starbuck Territorial Bank, Bob and his new deputies were eagerly greeted by Abe Starbuck. Always dressed impeccably for business, Starbuck looked more starched and polished than usual. The reason, as he quickly made evident, was his anticipation of the Cheyenne newspaper reporter who was due in on the train.

"You lads are most fortunate to be joining such a fine law enforcement team," he told Peter and Vern. "What's more, the timing of you coming aboard coincides nicely with some scheduled publicity for Marshal Hatfield and Deputy Fred that will no doubt add to wider recognition and appreciation for the fine job they've been doing here in our fair city. Your addition to the team will doubtlessly be made note of, too."

"That's a generous thought, Mr. Starbuck," said Peter, "but it ain't hardly our way to crowd in on somebody else's glory."

"That's right," added Vern. "That newspaper fella is comin' on account of what the marshal and Fred did, not us. After we've done something to earn our own recognition will be a different matter. For today, we're just a couple more onlookers who consider ourselves, like you say, fortunate."

Starbuck smiled tolerantly and said to Bob, "Refreshingly modest, aren't they? They seem to be forgetting how—based on what you told me and other council members—they helped you up in New Town on the night of the raid, when they wore no badges and had no real obligation to get involved at all."

"They were a big help to me, no denying that. It's their right to steer clear of the newspaper fella when he shows up, if that's the way they want it." Bob fervently wished he could find a good excuse for steering clear.

"Very well. If that's what everyone insists," Starbuck said with a sigh. "After all, it's not as if there isn't still a whale of a story for that reporter to tell based strictly on the exploits of you and Deputy Fred."

"Yeah. Exploits," Bob muttered.

"On a less negotiable point," Starbuck continued, "which of these stalwart lads will I be getting as the guard for my bank?"

"Probably both of them," Bob answered, "which is to say, I see them as being interchangeable in that role."

Starbuck nodded. "Excellent. I have no problem with that."

"The thing is, though, there'll be a slight delay before either one starts working into that routine," Bob said.

Starbuck scowled. "How so? We had an agreement that—"

"I'm well aware of our agreement, Mr. Starbuck," Bob cut him off. "And I fully intend to honor it. For right now, in these first few days, a number of other procedures are needed to get Peter and Vern thoroughly trained. And, for reasons I'd rather not go too deeply into nor do I want to have spread around, I'm concerned about what's left of the Sanders gang returning to break Sanders out of our jail. I mean to concentrate all of our forces on preventing that."

"Well, naturally I can understand that," Starbuck harrumphed. "And you, of course, know best how to place your men. If you're concerned about the gang hitting our town again, what about my bank? You don't think there's the chance they'd make another try on it, too?"

"There's always the chance. But, like I said, I'm convinced coming after their leader is their first priority, and I'm further convinced that their forces have been cut down too low for them to try both."

"In that case," said Starbuck rather grudgingly, "I'll bow to your judgment. Er, what about this U.S. marshal who's arrived in town? Is he working in conjunction with you on this?"

"Let's just say he agrees there's the likely chance that Sanders's men will be making a try at springing him," Bob replied in a flat tone.

Starbuck frowned as if finding the answer rather curious. Apparently deciding it wasn't worth pursuing, he cleared his throat and said, "I dare say we both have other matters to attend to before that reporter arrives, so I'll leave you on your way. Nice to have met you, Peter and Vern. I'm looking forward to seeing you around on a regular basis. When the train comes in, I trust I will be seeing you at the depot, Marshal?"

"Unless a jailbreak or some other *exploit* is keeping me too busy," Bob replied dryly.

Chapter 24

The train came puffing and hissing up the spur track at half past noon, right on schedule. It announced itself with several whistle toots and braked to a halt in front of the depot amid a good deal of metallic screeching and thumping of couplings as the individual cars shifted back and forth. Bob was there, watching and waiting alongside a smiling, eager-looking Abe Starbuck. Fred was present, also smiling. Only Bob, in his reluctance to be any part of it, was somber-faced.

Since the depot was at the south end of town, only a short distance from the jail, he had decided to change his plan for either Fred or himself to be there at all times. For one thing, he was fully confident of the Macy brothers' competence in their absence. For another, no way he was going to deny Fred his chance for a well-earned share of the praise the reporter would allegedly be including in his coverage. Much as Bob *didn't* want to be part of said coverage, Fred—who'd suffered much of his life because of his weight and the cruel remarks it sometimes drew—badly craved the positive attention.

Although he had his reasons for not wanting to be present, normally, Bob made a habit of being on hand for each train arriving in Rattlesnake Wells. He felt it was worthwhile to check out any newcomers getting off to stay. With the gold boom, newcomers were pouring in practically every day. More of them arrived on horseback or in wagons than by train, which meant the marshal had little chance to monitor all new arrivals, but that didn't mean he couldn't keep track of as many as possible.

As folks began stepping down out of the passenger car, it was easy to spot the newspapermen. The one Bob took for the reporter was a studious-looking gent of about thirty, curly brown sideburns bracketing a face full of average features. Clad in a powder blue suit, he wore a cream-colored, wide-brimmed plantation-style hat.

In recent years, newspapers had started publishing actual photographs rather than illustrations, so a photographer had been sent along with the reporter. He was clearly marked by the tripod and cumbersome camera case he was lugging. He was half a dozen years younger than the reporter, fresh-faced, wearing a brightly patterned sweater vest and a short-billed cap. Bob gave them a quick once-over but didn't spend a lot of time studying them beyond that. He figured he'd have plenty of opportunity for a closer look during the scrutiny he'd soon be enduring.

The most noteworthy of the remaining passengers was a handsome, somewhat older woman who appeared to be traveling by herself. Under a minimal bonnet, blue in color, she had pale gold hair starting to come loose from the bun that had once contained it. Her dress was also blue, though not quite a matching shade, and she clutched a large, multipatterned carpetbag. She had alert brown eyes and a face that was still attractive yet showing traces of years that hadn't always been easy.

As Bob watched, she spoke with the uniformed conductor. He pointed up Front Street as he jabbered an answer to whatever she'd asked of him. The woman gave a brief, grateful smile, seemingly satisfied with the response, and then started resolutely up the street. Evidently the carpetbag was the only thing she had in the way of luggage.

Bob found all of that a mite curious. He speculated she possibly was another working gal come to ply her wares—herself, in other words—amid the free-spending gold hunters. A freelance whore traveling by train, however, didn't quite fit. On the other hand, a lone woman traveling by train with only a carpetbag didn't quite fit anything else he could think of, either.

Only eight other passengers—including the newspapermen—had arrived on the train. Two of them were Rattlesnake Wells equipment dealers returning from a big trade show in Cheyenne.

A narrow-eyed, string-tie-wearing stranger who had the look of a cardsharp got off by himself. He wore a six-gun in a cross-draw rig under his coat—Bob could see the bulge and the butt of the gun when he moved a certain way—and carried only a small, flat, black leather case. He paused for a moment on the depot platform, taking a long look up Front Street and breathing in deeply, like a predatory animal trying to catch the scent of prey, then marched confidently toward the saloons and gambling dens that lay in that direction.

That left three burly, boisterous specimens dressed in the coarse, rugged clothes and heavy work boots of rail yard roughnecks. They clearly knew each other well and the way they threw elbows and shouldered one another aside as they clomped across the platform made it just as clear they were good pals. Despite the fact they carried no sign of baggage or personal belongings, Bob's guess was that they were three adventurous souls who'd impulsively—aided by the consumption of a generous amount of alcohol, no doubt—decided to chuck their current lives and jobs and strike out to find their fortunes and their futures in the Prophecy Mountains, where everybody knew all you had to do was walk across the ground and you were bound to trip over clumps of gold bigger than Aunt Bessie's mams. Bob had watched the arrival of their kind before . . . and, in most cases, he'd watched their departure only a short time later.

"Well, then. A gentleman of obvious prominence flanked by two stalwarts wearing badges can only mean one thing—I have arrived in the presence of Mr. Abraham Starbuck and the esteemed lawmen of this fair city." With that pronouncement, the man in the powder blue suit planted himself in front of Bob, Fred, and Starbuck. His smile was earnest and ingratiating.

Bob was too unfavorably inclined toward the whole exercise to find any likability in the hombre who'd be carrying it out.

"Allow me to introduce myself," Blue Suit continued.

"I am Carson Bailey of the *Cheyenne Sun.* This young fellow is my photographer, Tom Stevens."

Starbuck extended his hand. "And I, as you've already concluded, am Abraham Starbuck. To my right, Marshal Bob Hatfield. To my left, Chief Deputy Fred Ordway."

Handshakes and pleased-to-meet-yous were exchanged all around.

"Very good," said Bailey at the conclusion of the arm-pumping. "I must tell you that the very accommodating engineer and conductor of our train have agreed—at the cost of a small bribe ensuring them favorable coverage in our newspaper—to hold the train's departure for an extra couple hours, if needed, to allow us ample time to conduct our business. However, so as not to take advantage of their generosity, I propose we repair posthaste to a place where we can proceed with the matter at hand. Is that agreeable?"

"Indeed it is," said Starbuck.

"On the train, an establishment called Bullock's was recommended to me as a place where we might enjoy some lunch and liquid refreshment while we talk. Is that also agreeable?"

Again, Starbuck gave assurance that it was, concluding, "It's just across the street from my bank, where the robbery-minded villains had me under threat of death before our brave law enforcement team showed up to save the day . . . meaning they saved my life, as well as the money in the bank. It would be very convenient in case you want to take some photographs of the, er, scene of the crime, as it were."

"Excellent, excellent," said Bailey. "I can see you

have a distinct flair for getting to the real meat of a story."

The lunch-hour crowd at Bullock's was starting to thin, but Maudie Sartain was on hand to rearrange some things and get them seated at a large round table off in one corner where they could have their conversation in relative quiet and young Stevens could set up his tripod and camera.

Before taking her leave, Maudie said to Bailey with a wink, "After you've listened to the yarns these characters spin for you, come around to see me and I'll give you the real story on them."

"The prospect of coming around to see you, lovely lady," Bailey replied, "strikes me as such a hypnotically pleasurable one, I fear I would forget how to spell my own name, let alone write down anything you told me."

Maudie gave a laugh. "Mister, with a line of lingo like that, you oughta be fertilizing farmland back in Iowa or Illinois somewhere instead of wasting your time with dull old journalism."

"The way *I* write journalism," Bailey said rather stiffly as if he was mildly offended, "I assure you is neither dull nor a waste of time."

Bob groaned inwardly. Things was getting worse by the minute. All he needed was some high-minded word slinger to wildly embellish things in order to add color and excitement to the simplest story.

After they'd all made a trip to the spread of cold cuts, cheeses, bread, and various side dishes, they returned to their table, where they were served tall mugs of cold beer, and coffee for Bob and Fred, who were on duty. As they ate and drank, Bailey produced a pencil and notebook and began his questioning. Between sporadic bites off his plate and infrequent sips of his beer, Stevens set up the tripod and camera.

In contrast to what his remark to Maudie might have implied, Bailey asked probing, thoughtful questions about the raid and attempted robbery. He seemed well prepared and knowledgeable on the gang and on Arlo Sanders, as well as the history of Rattlesnake Wells. When he learned something new or got answers to his direct questions, he furiously wrote detailed notes and often read them back to make sure he'd gotten it right.

As the interview went on, Bob started to relax a little. Maybe it wasn't going to turn out so bad after all, he tried to convince himself. If only he could avoid getting photographed . . .

It was when Fred stood and went back for seconds that everything changed. And it had nothing to do with the interview or a photograph or any of that.

As he was returning to their table with his plate full, Bob heard the outburst of loud, braying laughter coming from the bar area. Unfortunately, it was directed at Fred, who heard it, too. It was the kind of thing he had been experiencing all his life. His shoulders slumped, his chin sagged, and the sting was always the same.

Bob felt the sting too—felt it *for* his deputy and friend. Heat instantly crawled up his neck and over his face, his cheeks turning as fiery red as his hair.

Seeing the transformation, Bailey stopped in the middle of asking a question and blurted out a different one. "Marshal? What's wrong?"

Sinking into his seat beside Bob, Fred softly said, "Leave it go, Marshal. They're just a bunch of loud-mouthed jackasses. They aren't worth the trouble."

"What jackasses? What trouble?" Bailey demanded. "What's going on?"

Before Bob could answer, he saw movement from within the knot of men over by the bar where the derisive laughter had come from. One of the men separated himself and started in their direction. Right behind him came two others. Bob recognized them as the three rail yard roughnecks he'd seen getting off the train earlier.

"Aw, shoot," Fred muttered under his breath.

Chapter 25

"'Scuse me, gents. Don't mean to interrupt, but I need just a minute of y'all's time."

The man who approached their table was a shade wider through the shoulders than his two comrades, neither of whom were exactly scrawny. They moved up behind the speaker, halting a distance of a yard or so. The speaker was a burly number, mid-twenties, with a lantern jaw covered by bristly black stubble, intense dark eyes, and greasy black hair spilling down behind his ears from a long-billed workman's cap. The other two were of a similar age and dressed the same. One was clean shaven with evidence of close-cropped hair, based on what wasn't covered by his cap. The third had a blond mustache and bushy sideburns of the same color.

"I'm sorry," said Bailey in response to Black Whiskers. "You *are* meaning to interrupt or else you would have held off until you saw we were finishing up. It happens we are in the middle of an important business meeting here and therefore—"

"Well, that fits just fine then," said Black Whiskers,

cutting him off. "Because what I want to talk about is important, too."

"You, sir, are being very rude and impertinent," huffed Starbuck.

Black Whiskers grinned. "It probably wouldn't surprise you to know, Gramps, that you're a long way from bein' the first person to ever call me *rude*. But as for that other word . . . *impertinent*? I don't even know what that means." He cut his gaze to Fred. "That ain't something illegal, is it, Deputy?"

Bob was quick to answer instead. "You push it far enough, we can arrange for it to be."

Black Whiskers put away the grin. "See, it's the same story in every pissant little town I ever been to. They pin a tin star on some shuffle-footed sucker who's never been of any consequence or importance in his life, and all of a sudden he thinks he *is* important." He tossed a glance over his shoulder. "Ain't that just the way, boys?"

The other two snickered obligingly.

Fred's face flushed a bright red, making his round cheeks practically glow in sharp contrast to the purple-black circles around his eyes. He came to his feet. "On his worst day, you bigmouthed lout, Marshal Bob Hatfield is more important than you and those other two skunks combined."

Black Whiskers' eyebrows shot up. "Hey now, Tubby, you *can* talk. Next you'll be tellin' me that it's true—like some of those other fellas over there at the bar are claimin.' How you're the fee-rocious law dog who helped the marshal of great consequence here put the run on the Sanders gang and slapped ol' Arlo hisself behind bars. That's what I came over here to get straight on. I'm sayin' there ain't no way in hell a lard bucket like you could've been any part of gettin' the drop on the likes of Arlo Sanders."

"Then you're saying exactly wrong, bub," Fred told him. "So, now that you got your answer, beat it. Go on your way and leave us to our business."

Black Whiskers shook his head stubbornly. "That ain't good enough. Not by a barrelful it ain't. I'm callin' you a damn liar."

Quick as a handclap, Fred balled his meaty right fist and swung a clubbing blow to the side of Black Whiskers' face. The taunting man was knocked backwards, staggering. Only the hands of his two pals reaching out to steady him kept him from being knocked down.

Bob sprang to his feet and swept the Colt from his holster.

Fred was quick to extend an arm, palm out. "Not this time. Put it away, Marshal. These jackasses ain't wearing guns, so that's how we'll keep it."

After lifting his own gun from its holster and tossing it on the table, Fred waded straight into the three rowdies with both fists raised and ready. Bob looked on momentarily slack jawed. He was surprised and impressed and . . . well, *proud*. He felt the corners of his mouth stretching into a wide grin.

Fred traded a series of punches with Black Whiskers, landing as good as he got and then some. When he sent the man staggering nearly off his feet again, one of the other two—the one with the blond mustache—blocked what would have been Fred's follow-up punch and threw one of his own in return. Bob suddenly realized that's what he'd been waiting for. Hell, maybe *hoping* for. Still grinning, he tossed his Colt on the table and lunged into the fray.

For the next several minutes, the five men surged back and forth, slugging and kicking, slamming the occasional head butt, overturning tables, and smashing chairs as other patrons scrambled frantically to get out of the way and give them fighting room. Eventually a semicircle formed at a safe distance and those within looked on with excited, sometimes wincing expressions as their cheers and jeers filled the room to the accompaniment of thudding blows, grunts, and curses.

From behind the bar, Mike Bullock shouted, "Stop it, you men! Stop it, I say!" all the while loudly pounding the bar top with his bung starter. When his shouts met with no result, he seemed to relax, and a thin, satisfied smile formed on his mouth as he watched Bob and Fred position themselves back-to-back, slowly circling, repeatedly beating off the three-on-two assaults.

When Maudie wailed, "Aren't you going to do something?" Mike's smile only widened.

"It's already being done, gal . . . and being handled quite well, I might add."

As the two lawmen circled, Bob lashed out with lightning-quick jabs and sharp right and left crosses. Fred threw heavy-handed roundhouses and clubbing backhands. One nostril of Fred's already broken nose was streaming blood, and Bob had blood dribbling steadily from a split lip.

Their three opponents were suffering the worst of it. Blond Mustache, who'd lost a tooth and bitten his tongue near in two, was hacking up gobs of bloody mucus. One of Clean Shaven's eyes was puffed nearly shut and trails of blood were streaming from both corners of his mouth. Blood was pouring out of both sides of Black Whiskers' broken nose, and he was doubled over, hugging his left arm to his side where one of Fred's ham-fisted punches had cracked a pair of ribs.

Finally, Blond Mustache hit the floor. He made one valiant effort to get up, then collapsed onto his stomach and just lay there, bubbling blood.

Clean Shaven was the next to go. Half blinded by his swollen left eye, he was able to neither block nor duck a slashing right cross from Bob that landed solidly, knocking him cold and dropping him flat onto his back.

That left Black Whiskers. Still doubled over in an attempt to cover and protect his busted ribs, he was breathing hard and spraying blood with each labored exhale. Focused blearily on Fred's fists getting set to deliver more, Black Whiskers suddenly threw up one hand, palm out. "That's enough! We're done. You win . . . I take back the things I said."

His own breath coming in ragged gasps, Fred said, "Maybe you're done . . . but what if I'm not?"

Black Whiskers swung his gaze to Carson Bailey, who stood huddled at a safe distance with Starbuck and Stevens. "You heard me . . . You can see . . . for yourself . . . that we're whipped . . . Damn it . . . You swore you'd stop it . . . if it started to get . . . out of hand."

Bob, Fred, and several other faces turned to look at Bailey.

"What's he talking about?" Bob wanted to know. "What have you got to do with starting or stopping this?"

Bailey's mouth worked silently for a moment before

he got any words out. "I . . . I assure you . . . You've got to understand—"

"Understand what?" Bob demanded. "You'd better start making sense, and you'd better start doing it pretty damned quick."

"He hired us . . . to start this ruckus," Black Whiskers said. "Back in Cheyenne . . . Said he was comin' here to do a story . . . on you . . . and wanted to make sure . . . you was as tough as he'd been told . . . so he didn't risk lookin' the fool."

"What he says is true. I heard Bailey make the deal," Stevens suddenly spoke up in a slightly quavering voice. "The whole thing was a foolish, manipulative idea and now look!" He thrust his hands despairingly toward his camera, which had gotten knocked off its tripod during the scuffle and was broken wide open on the floor. "That's my own personal equipment. And now it's destroyed because Mr. Flamboyant Reporter insisted on trying to add some firsthand color to his stupid story."

Starbuck scowled fiercely at Bailey. "Do you deny any of this, you scoundrel?" he demanded.

Bailey scowled back, getting defensive. "What if I don't? You think I'd come all this way, risk wasting my time to do a story based merely on the embellishments you put in that telegram of yours? If all you claimed was accurate, so much the better—but I wanted to make damned sure that I'd have some firsthand excitement and color to write about, one way or the other."

"How about if I bust your stinkin' jaw," said Bob, taking a step toward the reporter. "You'd still be able to write, and that would give you some real *firsthand* excitement to tell about."

Bailey shrank back. "You wouldn't dare! That would be assault. There are witnesses."

"I'm the law in this town. I decide who's a credible witness and who's not," Bob told him. "As far as assaulting you, because you hired those men I could charge you with inciting a riot—and probably a lot more, if I put my mind to it—which would give me plenty of grounds for throwing you in the clink. If you resisted arrest and got roughed up a little in the process, how could that be assault?"

"B-but I'm not . . . Y-you couldn't . . ." Bailey stammered.

"Don't kid yourself, Mr. Reporter," Bob said through clenched teeth. "There's a long list of what I could do to you as a result of your shenanigans here this afternoon. But I won't, and it's for two simple reasons. Number one, I've got way more important things on my plate, and number two, the sight of you makes me sick, and I don't want you around to look at for any longer than I have to. Haul your bony ass back down to the depot, get on that train, and out of here as fast as you can, understand?"

Bailey licked his lips and nodded meekly.

"A couple more things," Bob said. "You get back to Cheyenne and start feeling brave enough to write some kind of trash piece about me or this town, I'll hear about it." He cut a quick glance to Stevens. "Won't I, kid?"

The photographer nodded. "You can count on it."

"Comes to that," Bob said, addressing Bailey again, "I'll be the one paying *you* a visit, and I guarantee you won't be happy to see me. Far as the kid's camera goes, either you personally or your paper is gonna reimburse him for it. Ain't that right?"

"I'll see to it," said Bailey with a weak nod.

"What about us, Marshal?" asked Black Whiskers as he helped Blond Mustache up to his feet. "You gonna charge us with anything?"

Bob twisted his mouth wryly. "What would it be? Acting stupid in public? Agreeing to be part of a stupid idea?"

Black Whiskers looked sullen but made no reply.

Bob looked at Fred. "What do you think?"

Fred backhanded blood from under his nose and glared at Black Whiskers. "You get paid decent for coming here to cause this trouble?"

"Seemed like it at the time." Black Whiskers gently rubbed his ribs. "But now I ain't so sure. Never expected to run into a punch as mule-kick hard as yours."

The corner of Fred's mouth twitched, almost like he wanted to smile. "You act like a jackass, I hit like a mule . . . Reckon we can call it even."

Black Whiskers nodded, looking relieved.

"We call it even as long as you and your two compadres are also on that train leaving here in short order." Bob added. "The ride back might give you time to renegotiate your deal with Bailey . . . if you're so inclined."

"It might at that," Black Whiskers agreed.

"What about the damage to my place?" called Mike Bullock from behind the bar, his voice cutting through the ring of onlookers who'd been standing quietly once the fight ended.

Before anybody else could say anything, Abe Starbuck jerked a hand in the air. "I'll take care of that, Michael! Since I had the poor judgment to send for this fool"—another jerk of his hand indicated Bailey—"it seems only fitting I should compensate you in some way. Plus," he added with an uncharacteristic twinkle in his eye, "I'm doubly willing to pay for the rousing fight I just witnessed."

Bullock issued a booming laugh. "There's a sentiment after my own heart! To which I can only add— a round of drinks on the house!"

Chapter 26

"You!" Upon answering the knock on her hotel room door, the woman in the blue dress took an abrupt step backwards, her expression alternating between surprise and concern.

The tall man, whose knock she had answered and who was subsequently causing the uncertain reaction from her, moved into the room, crowding her and forcing her to take more steps back. He heeled the door shut behind him and then smiled, his white teeth flashing under his walrus mustache. "Hello, Libby. Long time no see," said Vernon Brock.

"A long time doesn't necessarily make it long enough," said the woman called Libby.

"That almost sounded unfriendly. Is that any way to be?"

"I wasn't aware we were ever friends, so why should I be friendly?"

Brock shrugged elaborately. "The term *friend* can be stretched to cover a lot of things. We surely have a common interest, don't we? Doesn't that come close enough?"

Libby just looked at him, made no reply.

Brock's gaze swept the room, coming to rest on the large carpetbag lying on the bed. One corner of his mouth lifted in another smile, at least a partial one. "I'd be surprised if you don't have some spirits in there. Aren't you going to at least offer a visitor . . . an old acquaintance, if not exactly a friend . . . a drink?"

Libby shook her head. "There's nothing to drink in there."

"Don't tell me you've become a teetotaler?"

"I ran out on the train. The clerk is supposed to be sending something up. When you knocked, I thought that's who it was."

"Ah. That's more like it."

Libby's eyes narrowed. "What are you doing here, Brock? And how did you know I was here? I just got in a short while ago."

"It should be obvious that my reason for being here is the same as yours. As far as knowing of your presence, it was just my good fortune that I was in the hotel bar and happened to look into the lobby as you arrived to check in."

"Your good fortune, my lousy luck," Libby muttered.

Brock's face went tight. "If you gave it half a chance and quit trying so hard to annoy me, it might be good fortune for both of us."

Before Libby could reply, there was another knock on the door. An elderly gent bore a tray containing a bottle of tequila and a cup of sliced limes. Libby took the tray and set it on a small stand beside the bed. Brock dug a coin out of his pocket, flipped it to the old man for a tip, and the man returned downstairs.

After the door had closed, Libby promptly began working the cap off the bottle and said to Brock,

"There are clean glasses over by the washbasin. Grab one for each of us."

A minute later, Libby was thirstily tipping up her glass while Brock was taking a more modest sip from his. "I can tolerate this stuff," he proclaimed as he lowered his arm, "but I'm damned if I can see how anybody makes it their drink of choice."

Immediately pouring some more for herself, Libby said, "We each find our own poisons . . . and, boy, don't I know about that."

"Hey, take it easy," Brock advised as she took another thirsty pull.

She lowered her glass and stared down in it for a long moment. When she spoke again, her voice was almost a whisper. "Have you seen him?"

Brock nodded. "Yeah. Briefly. Needless to say, he wasn't very glad to see me."

"What are their plans for him? Hanging?"

"Oh, yeah. There are all kinds of righteous, God-fearing folks who want to see him swing real bad. But not here. That is to say, the hanging won't be taking place here."

"How can you be so sure?"

"Because the town marshal of this burg has contacted a number of different jurisdictions and is bent on farming Arlo's hanging out to whoever can make the most convincing claim."

"That's a list that could stretch from here to God knows where."

"Tell me about it. I made my pitch for taking Arlo into my custody, but the good marshal wasn't having any of that. Me and him sort of ended up at odds with one another."

Libby tipped her head. "I see you're still wearing

that U.S. marshal's badge. You couldn't sell that dodge to this hick marshal, eh? You must be losing your touch."

"Maybe, maybe not. We'll see how good a touch *you* still got when you take a turn . . . By the way, Mrs. Sanders, exactly what is your dodge when it comes to that lowdown cur you call a husband?"

Chapter 27

"Doggone it, Con, didn't I ask you not to come around here for the next few days? I explained how—"

"I know what you asked," Consuela cut Bob off in mid-sentence, "and I know what you explained." She marched defiantly into the marshal's office with a bulky item in her arms, moved to the front of Bob's desk, and held the item out to him. "Here is part of my reason for not paying attention—it's your good rain slicker. There's a bad storm moving in, and I figured you would want this for when you go out on your rounds."

Bob took the slicker. "I'm grateful for you thinking of this, although there are a couple of old slickers in the back I could have made do with."

"I've seen those the times I came here to do some cleaning," Consuela replied. "I was tempted to throw them away each time I came across them. They're so old and tattered they surely would leak almost as bad as not having them on at all."

"I reckon you're right. But still . . . Never mind. It's done. And no doubt I'll be glad to have this if the weather turns as bad as it looks like it's gonna." Bob shook out the slicker, carried it over, and hung it on a peg next to the cell block door. Turning back, he said, "You mentioned bringing this was *part* of the reason you came. What's the rest?"

Consuela arched a brow. "The rest is that the agreement I made not to come here was with a mature, responsible officer of the law. From what I've been hearing all over town as I went about some afternoon shopping, that man has apparently been replaced by a reckless, saloon-brawling, furniture-smashing individual who I'm not sure I ever met. Therefore, I came to see for myself."

Bob grinned sheepishly. "Oh, that. You know how things can get exaggerated all out of shape."

Consuela swept her gaze from Bob to Fred, who was sitting quietly in a chair off to one side, and back to Bob again. "From the looks of you two, it doesn't appear that much exaggeration was necessary."

Now that he'd been dragged into it, Fred got up out of his chair and went to stand at the end of Bob's desk. "Aw, Miss Consuela, none of it is really as bad as it looks or probably sounds. Some rowdies in Bullock's were looking for trouble so we had to tame them down, that's all."

Consuela continued to look skeptical. "And how did you tame them—by repeatedly striking their fists with your faces?"

Fred gave a little laugh. "Hitting their fists with our faces. That's a good one."

"No, it is not good," Consuela insisted. "Look at the two of you. How can that be good?"

"The other fellas look worse. That's how," Bob told her.

"I'd have to see it to believe it," Consuela huffed. "You, with your split lip and bruised cheek and the Lord knows what else. And you, Fred. Are you trying to set some kind of record for how many times you can get your nose broken in the fewest number of days?"

Fred was still smiling. "Actually, you *should* have seen us, Miss Consuela. The marshal and me stood back-to-back, just like they write about in the dime novels, and fought all three of those troublemakers to a standstill. They weren't exactly three *puny* hombres, either."

"Except puny in their brains maybe. Saloon brawlers! And you two allowing yourselves to be drawn into it." Consuela focused on Bob. "What would you say if Bucky came home with a tale like that?"

"For starters, I'd chew him out for being in a saloon."

"I'm serious."

Bob spread his hands. "Okay. It would depend on the circumstances. If Bucky got in a fight standing up for himself or a friend, I expect I'd be proud of him and hope that he'd won the fight. I don't see another way to look at it."

Consuela shook her head. "You're hopeless." She paused, looking around the office as if she'd lost something. "Where are your new deputies? Did you send them out to find a brawl they could get into so you can be proud of them too?"

"Okay. That's enough, Con," Bob said. "As for the two deputies, they're out grabbing a late lunch and are due back shortly. As for the brawl, the whole thing was set up by that jackass of a newspaper reporter who I never wanted to meet with in the first place. Now he's out of my hair and, far as I'm concerned, the few scrapes and bruises I got to help make that happen were well worth it."

"I second that," said Fred. "Although I wouldn't have minded the newspaper story."

Grudgingly, Consuela managed to find a smile of her own. "Like I said, you're both hopeless. I guess that's all there is to it."

"Does that mean you're done scolding us?" Bob wanted to know.

Consuela's smile grew uncertain and then twin spots of color appeared on her smooth olive cheeks. "I—I didn't mean for it to sound that way. I have no right to scold either of you, of course. I only wanted to bring the slicker and . . . well, to make sure you were okay."

"We're fine, Con. Really we are," said Bob. "The saloon scuffle wasn't nearly as brutal or bloody as I expect it was painted to be by the time you heard about it. It was still nice of you to care, though."

"Yes, it was," seconded Fred, gazing at Consuela with eyes that said he would welcome all the caring and even scolding she cared to send his way. Although it was plain to most everyone, including Fred, that Consuela's heart belonged to Bob—one of the few who appeared maddeningly unaware of it . . . or at least unwilling to act on it—Fred nevertheless maintained a huge crush on the Mexican beauty, his feelings as ill-concealed as hers for the marshal.

"I'd still rather you didn't come around here—not

until this business with Arlo Sanders is wrapped up," Bob said to Consuela. "And, since Bucky is bound to be hearing exaggerated accounts of the saloon fight as soon as he gets out of school, I'd appreciate it if you'd intercept him again and steer him clear of coming here as well."

Consuela nodded. "I will. But it won't be easy. He misses you badly."

"I know. I feel the same way. This is the best and the safest . . . Now you'd better get along before you end up getting caught in that storm when it hits."

Bob was so relieved at how his concerns over the newspaper article had gotten resolved that, even with the looming potential of the Sanders gang striking again, he was experiencing the best mood he'd been in since before the initial raid. He naturally didn't like being isolated from his son and Consuela, as her brief visit had served to remind him, but he held fast to his belief it was for the best. He also remained convinced the whole thing would end soon—anything more the Sanders gang decided to try would come quick.

In the meantime, it was heartening to see a fast camaraderie developing between Fred and the Macy brothers. Peter and Vern were hungry for details on the raid, the attempted bank robbery, the recent saloon brawl, and other events of the kind they might expect in their new roles as deputies. Fred, basking in a more positive light than he was used to, was happy to supply them. For their part, the Macys had some colorful tales of their own to tell about their previous life on the banks of the Mississippi River and their journey across Iowa and Nebraska to make it to Wyoming Territory.

At one point, encouraged by his brother, Peter took a harmonica out of his pocket and played some tunes on it. Fred, who had a fine singing voice and often soloed in the church choir, sang along with a couple that he knew, and Vern joined him in harmony on the refrains. It all made for an impromptu, unexpected few minutes that helped pass the time and deepened the sense of camaraderie.

Bob participated sparingly in the verbal exchanges, holding himself apart, not out of aloofness or due to his leadership position but mainly because he made a habit of keeping his past his own business. By nature, he wasn't one to engage in embellishments even of more recent experiences.

When it came to the music, he enjoyed it and even found himself tapping his toe on some of the songs. As far as joining in, he opted out of that even more firmly than the talking for the simple reason he had a lousy singing voice and couldn't carry a tune in a bushel basket. Still, he enjoyed listening to the others banter and tell their stories and perform musically. With the four of them facing stretches of close-quarters time together, it was touches like that would make the passage of time a lot more tolerable.

Later in the afternoon, with the wind kicking up wildly outside and the sky steadily transitioning into a roiling, thickening mass of sooty black clouds that turned the day into the dimness of evening, Bob sent Fred and Peter out to make a quick turn around the town. He also gave Fred instructions to stop by Krepdorf's General Store and pick up some good-quality rain slickers for the Macys, billed to the town's account.

Shortly after the pair took their leave, a knock sounded on the office's outer door. Vern answered it.

The woman in the blue dress Bob had seen get off the train earlier entered. She looked decidedly windblown in spite of the scarf tied over her head and the heavy shawl wrapped around her shoulders, but there was no mistaking her identity. She still clutched the multipatterned carpetbag she'd gotten off the train with.

Bob stood up behind his desk. "Can we help you with something, ma'am?"

The woman appeared tense, somewhat uncertain. "Yes. Yes, I believe you can . . . It's a matter of whether or not you're willing."

Bob found that a curious remark. "We try to be accommodating to most folks, ma'am." Then, with what he hoped was an ingratiating smile, he added, "Unless you've broken the law."

The woman's gaze went momentarily to the heavy door leading back to the cell block, then returned to the marshal. "No, I'm not a lawbreaker . . . I'm just married to someone who is."

"Come again?" said Bob, caught off balance by her words.

The woman tipped her head toward the cell block door. "It's my understanding that you have the notorious outlaw Arlo Sanders behind bars in there. Is that true?"

"It is."

"My name is Libby Sanders. I'm Arlo's wife."

That put Bob even a bit more off balance, not to mention at a loss for what to say in response. Finally, he suggested, "Why don't you take a seat, Mrs. Sanders?"

From where he stood off to one side, Vern said, "Can I get you a cup of coffee, ma'am? Or maybe a glass of water?"

Libby Sanders shook her head. "That's all right. I'm fine, thank you. What I was hoping is that you would allow me to see Arlo for a few minutes. You see, I was in Cheyenne yesterday when word began buzzing around the hotel where I was staying that he had been captured up here in your town. I guess I should explain that we—Arlo and me, that is—have been separated for a number of years. Estranged, as they say. We both had a share in why it came to that, but it shouldn't come as a surprise that his outlaw ways certainly played a part."

"I reckon that's pretty understandable," Bob said.

Libby tugged her shawl suddenly tighter about her as if she'd felt a sudden chill. "Have you ever suffered a lost love, Marshal?"

Bob's mouth tightened. "I'm a widower, Mrs. Sanders. Yes, I know about lost love."

"I . . . I'm sorry. Then you understand . . . The thing is, for all that didn't work out between us, I never really stopped loving Arlo. I don't know how he feels about me. We haven't been in touch since we split, not at all. But when I heard he'd been captured and I was right there in Cheyenne, so close and all, I . . . well, I felt like I had to see him again. Maybe one last time. I mean, I know after all the things he and his gang have done he's bound for a hangman's rope. Isn't that right?"

"Not for me to say," Bob told her. "But, all things considered, I reckon that's a pretty strong likelihood."

Libby took a corner of her bottom lip between her teeth and nibbled at it. Then, with an imploring gaze, she said, "Well? Can it be arranged? Will you allow me to see him for a little while?"

Chapter 28

Every instinct inside Bob told him to say no, not to grant Sanders's wife a visit. It wasn't a good idea, and Sanders didn't deserve any favors.

But the woman had softened him with her talk of lost love, making him think of Priscilla. And the imploring gaze from those brown eyes set wide on a still-pretty face nevertheless bore the wear of sadness and times that hadn't always been easy . . .

"Excuse my bluntness," said Bob. "but will he *want* to see you?"

Libby blinked as if such a possibility had never occurred to her. Then, mustering a firmness that didn't quite fit her uncertain expression, she said, "I believe he will, yes. I won't permit myself to think otherwise."

Bob nodded. "Okay, I'll allow it. Briefly." He gestured to Vern. "Go back and let Sanders know he has a visitor." Turning back to Libby, he said, "During your visit, I'll need to remain there in the cell block with you."

"I understand. I'm very grateful, Marshal," said Libby.

Sanders's response to Vern had been that he not only was willing to see his estranged wife, but plainly eager.

Before going in, Libby asked to borrow a mirror—which Vern fetched for her from the washstand in the cell block—to fix her appearance. "I must look a sight after being out in that dreadful wind," she lamented. Once she had herself satisfactorily rearranged, she was ready.

At Bob's request, she left her scarf, shawl, and carpetbag in the office. A visual scan of the tight bodice and sleeves of her dress revealed no indication of anything she might have tucked away to slip to Sanders—which was the best Bob could do since a more effective search of her person was hardly an option.

A handful of minutes later, he ushered her into the cell block.

Sanders was leaning against the bars at the front of his cell, fists tightly gripping a pair of them, face pressed into the space between two others. His eyes hungrily followed Libby's approach. "Oh, God, Lib," he said somewhat breathlessly. "I can't believe this. You look fantastic. What a sight for sore eyes you are."

"I was in Cheyenne when I heard the news," Libby said softly. "I knew it would hurt to see you this way, but I had to come."

"I'm sorry, for your sake, we had to meet again under these circumstances," Sanders told her. "It's been so long. Too long. But, damn, you don't know how good it is to see you."

Libby slipped her hands over his fists, where they still gripped the bars, and squeezed gently.

Bob remained standing a ways back, just inside the cell block door. He felt awkward hanging close by like that, like some creepy eavesdropper or Peeping Tom or something. But it was necessary. It was his duty.

"You don't know how many cold, lonely nights I've thought about you touching me like that," Sanders said. "The feel of you touching me, the feel of you under my touch . . . Sometimes it was the only thing that got me through. Other times it damn near drove me crazy, the thought of having let it all slip away."

"Why did we, Arlo? Why?" Libby asked.

"Because we're two headstrong people, Lib. Too much so for our own good sometimes. Hell, most of the time." Sanders shook his head. "But let's not go over that now. Not the bad moves, not the regrets. Let's just savor this moment we got . . . God, I'm so glad you came to see me."

"So am I."

"You realize, of course, that I'm in a pretty sorry circumstance. Things don't look good for me, not at all."

"Let's not talk about that, either. Not the bad moves or regrets, remember? Let's just have this moment and block out everything else."

"Okay, but first I gotta say one thing. I gotta tell you how sorry I am for ditching you in that Colorado mining town the way I done. I thought about it a lot afterwards . . . after it was too late. It sickened me to have to face what a lowdown thing I done. I . . . I hated to think it, but I didn't even know if you'd survived. Seeing you now, I thank God that you did. I still don't know how, but—"

"That's enough, Arlo," Libby cut him off. "It wasn't

easy, and I can tell you that God didn't have a whole lot to do with it. But I don't want to go back over it now. I spent a long time getting past it and taking part of the blame on myself . . . I managed. That's all that counts."

"Yes. Yes, you did," said Sanders, half-sobbing. "You managed, you survived. And now you're here. You came to me in my hour of need."

"You realize I can't do much for you but offer some words of comfort and tell you that . . . well, I never stopped loving you."

"It's hard to believe how you could . . . but it's soothing to hear."

"Oh, you can bet there was a long spell where I told myself I hated you. It never really took, not down deep. And, like I said, I saw where I had to shoulder part of the blame myself."

"Not as much as me. Never close. I was the dirty dog who ran out and left you."

"Well, I don't intend to run out on you," Libby assured him. "Not now. Not until . . . well, until this is over. I'll be here in town. I've got a room at the Shirley House Hotel. I'll come see you every day." She turned her head and looked at Bob. "Will that be all right, Marshal?"

"I suppose," Bob said somewhat reluctantly. "As long as you keep your visits short and don't stir up any trouble. That goes for you, too, Sanders. You give me or my deputies trouble over anything, I'll put a stop on the visits in a hurry."

"I'll be sure to keep that in mind, Marshal," Sanders said.

Bob thought he caught a trace of sarcasm in the tone. He pushed away from his leaning position against the wall and said to Libby, "I think that's enough for now, Mrs. Sanders, if for no other reason than—from the way it sounds outside—that storm's gonna hit any minute and you'd best be back at your hotel before it does."

For a moment she looked like she wanted to argue the point, then gave Sanders a quick kiss through the bars. "I'll see you tomorrow, hon." Turning away from his cell, she fell in step behind Bob and they went on out into the office area, closing the heavy door behind them.

Sanders sat down on the cot and waited a full five minutes, making sure no one was going to pop back in, before he carefully opened the tightly folded piece of paper Libby had slipped into his right fist the very first moment she'd placed her hands over his. In tiny letters, a message was printed that read *Be ready. We're coming to get you out later tonight.*

Sanders read the message through twice and then sat there for a long time, not moving, his mouth curved in a wide, thin wolf's smile.

Chapter 29

Fred and Peter returned from making their rounds just as the front edge of the storm reached the town.

"Whooee!" exclaimed Fred as he hurried into the office with thin rivulets of rain running off the brim of his hat. "It is turning nasty out there!"

Entering behind him, slamming the door hard against the howling gusts of wind, Peter added, "Turning nasty now, with worse yet on the way. You oughta see the lightning show off to the west—poppin' and sizzlin' out of the sky like the Fourth of July."

In accordance with the instructions Bob had given Fred, Peter had on a new rain slicker, already shiny wet. He had a second such garment, neatly folded, under one arm. This he tossed to his brother, saying, "Here. You're gonna need this if you go out on the next set of rounds."

"Apart from the weather, how is it out there?" said Bob. "What kind of activity is taking place around town?"

"Awful quiet," replied Fred, shrugging out of his

own bulky slicker and carrying it over to hang it on a peg next to where Bob had hung his earlier. "The storm's got everybody sort of hunkered in close and tight. Only a handful of customers in Bullock's, nothing like it usually would be. Little livelier up in New Town. You know how those miners are hell-bent on having their fun, no matter what, when they get down out of the hills. But even there, in the saloons and gambling dens, it's a little slower than normal. And all those tents up and down Gold Avenue? Boy, are they flapping and shivering and shuddering in this wind. Wouldn't be surprised if some of them don't tear loose and end up over in Nebraska somewhere before this is over."

"I checked on ours while we were in the area," Peter reported to his brother. "It seemed staked down good and tight. I think it'll be okay."

"I hope so," said Vern. "Hate to have to go all the way back to Nebraska to chase it down."

Turning back from hanging up his slicker, Fred pulled a couple folded sheets of paper out of his shirt pocket and handed them to Bob. "Feeney hailed me when we were going by and asked me to bring these to you. One of them telegraphs is about your friend Marshal Brock, the other's about a prison break at the federal pen outside Laramie. Sounds like they're having their own share of excitement down that way."

Bob took the damp-edged papers and gave them a quick read-through. "Well, well. This one concerning Brock is in response to a wire I sent out early this morning. Turns out the things Sanders told me about him and my own hunch that he seemed fishy somehow were solid. According to this, Brock hasn't had the legal standing to pack that U.S. marshal's badge for more than a year now. For reasons of 'misrepresentation,' it says."

"The way he's been flashing it under everybody's nose ever since he hit town, is a continuation of the very same," said Fred. "Making it illegal, right?"

"Yup."

"So we gonna arrest him for it?"

Bob said, "Since the thing Brock seems to want most of all is to get his hands on Sanders, slapping him into a cell right next door could amount to playing right into his hands, don't you think?"

Fred scowled. "Yeah, I guess it would."

"So, unless he pushes it too far, I think we'll hold off on taking any action against him."

"Mind cluing us in on who and what you're talkin' about?" said Vern.

Bob gave the brothers a quick rundown on the phony marshal, concluding with, "Although Sanders won't say what, he did something in the past that left Brock with a deep, long-simmering grudge that he's driven to try and settle—even if he has to step outside the boundaries of the law to get it done."

"Yeah, that's the way with those fellas named Vern or Vernon," said Peter, throwing a friendly dig into his brother. "They can be as stubborn and single-minded as a mule . . . and usually not much better lookin'."

Vern calmly reached out and flipped up the shoulder flap of the slicker Peter still had on, causing some of the accumulated rainwater to splash over the back of Peter's neck and down inside his shirt collar.

Peter danced away, howling as the cold water trickled down his spine.

"Go ahead and enjoy some horseplay now if you want," Bob told them, "but if you run across this Vernon Brock, don't take him lightly. He's shifty and he's been on Sanders's trail for quite a spell. Means he's not the type to give up easy."

"You sure he's even still in town?" said Fred. "I haven't seen him around all day."

"He's around," Bob said. "He's staying at the Shirley House Hotel and was hanging out in the bar there earlier this afternoon."

"Don't worry, Marshal. We'll keep our eyes peeled and we'll take it mighty serious if we run across him," said a suddenly somber Vern.

Fred frowned. "What about those escaped convicts? I said that was excitement for down Laramie way but, when you stop and think about it, that ain't all that far from us. You don't think there's any chance they could show up around here, do you?"

"It's not impossible, I suppose," said Bob, "but I'd say it's pretty unlikely. Make more sense that they'd head for the tall and uncut off to the west."

"Yeah, I reckon. If this storm is reaching down that far, they're probably holed up somewhere and not on the move at all."

Speaking of the storm, it was howling with steadily increasing ferocity outside. Through the seams of the jail building's shuttered windows, brilliant flashes of lightning could be seen. And the low, almost constant grumble of thunder was frequently emphasized with resoundingly loud booms.

"Comes to being on the move in this storm," said

Peter, "how do you expect it might figure in the plans of the Sanders gang? Think they might still try something with it ragin' outside like it is? Or are they more likely to hold off?"

"That's a good question. One I've been wondering about myself," said Bob. "Was me, I'm thinking I might try to use this storm to my advantage . . . with the whole town hunkered in tight and the thunder and rain hiding the sound of any movement. Be a bear to be out in, but for rugged, desperate men, it could suit their intentions just fine."

"Boy, there's an unpleasant thought," said a sour-faced Fred.

"That's why we're forted up here," Bob reminded him sternly. "Let 'em try what they will. We'll be ready for 'em."

On the bed in Vernon Brock's hotel room, Brock and Libby Sanders lay partially covered by a thin, badly wrinkled sheet. Brock lay on his back, breathing evenly now, a few beads of sweat still gleaming in the mat of dark hair across his chest. Libby was nestled quietly, contentedly against his side—until, abruptly, she pushed herself up on one elbow, the sheet slipping from her bare shoulders as she reached out to seize the nearly empty bottle of tequila from where it stood on the nightstand.

"Hey. Better start takin' it easy on that stuff," Brock advised as she tipped the bottle high and took a long pull.

"Why?" said Libby after lowering the bottle. "We can always get more."

"It's not running out of that rotgut I'm worried about," Brock replied. "You need to stay sharp, keep your wits about you for the business we've got ahead of us before much longer."

Libby replaced the bottle on the stand and resumed her nestling against Brock. "Don't worry. I can handle my tequila. I took care of business pretty good just a little while ago, didn't I?"

Brock grinned lewdly. "Yeah, you sure did, but I think that was as much to spite your old man as it was to please me."

"What difference does it make? You *got* pleased, didn't you? Ain't that the main thing?"

Brock's grin went away and his mouth compressed into a thin, straight line. "No, it's not," he said tightly. "The main thing is gettin' Arlo out of that jail . . . Then the fun can really begin."

On the front range of the Shirley Mountains, in a narrow, steep-walled crevice overhung with pine boughs and rock ledges that shielded most of the pouring rain, five men huddled in a ragged cluster. Their faces were starkly etched by bright flashes of lightning that seemed to sizzle endlessly across the turbulent sky. Their expressions were grim.

"This storm is a bad omen if I ever saw one," grumbled Bad Luck Chuck Ainsley. "Nothing good can come of tryin' to pull a job on a night like this."

"Shut up, Ainsley," Reese Modello told him. "Nothing good ever comes from your constant bitchin' and bellyachin', either, but that never stops you from spoutin' a steady stream of it."

"Storm is good," said Johnny Three Ponies. "Give

us extra cover when we go in, wash away our tracks when we go out."

Ace Greer emitted a raspy chuckle. "Everybody hear that? Johnny don't say but about ten words a day, but when he *does* speak, you can bet he knows what he's talkin' about. In other words, this is a fine night to pull a bank job . . . providin' we don't all drown first."

"Long as we keep our powder—and, above all, that dynamite—dry," said Salt River Jackson, "a little rain ain't gonna hurt us. Matter of fact, for the overripe among us who ain't partial to soap and water under any other circumstances, it might do some much-needed good."

Ainsley scowled. "You talkin' about me, you old mossy horn? I don't see no swarms of honeybees buzzin' around you on account of your sweet smell, neither."

"Don't start, you two," warned Modello. "Once we get that bank vault cleaned out, you'll each have a gob of money in your pocket that will cure any question about lack of soap or overripeness or anything else. Nothing works magic like money. It can make the stinkiest old fart smell fresh as a daisy, or the homeliest mug look handsome as Prince Charming."

Salt River huffed. "In some cases, I'd say you're talkin' more like needin' a wheelbarrow full of money, not just a pocketful."

"See?" lamented Ainsley. "He won't let up."

"Seems to me," spoke up Greer, "that before we fret too much over the magical benefits of *havin'* money, we'd better first concentrate on what it's gonna take to *get* some."

"Ace is right," agreed Modello. "We've got near two

hours until midnight, when we'll ride out of here and make for town. It wouldn't hurt to go over one more time the part each of us is gonna play once we reach the bank."

"Seems unnecessary to me," grumbled Salt River. "But what the hell, I guess we got nothing better to do."

"Even though we figure the sidewalks are gonna be rolled up and the town shut down for the night—especially with this storm," Modello began, "we still want to move fast and precise. In and out, quick as can be."

"What if the storm has blown on through by the time we get to town?" asked Ainsley.

Modello shook his head. "Won't really matter. We never figured on it to begin with. Right?"

"Storm will still be there," said Three Ponies confidently. "It is slow moving, squatting over us now for several more hours."

"Either way," Modello went on, "our aim is the same. A quick in and out. You three shooters scramble into place—Three Ponies up on the roof, Ainsley on the edge of the street at the rear, Salt River in the alley at the front—to be ready for dealing with the law dogs and citizens when they come pouring out. While you're getting in position, Ace and me will be setting the dynamite. As soon as everybody's ready, we blow the back wall of the building and on through the rear of the safe. You shooters cover us while we're hauling out the money, then we all ride the hell clear of there."

"Sounds slick as snot on a pump handle," declared Greer. "Smash and grab—it's always the best way."

Salt River nodded. "I agree with that much. My only concern, and I'm not saying it's a big one, mind you, is how much we're counting on rupturing the back panel of the safe when you blast through the wall."

"It's worked that way for us in the past," pointed out Modello. "Plus we're taking along pry bars and picks. All we need is a rupture, a split, and we can force the opening some more if we have to. Enough for either me or Ace to slip in and start handing money out to the other."

"Yes, yes. Like you said, that way has worked for us in the past," Salt River said. "I just wish we had a little more dynamite, that's all."

"Now who's bellyaching and complaining," muttered Ainsley.

Modello ignored him and said, "Yeah, I wish we had a little more of a lot of things. But we don't. We lost men and part of our dynamite the other night during our first crack at that damn joint. All we've got is what we got. I think it's plenty to do the job. If I didn't, I wouldn't recommend us stickin' our necks out to try it again."

Nobody spoke for a minute or so. Lightning sizzled in the sky, thunder cracked.

Finally, Greer said, "Well, by damn, that's good enough for me. When it's time, Reese, you say the word . . . we'll all be ridin' in there right beside you to bust that sumbitch wide open."

Chapter 30

For supper, Fred fixed a pot of beans and chopped ham served with warmed-over sourdough biscuits purchased earlier in the day from the Blue Bird Café just up the street. It was a tasty and filling meal, a good choice for the stormy night. The only potential drawback, as wryly pointed out by Peter—who was proving himself to be a frequent source of good-natured ribbing—was the questionable wisdom of serving beans as the main dish to five men who would be spending the night cooped up together.

Bob, showing his own touch of wry humor, responded, "You fellas have got way more to worry about than me. Fred and Sanders will be together in the cell block; Peter and Vern will be together here in the office area. Me, I'm back in the storeroom by myself and I can close the door."

A little before ten, Bob and Vern went out to make the late rounds.

No one could call it a quiet night, not with the storm kicking up the way it was. As far as people activity, things were about as subdued as Bob could ever remember. Even along Gold Avenue not much was going on. Usually, when the miners and prospectors came down out of the lonely hills determined to spend their wages or scrapings of color and let the wolf howl throughout as many nights as it took until they were tapped out again, it was loud and raucous. The most excitement the two lawmen encountered—in a version of what Fred and Peter had described from their earlier outing—was watching three drunks frantically trying to keep their sleeping tent from blowing away in the fierce wind.

In Old Town, not even Bullock's was drawing much of a crowd. In fact, it was down to one table of five die-hard gamblers trying to make it a profitable night with rounds of five-card stud. A single hostess, either out of a dedicated interest in the game or in hopes of increasing her own night's profit, was looking on while somewhat wearily attempting to maintain a slinky, tempting presence.

Seated on stools at the bar, Maudie Sartain and Mike Bullock were trying hard not to appear bored but not pulling it off very well.

Bob and Vern walked in, shaking off some of the rain from their slickers and hats.

Bullock straightened up on his stool. "Well, hallelujah. I knew if I kept the lights burning long enough on this beast of a night, there was the chance my tenacity would be rewarded and my fortune would be achieved. And, lo and behold, here you are. The marshal of our fair city—and, just incidentally, bare-knuckle champeen of the territory—honoring us with a second visit of the day."

"Even if I couldn't *see* what a slow night you're having," Bob said dryly, "I could tell it by the line of bull crap you've obviously got stored up because nobody's been around to unload it on."

"Now wait just a minute," Bullock responded with mock severity. "Here at Bullock's we are renowned not for peddling bull crap but for dispensing as fine an assortment of alcoholic beverages as can be found in all of Wyoming Territory."

"He's right," agreed Maudie. "We don't peddle bull crap here . . . but under this roof, a lot of it sure gets shoveled for free."

Bullock frowned as if he'd just heard some startling news. "I never noticed. Must happen when I'm not around."

Maudie rolled her eyes. "See what I mean?"

Bob hiked a leg and settled onto one of the stools. Gesturing between the two, he said, "Vern, this is Maudie Sartain, one of the prettiest sights you'll find in all of Rattlesnake Wells. Maudie, this is Vern Macy, one of my new deputies."

Maudie smiled and extended her hand. "Pleased to meet you, Vern. I was introduced to your brother earlier when Fred brought him around."

"The pleasure's all mine, ma'am." Vern shook her hand, even bending a bit at the waist in a sort of gentlemanly bow.

Bob couldn't help smiling inwardly upon noting how much trouble it was for the young man to keep from gawking openly at Maudie's curvaceous figure and the generous amount of cleavage she made a habit of proudly displaying. In all but the crudest of louts who made no attempt to hide it, this struggle to look Maudie in the eye when carrying on a conversation with her was a common challenge for the men around town. Even Bob was no exception.

"Looks to me like you've picked two fine additions to help keep law and order in our town, Bob," said Maudie. "I feel safer already."

"Vern and his brother have quickly proved their mettle on a couple different occasions," Bob acknowledged. "I've no doubt they're gonna work out just fine."

"I'd say you're not wasting any time putting 'em to a pretty harsh test," Bullock said. "I admire your dedication to duty when it comes to patrolling our streets and all. On a night like this? Who in their right mind would be out looking to do mischief in this kind of weather?"

Bob shrugged. "You never know. Some enterprising troublemaker with a shrewd mind might be expecting us to figure it just that way and decide it would be exactly the right time to pull something."

Bullock scowled. "You mean somebody like Sanders's gang—or what's left of 'em, anyway?"

"Could be. I can't shake the hunch that they're gonna try to bust Arlo out of jail, Mike," said Bob. "Not only do I not see a little nasty weather stopping them when they're ready to make their move, they could even look at it as giving them an advantage as far as masking their movement and helping in their getaway."

"Okay. Yeah, I guess I can see how that might make a certain amount of sense from their perspective."

"I'll tell you what makes sense to me," spoke up Maudie. "That would be offering you two gents a drink of something to help ward off the chill and damp that you've been slogging through outside. And, since we're doing such a rip-roaring, high-profit level of business in here tonight, I bet I can even convince the boss to let me serve it on the house. What do you say?"

Bullock made a *by-all-means* gesture with his hands.

"Normally," Bob said, "I'd remind you we're on duty and so have to turn you down. But you know what? Since it *is* an exceptionally nasty night out there and we're only a couple blocks from finishing our rounds and calling it a day—barring a visit from the Sanders gang, that is—I'm going to bend the rules and take you up on that offer. A shot of bourbon, if you please, and a short beer to chase it." Turning to his deputy, he added, "Vern? How about you?"

Vern suddenly looked uncomfortable and actually blushed a bit. "I appreciate the offer, Marshal, but I . . . uh . . . I've never really acquired a taste for spirits. Me nor Peter neither one. If you don't mind, I'll just pass."

"I don't mind. Nobody does," Bob assured him. "To tell the truth, I don't imbibe a whole lot myself and it's probably a smarter path to walk clear of the who-hit-John, anyway."

Bullock cleared his throat. "It would be a sorry day for me and my business if too many folks felt that way. I ain't one to be forcing it on anybody, neither."

Maudie tapped the cup on the bar top from which she'd been sipping. "How about, as an alternative, some hot tea? That would still give you a touch of warmth to counter the cold night."

"Tea would be great, if it's not too much trouble," Vern said.

"Not at all. I'll top mine off, too, while I'm at it."

While Maudie went to get the tea, Bob threw down his shot of redeye and followed it with a pull of the beer. Like he'd told Vern, he didn't do a lot of drinking but he did enjoy a snort now and then. On a night like tonight, the heat of the whiskey flooding through him felt particularly good. While on the rounds, even in his good, heavy slicker that Consuela made sure he had, the cold and damp had bit deeper into him than he cared to admit, right down to the bone. Must be getting old, he thought sourly to himself.

Maudie returned with two cups of tea. As she handed one to Vern, she said, "I didn't think to ask if you wanted anything in it. Some sugar or milk?"

"No, just like this is fine."

After taking a sip from her own cup, Maudie said to Bob, "By the way, I have some welcome and surprising news regarding the little Chinese gal you rescued."

"I could use some good news, not to mention that I'm sure Mee-Kee could too. What is it?"

"It appears we've found a place for her to stay and even a way, a good way, for her to earn her keep. You want to tell him, Mike?"

"Angus McTeague stopped in this afternoon," Bullock said. "He came by mainly because he'd heard about the fisticuffs show you and Fred put on with those roughnecks from Cheyenne and he wanted to get the details. While I was filling him in, Kim happened through with Mee-Kee in tow. Somehow McTeague hadn't heard the story of how you'd found her in the wreckage and what she'd been through with those vermin who had her before then. When I filled him in on that, too, you should have seen his reaction."

"He melted like a stick of butter in the hot sun," Maudie interjected. "I never would have thought it of the old rascal."

"Can't say I would have, either," Bullock agreed. "He came up with the offer to take Mee-Kee in as a housekeeper and maybe cook. He's building that nice new house just off Gold Avenue, you know. It's nearly finished and almost ready to move into. With him making frequent trips up to his mining camps, he won't be there sometimes. He said he'd been thinking about hiring on a housekeeper, anyway— you know, to be present and look after things when he wasn't around. He went ahead and made the pitch to Mee-Kee . . . with the proviso that Kim would work with the two of them for a while, as a sort of interpreter, until they had enough lingo worked out between 'em to get by on their own. Said he'd pay Kim for her time, too. And when Kim explained it all to Mee-Kee, she was willing to give it a try."

"I'll be darned. Like you've both said, I never would have pictured McTeague as being so big-hearted," said Bob.

"Just goes to show, I guess."

Bob abruptly scowled. "You don't think there's any chance his intentions are—"

"Don't even say it," Bullock cut him off. "No, I don't think that. Not for a minute."

"If you'd seen them together, Bob, you'd understand," said Maudie. "The way he looked at her . . .

I agree with Mike. McTeague might be a hard-nosed so-and-so in a lot of other ways, but where that frail, abused little girl is concerned, I believe with all my heart that his intentions are strictly charitable and honorable."

Bob didn't need to hear any more and gave a nod. "That's good enough for me, then."

Chapter 31

Through the rain-beaded second-floor window of his hotel room, Vernon Brock watched Marshal Hatfield and one of his new young deputies emerge from Bullock's and head down the street toward the jail. Although the storm had blown out about a third of the pole-mounted lamps that lined Front Street—in spite of the glass housings that were supposed to protect the flame of each—the frequent pops of brilliant lightning made tracking the pair's progress easy enough.

Brock produced a pocket watch and checked the time, also via the flickering illumination of the lightning. *Eleven o'clock. Not much longer.* He held the watch open for several more ticks of the second hand. His gaze had shifted from the time face to the image of a pretty, middle-aged woman whose likeness had been carefully cut out and fitted into the concave area on the inside of the watch cover. *Not much longer now, Adelia . . . Not much longer until at last your tormentor will be held to account.*

Brock snapped the watch shut suddenly and dropped it back into his pocket. He stood motionless after lowering his arm, continuing to glare out the window, his expression as stern and dark as the roiling sky. Finally, he pulled the shade down and turned away from the window. Feeling his way in the dark, he moved to the edge of the bed and turned up the glowing wick of the nightstand lamp. A soft glow filled the room, revealing the form of Libby Sanders lying on her stomach, snoring lightly, one bare arm dangling over the side of the bed.

Brock reached down and shook the arm. When he got no response, he shook it harder. "Libby. Come on. It's time to wake up."

She pulled the arm away, muttering a very unlady-like curse.

Brock slammed his knee against the edge of the mattress, jolting the whole bed. "Damn it. Wake up! I told you not to guzzle so much of that stinkin' rotgut tequila. Now snap out of it!"

Libby's eyes fluttered open. She scowled up at the form hovering over her, and the faded beauty of her features, under a spilling tangle of hair, looked puffy and faded, far from her bygone best days. "I'm awake, can't you see? You don't have to be so damn ornery about it."

She reached out and her hand groped atop the nightstand. She pulled it back empty and her scowl deepened.

"The bottle's gone," Brock told her. "You drained it, remember? You don't need any more now, anyway."

"I do, too!" Libby insisted. "I need a pick-me-up."

"You'll pick yourself up on your own and do it

damned quick or I'll drag you out of that bed by the hair of your head," Brock snarled. "Now get a move on!"

"Okay, okay." Libby flung the covers back and swung her feet to the floor. She sat on the edge of the bed for a minute, holding her head in her hands. "Jesus, I need a drink. Just one. I need it bad."

"No, you don't. What you need is to clear your head, not fog it even more. Get up, splash some water on your face, then get dressed and start getting ready to carry out the plan we put together—the one that's going to gain us both what we so badly want."

"What time is it?" Libby wanted to know.

"Past eleven. Going on midnight."

"Jesus, it sounds like it's still storming like hell outside."

Brock's face was a mask of grim determination. "It is. But that's not going to stop us. In fact, when we get out on the street and set things in motion, it might actually work to our benefit."

A few minutes short of midnight, Reese Modello gave the signal, and he and the four others spurred their horses out of the rocky crevice and set on a course for Rattlesnake Wells. Sheets of rain washed over them, lightning raked the sky, and rolling booms of thunder made the ground vibrate under the horses' pounding hooves.

The hilly, broken ground of the Shirley Mountains front range gave way to flatter, more open terrain as they closed on the town. Nearing the northern tip of Gold Avenue, they swung wide to the west and turned southward again, moving parallel down the length of

Gold and past the point of where it converged with Front Street in Old Town. After only a short way, they cut back in toward town, eventually merging onto the western end of First Street.

They slowed their horses to a walk as they began moving past darkened residential homes. Ahead, they could see a few flickering street lamps on Front Street, but it was the steady flashes of lightning that continued to illuminate their way.

The residences ended and they came up on the back side of the hulking Starbuck Territorial Bank building.

Half a block down from the bank, Brock and Libby had emerged from the rear of their hotel and were huddled under a narrow strip of overhang on the edge of the alley. Brock was clad in a heavy rain slicker. Libby wore only her blue dress, no hat, no shawl.

"I'm freezing to death," she lamented. "This is a piss-poor deal for me, while you're wrapped up nice and snug in that big ol' coat."

"It's just for a little while," Brock said, aiming to console her. "You looking bedraggled and desperate will help you play your part. As soon as we get clear, I've got warm, dry clothes and a bottle of tequila packed in a saddlebag for you."

"You'd better."

"Okay. You can stay here under this overhang for a couple minutes longer. Give me time to get across the street and move up to that bell. Don't wait too long, though, before you make your way closer to the jail. When I start ringing that warning bell and the marshal and his boys come pouring out of the jail, you wait until they've gone past you and then go on the rest of the way. Hatfield will be sure to leave one deputy behind. You've got to take care of him and secure the keys to Arlo's cell while I'm slipping down behind buildings on the other side of the street to get our horses and bring them out. You got all that?"

"Yes, yes. We've gone through it a hunnert times."

Abruptly, Brock reached out and tore away one shoulder of her dress, leaving the sleeve to dangle loosely.

"Damn you, what'd you do that for?" Libby wailed. "That was my good dress!"

"That will help sell your story to the deputy you have to get past at the jail," Brock explained. "Don't worry, I'll buy you a new dress—a better one."

"You're damned right you will!"

Behind the bank, what was left of the Sanders gang crowded close, holding a sheet of canvas to keep the rain off the bundle of dynamite Modello had pulled gently from under his coat and was snugging up close to the building. A short fuse, only slightly more than a foot, trailed out from the sticks of explosives.

"That thing ain't gonna give you much time after you light it," Ace Greer said.

"It'll be enough. Can't afford to make it any longer for fear of the rain dousing it. Hand me that lid we're gonna put over it."

Greer held out a flat piece of board and a broken brick.

Wordlessly, Modello took them and arranged them over the length of fuse—propping the board on the brick so that it made a protective covering. "Now go ahead and lay that piece of canvas down on the dynamite and the board. Leave this end open enough for me to light the fuse."

Once his instructions had been followed, Modello rocked back on his heels. "Okay, boys. It's as ready as it's gonna get. All it needs is for me to snap a match to it. Three Ponies, Ainsley, Salt River—get in your positions. Soon as you're in place, I'll set this baby off."

For the two older gents it was only a matter of seconds before they'd taken up their stations—Ainsley out on the edge of First Street, covering that side and rear of the bank; Salt River in the alley, covering that side and the front. For Three Ponies to climb the uneven outcrops of brick that ran up the corner of the building took maybe a minute longer.

Looking up, blinking against the rain, Greer watched the half-breed's legs swing out and then disappear as he made it onto the roof. Greer reached down and tapped a squatting Modello on the shoulder "Okay. All in place."

Just as Modello struck the match he was holding ready, cupping one hand over the flame that crackled to life, a bell started clanging loudly, cutting sharply even through the howl of the storm.

"What the hell's that?" Greer hissed.

"It's that damn warning bell. The same one they started ringing the last time we hit this place."

"But how could they already know we're here again this time? We haven't even—"

"It don't matter," Modello cut him off. "That bell ain't gonna tell 'em a damn thing this explosion won't. Let 'em come meet the hail of lead they're gonna find waiting for 'em!"

So saying, Modello touched the match flame to the tip of the fuse, and it flared to life with a puff of smoke and a spatter of sparks.

Chapter 32

In addition to being forted up together in anticipation of the Sanders gang trying something, Bob
had decided that he and his deputies also needed to
set up a watch of sorts. After all, it wouldn't do a hell
of a lot of good to be bunched together and allegedly
ready for trouble if they were all caught flat on their
backs and asleep when it hit. They moved one of the
temporary cots from the office to the cell block,
shuffled bed assignments, and he assigned one of
them to be awake at all times, taking two-hour turns.

Bob took the first turn himself, since he knew he
wasn't ready for sleep anyway. Sitting at his desk, he
idly wondered if, when he did sleep again, he would
dream of his days on the run from Texas law as the
Devil's River Kid. With the threat of potential exposure from the Cheyenne newspaper reporter now
past, he hoped those dreams were past, too . . . not
that thoughts of those days and an underlying fear
they would someday somehow be revealed were ever
totally over with. His biggest concern, if it came to
that, wasn't for himself but for Bucky. The boy would

have to face the emptiness of being without either of his parents. He'd have Consuela, of course, but that would only mean that Bob had let both of them down.

It was past one, the hour scheduled to wake Peter Macy for his turn to take the watch. The marshal was in no hurry to do so, however. He still wasn't ready to go to sleep. It seemed a waste to deprive someone else of their slumber when all he'd do was lie on the cot with his mind churning, wondering if tonight was the night the Sanders gang was going to make their move. Or another time. Or if he was wrong about it all and they'd already fled the territory, aiming for greener pastures.

The steady hiss of the rain and the frequent growl and boom of thunder had dragged on for so long any sense of them being something out of the ordinary was nearly numbed. Still, some of the thunderclaps were sharp enough and loud enough to—

Wait a minute.

A new sound was throbbing through the turbulent night. *Was that . . . a bell?*

In the alley beside the Blue Bird Café, Libby Sanders shivered violently and cursed Vernon Brock. She needed a drink and she needed warm, dry clothes . . . but if she backed out of the plan she'd agreed to, she didn't know where she would get either one.

Her spare clothes and money were in her carpet-bag Brock had packed on the getaway horses. She was in too deep with him to back out. Apart from being separated from her belongings, if she double-crossed him and he ever caught up with her . . . She shuddered to think what he would do to her.

As she shivered and waited, questions plagued her mind. Why hadn't she just gone ahead and used the little derringer she brought with her? Why hadn't she secreted it in her dress and then shot Arlo through the bars of his cell like she'd intended? The marshal might have shot her, too, right there on the spot, or he would have arrested her and put her in her own cell. Either one would have been better than ending up half-drowned and freezing in the alley.

She heard the warning bell start to ring and took faint hope. The bell meant they were closer to wrapping things up, as far as freeing Arlo from his cell. All she had to do was wait for the marshal and his men to rush by on their way to answer the bell.

It was up to her to get past the deputy Brock was sure would be left behind at the jail. She didn't much like the thought of what she'd have to do next, using her derringer on a complete stranger, but it was what she'd agreed to and, once again, she didn't have the guts to cross Brock.

Vernon Brock had just given his final yank on the bell rope when somebody started shooting at him. He never heard the sound of the first gun report, not above the din of the storm, and might never have known somebody was throwing lead his way at all if the slug hadn't hit the bell just above his head. Brock ducked low, thinking *what the hell!*? when a second bullet smacked into a soggy crossbeam only inches from his shoulder.

Hearing the bell, Bob jumped to his feet, a jolt of heightened alertness coursing through him. Ready to call his deputies into action, he started for the door when yet another new sound tore apart the night. It was a powerful, rumbling roar. But it wasn't thunder.

Brock turned as a monstrous roar of sound, louder and somehow different from the thunder, ruptured the night. As he reached the corner of Bullock's Saloon, with no more bullets chasing him as far as he could tell, he turned his head to look back. A pulsing glow flickered momentarily behind the hulking Starbuck Bank structure and then, in a flash of lightning, he saw a column of smoke boiling up and he knew what he'd heard. Somebody was blasting their way into the bank!

Brock cursed. The most likely culprits were the Sanders gang. He didn't give a damn what they did with the bank, but would their attack also include an attempt to bust Arlo out of jail? *That* he did care about.

Questions ran quickly through Brock's mind. Would this new development rattle Libby? Would she run and hide after the sound of the explosion? Would she even realize what was going on? He shook his head at that one. The simple, sorry answer was no telling what the drunken slut would think or how she would react.

Damn! More questions rattled his brain. Why had

he saddled himself with her anyway? How could he have thought it was a good idea?

No more questions, he thought. With no time to cry over spilled milk, he'd have to make the best of it and that meant, for starters, get down to where the horses were stashed.

The street would soon be filling with lawmen and brave citizens rushing to the defense of their town, the same as he'd meant to accomplish by ringing the warning bell. The fact that they'd have bullet-spewing bank robbers to deal with might actually be a good thing for his purposes. It would certainly engage the townsmen more thoroughly than standing around wondering who'd rung the bell and what the problem was.

If any of Arlo's men splintered off to make their own try at springing Sanders, well, that would be too bad for them. Brock didn't intend to let anything or anybody interfere with getting his hands on the bastard he'd hunted for so long.

The sound of the explosion startled Libby, instantly creating more questions. Where the hell did that come from? That wasn't part of the plan . . . was it? Had she forgotten something? Was Brock was right and she shouldn't have downed so much tequila?

Before she had time to fret over exactly what the explosion meant, she heard the sound of gruff voices and running feet as three men—the marshal and two of his deputies—came running up the street and past the mouth of her alley, toward the sounds of the bell and the explosion.

That was her cue. She didn't have to understand everything, all she had to do was play her role and do her part to free Arlo and deliver him into the hands of Brock . . . and herself.

Libby pushed out of the alley and turned toward the jail.

Chapter 33

Bob, Fred, and Vern went running up Front Street. At Bob's signal, they slowed upon reaching the intersection with First, the northwest corner of which was dominated by the looming Starbuck Bank building.

In the slicing rain and bursts of lightning, Bob quickly assessed the situation. "There's nothing going on in front, so they must have set their blast at the rear. They're bound to have shooters posted to hold off anybody who shows up so keep to cover and be damned careful."

As if to emphasize the need for his cautionary words, a pair of rifle shots cracked from the roof of the bank building, the slugs cutting down and tearing gouges in the middle of the muddy street just ahead of their slowed advance.

"Fan out!" Bob ordered. "Fred, you take the west side of the street. Vern, stick with me."

Everybody scrambled accordingly. Fred ducked into the recessed doorway to the Shirley House Hotel, Bob and Vern wormed in behind a watering trough out front of Bullock's Saloon.

The sound of more gunfire was all but swallowed by claps of thunder, but there was no mistaking the *whack!* of bullets hitting the building fronts or kicking up geysers of water out of the trough. In addition to the gunman on the roof, another shooter opened fire from the alley running along the north side of the bank.

Bob snapped off a pair of return rounds, as did Vern. Fred leaned out of his recess and triggered a couple more.

Townsmen had started showing up in answer to the bell and the sound of the explosion. Wanting to make sure they understood they were entering a shooting scene, so they'd proceed with necessary caution, Bob rapid-fired the rest of his cylinder and drew a return volley from the two shooters guarding the robbery in progress.

Ducking back down as slugs zipped just above his head or slammed against the heavy-walled trough, Bob quickly thumbed fresh cartridges into his .44. At the same time, he hollered across the street to his chief deputy. "Fred! Get out of there and use Second Street to maneuver farther to the west. You should meet some men responding from that direction— Herb Beckus and Rob Dilmore, to name a couple. Gather them up, work your way around to the rear of the bank, and come at the robbers from that direction. If they've managed to break into the vault, don't let them make a getaway!"

"I'll make sure they don't get past us, Marshal," promised Fred.

With Bob and Vern providing cover fire, he shoved out of the doorway and ran to the south side of the building, disappearing around the corner. Some of the other just-arriving men quickly moved up and two of them scrambled into Fred's former position in the recessed doorway.

More and more townsmen were showing up. The crackle of gunfire began to fill the street, rivaling the peals of thunder that continued rolling back and forth across the sky. The new arrivals, just like Bob and Vern, were being held at bay, unable to close in on the bank due to the strategically placed shooters buying time for those going after the money.

"That hombre up on the roof is the one really raising hell," Vern said to Bob. "Shooting back at him from ground level is getting us nowhere fast."

"You got any ideas?" Bob said.

"Yeah, I think I might. I think I can shinny up the back side of that tree alongside Bullock's building and make a jump onto the saloon roof. That will put me level with the high shooter across the way. All things being equal, I figure I'd have a good chance to pick him off."

Bob craned his neck to look around at what Vern was talking about. "Might be easier to gain this roof from inside."

"Maybe. But not as quick. I can do it, Marshal. Back home, Peter and me used to race up silos taller and slicker than that tree, just for fun. All I need is a little cover fire from you, like we gave Fred a minute ago."

Without waiting for a response, Vern got his feet under him and sprang away. He dropped into a low crouch as he raced toward the tree. A bullet chipped away the corner of Bullock's building in his wake and another chewed bark as he slipped behind the tree trunk. Bob poured lead in return, diverting any effort to concentrate fire on his young deputy. Several of the townsmen saw what was going on and joined in, making it too hot for the outlaw shooters to do anything but pop their heads up momentarily and trigger hastily aimed rounds.

On the back side of the tree, Vern shoved his Winchester down through his belt at the small of his back, securing it so his hands were free. True to his word, he shinnied up the tree and onto the roof with all the agility of a squirrel.

"I'll be damned," Bob muttered under his breath.

A moment later, Mike Bullock burst out the front door of his establishment, clutching his snub-nosed .38. With his mouth twisted into a grimace, he dropped heavily down behind the watering trough next to Bob. "Well, I see your hunch was right about the Sanders gang making a return visit," he said, puffing a little.

"Don't pile the congratulations too high," Bob responded bitterly. "I was right about 'em paying a visit, but I sure as hell missed the mark on where they were gonna hit."

Bullock raised up to take a shot, then dropped back down. "Don't beat yourself up too bad. They haven't got away with anything yet."

Bob squeezed off a couple more rounds himself and added, "And by God they ain't gonna, either!"

Prowling back and forth in the marshal's office like a caged wild beast, Peter Macy understood that it was only smart for somebody to stay behind and guard the lockup and the prisoner in case whatever was going on outside was another ruse, but it was frustrating that he'd been the one chosen for the job. He'd much rather be out where the action was, where they'd heard the sound of the explosion and gunfire was popping. Given that Marshal Hatfield was the boss, and Peter had nothing but respect for him, he stayed as instructed.

At first, the sounds of the gunshots from up the street had been faint and intermittent, often drowned out by the thunder. But more and more guns were going off and their part of the noisy night was becoming more and more distinct. A hell of a shoot-out was clearly taking place, making Peter agonize all the more over not being part of it.

The first time the pounding came at the front door, he almost mistook it for thunder or more of the shooting noise. Stepping closer to the heavy, barred door, his right hand drifting to rest on the grips of the Colt holstered at his hip, he was in position to make no mistake about the sound when it came a second time. Somebody was definitely on the other side knocking, pounding insistently. A faint voice was accompanying the knocking.

"Help me! You have to let me in, I'm frightened and in trouble. Men with guns are running around out here, shooting up everything!"

It was a woman's voice . . . or somebody doing a darn good imitation of one.

"Bolt the door and don't open it for anybody until we get back!" Those had been Marshal Hatfield's last words as he rushed out with Fred and Vern.

But a woman was on the other side . . . *a badly frightened woman* out there alone in the howling night . . . and for damn sure men were running around and shooting things up out there.

Peter hated what he had to say next, but he had

to at least *try* to follow orders. "I can't unlock this door for fear of allowing the trouble to get in here," he called back. "Run and hide. Find safety somewhere else."

"They were right outside my hotel room window, cursing and shooting. I was so frightened I ran out into the night. I don't know where else to go . . . You have to help me!"

Knowing the small barred window with a hinged cover about five feet from the bottom of the bolted door was for peering out in times of trouble, Peter reckoned the circumstance fit . . . if anything did. He stood off center of the window and swung down the cover. "Stand in the light where I can see you," he ordered the woman.

She did as he said and, when Peter got a good look at her, his heart sank. She was a middle-aged woman who might still have been rather attractive if not for her drenched, bedraggled condition and the mournful, terrified expression on her face. All she had on was a soaked blue dress of some thin material with one sleeve torn away at the shoulder, and she was shivering badly from a combination of being cold and frightened.

He couldn't do it. Couldn't keep her locked out after seeing her like that. "Okay. I'm going to let you in. When I open the door, you hustle in quicklike."

"D-Don't worry. I w-will," she said through chattering teeth.

True to her word, as soon as Peter threw the bolt and swung the door open, the woman rushed in. A gust of cold wind and lashing rain also entered before he could get the door closed and locked again.

Tuning to her, he said, "It's warmer over there by the stove. I'll get you a cup of hot coffee and a blanket you can wrap—"

Libby Sanders produced the two-shot over-under derringer and fired both barrels into the chest of the young deputy. He staggered back two steps, buckling slowly at the knees as a red stain began spreading outward on the front of his shirt, then he toppled and fell heavily to the floor.

She didn't pause to look at the deputy after he went down, just as she hadn't looked at the face or into the eyes of the trusting fool who showed her a kindness when he let her in out of the storm and the gunfire. She'd feared that if she looked at him, she might not have been able to pull the trigger. Even though that part—the worst part—was over and there could be no turning back, she didn't want to dwell on him or what she'd done.

Shoving the derringer back into the pocket of her dress, Libby stepped to the front door and threw the bolt back so it was unlocked once more, then hurried over to the door of the cell block. Hooking the ring of keys hanging on a peg beside the door, she took them with her as she pulled open the door and entered the cell block.

Arlo was on his feet inside his cell, gripping the bars, looking out anxiously. At the sight of her, his face split with a wide smile. "I knew it! I thought I heard your voice. But then I heard the gun going off and I feared . . . Oh, thank God it's you and you're all right!"

"I told you we'd be coming for you," said Libby with a false bravado.

As she began trying different keys in the lock to the cell, Sanders said, "Where are the boys? Aren't they with you?"

"Didn't you hear the explosion a little while ago? And all the shooting out there? Yeah, the boys are around—but they're just a little busy with some other things right now."

Sanders beamed all the more. "You mean they're finishing the job on the bank, too? Hot damn! I love those crazy bastards!"

Libby finally found the right key and as it turned in the slot she said, "Don't get too excited. We're not in the clear yet. Part of all that shooting you hear is the marshal and his backup crew of deputies and townsmen doing a little protesting about what's going on."

"Let 'em protest all they want," Sanders said, baring his teeth. "They ain't gonna stop us again this time!"

The lock clicked open and the door swung out with a metallic groan. Sanders stepped out eagerly and immediately pulled Libby into an embrace. "Oh God, you can't imagine how good you feel in my arms again. You don't know how good it is to have you back, to have you willing to help me after the way I treated you. I'm so sorry, and so grateful I just can't—"

"Save it for later, baby." Libby managed a smile as she pulled gently but firmly away from him. "There'll be plenty of time for that in a little while."

"Right, right," Sanders agreed. "Let's get out of here."

Libby led the way out of the cell block and into the office area.

Vernon Brock was waiting for them. He sat on the corner of the marshal's desk, his .45 drawn and ready, aimed casually in the direction of Sanders. A wide, taunting grin was plastered on his face. "Howdy there, Arlo. You grateful to see me, too?"

Chapter 34

At the rear of the bank, Reese Modello and Ace Greer were working feverishly to gain entry into the money vault. The explosion had blown away a high, wide portion of the outer brick wall and had torn a split along a riveted seam of the vault's thick iron shell just within. Exactly as Salt River Jackson had feared, the force of the blast hadn't been sufficient to rupture a big enough tear in the iron shield for a man to fit through. It was so agonizingly close—Greer could squeeze his head and one arm and shoulder through, but nothing more—and yet so discouragingly far.

And so, with pry bars and a pick and sledgehammer, the two men had been straining and pounding frantically to increase the size of the split. Another foot, maybe even six inches, would do the trick, but the thick iron, jagged-edged and slick from the driving rain, remained stubbornly unyielding. Both men had gashes on their hands and arms, torn through leather gloves and shirt sleeves, with no discernible measure of success to show for it.

All the while, they were keenly aware that in addition to the battering of the storm, precious minutes were ticking by and the intensity of the gun battle waged by the other gang members was fiercely intensifying.

When his pry bar slipped for the sixth or seventh time, Greer was pitched off balance and fell against the scraping rubble of broken bricks. He turned the air blue with a curse and flung the ineffective tool hard against the twisted metal. "It ain't happenin', Reese," he said dejectedly. "We ain't gained one inch since we started. We can strain our muscles and scrape our knuckles until the sun comes up and we ain't gonna be able to make that hole no bigger with the tools we got. We're whipped."

"We can't give up!" Modello insisted.

"You hear that gunfire out there? Must be twenty guns firin' on our boys by now. They can't keep up for much longer. They'll either run out of ammo or just plain get overrun and gunned down. It's time to light a shuck out of here while there's still any of us left."

"Damn!" Modello took a savage but futile swing at the iron barrier with his sledgehammer. The hammer's heavy head hit with a loud clang and bounced erratically back, nearly striking him in the face.

From the roof of Bullock's Saloon, Vern Macy had been swapping lead with the shooter across the street on top of the bank. Vern had no way of knowing the identity of Johnny Three Ponies, but he knew one thing. Whoever he was, he was a slippery, lucky rascal when it came to dodging bullets and keeping up his own return fire. More than once, a slug had torn through the air so close to Vern's face he felt the heat of its passing. On top of that, the shooter on the bank roof and his partner down in the alley were still managing to throw enough lead into the street to keep the marshal and the townsmen from closing on the bank.

Knowing it was critical to take out the roof shooter like he'd promised the marshal he could and would, Vern decided to risk a desperation move by trying one of the oldest tricks in the book. He drew certain fire by exposing himself for a fraction of a second longer than he had at any previous point. When the expected bullets came, again passing so close their whine was wincingly loud, he threw up his arms in a dramatic fashion and fell back, even crying out for added effect. Not that the opposing shooter could probably hear him, but if he saw Vern's dramatic fall in the lightning pops that cooperated in a timely manner, it ought to be enough to convince him he'd scored a hit.

Cautiously, slowly pushing himself up off the pebbled surface of Bullock's roof, Vern bellied to a spot several feet from where he'd fallen. Rising ever so slow and careful, he lifted his head above the ledge of the saloon's front edifice until he could peer across to the bank. The rifleman was continuing to shoot and duck but was once again concentrating solely on the street below. He'd clearly bought Vern's act and no longer had any concern for further threat from atop the saloon.

Vern wasted no time showing him the error of his judgment. He thrust up higher, slamming the Winchester's stock to his shoulder, and levered off two rounds in quick succession. His first bullet hit his target in the middle of the chest, causing him to jerk upright. The second slug pounded in slightly off center, spinning him around awkwardly. He pitched into a fall that carried him outward and on down to the street where he landed, arms and legs akimbo, without so much as a twitch of life left in him.

Vern's quick glance straight downward revealed Marshal Hatfield looking back up at him. A flash of lightning showed the marshal's face shiny and wet from the rain, and wearing a grin. "Good job, kid," he hollered up then the grin faded. "Now get your butt back down here. We still got more work to do!"

A moment after the sledgehammer nearly struck Reese Modello in the face, Bad Luck Chuck Ainsley came running back from where he'd been holding a position on the cross street. "Jesus, they just got Johnny Three Ponies," he blurted. "Blew him clean off the roof! We're in for it now. There must be a couple dozen men out there. No way in hell we can hold 'em back now, not without Johnny coverin' from the roof."

Modello wheeled on him. "You sure as hell ain't helping to hold 'em by comin' over here and babbling to us instead of bein' out there layin' down lead the way you're supposed to. Get back to your position, you sniveling weasel!"

Ainsley poised uncertainly. His eyes went from Modello's face to the rupture in the vault that clearly hadn't been made any bigger, and then back to Modello again.

"N-No." His voice quavered in spite of his attempt

to hold it firm. "No, I won't. It's sure suicide to go back there and try to hold off all those men. It's a lost cause, and I'm gettin' the hell out of here. So will the rest of you if you have any sense."

Modello drew his gun and thrust his arm forward, aiming straight at Ainsley. "You get your bony ass back out there, you yellow dog, or I'll plug you right here myself." The sound of the hammer being cocked on the steadily leveled six-gun seemed unusually loud and distinct in the midst of the raging storm.

Curiously, the crack of the rifle that came an instant later from only a short distance away was somehow not nearly as sharp. The impact of the slug striking Modello's side just under his outstretched arm was meaty and solid.

So was the wet-sounding "Huh!" that escaped his lips as he was knocked off his feet and slammed down onto a pile of broken bricks.

"Oh my God! They're behind us!" wailed Ainsley.

Greer spun around, hesitating a fraction of a second to gawk bug-eyed at the fallen Modello, then quickly dropped the pry bar he'd picked back up and made a grab for the revolver on his hip.

"Freeze or die!" commanded the disembodied voice of Deputy Fred Ordway. "You've got a half dozen guns trained on you and you don't have a prayer if you pull that gun."

Greer hesitated once more for a fraction of a second. Whatever flashed through his mind in that eyeblink of time did not produce a wise decision. "To hell with all of you!" he hollered, and continued his grab for the gun.

Five shots rang out in rapid succession. The muzzle

flashes were blurred by the driving rain, but the bullets they hurled were not deterred one bit. The slugs riddled Greer, spinning him partway around and causing him to take a couple of awkward, jerky steps before he crumpled and fell, landing across the legs of Modello.

Ainsley, in the meantime, threw his hands up wildly and shouted, "No, no! Not me!"

The sudden, frantic movement was misinterpreted in the slicing rain and sizzling flashes of lightning. Another volley of shots was loosed, riddling him, too, and knocking him flat. His body skidded a foot or so on the muddy ground and then was still.

In the alley near the front of the bank building, Salt River Jackson heard the outbreak of shooting behind him and knew that some men must have circled around on Modello and Greer. Probably Ainsley, too. And he knew that Three Ponies was already dead. Like Ainsley, he'd heard the half-breed cry out when a bullet found him, and Salt River had seen him pitch off the roof to land in the middle of Front Street, where his twisted body continued to sprawl.

Salt River knew it was over.

He thought about throwing out his gun and raising his hands, surrendering, but to hell with that. They'd probably shoot him anyway . . . or hang him. He'd sworn a long time ago that he'd never check out with a rope around his neck. If he was going to go out in a hail of lead, damn it, he might as well go throwing some in return.

Diagonally across the street, that damned town

marshal had rallied some of the townsmen and they were wheeling out a water wagon from an old shed just past the community warning bell. Idly, the old outlaw wondered who had rung that bell just before the dynamite had gone off. It hadn't really made much difference, but he wished he could know the answer before he died.

He could see what they were up to with the water wagon and thought it was actually kind of clever. Using the wagon's tongue at the opposite end to steer, they set the rig in motion straight for Salt River's alley. It was a combination battering ram and mobile shield, with three or four men running along behind it, pouring lead as they went.

From behind his barricade of wooden crates and an oversized rain barrel, Salt River tipped his face up to the rain and thunder and lightning, and laughed wildly. He leveled his gaze on the men rushing him, extended both arms, gripping a pistol in each, and bellowed as he began pulling the triggers, "Come ahead, you sonsabitches! Bring your little push toy and see what it gets you!"

Bring their little push toy the marshal and the others surely did. Picking up momentum as it rolled across the street, the high wheels of the wagon hit the edge of the narrow strip of boardwalk running in front of the alley, hopped up and over and came down on the other side, crashing through Salt River's barricade like it was made up of so many dry twigs.

The old outlaw was pounded back by the impact, ground down amid broken wood and splintered barrel staves, repeatedly squeezing the triggers of his guns even after the hammers were falling on nothing but empty chambers. When they dug him out some time later, there wasn't a bullet hole in him, but his spine had been wrenched and snapped. He was every bit as dead as his cronies who'd been ventilated by lead.

Chapter 35

"One of the bullets hit square on the harmonica in his pocket," Dr. Tibbs was explaining. "It stayed there, not penetrating through. The other bullet hit the harmonica, too, but deflected off. Luckily, it veered up and outward, away from his heart. It lodged under the ball of his shoulder."

"So what's the verdict?" Vern Macy wanted to know. "Will he recover okay?"

"In time, yes. Fully. He lost a fair amount of blood, so he's bound to be weak for a while. He'll have some bruising and muscle soreness where the harmonica was punched against his chest. And, naturally, he'll be stiff and sore from where I cut the bullet out, but he's young and strong. It will all heal and before long he'll be good as new."

"How much time before he'll wake up from that chloroform you gave him?" said Bob.

"He should start coming around in a little bit, be out of it altogether within the hour. Get some coffee, or better yet, some strong broth in him as soon as you can. He'll be sore and hurting at first. Once I get back to my office, I'll fix up something he can take for the pain. Somebody will have to stop over and get it. After that, just see to it he starts out a little easy and then works steadily back into his normal routine."

The doctor, Vern, Bob, and Fred were gathered in the marshal's office. Peter, the patient under discussion, was lying on the cot where he'd started out to get the night's sleep that never happened and to where Tibbs had been summoned to minister to Peter's wounds and remove the bullet from him.

Outside, daylight was settling over the town. The slow-moving thunderstorm had finally passed on, but the sky remained an overcast, sooty gray and the air had turned colder, filled with a dampness that many speculated held the threat of snow.

The shoot-out with the bank robbers had been over for almost an hour before anybody got around to returning to the jail and discovering what had happened there. Before the doctor had put him under with chloroform in order to go in after the bullet, Peter had regained consciousness long enough to describe in detail the blond woman who'd shot him.

Knowing Peter was in good hands, Bob had left and made an inquiry at the Shirley House Hotel where Libby Sanders had mentioned she was staying. That had turned up no evidence of her any longer in residence, even though she was still registered. He'd noticed another name on the register—*Vernon Brock*—which gave Bob cause to do some additional checking. That had turned up neither hide nor hair of the phony U.S. marshal, either. In checking Peterson's livery stable, Bob had found three horses were missing, one of them the roan Brock had ridden into town on, pretty much making it conclusive. Brock and Libby had joined forces to break Sanders out of jail.

Bob had returned to the jail, discovering surgery was over and Peter had not yet come around.

Once Doc Tibbs had departed, Bob, Fred, and Vern fell into a kind of exhausted, half-numb silence for several minutes. It was the first chance just the three of them—and Peter, too, even though he was temporarily out of it—had the opportunity to spend more than a fleeting moment or two together since the night had literally exploded and propelled them into frenzied, nonstop activity.

At last, it had reached a leveling-off point. The bodies had been cleared from the streets and hauled away to the undertaker; the bank's money had once again been saved; a bricklayer and blacksmith were already lined up to start fixing the damage from the dynamite; and a general cleanup and repair of broken glass and bullet-scarred building fronts was underway in the light of the new day.

Miraculously, except for a few cuts from flying glass, a handful of scrapes and bruises from slipping and falling on the sloppy wet ground, and two or three close-call bullet burns, none of the local responders to the ruckus had come away seriously hurt.

In an attempt to nail down the remaining loose ends, Fred broke what suddenly seemed like an unnerving silence in the office. "The thing I still can't quite wrap my head around is the notion of Brock and Sanders's wife working together on the jailbreak. I mean, according to what Arlo claimed and the information you got, Marshal, in that telegram from Cheyenne, Brock has a personal score to settle with

Sanders. He may be out to cheat the hangman, but not in a way that Sanders is likely to be thankful for. Yet you said Sanders's estranged wife was gushing and carrying on about how she still loved her man. If that's the case, you wouldn't think she'd be helping Brock if she knew what he had in mind."

"Reckon that's the key," Bob said. "Either Libby *don't* know what Brock's got in mind . . . or all that gushing she did when she showed up to visit Sanders was an act and she has her own score to settle with him. They'd been separated for quite a spell, remember. From what I overheard when I was in the cell block with them, their parting wasn't exactly without some rough edges."

"So them breaking Sanders out of jail wasn't tied in any way to the attempted bank robbery?" Vern asked.

"I don't think so," said Bob. "It was just by the screwiest of coincidences both got planned for the same night at roughly the same time. Brock wouldn't have anything to do with the outlaw gang, I'm certain of that. In a strange kind of way, I figure he still sees himself as being on the right side of the law. Nor would the gang have cooperated with him knowing he had only revenge in mind for Arlo. As for Libby . . . if I'm right in the way I'm beginning to see her, she'd go along with just about anybody for her own chance to get even with Arlo."

"So," Fred summed up, "the Sanders gang has been wiped out and Arlo himself, even though he may not make it to the gallows where he surely was headed before, still seems bound for an execution of some sort before it's all said and done."

"Not if I can help it," Bob responded in a flat, somber tone.

"How's that?" Fred voiced the words, but he and Vern had both swiveled their heads to look questioningly at the marshal.

"You heard me," Bob answered. "I don't intend for Brock and Libby to get away with whatever it is they're planning to do with Sanders. I'm going after 'em."

"When? How?"

"Right away. As far as how . . . I'm gonna climb on a damn horse and head out to pick up their trail. How else do you think?"

Fred's brows pulled together tight, wrinkling his forehead. "But, Bob . . . er, Marshal, I mean . . . They lit out three or four hours ago in the pouring rain. And now it looks like it's gonna pucker up and snow any minute. What chance have you got of tracking them after all that?"

"A lot better one than I'll have sitting here on my duff fretting over what they pulled," Bob said stubbornly.

"What about your jurisdiction? They're bound to be well out of that by now."

"To hell with jurisdiction! Boys, they took a prisoner out of my jail—*our* jail. And Peter was shot, left for dead, in the process. You think I'm willing to simply report that over the telegraph wire and then sit back on my haunches and leave it to others to run 'em down? Yeah, Sanders is a no-good snake who deserves to hang . . . but only after he'd faced a judge and jury and the sentence was handed down legally. It's not for the likes of Brock or Libby, no matter what their grudges are, to carry out."

Vern's brow puckered. "But if all they want is to kill Sanders, why didn't they just blast him in his cell?"

"That's a good question. Think about it," said Bob, his expression turning even grimmer. "The only thing I can come up with is that they—or at least Brock—don't want him to die quick and easy. They want him to suffer first."

"Aw, now that ain't right," said Fred. "Sanders is for certain a snake, exactly like you labeled him. Hanging would be one thing. To drag it out . . . torture him, in other words . . . nobody, not even a dumb animal, deserves that."

"I figure the same," Bob agreed. "That's just one more reason I mean to go after 'em. I know the weather and everything else is stacked against me. But I've got to try."

"Who are you taking with you?" Vern wanted to know.

"Nobody. I'm going it alone."

"That's my brother they shot."

"All the more reason for you to stay here and look after him. And help Fred look after the town while I'm away. That's your job now, remember?"

"So you can stretch the limits of what your job is supposed to be, but nobody else can. Is that it?" Vern ventured.

"Yeah, it is. And if you can't accept that, if you can't take orders, then you can't work for me. That means you can go charging out there on your own if you want. But if you do, you'd damn well better stay out of my way."

Fred held up his hands, palms out. "Hey, fellas. Marshal. Vern. Everybody needs to calm down, okay?"

Bob and Vern continued to glare at one another

for several beats. Then, finally, Vern looked away. Shoulders slumping, he said, "You're right, Marshal. It's your call to make. I was out of line. I'm sorry. It won't happen again."

Bob nodded. "That's better. And you got nothing to be sorry for. Neither one of you." He swept his eyes to include Fred. "You both did a helluva fine job last night. I couldn't be prouder . . . Now, I need to know I can count on you to keep doing that kind of job while I go do what I have to. Try to understand. If you can't do that, just trust me."

"I trust you, Marshal. I always have," said Fred.

Vern turned back to face them. "You can count on me, Marshal. I'll follow Fred's lead and we'll take good care of the town while you're away."

Chapter 36

Entering his own house shouldn't have felt so strange. After all, he hadn't been staying away for *that* long. Bob suddenly realized it was neither the returning nor the length of time he'd been away that was bothering him. It was the fact he was coming back only to be leaving again . . . and he'd have to explain his reasons once more, this time to Bucky and Consuela.

He figured they would have heard all about the events of last night, so it came as no surprise they were up and waiting for him in the kitchen. Ordinarily, since it was not a school day, Bucky would not have been out of bed for very long, but he looked as if he'd been awake for some time. Consuela appeared as fresh and lovely as she always did.

"Wow, Pa. You look like a half-drowned cat," Bucky greeted him.

"Bucky! What a disrespectful thing to say to your father," Consuela promptly chided.

"That's okay. Boy's just being honest." Bob grinned

as he took a seat at the table. "Besides, if that's how I look, then it's better than I feel."

Consuela said, "I have clean clothes laid out in your room. And I have pots of water ready to pour a hot bath."

"Do you see any wings on her, Bucky?" Bob said to his son. "I swear she's talking the language of an angel down from Heaven."

"She's the same Consuela as usual, Pa. She's always thinking ahead for us," Bucky reminded him. Then, scrunching up his face, he added, "All I ask is that you use up all that hot water or else she'll get the idea I oughta take a bath, too."

"Not that it would hurt you. But the first use I want to make of some hot water is a cup of that fresh-cooked coffee I can smell."

Consuela rose to get it for him.

"Are things gonna go back to normal now, Pa? Are you gonna be comin' home at nights and not makin' us stay clear of the jail like you have been?"

"That's the general idea, son." Bob hesitated before he tacked on the next part. He knew neither Bucky nor Consuela were going to like hearing it, not any more than he liked having to tell them. "Here's the thing. Before everything goes back to normal, I've still got some unfinished business to take care of. If you heard about the things that happened last night, you know the prisoner we had in jail was busted out."

"I heard one of your deputies got shot."

"That's true. But he's gonna recover okay."

Consuela placed a mug of coffee in front of Bob, along with the sugar bowl, some milk, and a spoon. Settling back into her seat, she said, "So you're going after the escaped prisoner and those who broke him out."

Bob looked at her. "How did you know? Who told you?"

She met his eyes. "No one told me. I know you, don't I? I would expect nothing less from you."

Bob stirred sugar and milk into his coffee, thinking that maybe the telling wasn't going to be so difficult after all.

"Is it true, Pa?" Bucky asked.

"Afraid so, pal. A man got loose from my jail. A dangerous man it was my job to keep behind bars, keep away from honest folks he might harm. Same for those who helped break him out. So now I need to fix what got broken—to go after those dangerous skunks, get 'em in custody again before they *do* harm any more innocents, and see to it they pay for what they've already done."

"You goin' after them alone?"

"There'll be others on the lookout for 'em, too. I sent notice out to make sure of that. But I'm the only who'll be chasing them from here. It's not a job for a posse, and I need Fred and Deputy Vern to stay and keep an eye on our town."

"When will you be leaving?" Consuela asked.

"Soon as I can get ready. But I *am* gonna take time for that bath and those warm, dry clothes," Bob assured her and took a big swallow of his coffee. "Have you two eaten breakfast yet?"

Consuela shook her head. "No. We were waiting, hoping you'd join us."

"Now there's *more* words that sound like they ought

to be accompanied by the flutter of angel wings," Bob declared. "And ones I'm not about to pass up on. Tell you what. Give me time for a quick soak to warm my bones and then, while I'm getting dressed, if you'll make good on that breakfast offer with a big batch of scrambled eggs and bacon, you won't be able to beat me out of here with a stick until I've eaten my share and more."

Half an hour later, following the bath, Bob was in his room getting dressed. In addition to the socks, long johns, trousers, and shirt that she'd laid out, Consuela had also included his heavy sheepskin-lined coat. On the bed she had also placed his old war bag, taken from deep within the closet. It was a sturdy affair made of fringed buckskin and had endured many hard miles—most of them in the possession of none other than the Devil's River Kid. Of the items that always stayed with the bag, most prominent was the backup Schofield revolver he periodically took out and oiled. Consuela had also added fresh, waxed-paper-wrapped packs of beef jerky and hardtack. Bob smiled, remembering Bucky's words. *"She's always thinking ahead for us."*

He packed the bag and carried it to the kitchen.

Breakfast was delicious and plentiful. It felt good to enjoy a meal together again, after avoiding it for the past couple days. But weighing to some degree on each of them was the knowledge that another lapse was in store before they would be doing it again.

When it was time, Bob put on his heavy coat, slung his war bag over his shoulder, and moved toward the door. He squatted down, facing Bucky. "Don't know how long I'll be gone, pal, but I'll be back. You can count on that." He reached out, ruffled the boy's fiery red hair. *Sundown Bucky.* "You behave while I'm away, keep those school grades up, okay? And take care of Consuela.

"Now, since I'm gonna be gone for I don't know how long a spell, I don't think you're too big to give your ol' pa a big hug before I head out, do you?"

The strength with which Bucky squeezed when he threw his arms around him told Bob that his son didn't mind hugging the old man too much at all.

Bob straightened up, surprised to find someone else who didn't mind giving him a hug. The delicate, never-spoken, never-acted-upon feelings he and Consuela shared went momentarily past their restraints when she stepped into his embrace and pressed her warm cheek to his.

"*Vaya con Dios, Señor Bob,*" she whispered. "Come back soon, and come back safe."

And then the moment was past and it was time to leave.

Light flakes of snow were starting to fall when Bob stepped outside.

Chapter 37

Homer Wilby scowled at the swirling, wind-whipped flakes of snow. "Well this is a fine howdee-do, that's all I got to say. A *fine* howdee-do! If good luck came in buckets, we wouldn't have enough to fill a teaspoon."

Conjuring up a menacing scowl of his own, Dewey Hinkson aimed it at Wilby. "Yeah, and if bellyachin' came in spoonfuls, you could fill a damn barrel. So, after a while, what's the point?"

"The point of what?" said Wilby, looking genuinely puzzled.

Hinkson rolled his eyes in an exasperated manner. "The point of bellyachin' all the stinkin' time. What ya think I was talkin' about?"

The two men were crouched under a sheet of canvas stretched between two rock faces and propped in place by broken-off tree branches wedged into crevices in the rocks. A fire had been built near the front of the tentlike shelter, but because it was fueled by nothing but damp wood, its feeble flames were giving off more smoke than heat.

Wilby was a heavyset man, fortyish, with prematurely gray hair, a lantern jaw, and dull blue eyes set too close on either side of a blunt nose. Hinkson had skin as dark as uncreamed coffee, a shaved head, a cruel slash of a mouth, and wide-set, suspicious brown eyes that seldom stopped moving. Both men wore coarse clothing patterned with horizontal stripes of faded blue and stenciled yellow lettering across the back that read PROPERTY OF LARAMIE FEDERAL PRISON.

From farther back in the shelter, a third man stirred and leaned up closer behind Hinkson and Wilby. He was dressed the same as the other two, younger, lean and narrow-faced, with commas of curly brown hair spilling over his forehead above thoughtful eyes and an earnest expression.

"Since it seems neither one of you fellows has noticed," Milt Macready said in a Tennessee drawl, "I'll point out that a ray of sunshine ain't exactly how I'd describe either one of you. How would you like to be in my position—listenin' to *both* of you sourpusses carry on all the time?"

Wilby grunted. "Right about now, I wouldn't mind bein' in just about anybody else's position . . . Well, except either one of you two, that is. On account of you ain't no better off than me."

"See, that's what I mean," said Macready. "Yeah, we ain't sittin' here in the lap of luxury. You think I don't know that? But we ain't behind prison bars no more, either. No concrete walls squeezin' in on a body, smotherin' our every breath, blockin' out the sun and stars twenty-three out of twenty-four hours every day. No guard bulls breathin' down our necks, clubbin' us down every time they want to have a good laugh. You tellin' me this ain't better than that?"

"If it was warm and dry maybe," muttered Hinkson.

"Well, dry . . . Those damn cells were always cold, even in the summer. I got that cold so deep in my bones I don't think I'll ever get it out. For sure not in this setup we got here."

"Havin' the weather take this lousy turn right after we busted out with no warm clothes on our backs ain't to nobody's liking," Macready said. "But my point about us bein' *out* is still valid. These are spring storms, both the rain and now this whirl of snow. It was warm a couple days ago, and it'll warm right back up in another day or two. All we got to do is hunker down and wait it out a little longer. Then we can be on the move again."

"Some coffee and decent grub would go a long way to make it through the hunkerin'," said Wilby. "I suppose the way you see it, Macready, we're lucky those horses we stole had tin cups in their saddlebags so's we can boil rainwater or melt snow for something to drink. Me, I say that's mighty slim luck when you ain't got nothing else to put in those cups."

"And that, my friend, is the difference between bein' thankful for what you've got and bellyachin' about what you *ain't* got," pointed out Macready.

"Well, since we ain't got shit, the way I see it," insisted Wilby, "ain't very hard to out-balance the thankful stuff."

Macready shook his head as if in disbelief. "Let me get this straight. When you say 'coffee and decent grub,' are you actually talkin' about what they served us back in prison? Good God, man, the so-called coffee they gave us was nothing but pot rinsings from the real coffee they fixed for themselves. And the 'decent grub'? You can't truly mean that slop that had maggots crawlin' in it half the time."

Hinkson emitted a wry, raspy chuckle. "Stop, now you're startin' to make *me* hungry. And what do you mean about havin' maggots in your grub only half the time? Once again the black man gets the dirtiest dealin'. Mine had maggots in it *all* the damn time." He chuckled some more.

"That ain't funny. That ain't funny nohow," said Wilby. "The pen food wasn't that bad. Didn't none of us die from it, did we? And how could it be any worse than the horse meat we been chokin' down for goin' on three days now?"

"For one thing, the horse meat ain't got maggots crawlin' on it," Macready answered. "And, once you get past the idea of it, ain't a dang thing wrong with horse meat. The Injuns used to thrive on it. They couldn't hardly wait to raid other tribes in order to build up their pony herd big enough so's they could spare a couple head to cook and eat."

Hinkson's face bunched up with his own dubious expression. "Next thing, Macready, you'll be tellin' us it was a stroke of good luck when Wilby's horse stepped in that crack and broke its leg so we had to shoot it."

"It gave us fresh meat while we've been holed up here, didn't it?"

"But that misstep—along with this blasted weather—are the main reasons we *needed* to hole up here."

"Yeah, and as far as the stupid Injuns, they ate dogs, too. So what?" Wilby made an exaggeration of craning his head and looking in all directions. "Where are all the noble red men now? Oh, that's right—they got their asses whupped and run off."

Macready shook his head again. "You two are hopeless. Here, I'm gonna hand up some twigs I had shoved under my blanket to dry 'em out some. Feed 'em slowlike into that fire. They should burn better on account of bein' drier. When they get goin' that'll help some of those bigger chunks burn better, too, and we'll get some heat out of that rascal of a fire yet."

"Boy, I could go for that," said Hinkson, rubbing his thick-fingered hands together.

"Slowlike now on feedin' in those twigs," Macready cautioned.

"Yeah, yeah. I heard you," Wilby said as he fed the fire.

After a few minutes, the flames were snapping and popping higher, giving off less smoke as the bigger pieces that had been mostly only smoldering before started to burn, too.

"Now that's more like it," said Hinkson, hitching a little closer and rubbing his hands together some more.

"Now we need to just keep feedin' in more fuel, slow and steady," Macready said. "We get her burnin' good and hot, even some of those wetter pieces we drug over—long as we don't shove in too many at once—will dry right there in the flames and burn just as good. I can hitch up there and take a turn feedin' some if you want, Wilby."

"Naw, I'm doin' okay for now," said Wilby, busy enjoying the heat.

"Well, okay. But before long," Macready told him, "I'm gonna want to move up and cook me a piece of that horse. Even if you don't, I like it fine and I'm blamed hungry."

"That don't sound like a half-bad idea, especially

now that we got us a decent fire," spoke up Hinkson. "What we ate last night, when it was howlin' rain, was smoky and half raw on account of the pitiful little fire we was tryin' to work with. Now, with some good hot cookin' flames, I believe I can manage me a taste for some more of that mangy ol' mare."

Wilby frowned and seemed to be considering something. After a minute, he said, "Okay. Since watchin' you two chawin' on horse is about as disgustin' as downin' some myself, I reckon I might as well go ahead and join you. See if I can't squeeze some nourishment out of it to help keep me goin'."

Macready grinned. "That's more like it. That's the spirit, Wilby. We've come this far, we *got* to keep goin'. Right?"

Wilby sighed, indicating his willing spirit wasn't all that strong. "Yeah, but keep goin' where? And when? Hell, as far as that goes, I don't even know where we've got to so far. What's the name of this place anyway? Anybody know?"

"I do," Macready was quick to answer. "I read about it back in the pen. One of the few decent things about that hellhole was the library they had. Even it wasn't much, to tell the truth, but it had a pretty good section on local stuff."

"Couldn't prove it by me," Hinkson muttered. "A library don't do much good to a fella who never got learned how to read."

Macready didn't know how to respond to that, so he just went ahead with what he did know. "So, anyway, this place is called the Orphan Peaks. Once we decided we'd head north after we broke out—

instead of west, like we figured everybody would expect—I had a hunch we'd run across it."

"What kind of name is Orphan Peaks?"

"It got called that," Macready explained, "on account of how it's this cluster of rock formations and peaks that sorta poke up out of the flats all of a sudden on their own. They ain't really part of the Rockies to the south or the Laramie Range farther west, they're just here in the middle of nothing. Like orphans. Get it?"

"Yeah," Hinkson mused, "that's sort of how they looked when we spotted 'em day before yesterday ahead of that storm movin' in, didn't they? Like a jumble of orphaned rocks out in the middle of nowhere."

"Somebody must have a better imagination than me," Wilby said. "All I saw was a place where we could hide out and hopefully find some shelter."

"Wait a minute. It gets better," said Macready. "The Injuns around this area had a little different name for 'em. I forget how it was pronounced in their native tongue exactly, but it translated out to the Bastard Peaks . . . Kind of the same thing, see? The little cluster of rocks that didn't belong to any of the families of the bigger mountain ranges around. For a lot of years, that's what the fur trappers and mountain men who passed through here called 'em, too. But then, when women and children started arrivin' in the area on wagon trains and so forth, somebody decided they'd better clean the name up some. That's when the whites started callin' 'em the Orphan Peaks."

"That's real interestin'. But me, I don't give a damn what anybody calls 'em," Wilby said. "All I want is to be lookin' at 'em over my shoulder when we're ridin' away from here."

"Can't say I'd mind that neither," agreed Hinkson. Focusing on Macready, he added, "Since you seem to have studied some on the area, how far do you figure we are from the Prophecies, where we want to end up?"

"I'd reckon we're more than halfway from where we started," Macready said. "About a day and a half's ride. Maybe two days, considerin' how we'll be ridin' double at least part of the way."

Hinkson frowned. "Why only part of the way? You figure we got any chance of stealin' another horse somewhere out here in all this nothingness?"

"Don't see why not. There's bound to be some ranches scattered between here and the Prophecies. That's what brung folks to this area to begin with, long before the gold got struck up in the hills."

"A ranch would provide a change of duds, too, if it's got any crew ridin' for it," said Wilby. "Two horses we can get by on if we have to. It'll just slow us down some. But, in addition to needin' something warmer to wear, if we expect to mingle in amongst the diggers in one of those Prophecy gold camps, like we planned, we sure as hell can't be showin' up in these prison stripes. It'll mark us plain as day."

"Yeah, and if we go to robbin' from some ranch— for horses or clothes, either one—we'll run the risk of markin' the fact that we ain't runnin' to the west like we want everybody to believe. What about that?" Hinkson said.

"We'll just have to be careful, that's all," Macready replied. "But Wilby's right. We've got to figure out some way to swap these prison stripes if we want to stay unspotted. Maybe we'll be lucky and come across some clothes hangin' on a line to dry. We snatch a few without bein' seen, the ranch wife who hung 'em up will think they blew away in the wind or something."

Hinkson shook his head in wonderment. "Boy, you are so full of optimism it's amazin' you don't blow up and bust from it. Hell, why not wish for some duds to blow off a clothesline somewhere for real? And then have 'em come swirlin' down on a breeze and land right here in our laps?"

Macready grinned. "I can wish for that if you want, Dewey. But you know what my ol' grandmaw used to say?"

"No. I don't know and I don't care. But I figure you're gonna tell me anyway."

"Wish in one hand and poop in t'other and see which one gets full first. That's what she'd say."

Wilby grunted. "Now there's an old gal who sounds like she had her head on straight. You sure you came out of the same bloodline?"

Chapter 38

"First you try to drown me in all that rain last night, now you're freezin' me by pushin' on in this snow," complained Arlo Sanders through clenched teeth he was trying to keep from chattering. "If you're gonna kill me, why not just shoot me and get it over with?"

"Oh, I'm gonna kill you, all right," Brock replied with a lazy grin. "But shootin's too fast and too good for you. I got special plans before you suck your last gulp of air."

Sanders turned his attention to Libby. "And you're gonna stand by and let him do that? Be part of it?"

Libby canted her head and said in an indifferent tone, "What do you expect me to do—plead mercy for you? Honey, it would have to be a whole lot colder in a place not exactly known for its cool breezes, if you know what I mean, before I'd lift a finger to save you from any kind of grief."

Sanders curled his lower lip contemptuously. "God, what's become of you? We were married once, we took vows . . ."

Libby matched his contempt with a short, harsh

laugh. "That marriage and those vows were supposed to still be in place when you dumped me in that Colorado mining camp three years ago. What about then? That was the dead of winter, not some freaky little spring snow squall like this. You left me with nothing but the clothes on my back."

"Yeah, and you don't have to tell me what you did with your back from there. You made your living off it, didn't you?"

"It's called survival, damn you. I did what I had to. You didn't leave me any choice."

"You were a tramp right from the get-go," Sanders accused. "You and your trampy ways, cheating on me with Smithfield like you done, is why I dumped you in the first place. I should've killed you like I did him."

"Yeah, you should have," said Libby, her eyes narrowing dangerously, "because now I'm going to see you killed. That's the other thing that drove me to survive. You know the sad irony of it all? There was never a damn thing going on between me and Smithfield or any of the other gang members. You killed a perfectly innocent man."

"Yeah, well, he ain't the first, I don't expect," Sanders replied bitterly. "I got no regrets—except, like I already said, for not doing you at the same time."

That exchange was taking place within a stand of tall pines Brock had chosen as a good windbreak and a suitable spot to rest the horses and allow them to find some graze not yet covered by snow. They'd made a small fire and cooked some coffee, a cup of which Sanders had been given grudgingly. Otherwise, no accommodation had been afforded him through the balance of the night. He was still in the clothing, rain-soaked and crusty with flecks of ice, he'd had on in his jail cell.

The former marshal had supplied a pair of handcuffs that, as he clasped them on, he'd sarcastically said were "to help keep your wrists snug and warm."

Brock, in the meantime, wore a heavy rain slicker with warm flannels underneath. And, as promised, he'd allowed Libby to change into warm, dry garb before they'd vacated the marshal's office.

The rain had stopped just before daybreak but within a couple hours, the snow had begun to fall. It wasn't a heavy snow yet, but it was wet and cold and had some wind-whip to it. The kind of early spring twist to the weather that wasn't uncommon with mountain ranges reaching in on all sides. In another day, maybe by the afternoon, the sun could break through and melt the snow covering to seep into the ground along with the preceding rain.

Whatever twist the weather took, Brock meant to forge on. He had a destination and a purpose and wasn't about to be deterred. Not when he finally had Arlo Sanders at his mercy.

"I hate to break up this charming lovers' spat," he said after taking a cautious sip of scalding coffee, "but you two might be advised to save your energy for other things. We'll be covering a stretch of miles before the day is done and I don't intend to do a lot of stopping until then. I also don't intend to listen to a lot of rehashing and blaming over spilled milk. Especially from you, Sanders. Seems to me you ought to have enough to fret about for what lies ahead, not the past."

"The past?" Sanders echoed. "Ain't that what this

is all about, Brock? Your past, my past . . . and the way they crossed."

"You know damn well it is."

"It was an *accident*! Can't you see that?" Sanders's tone suddenly turned plaintive. "Come on, you know my history as good or better than anybody. You know I never went for shootin' women." His eyes cut momentarily to Libby. "Not even when they deserved it."

"The one you *did* shoot sure as hell never deserved it," argued Brock.

"I know that. I was out to ambush you, not her."

"A double-barreled blast from a twelve-gauge kinda don't know the difference, does it?"

"My God," gasped Libby, looking at Sanders like she'd never really seen him before. "You killed a woman with a twelve-gauge shotgun?"

Sanders looked away in shameful exasperation.

"No, he didn't kill my Adelia. Not right away," said Brock, his narrowed eyes burning with a sudden intensity and his voice taking on a raspiness that hadn't been there before.

"The woman was your wife?" Libby asked.

Brock nodded dully and then went on. "It wasn't long after I'd begun marshaling out of the Kansas headquarters. I was hard on Arlo's trail, had been for months, but he kept slipping away. After one particularly long chase, he dodged me again. I went home, dejected, exhausted. I thought I'd rest, clear my head, spend some time with my wife. What I didn't know was that Arlo had backtracked, started followin' *me*. He decided he was sick of having me dog him all the time and the best way to solve it was to get rid of me.

"He set up a ruckus out back of my house one night and waited in the bushes with a shotgun. What he didn't know was that I was in the bathtub and so, before I could climb out to go see what was going on, my brave, foolish wife went to the door . . .

"Some might say she was lucky. Arlo's aim was off, and he didn't kill her. Not right away. She took the blast to her legs. It crippled her, naturally, left her in terrible pain for the rest of her days. She fought for as long as she could against having her beautiful legs amputated. But the doctors couldn't keep the infections away. They had to take 'em. Even after they were gone, though, she could *feel* them—feel the pain in them. Finally, it was all too much for her to bear. She just gave up."

"I never meant for any of that to happen. I swear!" Sanders wailed.

"It don't matter what you *meant*, damn you," Brock snarled. "What matters is what *happened*. On account of you, my wife died a slow, painful death . . . and now you're gonna get the same."

Except for the sigh of the wind through the pines and the crackle of the fire, everything went very quiet for a time.

Finally Libby said, "Yours is a tragic tale. Much more so than mine. But why wait any longer for whatever it is you're going to do? We're out here in the middle of nowhere, hours ahead of any posse that marshal might have put together. And, even if he did, what are the chances they could track us after the rain and now the snow? So why push so hard to get somewhere else?"

Brock shook his head. "You don't understand. There's more to it. There's a special kind of fate involved."

"Fate? What are you talking about?" sneered

Sanders. "All that's involved is pure hate—yours for me. I don't like bein' on the wrong end of it, but at least I can understand it bein' that way. Call it what it is, I say, and then, much as I hate to agree with this tramp you've partnered up with about anything, go ahead and be done with it."

"Like I already told you, this ain't the time or place. I'll tell you when and where," said Brock. "And until then—even though you *think* you're cold and freezing—you can sweat wondering about it."

"What are you gonna do? Kill me with riddles? Now I'm supposed to wonder about some special *place* where I'm gonna meet my fate?"

Brock's mouth curved into a smile without a trace of humor in it. "See, you're starting to sweat already." The smile fell away and his expression turned flat and hard as he continued on. "If you'd been paying attention to what I said before, you would've caught it when I mentioned how I'd been marshaling down in Kansas for only a short time before I locked my sights on bringing you down. Before then, it so happens, I was working out of the Cheyenne office right here in Wyoming Territory. Laramie is where I met and married my wife. You starting to see why I talk of fate, of things coming full circle?

"When I got the offer to transfer to Dodge, Adelia never really wanted to leave Wyoming, but it seemed like a good career move for me, so she stuck by my side. I've asked myself at least once a day every day since I lost her, 'What would have happened if I'd turned down that Kansas offer?' Would she still be alive today?"

Sanders looked uncomfortable, uncertain. "You're

the one's been talkin' about fate. Don't that tell you the answer?"

"It wasn't Adelia's fate to die!" Brock said vehemently. "Part of the fate I'm talking about is the fate that brought me back up this way to attend the funeral of an old friend. That's what caused me to be in Laramie the day news hit town about you being captured in Rattlesnake Wells. And *that*, you belly-crawlin' slime, is what brings us to the here and now."

"But that still don't explain," spoke up Libby, "why here and now ain't good enough for you to finish your business with him."

"Enough talk," said Brock, flinging away the remains of his coffee, which had grown cold inside the cup. He started kicking out the fire. "I've explained all I mean to. Leastways for now. You'll know more when we reach where we're headed. Get ready to ride."

Chapter 39

Bob Hatfield was well aware he was playing a long shot in his attempt to overtake the fugitives. Their head start and the inclement weather made it impossible to track them by ground sign, presenting obstacles that might very well prove insurmountable. The odds soared even higher against him being able to catch up before they'd already dispatched Sanders.

But being as he was the marshal, he had to try.

He was banking on two things—endurance and a hunch. His own personal endurance, supplemented by riding out with two horses so he could switch off every few hours in order to always have a fresh mount, would take him faster and farther than Brock could progress with a captive—handcuffed or bound, most likely—and a woman on only one horse each. That would matter only if his hunch was right about which way the fugitives had fled. He tried not to think about the inaccuracy of the last hunch he'd played— figuring the Sanders gang would hit the jail rather than make another attempt on the bank.

The way Bob saw it, the trio wouldn't go east or

south because there were too many towns and ranches within a relatively short distance where they'd run the risk of being spotted once the weather broke. If they went north, there'd be the traffic and activity associated with the gold strike in the Prophecies. Plus, word about the jailbreak would spread out of Rattlesnake Wells the quickest in that direction. They could head north and veer toward the Shirley Mountains, but that was terrain almost too desolate and harsh to be a reasonable destination—nowhere for Brock and Libby to go after they'd dealt with Arlo.

That left west—the direction Bob's hunch told him they were most likely to have gone. The area all the way to the Great Divide Basin and beyond was wide open. They could avoid been seen simply by skirting a few scattered ranches. And after they were finished with Arlo, Brock and Libby could continue on to Rock Springs or Green River and use either as a jumping-off point to lose themselves, perhaps forever.

Bob was set on preventing that. If he couldn't save Sanders, he at least meant to catch up with the other two . . . or maybe only one. Without knowing the exact relationship between the pair, it had crossed Bob's mind that a former lawman as ruthless as Brock appeared to be could very well see himself as someone with a lot more to lose than the estranged wife of a notorious outlaw. If Brock left behind a witness to the cruel and cold-blooded act he planned, he would also be leaving himself vulnerable in a way he might decide he couldn't afford.

The possibilities kept getting uglier . . . which made Bob all the more determined to keep on.

In order to hold to his intended course as he rode

through the swirling snow, he checked the compass he'd dug out of his war bag. Like the bag itself, the compass had once served the Devil's River Kid down in Texas. The irony of using it in pursuit of fugitives, in contrast to when he'd used it to avoid those pursuing *him*, was hardly lost on Bob. In fact, as he held his horses to a steady pace against the cold, wet flakes, his mind drifted some and began swirling like the snow itself, swirling back . . .

Texas, five years earlier

Throughout the fall and into the winter, Bob Hammond—also known as the Devil's River Kid—continued to plague and harass Bell interests and associates all across Calderone County. Cameron Bell brought in more hired guns, but the Kid always managed to elude them. Finally, throwing away all pretense of being anything but a hireling to Bell, Sam Ramsey turned in his deputy's badge and went to work directly for the cattle baron, acting as captain over the small army of gunmen. Sheriff Garwood basically stood back out of the way and left it to that bunch to deal with Hammond.

Through the Christmas season, Bob had to stay farther away from his family than ever, due to the close scrutiny they were under in case any such contact was attempted. Not being able to spend Christmas with his wife and son pained him greatly, nearly destroying his spirit to continue with what he'd started.

When he did see his family again, long after the new year had turned over, he was shocked and more dispirited to see the further deterioration in his frail wife.

The decision was made then and there that Priscilla and Bucky, accompanied by Consuela to care for both, would go back east—to Chicago—as soon as the weather broke. Since it was certain they would be kept under surveillance for a time, Bob would hold off joining them until he could be reasonably sure the coast was clear. When it was, he would give up his outlaw ways and his continued harassment of Cameron Bell's interests and reunite with his wife and child. After that, they would move on to someplace where they could assume different identities and start a new life together.

That was the plan.

In the spring, shortly before Priscilla and Bucky were scheduled to embark for Chicago, the Devil's River Kid attempted one more poke to remind Bell he could never let down his guard.

The morning was bright and sunny, but off to the northwest, dark clouds were sliding in over the horizon. They had a look that could mean either rain or maybe a late spring snowstorm. Neither held any particular concern for Bob as he aimed to have his business finished and be on his way back to his hideout in the Devil's River wilderness before any kind of bad weather hit.

His intent was to set fire to one of Bell's line shacks and use that as a distraction to draw back the two wranglers who'd left the shack earlier to check on the cattle. The fire would give him an opening to separate them from their horses and then scatter and stampede the small herd of prized Bell cattle about to be moved from winter grass.

After tying his horse in some trees about thirty yards back from the shack, he approached on foot with a certain amount of caution. That wisdom might not have been enough if one of the men hiding in a nest of boulders off to one side of the shack hadn't scraped his gun barrel against the rock he was squatted behind.

Bob froze, dropping into a crouch in the open area in front of the shack. He had a bottle of coal oil in his left hand

and his Winchester in his right. He couldn't identify exactly what the scraping sound had been, but he knew it was out of place, wrong somehow.

His halted advance signaled to the men lying in wait that he'd been alerted. A couple of them panicked, hurrying into action before they should have, before they had Bob trapped quite as tightly as they'd meant to.

Some instinct or some sense of movement from inside the shack as well as in the bushes and rocks around the shack, caused Bob to spin away and throw himself to the ground just as a handful of guns exploded and sent bullets ripping through the air where he'd been standing only split seconds earlier. He scrambled frantically to a low, ragged spine of weed-choked rocks. The men shooting at him adjusted their aims almost as fast.

A volley of slugs slap-whined through the weeds while others smashed against and chewed at the rocky spine. Bob pressed himself flat to the ground, his mind reeling with the question of how anyone had known to be waiting for him, how they had known to set a trap for him. With no time to waste fretting and worrying over that, he had to figure out a way to get clear of the fix with his hide intact.

"We've got you now, Hammond, you sonofabitch!" shouted a familiar voice from within the shack. Former sheriff's deputy Sam Ramsey was crowing like a prize rooster. "Go ahead and crawl on your belly like the snake you are, but it won't do you any good. You ain't gettin' out of here alive!"

"I should've killed you when I had the chance a long time ago," Bob hollered back. "I should've known that just kicking you in the crotch wouldn't do much good, not considering how Cameron Bell has had your balls in his pocket for so long."

That brought on another volley that cut the air close above his head and pounded against the cover he'd wormed in behind.

"You're right about makin' the mistake of not killin' me when you had the chance," sang out Ramsey in the next lull of shooting, "because I'm damn sure gonna be responsible for killin' you now!"

As close as Bob could tell, he was up against about half a dozen guns. A couple were in the shack and the rest were scattered in the rocks and bushes bunched to either side. Plus, the two wranglers who'd left to check on the herd could possibly return. They weren't hired guns, so maybe they'd been instructed to stay clear of any trouble that might break out.

If they did return, they would come from behind where Bob had taken cover. Pinned down by the guns in front of him, he was in bad shape as it was. If somebody closed on him from behind, his situation would be damn near hopeless. Ramsey had made it plenty clear that surrendering— even if such a thing was in Bob's makeup—wasn't an option. The former deputy was out to gun him down, no matter what.

To get out of the tight situation, Bob had to come up with an idea, and he needed to do it mighty quick.

Moving fast, careful to keep low behind his cover as periodic bursts of bullets were sent his way, he tugged his shirttail out of his pants. Laying the Winchester aside for a moment, he tore off a fairly long chunk, uncorked the bottle of coal oil he'd managed to hold on to, and stuffed the piece of shirt down into it, leaving a bit of a tail hanging out. Striking a lucifer against the rock spine, he lit the tail and let it get burning pretty good.

He drew his .44 pistol and shifted it to his left hand. With the coal oil bottle and its burning wick in his right hand, he twisted onto his back, thrust the hand with the .44 up above the protective rocks and through the weeds, rapid-firing all six rounds in the general direction of the shack.

Hoping the reckless spray of bullets would cause Ramsey and the others to momentarily hold their own fire and do some ducking, Bob rolled onto his left elbow, thrust up his head and shoulders briefly, and threw the burning bottle at the shack as hard and straight as he could. Before ducking back down, he had the satisfaction of seeing the bottle strike just to the left of the front door, shattering and splattering in a wide pattern that immediately burst into orange-gold flames.

While that drew a retaliation of hammering, zinging bullets, he quickly reloaded, weathering the response by hunkering low and tight. Holstering his sidearm, he took up the Winchester again. If his firebomb got the full results he hoped for, it would provide him a slim, desperate chance to escape from his pinned-down position. It would last for a precious moment so he had to be ready to move and move fast.

Shifting once more onto his stomach, Bob cautiously raised his head to a level where the weeds prevented exposure yet gave him some slivers of space through which he could peer out. He didn't have to wait long.

The door to the shack—over which the flames were spreading hungrily, feasting on the dry, weathered wood—slammed open suddenly and Sam Ramsey and another man whom Bob did not recognize came running out.

"Hold your fire! Hold your fire!" Ramsey bellowed to his own men bracketing the shack. "Give us a chance to get clear!"

That was Bob's opening. He sprang to his feet and levered four fast, furious rounds from the Winchester, no longer *able to contain all the rage he had been bottling up to keep from doing more killing—not when it came to Ramsey. He hadn't been lying when he'd said he regretted not killing the ex-deputy before. He not only wasn't going to live with that regret any longer, neither was he going to give Ramsey a future chance to make good on his own kill threat.*

Ramsey jerked, stopped running, and went into a spinning, loose-limbed dance as the Winchester slugs tore into him. Twin geysers of blood sprayed from his chest before he fell heavily to the ground. The man who'd exited the burning shack with Ramsey also went down, punched backwards to land on the flat of his back with his own arc of thick scarlet spurting up to mark another fatal hit.

The shooting lull ordered by Ramsey just before he went down was prolonged by the sight of him and the other man getting cut low. But only for a moment.

That was the moment that gave Bob the opportunity to bolt for better cover and the chance to escape.

In a hard sprint, Bob covered the slice of open space between where he'd been pinned down and a growth of heavy brush and trees. He crashed through the brush, tumbling and rolling, chased by a hail of lead sent courtesy of the remaining men who'd been in place to trap and kill him. He wasn't completely clear of their damned trap yet, but he was in far better shape than he'd been in and he was by-God still alive and kicking.

The question was whether he should stay and make a fight of it, maybe eliminate more of those who were constantly dogging him, or if he should complete his escape and get out of there while the getting was possible. In the dense brush and trees, he had room to maneuver and repeatedly change his shooting position so that the incoming rounds were

*always chasing where he'd been instead of where he was . . .
if he wanted to play it that way.*

He didn't ponder very long, concluding it would be best
and smartest to call it a day and ride off as fast and hard
as he could.

With that in mind, he made it as far as the horse he'd left
tied farther down the tree line. While he was accomplishing
that much, the shooters from around the shack continued to
blindly blast the bushes in the general vicinity of where he'd
disappeared. Since he'd left his horse in a spot where it
couldn't be seen from the shack, Bob figured he was only a
few hoofbeats short of getting away clean.

Hearing the gunfire, the two wranglers who'd gone out to
check the herd came riding back. Cresting a low hill on the
approach to the shack, they spotted Bob mounting his horse
and immediately opened fire. Whether inadvertently or on
purpose, one of their slugs hit Bob's horse in the head and
instantly killed it.

The beast dropped like a boulder, nearly pinning Bob's leg
underneath its sprawled body. He barely managed to kick
free and promptly laid out close behind the carcass, using it
for cover. Steadying the Winchester's barrel across the dead
animal's haunch, he aimed and squeezed off two carefully
spaced rounds. A wrangler pitched from his saddle with each
shot.

That exchange brought the rest of the gunmen boiling
down from the shack.

With his horse down and no chance to catch the fleeing
animals the two wranglers had been riding, Bob had no
choice but to accept the fact he was now on foot. He could
have stayed and made a running fight of it—but he'd had
enough killing for one day. Shooting Ramsey and the other
hired gun was one thing. Having to shoot the wranglers, two
working stiffs who'd been unlucky and foolish enough to

get caught up in a lot more than they'd hired on for, bothered him. He'd never wanted to be part of anything like that.

So, snatching his war bag and bedroll off the dead horse, he faded into the dense trees and underbrush that ran up a gradually inclining ridge as far as the eye could see. If the remaining gunmen tried to follow on horseback, they would quickly find the trees too thick and the terrain too rugged. If they came on foot, he was confident he could easily elude and outdistance them. The ridge pointed like an arrow in the direction of the Devil's River wilderness . . . proven to be a welcoming home to the Devil's River Kid, even if he had to return there on foot.

From time to time, as he threaded his way toward the haven he'd relied on so many times before, he heard the faint sounds and shouts of the gunmen pursuing him. He could tell he was steadily outdistancing them, however, so they posed no real threat. Soon the clouds rolled in from the northwest and began dumping snow. It quickly became evident it wasn't a late spring storm that would last for only a few hours or maybe a day. No, it was a howling, full-force blizzard that was going to smother the land and not recede any time soon.

His concerns became something far different from the men trying to follow in his wake.

Although he had polished his wilderness survival skills from a young age and had grown to know the whole territory as well as or better than most men—especially during his recent time as a marauding outlaw—he was in an area not as thoroughly familiar to him as other parts. Nevertheless, he slogged on.

With the essentials he'd taken time to grab from his fallen horse, he was able to beat the blizzard conditions even after darkness fell. He cleared a small area deep in a pine growth where much of the knifing wind was blocked and the snow had not accumulated too substantially under the thick pine boughs. He built a close, warming fire, pitched a rudimentary tent with his bedroll and slicker, and hunkered down for the night.

In the morning, the sky remained overcast even though the snow had stopped falling, but the wind continued to howl, quickly covering any tracks Bob left as he went on the move again. It took him most of the day to reach the area he was familiar with and the small cave he had previously stocked with provisions for just such an emergency.

For the next week and more, even after the weather cleared and the snow melted away with the return of more typical springlike conditions, Bob stuck to his cave. There was little doubt that word of his recent killings had spread like wildfire and the hunt for him would be more intense than ever. His resolve to end the outlaw way of life, the foolish bloody mission he had set himself on, was stronger than ever. As soon as Priscilla and Bucky were in the clear and not being watched so closely . . .

Finally, on a partially overcast night with the moon only a ghostly sliver whenever it managed to peek through, Bob made the long, cautious trek to his parents' ranch, where he met a series of surprises. First off, he discovered that everybody thought he was dead. In spite of his body not being found, no one believed he could have survived the sudden, fierce blizzard that had overtaken him and his pursuers.

A second surprise was that two of those were confirmed victims of the storm.

After getting over the shock that he was alive, his parents were naturally overjoyed to see him. But they were the only ones present to welcome him. A third surprise—Priscilla, Bucky, and Consuela had departed for Chicago just the day before.

At first dismayed by the news, Bob soon came to realize

that the combination of everything could actually work out for the best. If everybody—or most people, at least—continued to believe he was dead, there would be little cause to closely monitor Priscilla and the others for the chance of him showing up. With the smaller risk of attracting attention, he could join them that much sooner, and they could proceed with their plan to relocate under new identities.

To play it safe as possible, Bob remained at his parents' home for three more weeks. Never venturing out, careful to stay away from windows and open doors, strictly laying low. They understood that when Bob did take his leave it would be for good, meaning they'd likely never see one another again. It was a time of deep, special bonding that made his departure somewhat easier to bear.

Bob made it to Chicago without incident and reunited with Priscilla, Bucky, and Consuela. Things went smoothly, but he kept looking over his shoulder, expecting and half-fearing someone would show up to nab him.

No one did and, except for Priscilla's ongoing struggle with her poor health, things continued to go smoothly as they went on with the rest of their plans—assuming the new family identity of Hatfield as opposed to Hammond and relocating eventually to Wyoming Territory in a place called Rattlesnake Wells.

Chapter 40

Bob came out of his long reverie and grinned wryly at the cold snow of the present gusting against his face. He considered how some people said certain things in life come back around in circles. He'd never quite understood that concept but was willing to give it a little more credence. After all, he could hardly deny that he was participating in another fugitive chase through a late spring snowstorm. His role was vastly different, but there were still similarities.

The circumstances had eventually worked out in his favor five years ago in Texas. He hoped that similarity would repeat again in his adopted Wyoming Territory.

As the day wore on, he kept going. He changed horses regularly, always with a fresh mount under him. While there was daylight, he stopped only once to feed the animals some grain and let them eat snow for water intake. As for himself, he chewed jerky and took sips of water as he rode, still counting on endurance—his and the horses'—to make his venture a success. He'd figured his sheer stubbornness would force him to measure up.

By mid-afternoon he had to face the fact that town life as the marshal of Rattlesnake Wells had softened him more than he'd reckoned when it came to long, steady hours on the trail.

Late in the afternoon, the snow stopped and the sky started to clear. Bob heaved a sigh of relief. With the continued aid of his compass and, with luck, some moon- and starlight to illuminate the rolling country-side, he could continue forging ahead after dark.

At one time he might have pushed on all through the night, but he saw the impracticality of such a notion. Allowing himself a few hours rest was sensible and necessary. It plain wouldn't be smart to catch up with his quarry in a stiff, sore, exhausted condition. Plus, although the horses were receiving periodic breaks from carrying his weight, they were still steadily on the move and could doubtlessly use a more complete rest themselves.

At no point had Bob believed he could ride straight toward his quarry and simply catch up to them. Having that much luck was never a realistic hope. What he *did* believe might be possible—provided his hunch was right about the general direction they'd gone—was that his steady, grinding pace could out-distance them. Ride *past* however far they made it, in other words. Then he could circle back, making wide sweeps in hopes of either catching actual sight of them or some sign of their passage.

A long shot, one he'd admitted from the beginning, but he'd committed himself to it and there was no turning back until he'd played it to the hilt.

* * *

"Thank God the rain and snow finally stopped," said Libby, leaning close to the campfire flames making shifting patterns of light across the strain and weariness that showed on her face. "I appreciate these nice warm clothes you fixed me up with, Brock, but I gotta admit I was still cold and miserable most of the day. I tried not to show it, but I was."

"You held up good, Libby," Brock said. "You're a real trouper."

"I hope so. I'm glad you noticed." Libby glanced up at the sparkling night sky. "If it stays clear like this, the sun ought to be bright and warm tomorrow, don't you think?"

"Most likely. That same clear sky and all this snow on the ground is gonna leave it pretty brisk through the night."

"That's all right. I'm so tired I expect to sleep like a log . . . and when we wake up, the sun will be out." She capped the sentiment by tipping up her bottle of tequila and taking a long swallow.

"You keep guzzlin' that Mex firewater like that," Sanders commented from where he sat a few yards apart from the other two, "you'll sleep like a log, all right. You'll be passed out."

"No skin off your nose, one way or the other," she told him.

"You might at least share a snort or two," Sanders said, his tone turning plaintive. "I got nothing but this lousy blanket and you've got me parked a mile away from the fire. A little heat on the inside would do me a powerful lot of good."

Brock had signaled a halt with the setting of the

sun. He'd found a good spot for their night camp in a stand of pine and cottonwood trees near an ice-edged little stream. Some fairly dry twigs at the base of the pines and an armful of thicker branches hacked from the underside of a fallen cottonwood trunk made for a good fire over which they'd cooked coffee and bacon. Sanders was given a cup of coffee and some hardtack, no bacon. He was also given a single coarse blanket to wrap himself in and then was hand-cuffed to the base of a pine.

"You don't need no booze or no inside heating-up," Brock responded to the prisoner's request. "You ought to consider yourself lucky to have got the hard-tack and coffee. It ain't like fattening you up is gonna make any difference when it comes to what I got in mind for you."

"Boy, you're all heart. You know that, Brock?" Sanders sneered.

The former marshal glared at him through narrowed eyes. "No. Thanks to you, my heart got yanked out in little pieces, watching my Adelia's life fade away."

"Hey, don't worry. I'm not about to share my tequila," said Libby, trying to curb Brock's intensity a bit. Not so much for Arlo's sake, but mostly because when Brock got that look on his face it frightened her.

"See to it you don't," Brock grunted. "Actually, it wouldn't be a bad idea for you to take it easy on that rotgut. Ain't nowhere close by where we're headed where you're gonna be able to pick up a fresh bottle, you know."

"No, I *don't* know," said Libby, bristling somewhat. "Where *are* we headed? And when are we going to get there?"

Brock didn't answer right away. He just looked

disapprovingly down at her for a long minute then turned partly away and let his gaze drift out at the night. "You'll find out in the morning. We should be there before noon."

"Look at that big ol' wide-open sky up there, fellas," said Milt Macready, peering out from under the canvas tarp that covered him and his fellow escaped convicts. "If it's clear like that in the mornin', we'll see plenty more of the sun that finally broke through late today. That means meltin' snow and warmth on our backs and the all clear to finally haul ourselves away from here."

"Yeah, melted snow leavin' slop and mud for us to wade through," grumbled Wilby with his typical sour outlook on things.

"So what?" Macready replied somewhat sharply, allowing his annoyance at Wilby's constant pessimism to show through. "The horses will be able to handle it. And mud and slop will do a good job, at least for a while, of fillin' in our tracks behind us. What's more, I expect the horses will be happy to get away from here, too. With the sun full and bright, that snow won't last no time and that'll even give 'em some grass pokin' through to graze on."

"To hell with how happy the horses might or might not be," spoke up Hinkson. "Me, I'll be so glad to put this rock pile behind us that I might just run on ahead of those nags."

"That'd be swell," said Wilby, a sarcastic smile matching his tone. "Then me or Macready won't have to ride double with you."

"In case you forgot," Hinkson came back, "you're the one whose horse went down. Any double-ridin' will be *you* crowdin' in on somebody."

"Thanks for remindin' me. That helps a whole lot."

"Aw, lighten up, you two. Jesus!" said Macready. "With this break in the weather, we're on the brink of takin' this whole escape thing all the way and actually makin' it work. We light outta here in the morning for those gold fields, find a ranch or small settlement on the way where we can swap out these stripes, and we'll dang near have it licked. We'll lose ourselves so deep in amongst those rock choppers and ground scratchers, nobody'll hardly notice us, let alone figure out who we are."

"You sure make it sound easy," said Hinkson.

"Never said it's gonna be easy. Never said it's been easy so far. Hell, the hardest part was bustin' out of the prison itself, right?" Macready set his jaw firm and didn't wait for an answer to his rhetorical question. "We had the grit and brains to pull that off, we surely oughta be able to finish the job."

Hinkson cut a glance over at Wilby. "The kid's right, you know. We *are* a good ways along with what most people didn't reckon could be done. The Laramie pen ain't exactly no cracker box. Ain't no reason to sell ourselves short and roll belly-up now."

"No, o' course not," Wilby said. "I could hold a lot more positive outlook with some decent food in me. Once we're on our way outta here—got this damn rock pile, as you put it, behind us—I'll be okay. I just need to get on the move again, elsewise bein' holed up here ain't been a whole lot different from still bein' in the pen."

"That's understandable. We all feel that way," said Macready. "Speakin' of food makes me think of that ol' horse we been gnawin' on and that makes me think of a piece of business we'd best take care of first thing in the mornin' before we move on out."

Hinkson frowned. "I didn't follow that. What are you sayin'?"

"I'm sayin' if we leave that horse carcass just layin' there like it is, it's bound to draw buzzards. They'd 've been swoopin' overhead already if the weather hadn't been so bad. Sun starts workin' on that carcass tomorrow, they'll be showin' up in no time."

"Who the hell cares?" grumbled Wilby. "They're welcome to whatever's left of that nag. I hope they enjoy her more than I ever did."

Macready shook his head. "That ain't the point. Stop and think how they'll be hangin' around this spot for three or four days, however long it takes 'em to pick the bones clean. A swarm of feathered varmints circlin' in the air like that will be able to be seen for miles. Anybody sniffin' on our back trail would be bound to notice 'em. They come around to investigate, it'll tell 'em way more than we want a posse of law dogs or guard bulls to know about which way we went."

"Damn," Hinkson muttered. "The kid's right again. We don't want that nohow. We can't run the risk."

"So what are we supposed to do?" Wilby said. "We ain't got no shovels or nothing to bury a whole stinkin' horse."

"No, but we got rocks all around us," Macready pointed out. "It shouldn't be too hard to find a rocky shelf of some kind we can kick at or pry on until it collapses . . . maybe a high, loose boulder we can send tumblin' down so it takes some others with it. We use the other horses to pull the dead one in under something like that, we can make it so's the rocks do our buryin' for us."

Wilby made a face. "Even so, it sounds like a helluva lot of work if you ask me."

"If it keeps a posse from ridin' up our rear end, ain't it worth it?"

"Who's to say a posse or anybody else will ever come close enough to even see those scavenger birds?" Wilby argued. "I thought we had it figured so's everybody would think we took off west when we broke from the prison. Why all of a sudden the change of mind about somebody sniffin' in this direction, anyway?"

Hinkson fixed Wilby with a hard glare. "Okay, mister. If you're too stinkin' lazy to help cover up that horse in the morning, like the kid suggests, you just go ahead and take it easy. You rest up real good. Because you're gonna need all that rest and energy in order to *walk* your ass outta here on account of you didn't earn the right to double up with one of us who *did* do the work."

Wilby held the black man's glare for a long count. Finally, he said, "One of these days, Hinkson, you're gonna push me too far."

"Then what?" Hinkson prodded.

Wilby turned his back. "You better hope you don't find out."

Chapter 41

Bob rode through much of the night until he came to a good spot to make camp. He grained the horses again then staked them where they could drink from slushy puddles of half-melted snow and even had a bit of grass poking through that they could graze on. He built a close fire and treated himself to some sugar-loaded coffee and a half dozen strips of bacon. With his belly warmed and fed, he wrapped himself in his bedroll and slept for three hours.

By the time the sun was up, he was on the move again. His plan, unless something occurred to alter it, was to once more push steadily through the day and into the night. If his hunch was right about which way Brock was taking his prisoner and the woman, Bob figured he surely should have them outdistanced by the next morning. At that point he would begin his reverse sweep, looking for sign he hoped would lead him to them.

The interim, of course, left considerable time for Brock to do whatever he had in mind for Sanders.

Bob hated to think what that might be, especially when there was really nothing more he could do to prevent it.

Yet somehow he had the feeling that Brock was in no hurry to close the book on Sanders. Dragging it out, in fact, might even be some added mental torture the former marshal was enjoying before he got to the actual physical punishment. It might be wishful thinking for Bob to believe that, he realized, but at least it gave him a shred of hope that he still could possibly catch up in time to save Sanders . . . save him for the gallows.

And, once more, he also thought about the woman. Libby Sanders. She was no prize, that was for sure—not the way she'd duped and cold-bloodedly shot Peter Macy. Nevertheless, she was a woman. Bob couldn't exactly say why he felt differently about someone who, if she'd been a man and done the same things, he would have little or no compassion for. But he did. And, the more he reflected on it, he grew increasingly convinced that Brock wouldn't hesitate at all over such a detail. Once he'd closed the book on Arlo, Libby wouldn't be far behind.

In the camp of the escaped convicts, Macready was the first to rise. He didn't bother trying to wake either Hinkson or Wilby. The longer he let them sleep, he figured, the less amount of time he'd have to listen to them bicker and bellyache. Plus, he'd have just as good luck exploring by himself for a likely spot to collapse some rocks over the dead horse.

The sun was just sliding above the eastern horizon as the young Tennessean began his search. He paused for a minute or so to watch it, marveling at its shimmering beauty and how far he could see in the crisp, clear air. Having been raised in the Smoky Mountains until he was well into his teens, he sometimes missed their hazy, eerie beauty at early hours and the rich greenness that was revealed when the fog started to lift and the sun broke through.

All in all, he reckoned he liked the wide-open spaciousness of the West a tad better—especially now that he was back in it again. It was hard to appreciate the beauty of any surroundings when bottled up in a concrete-walled prison cell.

As he ventured out, Macready took with him one of the two rifles he and the others had managed to snag—along with a Remington pistol—in the process of their escape. They'd also grabbed a holster and shell belt for the pistol and a bandolier of cartridges for the rifles, providing them a fair amount of firepower if they ran into any trouble. Should they have to make a prolonged fight of it, their ammunition wouldn't sustain them for long.

Macready took the rifle with him this morning for two simple reasons. One, for protection; two, in case he ran across any wild game he could bag for food. In spite of his lecturing about the suitability of horse meat and how lucky they were to have it, he couldn't honestly claim to like it. It was better than starving, and that was about all. Given no other choice, he would cook and eat another slab of it before they left, but bagging a pronghorn deer or even a jackrabbit would certainly be preferable. Hell, it might even bring a brief smile to the faces of Hinkson and Wilby.

Thinking about eating, whatever the fare turned

out to be, made Macready's stomach growl a fierce reminder of how empty it was. To counter that emptiness with at least something, he scooped up a couple handfuls of clean, slushy snow and put it in his mouth, letting it melt and slowly trickle down his throat. It was good and even a bit refreshing, but it was a far cry from a satisfying meal.

As he continued on, Macready's thoughts kept returning to his two companions. Instead of crawling out from under their canvas tarp when he first woke up, he'd lain there and started his day by doing some serious pondering about them. He hadn't had the kind of thoughts he'd begun thinking until after the exchange between Hinkson and Wilby that ended with "You'd better hope you don't find out" when Wilby was challenged to state what he'd do if pushed too far.

That both men were violent and dangerous there could be no doubt. Being a friendly, warmhearted person didn't land you in the Laramie pen. And while Macready had a dangerous side as well, accounting for his own incarceration, he didn't consider himself as ruthless and coldhearted as his fellow escapees.

Maybe it was time to start. For his own good.

One man on two horses with meager provisions had a whole lot better chance of making good the rest of his escape than three men on two horses with the same limited amount of provisions. Those were hard, flat facts. As such thoughts crossed Macready's mind, he didn't believe for a minute that Hinkson and Wilby hadn't considered the same thing. The only question was, would any of them follow through with it?

After grinding on it during much of the night and in his waking minutes, Macready hadn't felt desperate to make such a move before leaving camp. All he could do was hope he didn't live to regret it.

"See that hump of rocks rising up away off there in the distance?" said Vernon Brock. "That's our destination. Take yourself a good look, Arlo. You're due to be spending a long, long time there after I'm done with you."

"Looks like a swell spot, Brock," replied Sanders sourly. "Appears I'll be havin' me a mighty impressive tombstone."

"You go ahead and joke all you want," Brock told him. "Put on your phony brave act, have yourself some fun. Pretty soon it will be my turn to have some fun, and yours will be plumb over."

Sanders glared at him with hate-filled eyes. "You ain't got me in the ground yet, you vengeful bastard."

"No, but it's just a matter of time," Brock promised, one side of his mouth curving in a cold smile.

The former marshal had signaled a halt on the crest of a low hill from which he scanned out ahead slow and careful before pointing to the distant rock formation. They'd quit their camp just after daybreak and had been on the trail for two hours. The sun was high and warm, quickly melting the snow on the hills and draining it to form shallow, muddy pools in the lower areas.

"Speaking of time," Libby interjected into the

exchange between the two men, "how much longer will it take to get there?"

"Couple more hours," Brock said. "Like I told you last night, we'll be there before noon."

"That place got a name?" Sanders asked. "Besides servin' as a tombstone marker for mine, I mean."

"Matter of fact, it does. It's called Orphan Peaks," Brock answered.

"That's a dumb name. When folks start referrin' to it as the burial ground for Arlo Sanders, that'll definitely be an improvement."

"No. No, it's not really a dumb name at all," said Libby. "I can see it. I can see why they got called that. There's big ol' mountains off to the north and big ol' mountains off to the south. But that little clump—not that they're really mountains at all, but they kinda are—they're plopped out there in the middle all by their lonesome. Like orphans, get it?"

Sanders rolled his eyes. "Well, you went and did it, Libby. You outdid yourself. You took a dumb name and tried to make an excuse for it with an even dumber explanation."

"You go to hell, Arlo," Libby snapped. "It's a perfectly good explanation and anybody with a lick of imagination could see it that way."

She looked away from Sanders and cut her gaze over to Brock, who was looking at her in a most curious way. "What's the matter?" she said, feeling as if she might have done something wrong.

Brock did an even more curious thing. He actually smiled a little bit. Not the cold, wolflike smile he aimed at Sanders frequently, but a regular smile that truly seemed to have some warmth in it. It faded quickly, but it had been there, Libby was certain of it.

Stranger still, she found it almost more disconcerting than the other kind.

"Nothing," Brock replied tersely to her question. "C'mon, let's get moving again. We keep dawdlin' here, we'll make a liar out of me saying we can get there before noon."

They started again, riding on for quite a spell in silence.

Despite his act of bravado, Sanders rode slumped in the saddle with a long, mournful expression on his face. His eyes hardly left the rocky hump drawing steadily closer.

Libby kept watching, too, as the Orphan Peaks grew more distinct in their shape and detail. Every once in a while, she glanced over at Brock, wondering about that fleeting, odd—well, odd for him— smile.

For his part, Brock appeared to give no notice to either of those riding with him. He just stared straight ahead, his expression somber, grim. Behind that expression, much more was going on. Listening to Libby talk about the Orphan Peaks had struck an unexpected chord in him. Her compassion for the "lonesome" pile of rocks had seemed genuine, echoing many of the same words his late wife had used to describe the favorite place of hers, where they had come often for picnics and exploring and—as it would sometimes turn out—bouts of uninhibited lovemaking under the sun. They talked of one day building a cabin within sight of the peaks and starting a small ranch or farm.

That was back when they'd intended to stay in the area . . . Back before Brock had taken the transfer to

Kansas . . . Back before he convinced Adelia to go along with him . . . to where she would end up crippled and killed by Arlo Sanders.

He was taking Sanders back to close the circle. To deliver retribution for what he'd done, to make him suffer as Adelia had suffered, and to wet the ground of her favorite place with his blood in order to satisfy her spirit's thirst for vengeance.

None of that had changed. Brock fully intended to carry out that plan. What had changed—or were at least in question—were his intentions where the Sanders woman was concerned. All along he'd been figuring he couldn't leave her alive as a potential witness against him.

But after he'd heard her speak of the Orphan Peaks the way she did and had heard the echo of Adelia's voice speaking with her . . . he wondered. Was that some kind of sign, an omen perhaps *not* to do with her as he'd planned?

Those questions, those uncertainties churned inside him. For so long he had been on a firm, never faltering course. He knew exactly what he needed to do. Not where or when necessarily, yet he held the conviction that the day would come. Sanders would pay . . . at his hands.

The day, and practically the hour, had arrived . . . but an unexpected complication with the woman had arrived with it.

Chapter 42

"Where in blazes you been?"

That was the greeting Macready got when he returned to camp. It came, not surprisingly, from a suspiciously scowling Wilby. Yet even Hinkson, who stood on the other side of the campfire that one or both of them had stoked to a crackling flame while Macready was gone, looked on as if he figured he was also owed an answer.

"I was out workin'," Macready responded testily, annoyed by the demanding attitude. "While you two was still sawin' logs, I found a spot where we can bury that dead horse."

"Whereabouts? Close or far?" Hinkson asked.

"Not far." Macready pointed. "Through that gully yonder. Ground slopes down just past where you can see, then cuts sharplike to one side under a shelf of sandstone and some flat stone slabs stacked like plates. We can drag the horse carcass in there close and then kick those plate rocks into collapsin' without too much trouble, I think. Should do the job."

"If it was that close and that easy to spot," said Wilby, "what caused you to be gone for so long?"

It was Macready's turn to scowl. Growing more annoyed, he said, "Hey, what's with all the questions? I just busted out of a place where every move and every twitch I made got watched and asked about, thank you. I'm free from there now and don't appreciate more of the same treatment."

"Yeah, we know the place you're talkin' about real good," said Wilby. "We busted out of there together, remember? And *stickin'* together—not one of us slidin' off sneakylike apart from the others—is how we figure it oughta stay."

"Wasn't nothing *sneaky* about what I went and did, for cryin' out loud," Macready argued. "Your lazy asses was sleepin', so I let you be and went to do my explorin'. If anything, you oughta be grateful. Just like I was grateful for you to *be* asleep, Wilby—meant it would be that much longer before I'd have to listen to you grumblin' and gripin' about something."

"Best watch that mouth of yours, son," Wilby warned.

"How about you watch your mouth for a change?" Macready snapped back. "As for why I took a little extra time with my explorin', I was on the hunt for some fresh game that would've benefited all of us. If I'd 've brought a deer or antelope or some such it would've meant no more horse meat for any of us to suffer through. And that means you in particular, Wilby, since you hate eatin' horse the most and it's become one of your favorite things to carry on about."

"Anybody with a lick of sense would complain about eatin' horse," Wilby said sullenly.

"Maybe so," Macready said, "but since I didn't have

any luck baggin' anything else and you two have gone ahead and got us a good fire goin' and horse is all we got, well, I for one am gonna settle for havin' some more. I'm so hungry my belly thinks my throat has been cut."

"I was thinkin' along those same lines—as far as bein' hungry and, on account of that, settlin' for some more of that doggone horse," Hinkson admitted.

Wilby frowned deeply. "Well, pardon me all to hell for not bein' so quick to jump on board. It sure don't mean I ain't powerful hungry. But here now, Macready . . . You sayin' you really think there's a chance of findin' wild game like you mentioned in this rock pile?"

"I don't just think so, I know it," said Macready. "I saw plenty of sign, just no critters right handy to go with 'em."

"Deer and antelope, like you said?"

"That and more. Rabbits. Sage hens . . ."

Wilby cut him off with an exaggerated groan. "Stop. Man, you're killin' me. Why the hell didn't you say something so's we could've done some huntin' before this?"

"Before this," Hinkson reminded him, "we was hunkered in out of the rain and snow. So was all the critters. Wasn't no chance to do no huntin' before now."

Wilby straightened up from where he'd been squatting close to the fire. As he rose, he scooped up the second rifle they'd confiscated. "Well then, I don't intend to give up so blasted easy. You fellas stay here and choke down some more of that old nag if you want. Me, I'm lookin' for something a whole lot better!"

Hinkson eyed him suspiciously. "Wouldn't be that you're just anglin' to get out of helpin' bury that horse, would it?"

"No, it ain't that at all," Wilby assured him. "I'll be back in half an hour . . . by the time you fellas are done eatin'. If I have any luck, I'll have something to share. If not . . . well, I reckon I'll be goin' hungry."

"Damn right you will," grunted Hinkson. "'Cause once we tumble rocks over that carcass, there ain't gonna be no diggin' back in for a cut of the meat."

"That's the whole point. I don't *want* a cut of that stinkin' meat." Wilby shouldered the rifle. "You just keep the fire goin'. I used to be a pretty fair hunter back when I was a lad. I don't figure I've lost that much of my touch. I aim to be comin' back with some fresh meat to cook."

The sun wasn't quite at its noon zenith when Brock and the others reached the outlying shoulders of rock and tumbled boulders that marked the southeast boundary of Orphan Peaks. The day had warmed significantly, especially in contrast to the preceding damp, chilly weather. On the rolling prairie, the snow was all gone from the crests of the hills and reduced to melted, slush-thickened puddles in the lower areas. The same appeared to be true within the rugged terrain of the Peaks, with the jagged upthrusts and rounded rock surfaces bare while the narrower, deeper crevices still held patches of white.

"This isn't at all what I expected," said Libby, craning her neck to look around after Brock had signaled a halt. "Even after we started getting closer, it looked like just a pile of rocks, but I also see signs of grass and bushes and lots of trees back in there."

"That's right," Brock agreed. "Deeper in are meadows and groves of trees, a couple spring-fed streams, even a small waterfall of sorts where one of the streams drops over a ledge. A lot of people skirt around and ride on by thinking it *is* nothing but a pile of rocks. But there's a lot more to it than that."

Sanders curled his top lip in a distasteful sneer. "You'll have to excuse me if I don't let my breath get took away by all the awe-inspirin' natural beauty. To me it still looks like a big ol' tombstone—*my* tombstone. There are worse places to get laid to rest, I reckon, but when you're the one fixin' to be put to bed with a pick and a shovel there ain't none of 'em likely to tickle your fancy."

"Too damn bad about you not gettin' your fancy tickled," snarled Brock. "I didn't bring you here to appreciate the scenery . . . but I can guarantee your breath will get took away before I'm done with you."

"Oh, that's right. I almost forgot," Sanders said. "I'm here on account of fate, ain't I?"

Libby saw Brock's narrowed eyes fill with more disgust and hatred than she would have thought possible to convey in one look.

"Make light while you can. You'll soon be singing a different tune," he told Sanders. "And the last note you hear will be your screams echoing in and out amongst these rocks."

Libby shivered at the words and the ominous tone with which they were delivered. Part of her was fearful to say what came out next, but part of her couldn't help it. "You never did explain about the fate thing. You said you would when we got here."

Brock cut his gaze to her and she shivered again in spite of the warm sun beating down on all of them. The hatred that had been in those eyes only moments ago was suddenly gone. It seemed as if, for her, it had melted.

And then he began to explain. "My wife and I used to come here often when we lived in these parts. It was one of her favorite spots. We'd picnic, explore, just be together. Just the two of us, like we were a million miles away from the rest of the world. We talked about building a cabin near here one day, someplace where we could always look out at the rocks and come over here and spend time whenever we wanted . . . But then I took the transfer to Kansas and that dream faded . . . And there, any and all the dreams we ever had turned into the nightmare of my Adelia's long, slow, agonizing death."

Brock's eyes swung once more to Sanders, but they didn't fill with simmering hatred and rage. They just seemed dark and empty, like two bottomless holes. "And now fate has brought me back . . . with the scurvy piece of vermin who killed my Adelia. Full circle, like I said before. A nightmare for a nightmare. A slow, agonizing death for a—" He stopped short, his words cut off by the dull, echoing boom of a rifle shot rolling and echoing out from somewhere deeper within the Orphan Peaks.

At the escaped convicts' camp, Macready and Hinkson were fixing to bite into the smoking slabs of meat they'd just finished cooking on sticks held over the fire when they, too, heard the echoing report of a rifle.

Hinkson's eyes went wide. He looked around over one shoulder and then back to Macready. "That's got to be Wilby. You reckon he bagged something?"

"Sounds like," Macready said.

They set aside their intended meal and rose to their feet. "If he managed to get a deer or antelope, he'll probably need help bringing it in, won't he?" said Hinkson.

"Most likely."

Hinkson turned and looked around some more. "Sound travels kinda funny in these rocks, but I think the shot came from that general direction, don't you?"

Macready's eyes followed where the black man's finger pointed. "Sounded like it to me, too. Plus, that's the way Wilby headed out. So yeah, let's us go that way and see what he brought down."

They picked up their guns. Macready again took the rifle he'd carried earlier, plus the bandolier; Hinkson strapped on the holstered pistol and shell belt.

"Look at us," Macready said with a bit of a self-conscious grin. "We look like we're headin' off to fight a war, not goin' to help bring in some fresh meat."

"Maybe so," said Hinkson as they started in the direction they'd agreed upon, "but we sure ain't gonna leave our guns here. They're the only possessions we got on this earth." Then he threw a grin over his shoulder. "Far as helpin' to bring in some fresh meat . . . man, oh man, I hope that's the case. I don't want to get my hopes up, but my mouth is already waterin' like a droolin' baby's."

"I hear that," said Macready. "I'm the one who's

been preachin' about how horse meat ain't so bad, but to tell the truth, if I never have to sink my teeth into another bite it'll be too dang soon."

They moved quickly, eagerly along, sometimes through narrow passageways or around large chunks of broken boulders, sometimes over weather-rounded humps of rock. Some of the rock formations loomed tall and high ahead of them, a few with sheer, flat faces. Before they'd gone very far, Wilby suddenly rounded one of those flat walls, hurrying in their direction. A kind of wide-eyed excitement showed on his face.

Reading the excited look as a good sign, Hinkson couldn't wait to hear what was behind it. "We heard the shot," he blurted. "Did you bag something? Did you get us some fresh meat?"

As Wilby reached them, breathing a little hard from his hurried pace, he shook his head. "No. No, I took a shot at a deer but missed."

"Damn!"

"But wait. Wait . . . I got something better."

"What are you talking about? What do you mean by something better?" Macready wanted to know.

Wilby grinned. "Remember when you said we might come across a ranch with a change of clothes for us hangin' on the wash line? And then I taunted you about how maybe those clothes would blow off the line and come floatin' through the air to land right here in our laps?"

"Damn it, Wilby, quit spoutin' crazy talk. What are you gettin' at?" Hinkson demanded.

His grin growing even wider, Wilby said, "What I'm tryin' to tell you is that we got company here in this godforsaken pile of rocks. There's men who've got clothes on their backs that can be ours for the takin'. What's more, they've got horses with bulgin' saddlebags that have probably got more clothes and food." Wilby paused, his eyes taking on a different kind of gleam. "And they even got a woman with 'em!"

Hinkson canted his head back and arched a brow skeptically. "Are you sure you didn't slip and fall somewhere and rap your head hard enough to shake loose the loco dust inside your noggin?"

"I'm tellin' you true," Wilby insisted. "After I missed that deer, I climbed up on some high rocks to get a better look where he might've bounded off to. I was hopin' maybe I'd hit him after all and he'd either fallen or was draggin' along wounded. As I got up on that higher place, see, some movement caught the corner of my eye off in another direction—off to the north and east some. And that's when I saw 'em. Two men and a woman, scramblin' down amongst some rocks and boulders out on the fringe. I figure they must have heard my shot and took to cover out of caution."

"Whatever they're doin' here, I hope they don't decide to bolt away before we can get to 'em," Macready said, his brow wrinkling with worry. "Main thing, o' course, is that we'd be losin' whatever provisions they got. But also, if they get away and carry the report of hearin' a rifle shot from here in these rocks to the wrong place, that might put a notion in the heads of some of those chasin' us that we could've come this way."

"So what?" said Hinkson. "One way or the other, we'll be long gone by then. If we do miss out on this bunch we can—"

"We ain't missin' nothin'!" Wilby cut him off. "If these that I saw had a mind to take off, they would've done it when they first heard my shot. But they didn't. They're here for some purpose of their own. Maybe they're hunters or some such. Like I said, they likely took to cover out of caution. And if there *is* any chance they might ride off, all the more reason we need to quit standin' here jawin' and get moved into positions closer to where they are. Then, if they try to bolt, we can just shoot 'em. Even a different shirt with a bullet hole in it is better than these prison stripes."

"Hate the thought of shootin' a woman, though," muttered Macready.

"Don't you worry, sonny," Wilby told him. "Shootin' the gal is for sure the *last* thing I got in mind for her. She's got far better uses than servin' as another bullet stopper . . . but before we get to any of that, we need to get a move-on. Come on. I'll point out to you where they're at and we can make our plans from there."

Chapter 43

The sound, after traveling considerable distance across the rolling plains, reached Bob Hatfield's ears as a faint, dull *pop* . . . but there was still no mistaking it. The marshal had heard the reports of too many gunshots in too many circumstances over the years not to recognize yet another. The only things to question were where it had come from and what it meant. And was it something he needed to concern himself with?

Bob reined his horses to a halt and sat his saddle for a full minute and more, listening intently for another shot or any other sound that might be related to it. He heard nothing but the soft sigh of the wind and the munching sounds of his horses taking the opportunity to stretch their necks down and graze on some of the glistening grass revealed by the freshly melted snow.

The shot could be tied to many perfectly innocent things. There could be a ranch or farm nearby where somebody had taken a potshot at some varmint. Or maybe to bag an antelope or sage hen for supper. Or even something as simple as target practice, although that more logically would have included additional shots.

With the likes of Arlo Sanders and a kill-minded Vernon Brock also somewhere out on these plains, it could also be tied to them.

Bob knew the pace he'd been maintaining had eaten up a big gulp of distance. Was it enough to have caught up with—or at least drawn reasonably close to—Brock and the others? He didn't want to get his hopes too high, but at the same time, he recognized it could very well be possible. Enough of a possibility, at any rate, that he decided he had no choice but to investigate the shot.

For starters, he nudged his horses to the crest of the highest of the rolling hills surrounding him, halted again, and pulled from his war bag a pair of high-quality binoculars—yet another tool once used by the Devil's River Kid. Focusing the dual lenses, he slowly and carefully scanned to the south. Sound could be tricky in wide-open spaces, but he was pretty sure the shot had come from that direction.

There was no sign of movement or any hint of a ranch or farm in that direction. But about two, two-and-a-half miles away was a sizeable cluster of rock formations thrusting up in the midst of what otherwise seemed to be nothing but emptiness. Bob had no familiarity with the area that far west of Rattlesnake Wells. He could recognize the hazy humps of the Laramie Range off to the north and the Rockies far to the south, but he had no idea what that odd formation was. That singularity, combined with the total lack of anything else to go on, resulted in his decision to swing toward the rocks and check them out.

* * *

Crowded into a brushy notch between two shoulders of weather-rounded rock that extended out from the base of the Orphan Peaks, Vernon Brock concentrated intently on listening for any follow-up sound to the shot they had heard. Libby, Sanders, and their horses were gathered in close around him.

Finally, after keeping silent for as long as she could stand, Libby whispered, "What do you think that shot meant, Brock?"

"How in blazes am I supposed to know?" he responded through clenched teeth. "It wasn't *aimed* at us, I can tell that much. And I reckon you got to count that as a good thing. Beyond that, I don't know what to think."

"Maybe fate brought somebody else here," Sanders said sarcastically.

"You shut up," Brock said.

Sanders thrust his chin out defiantly. "What if I don't? What if I start hollerin' my head off and draw attention to us hunkered down in here? Maybe that shot was a law dog nosin' around on account of what happened back in Rattlesnake Wells. Or somebody from a nearby ranch out huntin'. No matter who it is, what have I got to lose? My situation can't get no worse than what it is now with—"

Brock spun around suddenly and slammed the butt of the rifle he was holding in a savage blow to the side of Sanders's jaw, silencing him and sending him to the ground, knocked out cold. The former federal marshal took a step and hovered over the fallen man, holding the rifle ready for another blow in case he tried to get up or had more to say. Sanders was capable of neither.

Libby, who had backed away as far as she could from the sudden and unexpected attack, pressed herself tight against the rock shoulder and looked on with widened eyes.

Brock turned his head to look at her. "He kept askin' for it. He kept eggin' me on. I held off hurtin' him before this because I wanted to wait until the time and place was right. Even though I want him to suffer long and slow, the way my Adelia did, I'll kill him suddenlike if I have to, rather than risk letting him get away from me. And whoever's out there, whoever fired that shot . . . I'll kill them, too, if I have to. I don't want to, but I will. I won't let anybody get in the way of me deliverin' to Arlo what he's got coming. You understand, don't you, Libby?"

She nodded somewhat jerkily. "Yes. Yes, I do." She would have been afraid to answer differently, no matter what . . . but, actually, she felt she *had* come to understand Brock. The depth of his pain, the fierceness of his hatred for Arlo. That didn't change the fact that the man was quite savagely mad, but at least she understood why and what was driving him.

Brock took a step closer to her. "You've proven yourself every hard step of the way through this, Libby. I've come to believe I can count on you."

"You can," Libby assured him. "I'm in this just as deep as you, and I want Arlo dead almost as bad as you. I'll admit that I . . . I'm not completely at ease with the slow death you have in mind for him . . . but I figure I can look away or walk away from that part if I have to. The way he dumped me in the past was every bit as cruel and torturous in its own way. And what he did to your wife . . . yeah, I think we understand each other pretty damn well, Brock."

His eyes bored into her hard and deep. For a minute, neither of them said anything.

Then Brock spoke. "So now I'll make an admission to you. Up until just about this very minute, I was figuring I couldn't afford to leave you behind as a witness."

Libby met his gaze. "I had a hunch that might be coming. Once I knew I'd gotten even with Arlo, I guess I didn't care all that much. I just hoped you'd make it quick."

"You should have cared, Libby, quick or not. Damn it, you've still got things to live for." He shook his head. "In spite of every instinct telling me I ought to go through with how I originally planned it, I ain't gonna. I can't. I won't. Not after all you've done to help me get this far."

"Won't say I'm disappointed," Libby replied with a crooked grin.

"And now I've got to count on you even more."

"How so?"

"That shot . . . I've got to go see what's behind it," Brock told her. "Don't exactly know why, but I got a feelin' in my gut it ain't anything good. I want you to stay here out of sight. Keep hunkered down low and keep an eye on Arlo."

"If you've got a bad feeling, why don't we just ride away?"

Brock shook his head. "You know why." He turned back to Sanders, bent over and dragged the unconscious man closer to the base of a thick bush growing up the side of the rock shoulder. He momentarily unlocked the handcuffs on Sanders's wrists, ran the chain around behind the thick, gnarled root extending up through a crack in the rock, then clamped the cuffs back on.

Straightening up, puffing a little, Brock said, "There, that oughta hold him. That tough ol' root grew up through that rock and split it open. I don't expect Arlo will be yanking it free very easy. If he wakes up and tries, you chunk him on the head again with something or otherwise figure out a way to discourage him."

"I can do that," Libby said.

Brock reached into the saddlebag on his horse, pulled out a well-worn Colt .44 revolver, and held it out to Libby. "This is my trusty old spare. Take it. If I don't make it back, promise me you'll use it on Arlo. He dies here one way or another. Okay?"

Libby reluctantly took the Colt. "Why wouldn't you be coming back? I mean, you will—won't you?"

"I plan on it, but like I said, I got a bad feeling about that shot. Don't know what I'm gonna run into. You never can tell. Something could go wrong. That's all I'm saying."

"How will I know?"

"If things go bad enough wrong, I expect you'll hear more shooting. Comes to that and I ain't made it back after two or three hours, likely I ain't gonna. That's when I want you to take care of Arlo for me. For all of us—me, my Adelia, and for yourself. Then you get out of here and take care of yourself."

Libby's brow wrinkled. "How will I do that?"

"Skirt around this rock pile and head due south," Brock told her. "You know how to figure that, right? Keep the sun on either your left or right shoulder.

Eventually, you'll come to the railroad tracks. Turn left and follow them. They'll take you straight into Laramie."

Libby started to say something, but Brock stopped her. "No time. I've got to go. You stick tight and do what you have to, gal. As will I." He managed a flicker of a smile. "Besides, don't figure on being shed of me quite yet. I plan on doing my damnedest to make it back here . . . I'm a powerful stubborn cuss when I set my mind to something."

A moment later he'd turned and clambered up over the rocks and was gone from sight.

"They're down in that splayed-out notch," said Wilby, pointing. "See 'em? In amongst those bushes?"

"No," grunted Hinkson. "With all those bushes, I can't see— Hold it. Okay, yeah, I can get a glimpse now. Some fella in a dark hat doin' a lot of talkin'. And I can see the horses sort of stickin' out, too."

"Yeah, I'm gettin' about the same glimpse," said Macready. "I can't really make out a whole lot."

"You don't have to see every exact detail," insisted Wilby. "The main thing is that you got a fix on where they're at. Me, I had a good look before they got themselves tucked in there so deep. You'll have to take my word that there's two men, a woman, and three horses."

"Okay. We got that," said Hinkson. "Now how do we play it from here?"

Wilby frowned. "What's so complicated? We sneak down quietlike until we're close enough, and then we jump out and grab 'em."

"That ain't no plan," protested Hinkson. "For cryin' out loud, Wilby. I never did hear what you did to get yourself throwed in the pen, but with plannin' like that for whatever crime you committed, it ain't no blasted wonder where you ended up."

"Yeah? Well if you're so brilliant," said Wilby, "then how did your black ass get—"

"Knock it off you two. Jesus!" said Macready. "We're onto a really good break here. You tryin' to ruin it?"

Hinkson and Wilby glared silently at each other for several beats, then turned their heads to look at the young Tennessean.

"I suppose *you* got some kind of plan?" said Wilby.

"As a matter of fact I do," Macready responded. "What I was thinkin' was this. One of us should stay up high, sort of like a lookout and guard. Down a little closer than where we're at now, but still well above that notch. The other two make their way down on each side, sorta like Wilby said, and close in on 'em. Like a pincer, see?" Macready made a squeezing motion with one hand. "When the two on each side are in place, the up-high fella fires a shot down. That'll draw the attention of those in the notch, distractin' 'em, and at the same time be a signal for the side men to go ahead and jump 'em."

Wilby spread his hands. "Ain't that what I said?"

"Just a little thicker on detail, in case you didn't notice," said Hinkson. "But never mind that. I think the kid laid it out pretty good. The only question left is who stays up and who goes down on the sides?"

Chapter 44

Bob Hatfield rode toward the Orphan Peaks—although he had no idea the cluster of rocks even had a name—at a harder pace than he'd previously been following. He wanted to get there and explore that gunshot as quickly as possible. In case it turned out not to have anything to do with his quarry, of which there was probably a better than even chance, he wanted to determine that without wasting any more time than necessary.

All the while, of course, there remained another possibility. Not only that the gunshot he'd heard didn't have anything to do with those he was after, but Brock might be leading the rest in a whole different direction and they were a hundred miles away.

Bob shook off those negative thoughts. He'd plunged himself in this far, damn it, he wasn't ready to believe it was all for nothing.

Drawing close to the sprawling rock formation, he reined up once more and again put his binoculars to use. He scanned the high peaks, the tumbled rocks, and the gullies and other low places where growths of bushes and trees could be seen. The sprawl of the place was larger than he'd first judged. Just as some serious doubts were starting to build about how long it might take to fully explore what lay before him, Bob caught a flicker of movement off to one side.

He swung the binoculars and focused their magnified view on a moderately high point in the rocks where three men were crouched in serious conversation. All three were armed and decked out in clothing marked with prisoner stripes.

Bob's memory flashed back to the telegrams he'd received in Rattlesnake Wells on the afternoon just ahead of the second attempted bank robbery and the jailbreak. One had been an advisement on the legal status of Vernon Brock; the other, which he'd paid little mind to at the time, had been a notification about three prisoners who'd escaped from the Laramie prison.

Damn. He quickly fell to pondering how much of an obligation he felt toward getting involved with the discovery of the prisoners. They were clearly desperate and dangerous men. And he was a lawman, albeit one far out of his jurisdiction.

That detail hadn't stopped him from going after Brock and the others. Under different circumstances, he knew it wouldn't be enough to hinder him from confronting those escapees. The trouble was, the circumstances weren't different. If he took the time to brace the fugitives, he would—in addition to risking his life—almost certainly ruin any chance of ever catching up with *his own* fugitives.

Double damn.

Bob was leaning seriously toward leaving the three escapees alone, letting them continue to be somebody else's problem, when he noticed that the discussion they were having seemed focused on a particular spot below their elevated position. Scanning down, looking more closely, he saw what was drawing their attention.

In a brushy notch between two weather-rounded, outward-extending fingers of rock, somebody was trying to keep out of sight. Unfortunately, there wasn't quite enough room for them to stay completely hidden. Bob could make out a horse's rump and a flash of color from someone's clothing.

In other words, the escaped men were getting ready to converge on some innocent person or persons who'd had the misfortune to wander into a danger zone.

The choice of whether or not Bob should get involved was suddenly made for him. He had no other option. The possibility that whoever was in that notch would turn out to be Brock and the others occurred to him only fleetingly. That would be too wild of a coincidence to ever give serious consideration.

Because he was arguably the best rifleman of the three, Macready was chosen to man the high position while Wilby and Hinkson worked their way down the sides. Wilby went to Macready's right, Hinkson to his left. The young Tennessean, in the meantime, climbed down to a somewhat lower perch above the notch.

Macready willed himself to be patient, to hold in

check the excitement pulsing inside him. That was the worst part about being the one to hold the stationary position. If he'd been one of the others, stealthily working their way down closer, he could have concentrated on the stealth part and impatience wouldn't have figured in hardly at all.

On the other hand, when Wilby and Hinkson jumped the men in the notch they almost certainly would be involved in killing. Macready didn't mind being left out of that part. He'd kill if he had to, especially to make good the rest of his escape from that hellhole of a prison, but it wasn't something he took lightly. Not the way Wilby or Hinkson seemed to.

Almost as soon as Macready had settled into his new, lower position, any chance for him to grow impatient was suddenly removed when he saw the man in the dark hat unexpectedly leave the cover of the notch and start to climb up into the higher rocks. Macready's first reaction was to raise and aim his rifle. Almost as quick as he'd appeared, the man in the dark hat disappeared again in a crevice of some kind worn into the rocks he was ascending.

Macready swore under his breath. Now what was he supposed to do? Neither Wilby nor Hinkson had had enough time to get anywhere near close to where they'd set out for. If he fired a warning shot, especially with no chance to hit the man in the dark hat, all he'd accomplish would be to throw everything into a tizzy with no advantage gained by anybody.

Macready held his fire and calculated. The man ascending from the notch was on a course likely to bring him in contact with where Hinkson was going down. Macready could not currently see either of them. The best he could do, he decided, was to stay focused on a point where he estimated they might meet and be ready to cover Hinkson if he had to. He had to trust that Hinkson would be alert enough and good enough to deal with the man in the dark hat on his own.

So intent was Macready focused on watching and waiting for that development to play out he failed to notice the rider approaching fast from the outlying plains.

Hinkson paused on his descent to rest a moment and catch his breath. *Damn.* Wouldn't do no good to sneak down real quietlike, he told himself, if he was puffing like a steam engine when he got close to that notch. All those months of mostly being cooped up in his prison cell had really gotten him out of shape.

Just as he was ready to start down again, he heard the warning scrape of a boot dragging across a rock. Before the sound could fully register, a tall man in a dark hat suddenly came around a large boulder directly ahead.

Their eyes met and both men spat curses. In the same instant, their hands grabbed for the guns holstered on their hips.

Hinkson was pretty fair with a gun, both short and long, but he never considered himself close to being a fast draw. Neither did Vernon Brock, not compared to many he'd come across. Nevertheless, it was an action he had a good deal of familiarity and experience with.

Brock's Colt cleared leather and spoke first. Twice. Both slugs tore into Hinkson at close range, one in the center of his gut, one a bit higher, splitting his sternum.

Hinkson was punched backwards, staggering. Before he went down, he managed to get off one shot of his own. The bullet went wide and would have sailed harmlessly past Brock if it hadn't ricocheted off a ragged boulder that sent it veering straight into the side of the former marshal's neck.

Brock staggered slightly but then stood firm. For a moment. He was aware of a dull, stabbing pain in his neck and when he tried to swallow, it made him suddenly cough. Thick droplets of blood sprayed from his mouth, spattered the ground just ahead of him, and dribbled down the front of his shirt. He dropped to his knees.

"Damn it all," he said, more blood bubbling out with the words. Then he fell forward, his Colt clattering to the ground beside him.

The burst of gunfire heightened Macready's attention all the more. He still couldn't see either man—not Hinkson nor the man in the dark hat—but he was able to spot a hazy cloud of gun smoke rising from an area where it seemed logical they might have met. There'd been three shots, in quick succession. All from the same gun? Or had there been two different weapons involved? Macready couldn't make up his mind but sort of thought it sounded like the latter. What did that mean, exactly? What difference did it make, either way, as far as what he should do?

He continued to watch anxiously, hoping for some sign of Hinkson, some indication he was okay. A glance in the other direction didn't show where Wilby had gotten to. Macready wondered what his reaction would be to the new crash of gunfire.

Finally deciding that the shooting had changed everything and nothing was to be gained by staying put, he shoved from his spot and headed the way Hinkson had gone, down toward where he'd seen the gun smoke.

Chapter 45

Bob Hatfield had just reached the edge of the rock sprawl, about two hundred yards down from the notch where he'd seen people hiding, when the three gun blasts sounded—close enough that he instinctively tensed and ducked his head, thinking a bullet might be whizzing his way. None came.

But the shooting had been too close for comfort.

Bob swung down from his saddle and quickly pulled his horses in behind some broken boulders that had spilled down from the higher cliffs. He tied their reins at the base of some tough, tangled bushes, yanked his Winchester from its saddle scabbard, and dropped into a low crouch. Making his way up into the rocks, he angled toward the source of the gunshots.

In the notch where she sat near the still unconscious Sanders, Libby had flinched at the burst of gunfire and waited with increasing anxiety in the silence that followed. She knew Brock to be a dangerous, competent man and had every reason to believe he could hold his own in a shooting scrape. Especially when he'd gone prepared, gone anticipating trouble. At the same time, he wasn't invincible. Any man could be tricked or shot from ambush.

Damn it. Why didn't he come back and tell her what had happened? Let her know he was okay?

As if seeking some reassurance, her eyes fell to Sanders, her estranged husband, still lying motionless where Brock had dragged him and cuffed him to the bush. No solace there. She shook her head. *As if there would have been even if he was conscious.*

Libby wished she had some tequila left. She could have found some comfort *there . . .* but she'd emptied the last of the bottle hours ago. *Damn it.*

She heard a faint noise over her shoulder, like the rattle of loosened pebbles. She spun around, her expression brightening hopefully even though the sound had come from the side of the notch opposite that which Brock had gone.

"Brock?" she said tentatively. "Is that you?"

When there was no response, she turned back the other way, thinking all the surrounding rocks might have bounced the sound in a confusing way. "Brock?" she said again.

Again, no response.

Once more from behind her, came the sound of bushes rustling and the dull thump of heavy footfalls. She spun around with a sense of alarm, not hope, knifing through her stomach and found a large man looming before her. He was unkempt and heavyset, clad in the unmistakable striped garb of a prison inmate. His unshaven face was split by a wide, leering grin. In his hands he gripped a rifle.

Libby started to raise the pistol Brock had left her. The big man moved with surprising speed, let go of the rifle with one hand, and knocked the gun from her grip with a powerful swatting motion.

She jumped back, her hand stinging sharply.

The big man took a step forward, leaning to scoop up the fallen pistol. With the pistol clamped in one hand and still wielding the rifle in the other, he took another step closer. Libby backpedaled until she came against the unyielding rock shoulder.

Wilby motioned with his rifle toward the still sprawled Sanders. "What happened to him?" he demanded.

"H–he was knocked unconscious," Libby answered.

"Who handcuffed him?"

"The man who's traveling with us. He's a U.S. marshal." Libby clamped her mouth shut tight, instantly regretting that she'd answered the man so easily and willingly. Thinking fast, trying to regain some ground with the menacing brute, she came up with, "The marshal went to signal some of the other lawmen who are elsewhere in these rocks. A whole posse is looking for this fugitive the marshal captured."

Wilby scowled. "That's a lie and we both know it. You three just got here. I saw you right after you came in off the plains. There is no posse."

"There is too! Those shots a minute ago came from the marshal, signaling the others like I said."

Wilby's grin returned. "Those shots were a couple of my pals pickin' off your marshal, more like . . . if the other fella I saw ride in with you even *is* a marshal."

"He is, I tell you!"

"Yeah, and we both know you're a liar. So what does that leave?"

"You'll see soon enough when he returns."

Moving once more in a sudden rush of speed, Wilby covered the distance separating them and slammed into Libby, pinning her hard against the rock. He brought the confiscated pistol up and pressed the barrel under her chin. "And what your so-called marshal will soon enough see, if and when he ever shows up, is me ready to blow your pretty little head off in case of any trouble. You understand?"

Libby tried to nod, but the gun barrel prevented it. "I understand."

"Now it would be a real shame if it came to that," said Wilby, beginning to grind his body against hers in a lewd way. "There's a lot better things I can think of to do with you than blow your head off."

"I'd rather take the bullet," Libby said.

Wilby laughed nastily. "We'll see about that. All in good time. Until we find out who shows up—your marshal or my pals—I'm a man starvin' in more ways than one. What have you got as far as grub in those bulgin' saddlebags I see over there?"

"There's some beef jerky. And some—"

"Beef jerky will do for a start. That'll give me something to feast my belly on while I'm feastin' my eyes on you, darlin', and waitin' to see who makes it back here to join us. Now let's move together, real careful-like, over to those saddlebags and find me some of that jerky."

When Macready came upon the bodies of Hinkson and the man in the dark hat, he was rocked by the sight. Even though he'd seen violence before and had more or less been expecting a scene something like that following the gunfire that marked the meeting of the two men, it was still an unnerving sight. Especially the fact that it included Hinkson. Macready didn't exactly consider the black man a friend, but he'd always been tolerable and decent enough in his own way. Particularly compared to Wilby.

"Dang it, Hinkson, why'd it have to be you?" the Tennessean said in a husky whisper as he knelt down on one knee and reached to thumb closed the fallen man's eyelids.

He was still in that position when a tall, red-haired man aiming a Winchester stepped out of the bushes just ahead and off to one side.

"Every man has his time, kid," Sundown Bob Hatfield said. "That fella had his—and, if you try anything foolish, I'll have to see that you get yours."

Macready froze. His grip tightened on the rifle he'd lowered down to his side when he'd knelt next to Hinkson. Recognizing he was in a bad fix, he didn't try to bring it up. He knew when not to do anything to make it worse. That didn't keep him from asking, "Who the hell are you?"

"I'm a fella who's got the drop on you. That's all you need to worry about right now. Just toss that rifle way off to the side. And remember I've got a bead square on your brisket."

Macready had no choice but to do as instructed.

"Okay. Now—" Bob stopped short.

Brock, who lay on his stomach only a foot or so away, lifted his head and said in a thick, bubbly voice, "Adelia . . ."

Coming from a source Bob had thought was dead,

so surprised the marshal it caused him to momentarily divert his attention away from Macready.

Although also surprised and shocked by the reaction from a seeming dead man, Macready was alert enough and desperate enough to take advantage of the distraction. He launched from his kneeling position and hurled himself in a headlong dive, slamming hard into Bob's chest and midsection.

The marshal was driven backwards and bowled off his feet. Tangled together, they crashed through the bushes and went rolling down a steep incline strewn with gravel and broken chunks of rock. Bob felt the Winchester jarred from his grip and, even though much of the air had been driven out of him, he still managed to work up a healthy curse.

The men rolled to a stop at the bottom of the incline. Without attempting to rise to their feet, they began frantically kicking and punching one another, each hoping to land a stunning blow that would gain an advantage. Macready grabbed a melon-sized piece of rock and swung it down at Bob's face. Bob managed to jerk away at the last second. Macready flopped awkwardly off balance, giving Bob an opening, but he didn't have the leverage to throw a fist with any power behind it. He got a foot planted in Macready's chest and pushed his leg to full extension, separating the two of them and sending the Tennessean rolling several feet away.

Both men recognized the mistake—a near fatal one for Bob—at the same moment. Macready had stopped rolling within easy reach of Bob's Winchester.

Instantly jackknifing to a sitting position, Bob shoved to his feet as Macready was grabbing the rifle and scrambling to stand up. He planted his feet and wasted no time to raise the Winchester. As many who'd gone up against his lightning draw died finding out, Sundown Bob didn't need much time when it came to drawing and firing the Colt that rode in the holster on his hip.

There was no chance to talk the kid down. His intentions were made plain by the determination in his eyes and the sweep of the rising muzzle. Bob had only a split second to keep from being ventilated by a Winchester round and the only way to prevent it was by planting a pair of .44 caliber slugs in the center of Macready's chest.

Chapter 46

"There. That marks the end of your phony marshal for double-damn sure," said Wilby when the reports of two more shots reached the ears of him and Libby. "Ain't no way he coulda got past *both* of my pals." The leering smile he seemed unable to keep off his face whenever he was looking at her—which was practically every minute—stretched even wider. "Don't worry, though, darlin'. He may have failed you, but I won't. I'll be right here to treat you real good."

Libby cringed at the thought but said nothing. What could she say? All she could do was hope—hope that this vile creature was wrong and that Brock would return to fill him full of lead.

As if reading her thoughts, Wilby said, "But just to be on the safe side, let's you and me scooch a little deeper back in this here notch and keep an eye peeled until we see who comes visitin'. And while we're waitin' we can cuddle real close and tight, with you sorta in front of me in case somebody takes a notion to start throwin' lead recklesslike. It'd make me powerful sad if you was to stop a bullet meant for me, but it'd make me sadder still if I had to stop one on my own."

He grabbed Libby roughly and dragged her along with him into a narrower part of the notch. On the way, they stepped over the splayed legs of Sanders, who was finally beginning to stir ever so slightly as he started to come to from the vicious blow Brock had delivered.

Wedged back far enough, Wilby turned so he was facing outward and jerked her in front of him. Once again, he ground his body disgustingly against her. He had the .44 in one hand, the muzzle held close to her face, while the other arm was clamped across her breasts except for when he would lift it briefly to take a bite of the jerky clutched in his fist. His breath against the side of her face was fetid, even worse than the sour stink that emanated from his whole body.

It was all she could do to keep from gagging.

She thought longingly of the derringer she'd brought with her to Rattlesnake Wells, the one she'd kept in the pocket of her dress until she'd used it on the deputy. Oh, how she wished she was still carrying it instead of having put it in her big carpetbag where it was doing her no earthly good. She'd had reservations about shooting the deputy, but she'd have none of the same about shooting the man brutalizing her. No, she would enjoy emptying the little gun in him and knew exactly where she'd aim her shots.

"Oh, yeah. This is mighty cozy," Wilby said with a contented sigh. "I hope whoever's comin' takes his time, don't you, darlin'?"

It was only a matter of two or three minutes, however, before a voice called to them, "You in the notch! You're surrounded and you got no chance. Throw down your guns and give it up. Come out in the open with your arms raised and you won't be hurt."

"Of all the stinkin' luck! He *did* make it past Hinkson and the kid," Wilby muttered under his breath. Much louder, he shouted back, "You go to hell, law dog! I know you're a lyin' sack. You ain't got jack surrounded. Ain't nobody out there but you alone!"

"You'd be making a serious mistake to believe that," Bob responded.

"And you'll be makin' an even more serious one if you try to push me into a corner," Wilby hollered. "I got your woman in here. I got a gun held tight to her head. Guess what happens to that pretty little pumpkin if you ain't willin' to make a deal?"

Bob held off answering right away. Waiting. Giving the fellow time to sweat.

In that stretch of tense silence, Libby's mind raced. She knew the voice didn't belong to Brock, and yet it sounded vaguely familiar. So who was it? Where had she heard it before?

Suddenly the pistol snout was jammed harder against her temple. "Holler out there! You'd better convince your boyfriend that I ain't foolin' around."

Libby wanted to refuse his demand, wanted to tell him to go to hell. If it had truly been Brock out there, maybe she could have. But it wasn't, and she couldn't. What she wanted most was to not get her brains blown out.

"You've got to listen to him," she called. "Please don't let him kill me!"

Bob stayed quiet for a different reason. He had to consider the woman. He'd been worried about Brock killing her. He couldn't very well shrug off the even greater certainty of somebody else doing it.

"What kind of deal you got in mind?" he finally said.

"That did the trick, baby. You might even come out of this alive for real," Wilby whispered harshly in Libby's ear. Louder, he hollered to Bob "You give me an hour's start, with the woman as my insurance. When I know I'm in the clear, I'll let her go and you can come fetch her back."

"I'm supposed to just take your word on that?"

"It's all you're gonna get, law dog. Either that, or you can take my word on what I'll do to her otherwise."

Bob ground his teeth. Any way he mentally cut the deck, odds were mighty slim of drawing a high card. He'd been playing slim odds ever since his days as the Devil's River Kid. "What about Sanders?"

"If you mean this slob you coldcocked and handcuffed," Wilby replied, still thinking he was talking to the woman's alleged marshal, "he's still layin' here right like you left him. You can have him back the same way. He's no skin off my nose."

"Okay. I'm coming down with my hands empty. You meet me partway, we'll talk it through from there."

"You bet we will, law dog," Wilby whispered in Libby's ear, followed by a nasty chuckle. To Bob, he called, "Come on ahead!"

Wilby moved out from the narrow part of the notch, keeping Libby in front of him, keeping her clutched tight, keeping the gun pressed to her head. Once again, she thought of her derringer and how she wished she had it on her person.

Somewhat startled, she was surprised to see the marshal from Rattlesnake Wells step into view at the wide mouth of the notch. That explained why his voice had sounded familiar. A surge of renewed hope coursed through her. She didn't know how he'd caught up with them, but could it possibly mean that he *did* have a posse with him?

Bob came forward a few more steps and then stopped, holding his hands out wide at his sides. He'd left his Winchester back up in the rocks. His .44 was still in its holster on his hip and, invisible to Wilby and the woman, Hinkson's pistol was jammed in his belt at the small of his back.

Wilby pushed Libby forward a little farther and then halted, too. "That's a good start, Marshal. You said your hands would be empty, and I can see they are. But I can also see that hogleg on your hip is in mighty close reach. Lose it."

Bob's eyes narrowed. "That would leave me at a real disadvantage, hombre. I don't know if I'm ready to go quite that far."

"We do it my way or there's no deal at all!" Wilby said harshly. "We already went through this. Any craw-fishin' by you only brings the woman that much closer to gettin' blasted. Is that the way you want it?"

"How about taking me as your hostage and leaving the woman here?"

"No! I made my terms clear. Take the gun from your holster—real slow, usin' only two fingers—and lay it on the ground at your feet. I'll let you keep it that close, but that's as far as I go."

Bob took a deep breath, let it out slowly. Then, just as slowly, he reached down to squeeze the .44 between two fingers and lift it out of its holster. He never took his eyes off Wilby as he leaned over to place the gun on the ground beside his right boot. He knew exactly what was going to happen when he straightened back up and he tensed his muscles to be ready.

Sure enough, as soon as Bob had raised his head and shoulders, Wilby shoved Libby to one side and drew a bead on the marshal. Bob's split-second skill at the draw, even reaching behind him to grasp the gun secreted at the small of his back, once again allowed him to beat the odds.

The men fired simultaneously. As he swung the backup gun around and up, Bob let the momentum twist his body so that it presented the narrowest possible target to Wilby. The escapee's bullet grazed the rounded edge of Bob's left shoulder, leaving a deep bullet burn, maybe cracking a bone slightly, but nothing worse.

At the same time, Bob's bullet pounded square into Wilby's forehead, an inch above the bridge of his nose, snapping the big man's head back. He took a single backwards step and toppled over as straight and hard as a felled oak.

Chapter 47

Dusk was settling, throwing long eastward shadows out from the Orphan Peaks.

"So you're not going to change your mind about riding off into the night?" Libby asked one more time.

Bob shrugged. "Way I've been doing it. It's worked out pretty good so far."

"That explains how you were able to overtake us, even though we had a head start on you."

"Reckon so. In this case, heading out right away means that much quicker I can get back to my family that I plumb miss."

As soon as the words were out, he realized that as he'd said *family*, he was picturing Bucky and Consuela in his mind. Priscilla hadn't been part of that mental picture until she slipped in a moment later. He felt an immediate pang of guilt, followed by the nagging question of why he'd initially envisioned what he had. He had a hunch that, deep down, he probably knew the answer . . . but he wasn't ready to delve that deep just yet.

"Family's as good a reason as any. Better than most, I guess," said Libby. "Me, I ain't been part of a family since I was real young. And all I wanted back then was to get shed of the one I had."

"If a family is what you want, maybe it's not too late to build one around you," Bob said.

"Have kids, you mean?"

"Not necessarily. There are as many ways to build a family as there are lonely people wanting to be part of one. You just have to keep your eyes open for the right ones to latch on to."

Libby regarded him. "You're a strange man for a hick town marshal. You know that?"

Bob grinned. "You're hardly the first one to point that out."

"And deciding to let me go, I gotta say, ranks pretty high in your strange ways—not that I'm complaining, mind you."

"Just don't let me hear about something you do in the future that will make me regret it," Bob said.

"Like shooting any more deputies, you mean?"

"Yeah. Like that, for sure."

"Thank God I didn't kill him like I thought I did."

"What you need to do to help make up for your past wrong deeds is take what we found in Brock's money belt and, when you get back to Laramie, find a better path to walk from here on out."

At Libby's pleading, they had taken time to bury Brock. In the process, they'd found a full money belt around his waist. Bob had handed it over to Libby along with his sanction for her to go free, not be placed in cuffs and taken back to face charges. He couldn't say exactly why he'd made that decision. The best he could come up was that since she'd been through hell the past few days, including cheating death twice in just the past few hours maybe it was time for somebody to give her a break.

"I will find a better path to walk, Marshal. I promise," Libby said earnestly. "I'm not even gonna make a bottle of tequila the first thing I buy with that money when I get to Laramie. Maybe not the second or third, either."

"Sounds like a good start. You're sure you can find your way to Laramie okay?"

"Brock gave me good instructions." Her expression turned somewhat sad at the remembrance. "Don't worry about me making it through the night out here on my own. I've survived a hell of—excuse me—make that a *heck* of a lot worse. I'll build a big ol' fire and I've got guns and plenty of ammunition. I'll be fine. I'll strike out for Laramie first thing in the morning."

"When you get there, don't forget to give that note I wrote about the escaped convicts to the marshal there. Tell him I'll wire a more detailed follow-up as soon as I get back to Rattlesnake Wells."

Libby nodded. "Consider it done."

Bob turned to his horses—the two he'd arrived with plus a third upon which sat a slumped, silent, sullen-looking Arlo Sanders, once more handcuffed to the saddle horn. He'd been keeping quiet all during the exchange between Bob and Libby for one simple reason. He couldn't talk. Brock's smashing blow with the rifle butt had busted his jaw in at least three places, leaving the lower half of Arlo's face badly swollen and throbbing with pain. Trying to talk—which was futile anyway because anything he attempted to say came out unintelligible—only made the pain more excruciating. He just glared hatefully at everything and everybody.

Bob swung up into his saddle. Looking down at Libby, he said, "As soon as we turn and start to ride away, you ain't thinking about taking a shot with one of those guns you spoke of a minute ago in a last-ditch attempt to make good on your promise to Brock about killing Arlo, are you?"

Libby's mouth twisted wryly. "I gotta admit I did some thinking along those lines, but in the end, seeing how miserable he is with his busted jaw and all, and considering how far you've got to ride before he gets any medical attention . . . I decided that wasn't a bad trade-off. I think even Brock might understand."

"I don't know about that, but I think you made the right decision. I hope we both did." With that, he gave her a hat-pinch, then wheeled his horse about and nudged it, along with the others, eastward. Toward home, for him. Toward the gallows, eventually, for Sanders.

Save a man in order to take him back for hanging.

Bob wondered about the sense in that. He reckoned not all of his decisions made sense. But then, he *was* a strange one.

**Keep reading for a special preview
of the first book in a magnificent new series
by America's bestselling Western writers.**

Here is the towering saga of Breckenridge Wallace,
a new breed of intrepid pioneer who helped forge a
path through the wild American frontier . . .

THE FRONTIERSMAN
by William W. Johnstone
with J. A. Johnstone

In Tennessee, 17-year-old Breckinridge Wallace knew
the laws of nature. When his life was in danger, he
showed a fearless instinct to fight back. Killing a thug
who was sent to kill him got Breckinridge exiled from
his Smoky Mountain home. Brutally wounding an
Indian attacker earned him an enemy for life . . .

Now, from the bustling streets of St. Louis to the vast
stillness of the Missouri headwaters, Breckinridge is
discovering a new world of splendor, violence, promise
and betrayal. Most of all, he is clawing his way to
manhood behind the law of the gun. Because the
trouble he left back in Tennessee won't let him go.
A killer stalks his every move. And by the time he joins
a dangerous expedition, Breckinridge has had only a
small taste of the blood, horror, and violence he must
face next—to make his way to a new frontier . . .

Coming March 2017 from Pinnacle.

Chapter 1

Death lurked in the forest.

It wore buckskins, carried a long-barreled flintlock rifle, and had long, shaggy hair as red as the flame of sunset. Death's name was Breckinridge Wallace.

Utterly silent and motionless, Breckinridge knelt and peered through a gap in the thick brush underneath the trees that covered these Tennessee hills. He waited, his cheek pressed against the ornately engraved maple of the rifle stock as he held the weapon rock-steady. He had the sight lined up on a tiny clearing on the other side of a swift-flowing creek. His brilliant blue eyes never blinked as he watched for his prey.

Those eyes narrowed slightly as Breckinridge heard a faint crackling of brush that gradually grew louder. The quarry he had been stalking all morning was nearby and coming closer. All he had to do was be patient.

He was good at that. He had been hunting ever since the rifle he carried was longer than he was tall. His father had said more than once Breckinridge should have been born with a flintlock in his hands. It wasn't a statement of approval, either.

Breckinridge looped his thumb over the hammer and pulled it back so slowly that it made almost no sound. He was ready now. He had worked on the trigger until it required only the slightest pressure to fire.

The buck stepped from the brush into the clearing, his antlered head held high as he searched for any sight or scent of danger. Breckinridge knew he couldn't be seen easily where he was concealed in the brush, and the wind had held steady, carrying his smell away from the creek. Satisfied that it was safe, the buck moved toward the stream and started to lower his head to drink. He was broadside to Breck, in perfect position.

For an instant, Breckinridge felt a surge of regret that he was about to kill such a beautiful, magnificent animal. But the buck would help feed Breck's family for quite a while, and that was how the world worked. He remembered the old Chickasaw medicine man Snapping Turtle telling him he ought to pray to the animals he hunted and give thanks to them for the sustenance their lives provided. Breck did so, and his finger brushed the flintlock's trigger.

The crescent-shaped butt kicked back against his shoulder as the rifle cracked. Gray smoke gushed from the barrel. The buck's muzzle had just touched the water when the .50-caliber lead ball smashed into his side and penetrated his heart. The animal threw his head up and then crashed onto his side, dead when he hit the ground.

Breckinridge rose to his full height, towering well over six feet, and stepped out of the brush. His brawny shoulders stretched the fringed buckskin shirt he wore. His ma complained that he outgrew clothes faster than anybody she had ever seen.

That was true. Anybody just looking at Breckinridge who didn't know him would take him for a full-grown man. It was difficult to believe this was only his eighteenth summer.

Before he did anything else, he reloaded the rifle with a ball from his shot pouch, a greased patch from the brass-doored patchbox built into the right side of the rifle's stock, and a charge of powder from the horn he carried on a strap around his neck. He primed the rifle and carefully lowered the hammer.

Then he moved a few yards to his right where the trunk of a fallen tree spanned the creek. Breckinridge himself had felled that tree a couple of years earlier, dropping it so that it formed a natural bridge. He had done that a number of places in these foothills of the Smoky Mountains east of his family's farm to make his hunting expeditions easier. He'd been roaming the hills for years and knew every foot of them.

Pa was going to be mad at him for abandoning his chores to go hunting, but that wrath would be reduced to a certain extent when Breckinridge came in with that fine buck's carcass draped over his shoulders. Breck knew that, and he was smiling as he stepped onto the log and started to cross the creek.

He was only about halfway to the other side when an arrow flew out of the woods and nicked his left ear as it whipped past his head.

"Flamehair," Tall Tree breathed as he gazed across the little valley at the big white man moving along the ridge on the far side.

This was a half hour earlier. Tall Tree and the three men with him were hunting for game, but Flamehair was more interesting than fresh meat. The lean Chickasaw warrior didn't know anything about the red-haired man except he had seen Flamehair on a few occasions in the past when their paths had almost crossed in these woods. It was hard to mistake that bright hair, especially because the white man seldom wore a hat.

"We should go on," Big Head urged. "The buck will get away."

"I don't care about the buck," Tall Tree said without taking his eyes off Flamehair.

"I do," Bear Tongue put in. "We haven't had fresh meat in days, Tall Tree. Come. Let us hunt."

Reluctantly, Tall Tree agreed. Anyway, Flamehair had vanished into a thick clump of vegetation. Tall Tree moved on with the other two and the fourth warrior, Water Snake.

Bear Tongue was right, Tall Tree thought. They and the dozen other warriors back at their camp needed fresh meat.

Empty bellies made killing white men more difficult, and that was the work to which Tall Tree and his men were devoted.

Three years earlier, after many years of sporadic war with the whites, the leaders of the Chickasaw people had made a treaty with the United States government. It was possible they hadn't understood completely what the results of that agreement would be. The Chickasaw and the other members of the so-called Five Civilized Tribes had been forced to leave their ancestral lands and trek west to a new home in a place called Indian Territory.

Tall Tree and the men with him had no use for that. As far as they were concerned, the Smoky Mountains were their home and anyplace they roamed should be Indian Territory.

They had fled from their homes before the white man's army had a chance to round them up and force them to leave. While most of the Chickasaw and the other tribes were headed west on what some were calling the Trail of Tears, Tall Tree's band of warriors and others like them hid out in the mountains, dodging army patrols, raiding isolated farms, and slaughtering as many of the white invaders as they could find.

Tall Tree knew that someday he and his companions would be caught and killed, but when that happened they would die as free men, as warriors, not as slaves.

As long as he was able to spill plenty of the enemy's blood before that day arrived, he would die happily.

Now as he and the other three warriors trotted along a narrow game trail in pursuit of the buck they were stalking, Tall Tree's mind kept going back to the man he thought of as Flamehair. The man nearly always hunted alone, as if supremely confident in his ability to take care of himself. That arrogance infuriated Tall Tree. He wanted to teach the white man a lesson, and what better way to do that than by killing him?

He could think of one way, Tall Tree suddenly realized.

It would be even better to kill Flamehair slowly, to torture him for hours or even days, until the part of him left alive barely resembled anything human and he was screaming in agony for the sweet relief of death.

That thought put a smile on Tall Tree's face.

Water Snake, who hardly ever spoke, was in the lead because he was the group's best scout. He signaled a halt, then turned and motioned to Tall Tree, who joined him. Water Snake pointed to what he had seen.

Several hundred yards away, a buckskin-clad figure moved across a small open area. Tall Tree caught only a glimpse of him, but that was enough for him to again recognize Flamehair.

Tall Tree understood now what was going on. After Water Snake had pointed out the white man to Big Head and Bear Tongue, Tall Tree said, "Flamehair is after the same buck we are. Should we allow him to kill it and take it back to whatever squalid little farm he came from?"

"No!" Big Head exclaimed. "We should kill him."

Bear Tongue said, "I thought you wanted to hunt."

"I do, but Flamehair is only one man. We can kill him and then kill the buck."

"Even better," Tall Tree said, "we can let *him* kill the buck, then we will kill him and take it for ourselves and our friends back at camp."

The other three nodded eagerly, and he knew he had won them over.

Now they were stalking two different kinds of prey, one human, one animal. Tall Tree knew that eventually they would all come together. He sensed the spirits manipulating earthly events to create that intersection. His medicine was good. He had killed many white men. Today he would kill another.

Tall Tree knew the trail they were following led to

a small clearing along a creek that wildlife in this area used as a watering hole. Before his people had been so brutally torn away from their homes, so had they.

It was possible Flamehair knew of the spot as well. He came to these hills frequently, and it was likely that he was well acquainted with them. Tall Tree decided that was where he and his men would set their trap. The buck would be the bait.

They circled to reach the creek ahead of the buck and concealed themselves in the thick brush a short distance downstream from the clearing. A fallen tree lay across the creek. Tall Tree had looked at that log before and suspected Flamehair had been the one who cut it down.

As they waited, Tall Tree began to worry that the buck wasn't really headed here after all and would lead Flamehair somewhere else. In that case Tall Tree would just have to be patient and kill the white man some other day.

But he was looking forward to seeing if the man's blood was as red as his hair, and he hoped it was today.

A few minutes later he heard the buck moving through the brush and felt a surge of satisfaction and anticipation. He had guessed correctly, and soon the white man would be here, too. He leaned closer to his companions and whispered, "Try not to kill him. I want to take him alive and make his death long and painful."

Big Head and Bear Tongue frowned a little at that. They had killed plenty of whites, too, but not by torture. Water Snake just nodded, though.

A few more minutes passed, then the buck appeared. Almost immediately a shot rang out, and the buck went down hard, killed instantly. It was a good shot. Tall Tree spotted the powder smoke on the far side of the creek and knew that if all they wanted to do was kill Flamehair, they ought to riddle that spot with arrows.

Instead he motioned for the others to wait. He was convinced he knew what the white man was going to do next.

He was right, too. Flamehair appeared, looking even bigger than Tall Tree expected, and stood on the creek bank reloading his rifle, apparently unconcerned that he might be in danger. Reloading after firing a shot was just a simple precaution that any man took in the woods. Any man who was not a fool.

The other three warriors looked at Tall Tree, ready and anxious to fire their arrows at Flamehair. Again Tall Tree motioned for them to wait. A cruel smile curved his lips slightly as he watched Flamehair step onto the log bridge and start across the creek. He raised his bow and pulled it taut as he took aim.

This was the first time he had gotten such a close look at Flamehair, and a shock went through him as he realized the white man was barely a man at all. For all his great size, he was a stripling youth.

That surprise made Tall Tree hesitate instead of loosing his arrow as he had planned. He wanted to shoot Flamehair in the leg and dump him in the creek, which would make his long rifle useless and ruin the rest of his powder.

Instead, as Tall Tree failed to shoot, Big Head's fingers slipped on his bowstring and it twanged as it launched its arrow. Big Head's aim was off. The arrow flew at Flamehair's red-thatched head, missing as narrowly as possible.

But somehow it accomplished Tall Tree's goal anyway, because as Flamehair twisted on the log, possibly to make himself a smaller target in case more arrows were coming his way, the soles of his high-topped moccasins slipped. He wavered there for a second and fought desperately to keep his balance, but it deserted him and he toppled into the stream with a huge splash.

Tall Tree forgot about his plan to capture Flamehair and torture him to death. All that mattered to him now was that this white intruder on Chickasaw land should die. He leaped up and plunged out of the brush as he shouted in his native tongue, "Kill him!"

Chapter 2

Breckinridge had good instincts. They told him where there was one Indian there might be two—or more. He knew he was an easy target out here on this log, so he tried to turn and race back to the cover of the brush on the creek's other side.

Despite his size, he had always been a pretty graceful young man. That grace deserted him now, however, when he needed it most. He felt himself falling, tried to stop himself, but his momentum was too much. He slipped off the log and fell the five feet to the creek.

He knew how to swim, of course. Like shooting a gun, swimming was something he had learned how to do almost before he could walk.

So he wasn't worried about drowning, even though he had gone completely under the water. His main concern was the charge of powder in his rifle, as well as the one in the flintlock pistol he carried. They were wet and useless now. The powder in his horn was probably all right, but he figured his attackers wouldn't give him a chance to dry his weapons and reload.

Sure enough, as he came up and his head broke the surface, he saw four Chickasaw burst out of the brush. Three of them already had arrows nocked, and the fourth was reaching for a shaft in his quiver.

Breckinridge dragged in as deep a breath as he could and went under again.

He still had hold of his rifle—it was a fine gun and he was damned if he was going to let go of it—and its weight helped hold him down as he kicked strongly to propel himself along with the current. The creek was eight or ten feet deep at this point and twenty feet wide. Like most mountain streams, though, it was fairly clear, so the Indians could probably still see him.

Something hissed past Breckinridge in the water. He knew it was an arrow. They were still trying to kill him. He hadn't expected any different.

When he was a boy, he had befriended and played with some of the Chickasaw youngsters in the area. The medicine man Snapping Turtle had sort of taken Breckinridge under his wing for a while, teaching him Indian lore and wisdom. Breck liked the Chickasaw and had nothing against them. He didn't really understand why the army had come and made them all leave, but he'd been sorry to see them go.

Not all the Chickasaw had departed for Indian Territory, however. Some of them—stubborn holdouts, Breckinridge's pa called them—had managed to elude the army and were still hidden in the rugged mountains, venturing out now and then for bloody raids on the white settlers. Breck figured he had run into just such a bunch, eager to kill any white man they came across.

He had known when he started into the hills that he was risking an encounter like this, but he had never let the possibility of danger keep him from doing something he wanted. If that made him reckless, like his pa said, then so be it.

Now it looked like that impulsiveness might be the death of him.

His lungs were good, strengthened by hours and hours of running for the sheer pleasure of it. He had filled them with air, so he knew he could stay under the water for a couple of minutes, anyway, probably longer. He had to put that time to good use. Because of the thick brush, the Indians couldn't run along the bank as quickly as he could swim underwater. All he needed to do was avoid the arrows they fired at him, and he had to trust to luck for that since he couldn't see them coming while he was submerged.

Breckinridge continued kicking his feet and stroking with his left arm. Fish darted past him in the stream, disturbed by this human interloper. It was beautiful down here. Breck might have enjoyed the experience if he hadn't known that death might be waiting for him at the surface.

He didn't know how long he stayed under, but finally he had to come up for air. He let his legs drop so he could push off the rocky bottom with his feet. As he broke the surface he threw his head from side to side to sling the long red hair out of his eyes. When his vision had cleared he looked around for the Indians.

He didn't see them, but he heard shouting back upstream a short distance. He had gotten ahead of his pursuers, just as he'd hoped, and once he had grabbed a couple more deep breaths he intended to go under again and keep swimming downstream.

That plan was ruined when strong fingers suddenly clamped around his ankle and jerked him under the surface again.

Taken by surprise, Breckinridge was in the middle of taking a breath, so he got a mouthful of water that went down the wrong way and threatened to choke him. Not only that, but he had a dangerous opponent on his hands, too.

He could see well enough to know that the man struggling with him was one of the Chickasaw warriors. He must have jumped off the log bridge into the creek and taken off after Breckinridge as fast as he could swim. The warrior was long and lean, built like a swimmer. He slashed at Breck with the knife clutched in his right hand while keeping his left clenched around Breck's ankle.

Breckinridge twisted away from the blade. It scraped across the side of his buckskin shirt but didn't do any damage. His movements seemed maddeningly slow to him as he lifted his other leg and rammed his heel into the Indian's chest. The kick was strong enough to knock the man's grip loose.

The Chickasaw warrior shot backward in the water. Breckinridge knew he couldn't outswim the man, so he went after him instead. If he could kill the Indian in a hurry, he might still be able to give the slip to the others.

Breckinridge had never killed a man before, although he had been in plenty of brawls with fellows his own age and some considerably older. This time he was fighting for his life, though, so he wasn't going to have a problem doing whatever he had to in order to survive. Before the man he had kicked had a chance to recover, Breck got behind him and thrust the barrel of his rifle across the warrior's neck. He grabbed the barrel with his other hand and pulled it back, pressing it as hard as he could into the man's throat.

The Chickasaw flailed and thrashed, but Breckinridge's strength was incredible. He managed to plant his knee in the small of the Indian's back, giving him the leverage he needed to exert even more force.

The warrior slashed backward with his knife. Breckinridge felt the blade bite into his thigh. The wound wasn't deep because the Indian couldn't get much strength behind the thrust at this awkward angle, but it hurt enough to make red rage explode inside Breck. The muscles of his arms, shoulders, and back bunched under the tight buckskin shirt as he heaved up and back with the rifle lodged under the warrior's chin.

Even underwater, Breckinridge heard the sharp crack as the man's neck snapped.

The Chickasaw's body went limp. Breckinridge let go of it and kicked for the surface. As soon as his enemy was dead, Breck had realized that he was just about out of air. The stuff tasted mighty sweet as he shot up out of the water and gulped down a big breath.

An arrow slapped through that sweet air right beside his head.

Breckinridge twisted around to determine its direction. He saw right away that the other three Chickasaw had caught up while he was battling with the one in the creek. Two of them were on the bank even with him, while the third man had run on downstream, where he waited with a bow drawn back to put an arrow through him if he tried to swim past.

They thought they had him trapped, and that was probably true. But the realization just made Breckinridge angry. He had never been one to flee from trouble. He shouldn't have tried to today, he thought. He should have stood his ground. He should have taken the fight to the enemy.

That was what he did now. He dived underwater as the two Indians closest to him fired, but he didn't try to swim downstream. Instead he kicked toward the shore, found his footing on the creek bottom, and charged up out of the water bellowing like a maddened bull as the warriors reached for fresh arrows.

The rifle wouldn't fire until it had been dried out, cleaned, and reloaded, but in the hands of Breckinridge Wallace it was still a dangerous weapon. Breck proved that by smashing the curved brass butt plate against the forehead of the closest Indian. With Breck's already considerable strength fueled by anger, the blow had enough power behind it that the ends of the crescent-shaped butt shattered the warrior's skull and caved in the front of his head. He went over backward to land in a limp heap.

The other Indian loosed his arrow, and at this range Breckinridge was too big a target to miss. Luck was with him, though, and the flint arrowhead struck his shot pouch. The point penetrated the leather but bounced off the lead balls within.

Breckinridge switched his grip on the rifle, grabbing the barrel with both hands instead, and swung it like a club. He was proud of the fancy engraving and patchbox on the stock and didn't want to break it, but pride wasn't worth his life.

The Chickasaw dropped his bow and ducked under the sweeping blow. He charged forward and rammed his head and right shoulder into Breckinridge's midsection. Breck was considerably taller and heavier than the Indian was and normally would have shrugged off that attempted tackle, but his wet moccasins slipped on the muddy bank and he lost his balance. He went over backward.

The Chickasaw landed on top of him and grabbed the tomahawk that hung at his waist. He raised the weapon and was about to bring it crashing down into Breckinridge's face when Breck's big right fist shot straight up and landed on the warrior's jaw. The powerful blow lifted the Indian away from Breck and made him slump to the side, momentarily stunned.

Breckinridge rolled the other way to put a little distance between himself and the enemy. As he did an arrow buried its head in the ground where he had been a split second earlier. The fourth and final Chickasaw had fired that missile, and when he saw that it had missed, he screeched in fury and dropped his bow. He jerked out a knife and charged at Breck.

As he rolled to his feet, Breckinridge snatched up the tomahawk dropped by the Indian he had just walloped. He dodged the thrust of the fourth man's knife and brought the tomahawk up and over and down in a blindingly swift strike that caught the warrior on the left cheekbone. Breck intended to plant the tomahawk in the middle of the man's skull and cleave his head open, but the Indian had darted aside just enough to prevent that fatal blow.

Instead the tomahawk laid the warrior's cheek

open to the bone and traveled on down his neck to lodge in his shoulder. Blood spouted from the wounds as he stumbled and fell.

Breckinridge would have wrenched the tomahawk loose and finished off the injured Chickasaw, but at that moment the man he had punched rammed him again. This time the impact drove Breck off the bank and back into the creek. He floundered in the water for a moment, and by the time he was able to stand up again the two surviving warriors were disappearing into the woods. The one who had just knocked him in the stream was helping the wounded man escape.

Breckinridge felt confident that they didn't have any fight left in them. He might not have admitted it to anyone but himself, but he was glad they felt that way. He knew how lucky he was to have lived through a fight with four-against-one odds . . . especially when the one was an eighteen-year-old youngster and the four were seasoned Chickasaw warriors.

There was no telling if other renegades might be in the vicinity, so he figured he'd better get out of the hills and head for home pretty quick-like.

He wasn't going back without his quarry, though, so without delay he gathered up his rifle and started for the clearing where the buck had fallen. It would take time to put his rifle and pistol back in working order, and he didn't think it would be smart to linger that long.

When he reached the clearing the buck was still lying there, undisturbed as yet by scavengers. Breckinridge stooped, took hold of the carcass, and heaved it onto his shoulders. Even his great strength was taxed by the animal's weight as he began loping through the woods toward home.

He thought about the four warriors he had battled. Two of them were dead, he was sure of that, and the one he'd wounded with the tomahawk probably would die, too, as fast as he had been losing blood.

What would the fourth man do? Would he go back to the rest of the renegades—assuming there were any—and tell them that he and his companions had been nearly wiped out by a large force of well-armed white men?

Or would he admit that all the damage had been done by one young fella who hadn't even had a working firearm?

Breckinridge grinned. Lucky or not, he had done some pretty good fighting back there. He knew now that in a battle for his life he would do whatever it took to survive. He wondered if he ought to tell anybody the truth about what had happened. Chances were, they wouldn't believe him.

But he knew, and he would carry that knowledge with him from now on.

It was all Tall Tree could do not to cry out in pain as he leaned on Bear Tongue while they hurried through the forest. He was weak and dizzy and knew that was from losing all the blood that had poured out from the wounds in his face, neck, and shoulder.

"We must get you back to camp," Bear Tongue babbled. His voice was thick because his jaw was swollen from the powerful blow Flamehair had delivered to him. "If you don't get help, you will bleed to death."

"No," Tall Tree gasped, even though it caused fresh explosions of terrible agony in his face every time he moved his lips. The pain was nothing compared to the hatred that filled him. "I will not die. The spirits have told me . . . I cannot die . . . until I kill the white devil Flamehair!"

Connect with

U s

Visit us online at
KensingtonBooks.com
to read more from your favorite authors, see books
by series, view reading group guides, and more.

Join us on social media

for sneak peeks, chances to win books and prize packs,
and to share your thoughts with other readers.

facebook.com/kensingtonpublishing
twitter.com/kensingtonbooks

Tell us what you think!

To share your thoughts, submit a review,
or sign up for our eNewsletters, please visit:
KensingtonBooks.com/TellUs.